For Nelly and Erin—and the vital importance of sisters

THE HOUSE OF SAND

JULIAN SHAW

BY THE SAME AUTHOR

THE MEADOW SERIES

BEFORE YOU BEGIN...

If you enjoy fantasy with a metaphysical edge, I've got a free gift for you.

Whispers from the Meadow: An Insider's Companion to The Meadow Series
This exclusive companion eBook is filled with background lore, creative insights, and reflections behind *The Rains Came Down* (the first book in the series)—perfect as you begin (or revisit) your journey through the Meadow.

Download your free copy here:
https://subscribepage.io/CMivTJ

And if you enjoy *The House of Sand*, a short Amazon review means the world—it helps others discover the story too.

Thank you so much for reading,
Julian

Chapter 1

Family, Life After Death

Rain lashes the city relentlessly, swamping trees hanging over cobblestone streets and pooling in hollows of forgotten alleyways. The night sky is an ocean of tussling clouds, stretching thick and unbroken, veiling the stars in a shroud of leaden grey. London has been drowning like this for days.

Beneath the storm, in the nave under the vast dome of St. Paul's Cathedral, a hundred men lie in ranks, slumped and motionless. Had the dice of history fallen differently, these men would lie in the House of Commons—a consequence of Guy Fawkes' triumph. Instead, these unelected leaders of the realm between life and death choose this place. A grand sanctuary of stone and silence that materialised in the fallout of the Great Fire. The fire that reshaped London on Earth, but in many ways, gave life to London in The Meadow.

Among the men, one figure is upright.

A woman.

She sits poised and resolute, her presence a sharp contrast to the dormant men. A tight, sleek bun of fiery copper hair is tied at the back of her head. Its ordered precision is of more concern to her than the imminent opinions of the unconscious, entitled men. Between her fingers, she turns the fractured remains of a marble—a once-perfect sphere now cracked into sharp fragments. An unassuming little object, yet potent enough to drop an assembly of the most powerful men in this realm into an unshakable slumber.

Here, you don't play with marbles. You use them as vehicles to the past.

Forged in fire, a marble contains grains of sand, droplets of water, and *memories*. Perfect and accurate memories extracted from the soul that shaped it, swirling in liquid resin at its core. To place a marble on your tongue is to taste the emotions of its maker—ecstasy, terror, mischief, regret. But when a marble is shattered, its power is released. A mist unfurls, delicate and insidious, and the moment it touches your lungs, it drags you into the past. Not merely to witness, but to relive.

The men are ensnared in the woman's memory.

She remains awake, letting the last whispers of her marble's dark purple mist evaporate around her face. You don't enter the memory of your own marble. Not unless you have to.

The memory that had been captured is now free and from this point on will exist, as most memories do—as imperfect recollection. Its truth is now contestable. Its precision is now opaque. Its home, once again, is the fallible sanctuary of its maker's mind.

The woman isn't concerned. That memory wasn't important. Not to her. Not to who she is. She feels the leather pouch of marbles on her hip. God forbid one of those ever be cracked.

Beside the woman, one by one, the unconscious members of the Council of the Distillery wake. First is the President—an older man, hunched in a throne at the head of the council. His appearance is regal, draped in fur and silk indigo robes, but his face is scrunched like a used napkin; his eyes are cold, and the wrinkles that carve out his features speak of a life lived cruelly. Before the other men wake, he leans forward and addresses the woman, his voice just above a whisper.

"Did you have enough protection?" he asks her, his eyes wide and interrogating. "You know, I would be happier if your security were bolstered."

"Seriously?" whispers the woman, exasperated. "Any more security, and they would have thought we were invading!"

He grimaces, then glances anxiously up to the triforium—the gallery overlooking the nave—where a pair of cloaked figures observe the council. Dark hoods shroud their faces, but he knows they are watching and listening intently. They always are.

Gradually, the rest of the council members wake, shuffling uneasily back into consciousness. The last to wake is a bald, muscular man with a clean inch-long scar on his cheek and a tightly groomed beard, arrogantly neat like the chin strap of a police officer's helmet. His name is Andrew Callaghan. He is the President's son, but most know him by his title—*The Ferryman,* head of the secret police who go by the same name: the Ferry Men. There is a sneer visible across his lips even before he is fully conscious.

"Thank you, Governess," the President announces, his voice cutting through the uneasy silence. "That was an enlightening memory of your recent voyage across *the Channel.* I see the French continue to deny that we are in purgatory?"

"They consider our existence a collective dream," she replies curtly. "The residue of life, rather than its punishment."

"Ridiculous!" scoffs the Ferryman, laughing. The other councilmen murmur in agreement. "Did you notice the dirty resin stains all over their faces? Is that not evidence enough that they are living in sin?!"

"The colour of a person's resin is considered irrelevant in *La Prairie,*" the governess replies. "They carry no shame for their stains."

The Ferryman sneers in disgust while a chorus of revulsions echoes among the council members. *'Heathens!' 'Degenerates!' 'Sinners!'* They shout. One councillor even spits onto the stone floor in disgust.

"At least they have agreed to herd their Founderers onto the Drifter barges now," offers a bureaucrat, silencing the rest. "Our workhouses are overflowing."

The President nods approvingly.

"They'll all be Drifters by the time they get to North Wales, anyway," smirks the Ferryman.

There are titters around the nave.

"Do we know the port at Holyhead can cope with the extra arrivals?" asks another bureaucrat.

"That's your job to sort out," the Ferryman smiles. "You can always redirect a few French barges into the Swellies if the port gets too full."

The man looks back, eyes wide.

"I'm kidding," he smirks, menacingly. "Scuttling them in the whirlpools would be a waste of good ships."

The bureaucrat frowns and scribbles some notes onto the ream of paper in front of him.

"All I say is this," starts the President. "Thank God we have order in the Meadow… that we cleanse our people from the shameful, murky memories that leak from the pores of an impure mind. We hold our heads high, knowing our conscience—and our resin—is clear." He glances up at the triforium, as though he says this for the two figures up there. "Ok, that covers the set agenda of today's Distillery Council. Is there any other business before we adjourn?"

The Governess raises her hand. There are a few yawns and tuts from the men around the nave, but she ignores them. She doesn't care if they want to finish early.

"Yes, Governess," says the President.

"The first thing," she says, standing and addressing the room, "is the plight of the missing young men. Their numbers now exceed one hundred. Even my ship back from *La Prairie* had lost one of its young sailors recently. I'm asking for permission to look into these disappearances. I can ask around and see if we can give the people some answers…"

The Governess looks around the chamber, but none of the men seem remotely interested. "Come on," she implores them. "There are flyers up all around the city. Good men. Men with clear resin are being snatched off our streets…

"Snatched?! You shouldn't fuel such unverified rumours, Governess!" the President interrupts, his eyes flicking warily up to the hooded men in the gallery.

"Then let me *verify* them!" she responds. "It helps no one if this council buries its head in the sand. The rumours about kidnappers on horseback are disturbing, and they're gaining traction. If we could just show the rumours to be false…"

"We have bigger issues to deal with right now, Governess," the Ferryman interrupts, his voice calm and condescending. "We can't be worrying about a few missing young men."

There are nods of agreement around the nave.

The Governess goes to retort, but the President raises his hand. "This matter is closed," he says. "Is there anything else?"

"Actually, yes," says the Governess, breathing deeply, steadying herself. There are more groans, but the governess is unmoved—she has navigated the ignorance of these stubborn pricks for years. "It is in my role as Advocate for Women in the Meadow, and in solidarity with the *Colney Hatch Sisterhood*, that I demand answers about our Palaces."

The President sighs, pinching the bridge of his nose and shaking his head. "We have covered this ground many times before, Governess-"

"I'm aware of that, Father–President," she corrects herself sharply. "But my recent visit to *La Prairie* opened my eyes. They have palaces too. They have Flickers, just like ours—women wandering the streets without memory of their past. But the women there aren't silent victims. The streets of Paris are in open revolt, led by *Les Mariées Bleues—The Blue Brides—*Women who march in blue ballgowns, declaring their tragic absence of resin, demanding answers."

The President shakes his head dismissively. "As long as the *Blue Brides* stay over there, Governess, I see no reason to concern ourselves. Their rebellion isn't ours."

The Governess stares daggers at her father. "Their rebellion *should* be ours! Our women deserve more than silence. More than a dismissive mantra, '*no resin is better than dirty resin*'. Compliance in London isn't the same as consent!"

A few men around the chamber shuffle uncomfortably. A handful look up at the gallery anxiously. The two cloaked men have got to their feet, their hoods still hiding their faces.

"You have been warned before, Governess," one of the hooded figures booms down into the nave. "The palaces are the responsibility of *our* Council. The Council of the Almighty. Not yours. The sanctity of the palaces is for us, the *princes*, to keep. They are not for you to question. We keep them in line with *His Will.*"

"But…"

"No 'buts', Governess. And might we advise that this is the last time you raise this?"

The Governess grits her teeth in frustration. "I will stop raising issues with the palaces when your lot start giving me answers… when you stop hiding behind *His Will!*" she shouts up blindly into the dark gallery.

The President stares across at his daughter, a nerve twitching in his top lip, but he dares not interrupt.

"Mr President," one of the hooded figures calls down, his voice unerringly calculated. "Please, keep your daughter in check. Unless, of course, you want Eilish to journey north with us?"

"Talk to me! Not my father!" shouts the Governess.

"Enough!" booms the figure. His voice echoing off the cathedral stonework. "You talk of things you do not understand, Governess. Of course, you would. You have never been to the palaces. Your resin flows as free as any man's. But heed this, a final warning, if I may—*His will be done!* Even a Governess is fit for palace life… I mean it. We'll take you to *His* grandest palace. We'll take you to the *House of Sand.*"

"No, no, please," says the President, his face white, his eyes pleading desperately with his daughter. "Eilish, please."

Ignoring her father, the Governess stares up at the gallery. There is a fire in her eyes like the colour of her hair. She wants to stand her ground, but reluctantly, she stays silent.

In the triforium, both figures stare back down at the governess.

"We thought not," concludes one of the figures, sarcastically. He puts his arm on the shoulder of his colleague, who nods, and both cloaked men turn away into the darkness of the gallery. They leave without so much as an acknowledgement of their hosts in the nave, or a farewell.

The President shuffles some papers in front of him before clearing his throat.

"Ok, if there is no other business," he says, regaining composure, "then I invite you all to share marbles with me. Council adjourned."

There is a collective exhaling of breath, and the tension in the nave evaporates. The councillors shift themselves on their long wooden pews, start eager conversations, and reach for the ramekins full of marbles nestled beside them, throwing marble after marble into their hungry mouths.

The Governess does not move. She stands and glares at her father, her knuckles white with irritation. But she knows she stands there alone. The only anomaly among a salivating compliance of council members, high on the sensations they get from sucking marbles.

The Meadow, her home for twelve long and awful years, ever since the tragic plane crash that brought her family into this realm, is slipping deeper into tyranny and despair. Her father is the stubborn captain of a sinking ship, paying no heed to the approaching storm. A storm of absent resin and dirty resin. And his drive to cleanse this resin is doomed, but he can't see it. He won't see it. But she will. She will not condone his wilful ignorance. She will not meet the same end as her mother and sister. Not yet.

Eilish drops into her chair, feeling the frustration prickling into perspiration on her brow. Instinctively, she wipes the minute beads of resin with a delicate lace kerchief from her pocket. And, out of habit, she inspects the residue, privately. There it is, the usual dark, dirty smear of resin—the dreadful secret she must hide.

***

Chapter 2

The Blue Bride

Earth - Mynydd Aaru

S ome months later, *and* eleven years earlier, a harsh winter storm roars around *Mynydd Aaru*—the largest mountain in Wales on Earth—an offensive interruption to the solemn magnificence of the mountain. At the mountain's base, fully exposed but stubbornly sturdy, stands a dilapidated little café. And though its front door rattles on its hinges, permitting a cold, fierce air to rush in and dance under the feet of its customers, the atmosphere inside is warm and jovial.

A dozen or so rock climbers fill the café. It is their natural refuge on days like today, their comfortable place. A place to tell stories, boast about climbs they have done, and wax lyrical over climbs they wish to do. But not everyone in the café this afternoon is a mountaineer.

In a corner, by the window, sits a lady who has been lodging above the café for the past week. She doesn't speak with anyone, choosing to keep the hood of her jacket up, even indoors. She sits and watches. Watches everyone who comes and goes. And gazes up at the weather that batters the great mountain outside.

The café owner himself is a climber, or *was*. He rejected corporate life a decade ago in favour of a simpler life, surrounded by kindred spirits. He has tried to chat with the strange lady all week, but to no avail. She is as enigmatic as the infamous *Asphodel Face* of *Mynydd Aaru,* which looms over them outside, and just as impenetrable. She hasn't offered her name, despite numerous opportunities to do so, and seems determined to blend into the background despite the chronic injury that makes her limp awkwardly. She's not from around here, the café owner knows that much, but for some reason, she knows the mountain outside the window very well.

A car pulls up in the parking lot outside. Its headlights, necessary because of the storm and not the time of day, flash a yellow beam into the café. A dozen mounted photographs decorating the wall are each briefly given the spotlight; their smiling subjects, embracing on the summit of the mountain, shine. And a moment later, the front door swings open aggressively, caught by the wind.

In steps a young lady. She apologises immediately, not intending the dramatic entrance. The ferocity of the wind had taken her by surprise.

She is a tall lady. Young, maybe in her early thirties. She has long, black hair—black as a moonless night—which cascades down her back in stark contrast to her pale, almost ethereal skin. She is gaunt, as though her whole adult life so far has been filled with anxiety and worry. And her wide blue eyes sink into their sockets. She wears a long leather trench coat, concealing everything beneath, though her manner suggests she isn't wearing mountaineering gear. Slung over her shoulder is a heavy backpack.

The lady steps up to the counter and smiles nervously, catching the eyes of a few climbers accidentally.

"Excuse me," she says quietly. "Is there still time to get a coffee?"

The café owner smiles. "Of course," he says, his grin stretching between his stubbly cheeks. "I'll throw in a free flapjack as well. They won't shift before closing, and I don't need them." He pats his belly. It's barely a 'belly', but since an injury stopped him from climbing, he has developed a deprecating self-consciousness.

"That's very kind, thank you," says the lady, tucking a strand of hair behind her ear. She pulls out her purse and drops its contents into her palm. There's a ten-pound note and a handful of marbles.

"I'm afraid I only accept English pounds," says the owner, his grin widening further. "I've not got change for... marbles!"

The lady smiles politely but avoids eye contact. She hands him the note.

"Keep the change," she says.

"Really? Then you're more than paying for the flapjack!"

"It's ok," she says, dropping the marbles back into her purse.

The coffee machine compresses boiling water through coffee grounds into a cup as the café owner swills a jug of frothy milk. Bringing the two together, he carefully pours the milk, finishing the foam with a rehearsed flick of his wrist, leaving a milky white depiction of a mountain in the brown stain of coffee. He has been perfecting this little gimmick for years.

He places the coffee and the flapjack wrapped in a napkin proudly onto the table in front of the lady. A table beside the window, directly opposite the hooded lady—the lady who hasn't taken her eyes off the newcomer since she stepped in.

The lady tries to sip her coffee, but she is nervous, her hands visibly shaking. She rattles her cup onto its saucer and unfolds the napkin, breaking a piece off the flapjack. The mixture of sugar, honey, and oats is received gratefully by her tired body, washing energy through to the tips of her fingers and toes.

She looks out of the window at the storm. The snow and the wind dance like maniacs. Somewhere out there, no longer visible, is the mountain. It stares towards her, and she stares back. She knows what is coming, and now her knees begin to jiggle.

Rummaging through her backpack, she checks the contents carefully, as though terrified that she could have forgotten something important. Then she glances around the café, looking for something else.

"Excuse me," she whispers in the direction of the hooded lady. "Do you know where the bathroom is?"

The hooded lady nods, gesturing to a door beside the counter.

"Thank you."

While the lady is occupied in the bathroom, the hooded lady, unobserved by anyone else in the café, slips her hand into her jacket and pulls out a little pocket-sized book—a blue leather-bound copy of Lewis Carroll's *Through the Looking-Glass, and What Alice Found There*. Into it she slides a photograph. Something that she is keen no one observes. Then, stealthily, she leans over the absent lady's open backpack and drops her book into it.

When the black-haired lady returns, the hooded lady is leaning back in her chair, as though unmoved. The newcomer's trench coat is unfastened, revealing an elegant, silk blue ball gown. The hooded lady isn't surprised by this attire. She knew the lady would become the *Blue Bride* today.

A chauvinistic mountaineer wolf-whistles at the lady, making his friends turn and notice her.

"Dressed for the occasion, love?" he asks, derisively, his tone more of an announcement to his friends, showing off. A few of them snigger.

The lady smiles nervously, fastening her coat quickly.

"You haven't been up *Mynydd Aaru* in that, have you?" asks another man, as though somehow this unknown lady is now fair game for their conversation, despite her evident aversion to it.

The lady pauses, thinking of an appropriate answer. "Not *yet*," she settles on, smiling. Her feigned smile offers a glimmer of liberation from men like these.

The men, who don't know whether to take her seriously or not, go back to talking inanely amongst themselves.

Back at her table, the lady breaks off a final lump of flapjack and takes a long sip of her coffee, her hands no longer shaking. Her mind is clear and focused now. She picks up her backpack and slings it over her shoulder. Opposite her, the hooded lady stares earnestly, almost willing her to look back, but she doesn't notice.

"Thank you," the lady calls in the direction of the café owner, but her voice is too weak, and he doesn't hear. It doesn't matter anyway; she is already striding out of the café and into the storm.

The hooded lady sighs. She knows where the lady in the blue dress is going. She is off to climb the mountain. And she is going to take her own life.

***

Chapter 3

Potent Posturing

The Meadow - London

The evening is cold, and there is a bite in the frigid air, but the marbles on offer in the Presidential Estate are warm and fresh, still glowing from the marble-making kilns that burn deep under London. They secrete behind teeth, a lingering indulgence, as members of the Distillery Cabinet trade soft, surface-level remarks. One man mentions a delay in marble deliveries. Another replies with a bland commentary on resin permits. There is a little laughter, all of it careful and calculated. No one has yet spoken of the thing they were summoned to discuss.

Andrew Callaghan—*The Ferryman*—has not spoken.

He sits beside the hearth, deliberately and dominantly still. He doesn't fidget. He doesn't blink. He watches the room like it's already let him down. Across from him, skulking in his shadow, is Aidan Elfmann—*the Mineralist*—a gaunt man whose translucent skin seems sanded down to its last miserable layer. His sunken eyes bulge with cruel amusement, and when he smiles, it's the smile of a man who already knows something you'd rather he didn't.

Elfmann is always close to Andrew. Always eager to please him, and murmur in his low, slimy tones. Most people find excuses to avoid Elfmann. He can cool the energy in any room and seems to draw on others' unease. No one knows whether he chose to oversee the underground marble workhouses or if this role was delegated to him. No one else would choose such a life.

Another governor—Angus Callaghan-Crawford—shifts awkwardly in his seat beside the Mineralist. He is flush-faced and fidgety, the only member of the Cabinet without a marble in his mouth. He's too afraid of one bursting, despite endless assurances they won't. Instead, he picks absently at loose strands from a stick of bamboo that rests against his chair.

Angus feels the weight of it all—the fragile silence, the posturing of entitlement, the glint of books too old to touch—and knows he doesn't belong here. This room was sculpted for sharper people. He's here because he married into it, and even that now feels more arrangement than alliance. He watches Eilish, the President's daughter, the governess, his wife. She is, as always, so composed in the company of powerful men, her mind already several moves ahead of the room.

The President watches her, too. He is silent, his amber marble tucked into his cheek, but the weight of his gaze gives him away. He knows Eilish's mind, knows her instinct will pull her away from what Andrew is about to propose. And yet—he's already chosen to back his son tonight. Clearing the streets of dirty resin is, in his mind, an end to justify any means.

The fire crackles.

A councilman, finished with the sensation of his marble, drops it. The marble shatters and fizzles its mist up into the rafters, and with it, the last of the pleasantries fade. In the space left behind, the real meeting now starts to breathe.

The Ferryman shifts in his chair.

Elfmann leans in, his grin sharp as razor wire.

And the rest of the room waits.

"Angus," shouts the Ferryman, staring at the governess' husband, and throwing a sharp red marble into his mouth. "Your spies embarrassed us again at the council. We have rebels on our streets, and your intelligence from *Operation Jack and Jill* is pathetic."

There are murmurs of agreement around the room.

Angus mumbles something and lowers his gaze.

"Well, governor?"

"Sorry, what?" asks Angus, looking up, trying to work out what he's expected to say.

"These '*Well Wishers*'," says the Ferryman, "It has been ten years of decline since the infamous night of rebellion… yet they are on the rise again. How do you propose we quash them this time? It is your network of spies on the front-line, after all!"

"Err…" Angus stutters. "I don't really know what we can do, Your Excellency."

"You are worse than useless!" the Ferryman shouts. "You might not have chosen your position, but you are married to my sister. At least try to do her proud!" He slams his fists down, shooting an accusatory gaze at the Governess. "We have a rebellion growing in the Meadow again. I will not have my father's control of the Distillery threatened!"

Angus whimpers.

"I think you should try again, governor!" says the President, joining his son's attack on Angus. "How are your spies going to help us squash this rebellion?!"

Angus' breathing becomes short and sharp. He avoids everyone's gaze, wipes his brow nervously with a dark purple handkerchief, and rolls a marble across his palm.

"You are hopeless!" shouts the President, losing patience.

The Governess looks down at her husband. She hates it that he never stands up for himself against her brother or father. Never fights back.

"I can offer something?" she speaks up.

The President looks across at his daughter, his right eye twitching nervously.

"No need!" interrupts her brother. "The Mineralist has already given me the best idea…" He winks at Elfmann.

Shuffling into a more upright position and taking a moment to inspect the assembled councilmen, Andrew enjoys that all the attention is fixed firmly on him, waiting for him to continue.

"I think it is time we reintroduce an old custom," he announces. "One, long forgotten. A custom that gave the Distillery unrivalled control over the Meadow in the past. I think it is time that *public executions* start once more!"

There is near silence in the room. The President chuckles, enjoying the moment.

"What?" Andrew asks the room, threateningly. A grin stretches across his face, and he casts a disdainful eye on his sister. "The people here have been blessed with a second life in the Meadow. I think the *ungrateful* deserve to have that life taken away."

"Andrew, you are not serious?!" spits the Governess.

"Am I not?" he says, reaching with a twisted golden ladle into a font between him and his father, pulling out a dark black marble. He drops it into the gaping void of his mouth, and a sharp flash of crimson sparkles in his eyes.

"We *need* control," he says.

"Control? Your officers already have the power to take and destroy private marbles," Eilish says, glaring at the councillors whose votes secured this practice. "And your officers have canisters again. Is that not enough?" asks the governess.

Andrew clutches at the small metal canister in a holster on his hip. One spray of this Thermocline Mist would end a person's life in the Meadow.

"Deterrence is insufficient," he says defiantly. "We need absolute control!"

Eilish scoffs. "You're becoming a monster, Andrew. Can't you see it? What next? Forcing people to drink groundwater from the Lethe?"

The Mineralist sits up, looking at the Ferryman, as though seriously considering the Governess' sarcastic suggestion.

"Don't even think about it," she snaps at Elfmann.

"Well, I think this is an excellent idea, Andrew," says the President, ignoring his daughter's concerns and dabbing his brow with a handkerchief. "If we use such a punishment on convicted Well Wishers... well, the rest will surely step in line."

"Yes. Convicted Well Wishers... to *begin* with..." Andrew muses out loud.

"Father, stop him," says Eilish, looking to the President to rein her brother in. But the President remains unmoved, avoiding eye contact with his daughter.

"There are other blemishes in the Meadow which could certainly do with a more permanent heal..." Andrew looks around the room, leaving a long and menacing pause. "Dirty resin is a shameful blight on our streets. But in the main, these *stains* hide in the dark alleys and slums of the city, out of sight. But not all of them.

"I am, of course, referring to the *Sculptor Collectives*. For years, they have shamelessly leaked their dirty resin all over our city, hiding behind wealth in their lavish gated communities. But the people are tired of them… The taxes on their marbles and the shaming of their wealth haven't gone far enough. So, I say we cleanse their stains once and for all!"

"You want to *kill* the artisan marble makers?!" exclaims Eilish.

"The *Sculptors* are a *pariah* in the Meadow!" Andrew shouts angrily.

"Well said, your Excellency!" exults the Mineralist.

"Give me public executions, and I will break the *Sculptors*," shouts the Ferryman, casting his voice around the room. "I will expose their members as *Stained*. I will cleanse these shores of their filthy resin, and I *will* purify the Meadow!"

The governess looks at her brother appalled. Are there no depths to which he won't sink?

"You've completely lost your mind, Andrew," she hisses. "Have you no heart, either?"

"Wind your neck in, Eilish," snaps Andrew, sharply, losing his cool. "They're *stained*… they deserve what they get. And that's your problem, Eilish," he goes on the attack. "You get too *emotional* about these things!"

Eilish won't stand for this. She smashes her marble aggressively into the wall above Andrew, sending its rose mist climbing into the rafters above them. She doesn't care about making a scene. She doesn't care that this display of rage only serves to make Andrew feel vindicated in his attack on her emotions. She storms out of the room and slams the door in the faces of her father, brother, and the pathetic congregation of 'yes men' they surround themselves with.

She is furious. She is devastated. Devastated by what her family has become. Devastated that ever since they had arrived in the Meadow, ever since they had risen to prominence, and ever since they had learned of the *Stained*—those poor people whose resin will *never* run clear because their minds are too tormented. Tormented by suicide or murder—they had been on a vendetta against them.

Of course, Eilish knows why, but that doesn't justify any of it. Ciara, her sister, died with her twelve years ago, too. And suicide always tears through the families left behind, even if they weren't *actually* left behind. It tears in ways that cannot be predicted or controlled. But eventually the wounds must heal. Eilish has to believe it.

****

Chapter 4

An Angel's Whisper

The Meadow - London

"Public executions?! Oh my god! What is wrong with them?!"

The atmosphere in the grand riverside bar is indulgent and decadent. Through the windows, the River Lethe—the Meadow's equivalent to the river Thames from Earth—sparkles in the evening sun, looking dangerously enticing, flowing, as it does, with deadly groundwater. Water which, if consumed in any quantity more than a cupful, would dissolve the mind and send you 'on'.

Inside the bar, the privileged socialites of The Paddock—this area of London south of the river—slurp opulent marble cocktails from glittering glass flutes and converse boastfully with one another.

Away from prying eyes, tucked in beside a quiet window, Governess Eilish Callaghan sits facing her closest friend in the Meadow—Chloe Callaghan, her brother's wife. Chloe's skeletal figure is reminiscent of a shadow; fragile and vulnerable.

"Do you think it is just a threat?"

Eilish shakes her head. The years have long since passed when her father made idle threats to keep people in line.

"I'm fuming with myself," says Eilish.

"With yourself? Why?"

"I made a scene," she concedes. "Seriously, Chloe… Why? Why do I *always* make a scene? Why do I get so… so *emotional*?" She hates herself for using her brother's criticism.

"Because you care!" says Chloe, without hesitation. "You should never feel bad for caring!"

Eilish smiles. It always helps knowing that Chloe has her back. It doesn't kill her self-loathing, but at least it pushes it back in its place.

"Angus will be in charge of condemning the first victims," she frowns.

"Your Angus?! No. He wouldn't."

"I don't think he has a choice. My father is convinced that these latest rebellions are all because the Well Wishers have got too confident again. He says the Council of the Almighty have instructed him to quash the rebellion in any way possible–it's *His Will.*"

Chloe scoffs.

"Your father only pretends to have faith in *Him* to maintain power. Your brother is the same. Do either really believe?"

The governess shrugs.

"I can't tell… it benefits them to go along with it, either way."

Chloe shakes her head.

"Andrew has requested that the executions be also used on the *Sculptor Collectives*," says Eilish.

Chloe draws in a sharp intake of breath. "What? Why?! They're just craftspeople."

"It is his opinion that the Distillery should craft the only marbles in the Meadow now," says Eilish. "He says their artisan marble craft is a dangerous trade. He thinks that's why they are all afflicted with dirty resin. And he thinks their marbles are contributing to the darkening of other people's resin, too."

"That's no reason to execute them!"

"No, of course," Eilish retreats. "But you know how my brother and father have always hated them. They say they're with the people, hating the *Collectives'* unjustified wealth and hating their refusal to integrate with the rest of the Meadow. And now my brother is claiming to have evidence that the *Collectives'* resin isn't just dirty but permanently *stained.*"

Chloe rolls her eyes and dabs her forehead with a handkerchief. "I bet he does… but we've heard this accusation so many times before. It never sticks!"

"I know," says Eilish.

"The only way to confirm a *Stain* is either to get a confession or spend years interrogating them to prove, beyond doubt, that their resin will never run clear. Andrew won't have evidence… he's spouting the same old lies just to boost his popularity here in the Paddock."

The Governess looks out across the river towards the north bank, where life is such a contrast to the opulence of the Paddock. In the darkness, beyond the collage of rickety terraced rooftops, fires are glowing—fires of the rebellion.

"You're probably right," she says. "But you can see why. There's no doubt about it, discontent with the Distillery is growing."

"I know," Chloe concedes. "And you can hardly blame them. Life is getting very precarious once more. Marbles are bursting in people's mouths like they never used to, and few people have access to the supplies we do. It's not just addicts going 'on' anymore. Young men are going missing, and people are losing trust in marbles. They are losing trust in the Distillery."

A bright flash of light illuminates the sky outside. Somewhere in the distance, out west, a shaft of white beams from the sky to the ground. A shaft of light indicating that a new arrival has just entered the Meadow. A person who, through disaster, has crossed from Earth to the Meadow.

Both women look at it solemnly.

"It looks like a stormy one," says Chloe, observing dark clouds bursting out from the shaft of light. She looks over at Eilish, trying to guess what she's thinking.

Eilish's eyes have glazed over, falling into memory. Chloe knows which memory.

"You think your angel will come?" Chloe asks.

"She usually follows Arrivals."

"But can she withstand the storm?"

"Maybe."

"Just be careful," says Chloe, looking worried, knowing Eilish's mind is made up—she's going to the bridge, despite the weather.

"I will," smiles Eilish, reaching across and clasping Chloe's palm tightly. "Don't worry about me—I won't do anything dangerous. I promise. See you at the Festival!"

Chloe smiles. "I'm looking forward to it."

Eilish looks kindly into Chloe's eyes, and their shared warmth thaws her soul. "I love you, Chloe," she says.

"I love you, too, Eilish."

Eilish pulls away, puts on a fur hat and long-belted coat, tying it firmly around her waist, before stepping out into the blustery street, headed for London Bridge.

Chloe watches her go and lingers a while, gazing out at the darkening sky. The wind is whipping up, coming from the direction of the rapidly fading shaft of light. Troughs of small waves break the river's surface, and the branches of the trees lining the riverbank start to sway.

The breeze is quickly a gale. What had been a warm, quiet evening is turning into a treacherous winter storm that sweeps through the city. A rapid change in the weather like this is not uncommon in the Meadow. When a disaster happens on Earth, bringing new souls into this realm, it also brings climate and artefacts from Earth; rain, sun, or snow, and vehicles, objects, things—whatever a soul was touching when it fell.

Eilish hurries onto London Bridge, holding her coat tight as the biting rain drives into her face. The river, angry and swollen, churns in the channel, its surface flailing under the stone arches.

She leans against the railings alone, facing westwards into the wind and shivers, not from the stinging cold, but from the kaleidoscope of memories that begin to tumble into her mind.

A dark patch of the pregnant river stares at her. The place where it had all begun twelve years ago. She can still feel tension in her arms from tightly grasping her seat in the plane, and she can hear the horrific sounds of the crash as their Learjet smashed into the Thames. Her racing heart can still remember the desperate instinct to thrash her limbs frantically. Scrabbling for her life, splashing and scraping through the sinking fuselage on that dark, cold night.

'Forgive me,' she whispers desperately into the storm, but she can tell that her angel isn't coming. Not tonight. *'Forgive me… please.'*

She pulls off her hat in the frantic rain, leans her head back, and wails into the night.

"Something the matter?" a deep voice startles her.

Eilish turns sharply, embarrassed and shocked that someone else is out on this awful night. A large, bearded man is dragging himself across the bridge, lugging a heavy sack over his shoulder. His overwhelming size and the dishevelled mass of hair that covers his face give him an almost mythical appearance.

"I'm fine," she lies, quickly.

"You don't look fine," he says, eyeing her knowingly.

Despite the scars that tell of countless storms at sea, he has a kind face, and this disarms Eilish.

"You look like you could do with a marble," he says, dropping the sack from his shoulder. "*Sailor's Mist*—guaranteed to steady the nerves." He pulls out a handful of beautifully crafted marbles—the kinds of marbles only the *Sculptor Collectives* would have.

Eilish knows it is never sensible to take marbles from a stranger, especially not on a dark, rainy night on a bridge over the Lethe. But her intrigue betrays her caution, and she reaches out.

"Thank you," she murmurs.

He smiles.

"Can I walk you home?"

"No. No, thank you, sir," says Eilish defensively.

A grimace flashes across the man's face. "Fair enough," he says, nodding respectfully. "Well, take care." He shoots a quizzical look at Eilish in the darkness.

She drops her gaze, believing that the man hasn't yet recognised her.

"Thank you again," she says, stepping away.

"No problem. Good risen!" he calls back with a wave of his hand.

'Good risen', thinks Eilish. Gosh. She hasn't heard that phrase in ten years. Not since the last rebellion.

As Eilish leaves the bridge southwards, soaked and uneasy, the large, bearded man trudges alone over the cobblestones of the north bank of the Lethe, until he reaches the door of a pub—*The Angel's Whisper.*

Giving his overalls a shake, like a bedraggled old dog, he pushes open the door and steps in.

Inside, despite the dated decor—the heavy red curtains, the worn racing green carpet, and the sticky mahogany tables—*The Angel's Whisper* throbs with a snug warmth and homely energy. Ignoring the dozen young people, with soot and ash in their clothes, who prop up the bar and chat raucously, indulging marble after marble, the bearded man shuffles himself to a dark corner of the old pub. An area dimly lit by hanging candle lanterns, where huddles of patrons murmur in hushed conspiratorial tones.

"Did you hear that Sammy's brother's friend Danny is missing now?" says a young woman at the bar.

"For real?" asks her friend.

"Yup," the girl responds, looking around at her friends, all eyes on her. "Sammy's brother saw them."

"No way!?"

"Yes way!"

"Saw who?" asks a nervous-looking young man who sits on a barstool, biting his nails.

"The *Horsemen!*" the girl exclaims.

"They're real?"

"Oh, they're real alright… Sammy's brother says that they snatched Danny from his paper round."

"Keep your voice down, dear," says an old lady, tapping the girl on the shoulder, startling her. "There are lots of worried and superstitious parents around," she nods towards the bar where the landlord, a large man in his middle age, is busy cleaning marble ramekins.

The lady holds a status amongst the group of young people, for they part and reverently make space for her to reach the bar. The old lady smiles gratefully.

"Any chance of some service before we grow old and die?" the old lady calls out to the landlord, leaning nonchalantly against the bar.

The landlord turns, and a wide grin stretches across his face. "We're all dead," he chuckles. "What are you rattling on tonight, Kim-Joy? The usual?"

"And what would be my 'usual'?" smiles the old lady.

"Something *un*usual!" he grins.

"What's the rarest marble you've got? Any from the *Collectives*?" she winks.

The landlord casts a nervous look along the bar, then reaches down under the sink for a crate.

Kim-Joy inspects the delicately crafted spheres held in velvet in the crate as the landlord holds them up to the light. A handful of marbles resemble miniature globes, their colour swirling like weather systems over a wash of earthy green and ocean blue.

"They're not *Earth Marbles*, are they?" she asks, astonished.

"They are, indeed," smiles the landlord.

"I haven't had one of those in centuries! I'll take a couple for me and Cyril."

The landlord nods, carefully lifting two *Earth Marbles* with a pair of silver tongues and places them into a sterilised crystal ramekin.

"How much do I owe you?" asks Kim-Joy.

"It's on the house," says the landlord. "So long as you keep bringing your rabble here, it's always on the house."

Kim-Joy smiles appreciatively. "Well, you're always welcome at the *Tide and Time Tavern*," she says. "We have some rare marbles too."

"I'd love to," the landlord responds. "Though I'm keen to avoid the blemish on my record that a trip to your place would guarantee. Rumour has it your place is now watched day and night."

"Oh, yes," sniggers Kim-Joy. "They've been watching us for ten years. They will never find anything in my tavern. The Ferrymen can't see for looking!"

"You've always had the fire of a rebel," beams the landlord. "Do you not worry that the Distillery will one day use force to destroy the *Tide and Time*?"

"Oh, I'm sure they will," says Kim-Joy, her smile dropping from her face. "But we have plans for when they do…"

"Plans?"

"Don't worry, we won't be knocking on your door, Carl!"

Kim-Joy chuckles and wanders off with her two marbles rattling in the ramekin.

She approaches the dark corner of the old pub and smiles. Squashed into a cosy private booth, the bearded man waits for her, beaming.

"*Earth Marbles*," says Kim-Joy, placing the ramekin on the table. "These will take you back."

The trawlerman lifts his grizzled face. "I haven't had any of these in years!" He rolls the marble in his leathery hand. "Before we indulge, I have news."

"Go on."

"She was back on the bridge tonight."

"In this weather?"

"Aye… And I spoke to her."

"Cyril, you didn't?!" Kim-Joy exclaims.

"It's alright, I was careful. She would never recognise me."

"So, do you think she *is* a possibility?"

"Yes, I do. She's the only senior figure in the Distillery who seems to have a heart."

"But she's a Callaghan?!"

"I know. But she's not like the others. She is a beacon of hope."

Kim-Joy runs the marble between her thumb and forefinger in thought. "And did *she* visit again? Her *angel*?"

"No," says the trawlerman. "It was too windy."

"But you're convinced she's good news?"

"I think so," says the trawlerman.

"Well, listen," says Kim-Joy. "Keep tabs on the governess, but don't get caught. She might be reasonable, but the rest of the Callaghan family are not."

"Agreed," the trawlerman grimaces.

***

Chapter 5

An audience for a tragedy

Earth - London

Several months later, *and* ten years earlier, the St. Patrick's Day crowds swagger with a drunken joy down the side streets and bars that surround Hammersmith station in London, on Earth. The night sky is dark, but the spring air is pleasantly warm and alive. The lights of the city reflect in the polished surfaces of the cars and in the ravenous eyes of the men and women who saunter through tonight's party atmosphere. The only interruption to their breeziness, because of the proximity to Charing Cross Hospital, is the countless Ambulances that rush past. Tonight is the busiest night of the year for paramedics in London.

Young men in tight tops and skinny jeans strut around in packs, their cockerel chests pumped out with bravado spewing everywhere. Older men, with red-flushed cheeks and chubby hands, grasp half-finished pints of Guinness and laugh with filthy eagerness, endlessly trying to catch each other's eyes, hoping for approval. And the women on the street, both young and old, have squeezed into a shimmering array of sparkling dresses. Dresses that show off their curves or betray a reality their wearer wishes weren't true. Leaning against one another, bony elbows prodding into the air, these women slur their compliments to each other and cackle into bottles bought for them by repugnant admirers.

Standing on the corner of King Street, overlooking Hammersmith station, and all alone, is the mysterious hooded lady. She has been hobbling up and down this corner of the street since the sun dropped below the rooftops. Watching the people of the night with a casual interest, listening keenly to the sounds of the city, and checking her watch obsessively. She is waiting. Waiting for the sound of sirens. Waiting for the tragedy to unfold.

The lady spots a couple sitting on a bench nearby, outside a café. They're a couple she knows of but has never actually met. She hadn't realised they would be here tonight. But it makes sense, of course. The night is so crucial to both of them. The lady, Ashley Arnold, is in her eighties, a survivor of World War II. The young man—Gareth Edwards—her husband, is more than half a century her junior. He supports her fragile frame in his stooping, nervous arms. Their love is unusual. Forged in a different time and a different place.

There is a scream and a commotion on the street. Outside *Flannagan's* pub, two young men are squaring up to each other. One of the men appears to have a pint of Guinness dripping down the front of his shirt, the empty glass still in his clenched hand. The other man has blood pouring from his nose. Friends and desperate girlfriends are restraining both men.

"He's not worth it, Stevie!" shouts one of the girls, her sequinned black dress riding high up her thigh while her mascara runs down to meet it.

"You stay outa dis, Chelsea!" says her boyfriend, wriggling free, pulling his fists up in front of his face and wiping the blood off his nose onto his sleeve.

"Roy, be the bigger man!" pleads the lady holding onto the other baying male. "It's just a shirt! We can buy anuva one!"

"It's a shirt *and* it's my pint!" he says. "*And* the way he looked at you!"

"Ah, feck off!" shouts Stevie.

Roy doesn't need an invitation. He lunges forward, windmilling his right arm wildly, staggering with drunken coordination and somehow landing a heavy blow to Stevie's left cheek, making him fall back into the road.

Chelsea screams. At the moment that Stevie stumbles into the street, a moped delivery rider is coming past. His Learner 'L' plates are plastered to the front and back, though, even if he was an experienced rider, he would have struggled to avoid the staggering drunk.

The moped collides with Stevie, its front wheel striking his head, knocking him out cold. A gaping wound from his temple vomits blood all over the pavement. In an instant, a mixture of sweat, alcohol, fear, confusion, testosterone, and tarmac mix in a melee of chaos.

Stevie, who had been so fired up a moment ago, is quiet as he lies on the road, drifting out of consciousness. All around him, his friends and those who witnessed the incident have started to panic. A decision needs to be made. Do they carry Stevie down the street to the hospital, or do they call for an ambulance to come here? What would be best? What would be quickest? Alcohol is not a helpful ingredient for decision-making.

As a couple of Stevie's friends try to lift him, they slip on the petrol that is pouring out of the crashed moped, creating a hazardous slick across the road. Despite the awful situation, a few drunken girls cannot help but laugh at their slapstick clumsiness.

Standing just back from the commotion, the mysterious hooded lady is unmoved. She has recognised that this is the moment. *This* is the event that triggers the sirens. And indeed, across from her, the old lady at the café has her phone out. She is calling for help.

A moment later, sirens scream into the street before a bright yellow ambulance hurtles around the corner. The people all around Stevie wave frantically at it, as though it isn't apparent that this is where the accident has happened. But none of them anticipate what is coming.

As the heavy vehicle speeds over the petrol slick, the driver loses control. Its brakes screeching, the ambulance rocks over onto two wheels and careens into the crowd.

The screams of the people and the wail of the siren are crushed into the noise of the thundering impact of the ambulance with the pavement.

Despite this awful event unfolding in front of them, the hooded lady and the couple outside the café just watch, impassively. They knew this tragedy was coming. They needed it to happen.

***

Chapter 6

Sermon of Apocalypse

The Meadow - London

Hidden in the shadows of snow-laden pines north of the River Lethe, the ancient stones of *St. Magnus the Martyr* from Earth now house the *Almighty Sanctioned Reformed Church of Well-Wishing* in the Meadow.

Ten years ago, before the rebellion, Well-Wishing was outlawed. It's belief—that souls could travel between Earth and the Meadow—directly challenged the Distillery's doctrine: that the Meadow was purgatory, a one-way passage toward the afterlife. But after the rebellion, the Distillery was forced into negotiations. This church, now crowded with hundreds, was one of the first to gain official recognition.

Inside, candlelight flickers over the tense faces of Kim-Joy and Cyril Spate. Though the air is frigid, the way they stare towards the priests at the front of the church is colder. The rebellion left scars—some visible, most not—and trust among Well Wishers remains brittle.

The church leaders who brokered peace with the Distillery accepted personal privileges—access to the Palaces, among others—in exchange for their obedience, and the obedience of their congregations. These days, their sermons echo the Distillery's line: the Meadow is a place of cleansing, not passage. Talk of returning to Earth is theoretical at best—heretical at worst.

The priesthood of Well-Wishing, once radical, now mirrors the regime they once opposed. They speak of the Meadow as a necessary stop on the soul's journey, a space to shed old demons and rehearse a better life. Few of them remember when Well-Wishing meant freedom.

That said, this doesn't mean the community of Well Wishers align with their Priesthood. Those rebels who fought the Distillery ten years ago couldn't be bought out.

At the front of the church this evening, a priest stands with his arms raised, waving them like a sorceress casting his spell. He is trying, in vain, to capture the attention of his congregation, but they ignore him, happily bumping into friendly faces they know from across the city. Faces they haven't seen in a while. Friends they were worried might have 'gone on', and often comrades who had stood arm in arm with them during the rebellion.

When the congregation eventually goes silent, the priest, his voice low and melodious, addresses them. His words slither noxiously over them all.

"Welcome, family. Welcome, friends," he hisses. "What a great joy to see you all. What a great privilege to join together in freedom in this, our second life.

"This evening, we remember our loved ones lost. And we are graced with a lesson from our esteemed friend, High Councillor Craven. But first let us join together, as we always have, in song…

"May the seas warm, and the clouds form…"'

To which the congregation responds, "*…and may the rain fall, filling the rivers of Love.*"

At the front of the church, a band begin to play. A folk band, familiar to many in the congregation. *The General Electrics.* Three young women—dedicated Well Wishers—celebrated rebels who led the line in the rebellion ten years ago, and excellent musicians. They start the most popular song of the Well Wishers, its chorus familiar to all, though many of its verses have been sculpted recently to keep their music current and their message in tune.

Out of circadian, She heard us play,
Our tune brought life to her breath.
Her true winds stoked our fires,
While our music reached her depths.

Her loving rain is falling free,

The soil thirsts, the raindrops sink into the sea.

One righteous night, they stood their ground,
  Despite the rain, despite the fight.
Mist filled the hill, mist swirled around,
  Our heroes drank and entered light.

Her loving rain is falling free,
The soil thirsts, the raindrops sink into the sea.

Ten years, the spool of time unwound,
  An era of remembrance nears.
But back or forth, to realms newfound,
  Her story is hope. Never fear.

Her loving rain is falling free,
The soil thirsts, the raindrops sink into the sea.

After a dozen repeats of the chorus, each with as much energy as the last, the congregation applaud with a rapturous energy that fills the old dusty church with life. That is, until they all go quiet for the priest.

"We are gathered here today," he calls out, "to remember those from this city who have left the Meadow. Hold them in your hearts as we release marbles in their memory." He raises his hands high above his head, pinching a marble between thumb and forefinger. "With those names on our lips, let us break a marble in memory."

All around the church, people reach into pockets and pouches, selecting marbles which they raise into the air.

"We will never forget you!" shouts the priest, and he hurls his marble to the ground, shattering it into thousands of fragments. A deep purple mist fizzes up around him.

The congregation follow suit, and the noise of smashing marbles is deafening, before a kaleidoscope of mist fizzes up through the people, like a rising cloud of colour, losing everyone for a moment, before the mist climbs into the rafters and dissipates.

In the reverent silence, as the congregation remember their loved ones, an old man—an elder whose mind is failing—climbs the steps of the lectern to give the evening address.

"Brothers and sisters," he calls out, his voice sharp and frail, commanding a deathly silence. "Tonight, we confront a terrible truth. Nearly two hundred young men—good men with clear resin—have vanished without a trace."

There is hush in the church. Heads turn to loved ones. Usually, the address is a dry and pious affair. But the plight of the missing men is already on many of their minds—it strikes to the heart of almost every community in the city.

"The Distillery dismiss these disappearances as youthful folly, misadventure…"

'Boos' ring out from pockets of the congregation. The priest simply raises his hand and continues.

"…But you know the whispers—the sightings. The mysterious goings on at night. Horsemen riding pale, red, black, and white steeds. Kidnappers snatching men from the street."

The High Councillor turns and nods to a younger priest who stands at the lectern with a large leather-bound bible. The young priest opens the text to the final book—the book of Revelations—and reads aloud a passage full of bleak and unsettling imagery about a lamb opening seals and of four creatures, four horses—one ridden by Death. His voice is shrill, ringing uneasily over every disturbing detail, and falling clumsily onto the silent congregation.

There is confusion writ large on everyone's faces as the young priest closes his bible and retreats to the altar. The elderly priest, still standing, allows the words and images of the reading to swirl around the minds of the congregation before him for a moment.

"On Earth," he starts again, "many Christians take this passage from the Book of Revelations to depict the 'end times'. A time when the four horsemen of the Apocalypse—war, conquest, famine, and death—are to visit the Earth, signalling its imminent destruction before the final victory of Christ. Well, we come to tell you today that those four horsemen are *real!* And they are here. Here in the Meadow! They have come from the Beyond, and they are using our realm as the staging post for the final invasion of the Earth."

This bizarre announcement, so unclear and unexpected, causes the people to chatter in confusion. Many of the congregation are not convinced. Kim-Joy exchanges a troubled look with Cyril. They both feel the familiar chill of manipulation.

The High Councillor holds up his hand again. "You all know the rumours!" he shouts out, an air of accusation in his voice. "Think about it... Young, fit men... all of fighting age with perfectly clear resin in their pores signalling purity of mind, are disappearing in their dozens. And who is taking them? Four night-dwelling individuals on horseback, riding white, red, black, and pale horses. These *are* the four horsemen of the apocalypse. And they are taking our young men to prepare them to fight in the invasion of the earth."

"*How does this help me?* I hear you cry... the Book of Revelations is not just a prophecy about the end of the Earth. Not at all... For after the horsemen purge the Earth of its failings, the passages tell us that the stars in the sky will fall, and the heavens themselves will recede '*like a scroll being rolled up*'. The 'heavens'— our realm here in the Meadow and the Beyond—will recede. This will be the end times for *all* the realms as we know them. So, ignore the presence of the *horsemen* at your peril. They signal that the end is coming!"

As the High Councillor draws his address to a close, the priest tries, in vain, the quieten the congregation who are now talking anxiously. Usually, they would finish with a prayer, but the priest has no chance of initiating this tonight.

Towards the back of the hall, near the exit, Kim-Joy and Cyril are fighting their way out into the street.

"Well, fuck me!" says Cyril, striding into the fresh night air. "This is getting too much! It is madness! Missing men being taken by the horsemen of the apocalypse. That kind of scare tactics sounds just out of the Distillery playbook to me. And I don't like it!"

Kim-Joy nods in agreement, her eyes flashing with anger. "I think we can safely conclude," she says, "that the Reformed Church is now firmly in the control of the Distillery."

"Agreed," says Cyril. His eyes, which usually twinkle cheerfully, darken. "Shame."

"We can't let the people fall for these lies," says Kim-Joy. "They are good people who need help. These priests can't be their only guides."

"No," agrees Cyril.

"We're going to have to give Nailah more resources and support. If Well-Wishing is to survive, we need her more than ever!"

***

Chapter 7

Sand on the tracks

The Meadow - London

Many miles north of the church, in the icy quiet of the night, Euston Station lies hushed beneath an agony of frost that grips tight to the iron rails. A station operative cranks a handle on the rear carriage of a long, snaking train. The train, a dormant beast, waits obediently in the cold, bitter night, its flanks scratched with icicles. The man, wearing all purple—the purple of the Distillery—peers in through the barred windows of the carriage.

Dozens of gaunt, barely conscious men and women, their eyes unfocused, their breaths dribbling into the frigid air, are squashed, like cattle, into the carriage. These passengers are the recently deceased and dying souls of the Meadow—the souls who have no more than a fleeting time left in the realm. There are unconscious souls—these are the *Drifters*—and others, teetering on the edge of consciousness, they are the *Founderers*. Their minds have given up, and now their bodies are left to drift through the Meadow, heading towards a place where all souls inevitably go— the Source—a spring of water that cascades off the cliffs at the top of the highest mountain in the realm.

Dripping down the faces of the passengers, streaking in filthy stains, is dirty black resin. It is the discharge of a mind that has met its end. The body might not age in the Meadow, but the mind does. And there is no return for a mind leaking black resin.

The man sneers at the passengers, conditioned to be repulsed by the sight of their dirty resin. Anything but clear resin is abhorred by anyone in the Distillery.

The operator bashes the bars with his truncheon. "Safe journey!" he sniggers. "Enjoy the jump!"

None of the passengers react. They are indifferent to his cruelty.

"Right," the man calls out sharply, addressing a colleague further up the platform, "Flickers next."

His colleague raises an acknowledging hand and turns towards the station building, nodding to some other officers waiting inside.

The officers inside are surrounded by young women. Lost, bewildered, and tragically obedient women. These women are *Flickers*. They are 'foundering souls', but not the same as the *Founderers* in the train. They are conscious women who have lost all memory of their lives before the Meadow. And without memory, they are also without resin. But these particular women have lost more than memory and resin; they have lost hope.

As they are corralled out of the warm waiting room onto the bitterly cold platform, a woman asks, "Where are we going?" She looks confused to the point of fear.

"To the mountains," says the officer at her side, chuckling darkly. He flicks out the large metal baton that was tucked into his trousers and raises it threateningly.

"Go steady. We don't like bruised apples!" says his superior, waiting beside a luxurious first-class carriage.

The women are filed obediently into the carriage, where beautifully upholstered seats and bubbling marble-filled fonts await them. A façade of bountiful indulgence that contrasts with their emptiness and despair.

The two operatives who remain on the platform peer enviously into the warm carriage where their colleagues sit comfortably among the young women. The younger man shivers as he fastens the carriage door tightly shut.

"Lucky bastards," he mutters to himself, bitterly.

"Stay sharp," snaps his superior. "This one's getting a Presidential Carriage too."

"A *Presidential Carriage*?!" His pulse quickens. Presidential carriages are rare and mean secrecy.

The superior points down the platform.

In the mist beyond the front of the train, a carriage is emerging, pulled by a dozen strong shire horses, led by equally strong, muscular Ferrymen in jeans and bomber jackets. Each of the horses is draped in purple coats, encrusted with the Speared Drop—the symbol of the Distillery.

"Evening, gentlemen," shouts the officer as the carriage party approaches.

"Evening, Sir!" the front Ferryman shouts back, cupping his right hand to his mouth—a salute. The other Ferrymen follow suit, before they start coupling the new carriage to the train.

"Right. Inspection time," says the superior officer, gesturing his subordinate towards the new carriage.

The Presidential carriage is exquisite. Every panel is varnished to a bright sparkle, and brass fittings gleam. Curtains of delicate lace hang in the windows, and lamps accompanying each seat are fringed with dancing thread. Soft armchairs, upholstered with purple velvet, face in towards one another, each with its marble font made of sharp crystal. A rainbow of marbles already tumbles over one another in the warm, clear water.

In the centre of the carriage, standing from the floor to the ceiling, is a peculiar capsule.

"What's that?" asks the younger man.

"None of our business," snaps his superior. "Just check it's empty."

The young man peers into the capsule. Like a phone booth, the upright compartment has glass windows and a sturdy metal frame. It is about the right size to fit a single person inside. The doorway to the capsule is sealed tightly, and handles fasten it shut on the outside, as if it is designed to keep someone in. He peers at the floor of the capsule, where little mounds of fine silty sand are piled. An aroma emanates from the sand. A potent human odour. A mix of sweat and virility. It's very odd.

"Are we good?" asks the superior.

The young man turns and nods.

"Let's take up our positions. The welcome party will be here soon."

A moment later, four cloaked men emerge from the station house. Between them, they are carrying a long, heavy box—a coffin. Behind the pallbearers are the Ferryman, the Mineralist, and the President. Each stride into the cool night, their shoulders hunched, and their heads bowed solemnly.

The abdominal muscles of the station operatives clench nervously. A Presidential Carriage is rare, but one with this status is unheard of. Together they stand to attention beside the vestibule door and, in unison, cup their right hands over their mouths.

The royal party are silent as they pass, and do not even acknowledge the station staff as they step into the carriage and swiftly draw the blinds to all the windows.

Inside, the President lights an oil lantern, throwing an orange glow through the carriage, illuminating the four cloaked men struggling past the armchairs with the heavy coffin.

"Ok, have you got him?" asks one of the figures rhetorically, leaving the coffin for the other three to hold, and turning to the capsule in the centre of the carriage. He carefully unfastens each of the airtight latches and gives the door a firm tug, breaking the seal.

Stepping in, the man inspects the compartment, top to bottom, smoothing out the odorous mounds of sand on the floor. Then, between them, the cloaked figures lift the coffin upright and slide it into the capsule, before stepping back and sealing the doorway.

The President and the Ferryman draw near. The Mineralist lurks in the shadows. The cloaked figures drop their hoods before one of them taps on the glass of the capsule with five rhythmic beats.

Inside, the coffin wobbles. Then the lid creaks and gently swings open. From inside, a fifth cloaked man steps forward, leaning himself up against the glass of the capsule. His features are smooth and soft. His bald head speckled with grains of sand. He scans the men in the carriage thoughtfully before reaching up to a vent embedded in the capsule's frame.

Sliding out from his cloak, the man's arm is grotesquely bruised, with the metallic plugs of multiple medical cannulas taped to his veins, and his hand is deformed. He has a single intact finger. The rest, mere crumbling stumps.

As the man grasps the vent with his remaining finger, sliding it open, the tip of this finger too crumbles, fracturing like a fragile sandcastle, filtering onto the floor beside him.

"My apologies for this unorthodox meeting," rasps the man in the capsule with a dry rattling voice. "As you can see, my host is failing me." He grimaces as more grains of sand crumble from his lip.

"It is no problem, your highness," says the President, bowing. "We are grateful for your audience nonetheless."

"Yes, well… this may be our last meeting for a while. The princes and I…" he nods to the men in cloaks. "We will be returning to Elysian while you get me a new host. But I'm sure you are capable of looking after the Meadow without us for a while?!"

"Of course," responds the Ferryman. "With our new powers, we will."

"Yes… about that…" the man hisses from the capsule. "We have word from *Him* about your plans for public executions… *reservations,* I might say."

The Ferryman looks at his father, who, in turn, glances quizzically at the Mineralist.

"Reservations, your highness?"

"Yes… Strong reservations," says the man. "How many executions do you anticipate carrying out?"

"That depends," says the Ferryman. "We plan to do whatever it takes to stop the current rebellion."

"So, it could be hundreds, maybe even thousands each month."

The Ferryman shrugs nonchalantly. "Yes, I suppose it could."

"Well, *He* would not welcome such numbers."

"Your highness?"

The man in the capsule looks tired, as though conversing is too draining for his failing body, so nods to one of the cloaked figures outside.

The man flicks back his thick brown hair, turning to the President. "Every soul released prematurely from the Meadow disrupts the balance of our realm. It places an unwelcome burden on Elysian."

"A burden?" asks the Ferryman.

"The last time your realm used such measures, the heavens were flooded with trouble, and *He* was forced into wrath. A wrath that scorched this realm."

"You are referring to the *Mighty Fire*? The fire that engulfed the Mountains ten years ago?" asks the President.

"That's right," says the man.

The President and the Ferryman look to the Mineralist nervously, but don't say a word.

"That wrath must not be required again."

The cloaked figures leave a moment before the President speaks.

"So, are we to limit our executions?"

He turns to his son.

"Then your plans for the *Sculptors* may have to wait."

The man in the capsule raises his stumped arm. The President falls silent.

"His Almighty has another solution for you. The wrath of the Almighty has always bubbled against the *Stained*… many of them are your 'Sculptors', right?"

"We believe so," says the Ferryman.

"His Almighty detests any soul who tries to extinguish their spark of life. Nothing angers Him more. And so, He proposes to you a more destructive sentence for these souls in the Meadow…"

The Ferryman leans in eagerly.

"His Almighty proposes that, like *He* did with the *Mighty Fire*, you make use of the power of extinction on the *Stained*."

"Extinction?" the Ferryman asks.

"Untimely death on Earth brings a soul here to the Meadow," the man says. "And an untimely death here takes you into our realm. But there is another path that a soul can take. The path taken by those who perished in the fire. A path of extinction. A dead-end for the spark of life." He pauses.

"If a person here in the Meadow is trapped in flames, that person's body will eventually disintegrate into ash. It will be destroyed. The soul that resided within it will have lost its vessel. And a soul without a host is fragile like glass and cannot leave this realm. A gust of wind can shatter it out of existence. It will never come to our realm, and it will never trouble the Meadow again."

"The Almighty sanctions your use of extinction on the Stained... on your Sculptors." The man in the capsule ushers the President and the Ferryman closer to the glass. "Though, be warned, your authority in the Meadow will be hard to maintain if the people here get wind of this punishment."

"So, you're saying," says the President, "this punishment must be secret?"

"It would be in your interest," smiles the man in the capsule.

Out from the shadows, the Mineralist steps into view. "Might I suggest my workhouses be used for such an important operation?" His slimy smile stretches across his tight face. The creases in his sallow skin cut red lines across his brow.

The President nods.

***

Chapter 8

Symbolic Complaint

Earth - London

A week later, and ten years earlier, Detective Marty Fredrickson, leaning against the gale force winds which are buffeting London on Earth, strides up the steps to Chiswick Police Station. The station is nestled among the grand town houses of the wealthy inhabitants of West London, but is in no way grand itself. Not anymore. It has been fifty years since any government put money into its upkeep. Even the front door is a shameful indictment of the country's investment in public services. The 'P' in Police fell off years ago, and the rusty screw that remains has left an orange stain.

Inside, Marty hears the lobby grandfather clock chiming for nine o'clock. He's on time, for once.

Marty Fredrickson is not what you would expect of a warranted police detective of the Metropolitan Police Service. His appearance is a mess. His blonde hair is long and chaotic—and not just because of the wind—and his chin is covered in a lazy stubble. But his eyes are sharp and glint with a sapphire blue, taking in every detail of his surroundings. He never switches off.

Detectives don't wear uniforms. Well, not the lower ranks. While Marty's colleagues opt for smart suits instead, he does things his way. He wears baggy skater jeans, a ripped red hoodie, and old, scuffed, white trainers, mucky from the street.

"Morning, Detective," says Constable Sharon Leslie, leaning lethargically over the front desk as Marty strides into the station. "Windy, isn't it!"

"Morning, Constable," says Marty, trying, in vain, to pat down his hair. "It is *insanely* windy."

"Busy day?" asks Sharon.

"Looks like it could be," says Marty, picking up the heavy case file that Sharon has just placed in front of him.

"And how's your boy doing?" she asks, considerately.

Marty glances at Sharon and grimaces.

She knows not to probe any further—poor guy.

"I hear they're asking us to look into this potential case of negligence from our pals in green?" Marty says, reverting to his comfort zone: work.

"Yeah, that's what I've been told. The ambulance crew won't be in trouble, will they?"

Marty shrugs. He knows full well that the Chiswick team from the London Ambulance Service, the boys and girls who run the sister station next door, could well be in a spot of bother. He's the investigating officer on the multiple fatality collision that happened when one of their ambulances crashed in Hammersmith last week. Five fatalities in all. Two innocent passengers from the back of the ambulance and three drunk bystanders on the street. Any fatal incident involving a public service would undoubtedly lead to a formal police investigation.

The case didn't look good. The young ambulance driver should not have been responding to an emergency while still having a patient on board. And he certainly should not have been driving at such speeds in a busy pedestrian area. But such were the demands on LAS these days. Ambulance staff took risks to cover up for the inadequacies of their service amidst rising public demand. The Police were no different.

"Is that the Hammersmith file, boss?" says Detective Constable Bates, one of Marty's young colleagues. He is the youngest and freshest face on the investigations command, based on the top floor of Chiswick Police Station.

All around them, fellow detectives clatter about, their shined Oxfords echoing on the tiled floor as they carry case files and redacted reports. The air is stuffy and tired with the smell of coffee and printer ink, as though the atmosphere itself is considering industrial action.

Marty nods.

"It has gone to Official Complaints, hasn't it?!"

Marty sighs. It's all they seem to care about on the station these days. Not justice. Just who is in trouble with whom?

Marty lifts the mug of coffee he has collected on his way up to his desk and takes a sip as he opens the heavy case file slowly and deliberately.

"What's your hunch, boss?" asks DC Bates, pulling up a chair beside Marty.

"I don't go by *hunches,* you know that, Jordan."

DC Bates smiles nervously. He talks too much, and he knows it. But he also can't help it.

"Did you find anything on the Ambulance?" asks Marty, knowing the DC Bates had been assigned to gather evidence from the crashed vehicle.

"Nothing, really," DC Bates frowns. "I wish we could have found a fault with the vehicle. That would have made our job, and the ambulance crew's situation, much easier."

Marty frowns. Jordan has only been in the job a year, and he is already looking for the easy way.

"Aside from all the medical gear, all we found was a load of empty energy drinks, sweet wrappers, and an out-of-date newspaper. And not an interesting paper. A copy of one of those boring papers… the ones with lots of writing in. Who reads those anymore?"

"What was the paper?" asks Marty.

"I don't know… The Guardian or Telegraph or something."

Marty frowns as Jordan wanders over to his desk to get the evidence. Of course, DC Bates wouldn't know the stark difference in political leanings between the newspapers. It was a shame that he thinks no one reads them anymore. Marty does.

"It's strange," says Marty, inspecting the copy of The Times that Jordan passes him. "The paper is from last year, and it looks like it hasn't even been read?"

"Yeah," says Jordan. "The crew probably bought it on a quiet day last year and haven't had a quiet day since!"

"We need to check if there's anything significant about this date," says Marty, putting down his mug and pointing at the date on the top of the paper.

"Why, sir?"

"Anything that doesn't add up on its own, Detective, we need to do the maths ourselves."

"But the crash was an accident," says Jordan. "We've seen the CCTV. The driver took the corner too fast and didn't anticipate the petrol spillage. He had no chance of avoiding it after that. Just a very tragic accident."

"Nothing is ever as simple as it seems, Jordan," says Marty, frowning again, looking down at the old newspaper.

The front page holds a story about another tragedy—a train crash at Euston last year, a train crash where dozens died. Marty had also been involved in that investigation. Then he notices a mark in the top corner of the paper—a strange symbol, scrawled in ink. The ink had run slightly, so it wasn't easy to tell what it was. But he could make out a circle and an arrow.

"It's *that* symbol again!" says Marty, handing the paper to Jordan.

"Boss?"

"Third time this month. A strange symbol that looks like a water drop with an encircling arrow. Every time I've come across it at a scene, it is always there with no context, and no suspicion." Marty stares at the symbol for a moment in silence.

"Is it on the board?"

Marty nods. In the corner of the investigations floor, the detectives have collated bits and pieces that seem particularly strange from across a whole range of crimes and incidents over the last ten years. This symbol is one of them. Versions of it have been picked up on evidence from numerous disasters and accidents in the city.

Much to the detectives' annoyance, the response officers recently got wind of the board of unusual evidence and jokingly call it the *Wacky Wall* or the *Bonkers Board*, laughing that the detective ranks have lost their grip on reality. To be fair, a lot of what is on there is odd. Witness statements and testimonies have been gathered from crash victims. There are cuttings from tabloid press interviews with tragedy survivors, all of whom claim to have travelled to another world—somewhere called *The Meadow*. There are only bits and pieces mentioned in each statement, but considered together, they chaotically describe a place that exists between life and death, where water is deadly, people never grow old, and all eras of human history coexist. They are such strange tales that even the tabloids haven't embellished their testimonies. But Marty, an experienced detective, isn't drawn into fantastical thinking. He is intrigued by the possibility of a hidden logic that must be there, somewhere.

"Listen, Jordan, I'm off out now," he says. "I've got to go and see the husband and father of the deceased from the ambulance. He wants an update on the investigation. While I'm gone, see if you can run the CCTV from the route of the ambulance before the crash. Let's find out when and where they got the paper, and who put the symbol on it. There's probably nothing to it, but I'd like to know."

"Yes, boss," says DC Bates, relieved to be given a clear direction for once. "Good luck with the visit. It's Mr van Koopler who requested the Official Complaints enquiry, you know!?"

"Do you blame him?" says Marty. "He lost his wife and son needlessly."

Jordan frowns. "Yeah, I know," he concedes.

***

Chapter 9

Forbidden thoughts and secrets said

The Meadow - London

A heavy grey sky hangs, tired, over Holborn Boulevard in the Meadow. Shutters are closed, muffling the morning chatter of birds in the conifers lining the street. At the far end, a young man from *The Shipping Forecast* tosses newspapers onto doorsteps, pulling a trolley plastered with slogans: '*Firm, Fair, Forceful—Ferrymen for the people,*' and '*Distillery Marbles—Only trust the best.*'

Halfway down the street, a lone figure dressed entirely in black stands waiting, anxiously. Though appearing youthful, he has lived nearly eighty years: thirty years on Earth before a fatal fall at a Scout Jamboree, followed by five decades in the Meadow. Now he is a Minister of sorts—a Well-Wishing priest with a secret.

A smart, horse-drawn carriage approaches softly over the leaf-covered street. The minister signals it, and the rider in an ill-fitting purple uniform halts beside him, nodding silently toward the carriage door. The minister climbs in quickly, glancing nervously around.

"Your Wellness, thank you for agreeing to meet me," says a voice from inside. Governor Angus Callaghan-Crawford is there, sitting with his legs crossed, holding a short bamboo pole, beckoning the minister to sit beside him.

"Of course, Your Excellency. Always happy to see you."

The Governor taps the ceiling with his bamboo pole and smiles as they start to move again, swaying over the leaf-covered cobbles of Holborn Boulevard, rattling forward in the contrived intimacy of the carriage.

"If this is about the fires again," starts the Priest, nervously, feeling the governor's eye leaping upon him. "Like I told you before, I know as much as you. Dissatisfied youth... that's my guess—nothing to do with my congregation of Well Wishers."

Angus places a reassuring hand on the minister's lap.

"No, Paul, it's not that. I believe what you say. The President is just concerned that a broader rebellion is brewing—like last time, when your Well Wishers believed they had evidence of souls returning to Earth."

Paul nods knowingly.

"After the bloodshed and the *Mighty Fire,* the Distillery made a deal with you. A deal that allowed you to keep your beliefs so long as you drove, with us, to keep dirty resin off our streets... sharing with us the details of members of your congregation whose resin has darkened. In exchange for this, you and your fellow priests have been given unique privileges. The President wants reassurance," Angus presses. "Are all the *Stained* individuals being reported?"

Paul grips Angus's hand earnestly. "I promise. I really promise. We are not sheltering *Stained.* We preach the importance of a clear conscience every day. And of course, we are grateful for our privileges."

"Good," says Angus, relaxing. "The President will be pleased. But there's something else. We have reason to believe that the current rebellion is being supported by the *Sculptors.* Do you have any knowledge of this? Anything at all?"

Paul hesitates, breathing heavily. "I've heard rumours."

"Go on..."

"You are familiar with Professor Pelling?"

"The astronomer?"

"Yes," says Paul. "He has a home in the northern enclave of *Sculptors.* His support for the past rebellion is well known. He has wealth and influence. If anyone knows, he does."

Angus looks conflicted. "Thank you," he says. "That is really helpful."

Silence fills the carriage briefly before Angus leans closer again, lowering his voice. "I also wanted to ask... Have you seen any signs from the Returners yet?"

"Your Excellency?"

"Those Well Wishers who drove the last rebellion and 'returned' to Earth... I know you will still be looking for signs of their successful return. Have you seen anything?"

Paul looks anxiously into Angus's eyes.

"This is just a personal interest of mine. The President won't hear of it. I promise. You have my word."

Paul gazes out of the window. "Bits and pieces," he admits. "Nothing conclusive. We thought one of them might try to come back... we are still waiting."

"What bits and pieces have you seen?"

"There are some artefacts from Earth coming through openings—newspapers, magazines, that kind of thing. They mention survivors from the train crash. Near-death experiences. But the journalists on Earth always dismiss any delusions of an afterlife."

"Would you return, if you could?" Angus presses eagerly.

Paul tenses, startled.

Angus squeezes his thigh.

"Paul, trust me. This is just between us."

"I don't know. Life here is good—better than I had on Earth. And *returning,* if it does work as we imagine, is a risk. We know that not all who have tried to go back have returned successfully, even if they disappear from this realm. It seems to depend somewhat on the state of your body left on Earth."

Angus smiles wistfully. "I'd take the risk."

The carriage rocks to a stop. Angus peers out of the window. "Well, it has been lovely to see you again, Paul..."

"Likewise, Angus," says Paul, relaxing now that the secret meeting is coming to an end.

Paul steps down from the carriage, assisted gently by Angus. Their hands linger momentarily, until Paul pulls away and raises his hood, stepping back into the thicket of conifers that line the boulevard.

Inside the carriage, Angus removes a marble from his mouth and drops it into a bamboo pole labelled *Operation Jack and Jill*, where it clinks on top of a dozen other intelligence marbles he has produced this week. He won't lack Intelligence at the next Distillery Council meeting.

***

Chapter 10

Festival of the Mind

The Meadow - London

Filling the chaotic north banks of the Lethe, traders display their wares—artefacts from Earth, rare and unusual marbles, and homemade crafts. All around, the Festival of the Mind sweeps through the streets like a river of energy. It is the one time that the people north of the river Lethe socialise with the people of the South who have traipsed across the bridges in their droves. An annual celebration that brings together everyone in the city of London to share marbles, remember the souls who have recently left the Meadow, and celebrate the fortune of having a second life after death on Earth.

It has become tradition in the last few years for people to dress at the Festival in the clothes that they arrived in the Meadow wearing. This practice alone spotlights the breadth of history that dwells in the Meadow, as fabrics of all textures and a riot of colour whirl around. Mingling with this feast for the eyes, music, drumming, and feverish conversations of excited citizens, mix into a palette of sound.

Making their way through the festival crowds, receiving the occasional reverent look and bow, Governess Eilish Callaghan and her sister-in-law, Chloe, peruse the market stalls.

"How is Angus?" Chloe asks, mopping her brow with a handkerchief.

"He is worse than ever, I'm afraid," replies Eilish, her posture rigid and tense in the convivial exposure that comes with the public street. "He has been distant in the past. But since the raid on the *Sculptors'* enclave, he has barely spoken."

"I'm sorry, Eilish. The raid shocked me, too. I wish I could challenge my husband."

"No, I'm sorry," says the governess. "I cannot convince my brother, any more than you, to be different towards them, even if they all do turn out to be *Stained*."

"Well, he's *my* husband," Chloe cuts in, ashamedly. "I should be able to talk to him."

"No," says the Governess, abruptly. "I'm so sorry… no one can talk to him, and I don't want him to hurt you anymore."

"How are you so different from your father and brother?" asks Chloe, delicately.

The governess smiles. "I'm glad you still think I'm different." She looks out over the river, biting her lip nervously. "I think Angus is so affected by these raids," she continues, "because of the part he played in it."

"What do you mean?"

"Well, he gave information to my father. Information that suggested Professor Pelling, the astronomer who lives in the enclave, was helping the current rebellion."

"It was Angus who exposed Professor Pelling?!"

The governess nods.

"But I thought Angus idolised him?"

"He does… He never thought it would go like it did… My father was pressuring him to show the worth of his network of spies. Angus never imagined my father would sanction such a retaliation. He is devastated."

"Hasn't the Professor been arrested? Isn't he to be the first to be publicly executed?!"

"Not him, he's sentenced to hard labour, but the young rebels that he was sheltering in his home, they're sentenced to death," concedes the governess sorrowfully. "That is why Angus is so silent now."

"Is there nothing we can do to change my husband's mind on these executions?" asks Chloe.

"I've tried everything," says Eilish, desperately. "But he is furious. A rage like nothing I have ever seen in him before. Not even on Earth. This link to the *Stained*, now well established, is fuelling his fury, and he will stop at nothing to ruin them and the rebels."

"I'm scared," Chloe concedes, wiping her forehead with her sleeve, her voice measured and deliberate. "I think my husband would even execute me if he thought I was a problem."

The Governess grasps Chloe's hand. "*That* will never happen," she says firmly. "He will never lay a hand on you again. I promise."

Chloe twitches nervously. In her deep blue eyes, her soul cries out silently, burdened with unspeakable sorrow, but no one can hear. So much for a feeling of celebration at the festival. She looks around at the crowds, dancing jubilantly in the street, indulging in marbles of every colour and sensation imaginable. These people must not care about the raid on the *Sculptors'* enclave last night. No one cares about them anymore.

Up ahead of the two women, a stall catches Eilish's attention—*Rare Resin: Unusual Crafts of the Realm*. She ushers Chloe forward. She is like a child outside a sweet shop when it comes to these kinds of items. Ever since arriving in the Meadow, she has had a fascination with the artisan marble sculptors, no matter her brother's opinion of them, and resin craft more generally. On her hip, even now, is her precious pouch of marbles. She always carries it wherever she goes. While most people just keep their Interrogation Marble on their person—the 'passport' and 'proof of identity' for citizens of the Meadow—Eilish keeps a whole pouch of her favourite and rarest marbles on her, like a collection of seashells from memorable beach trips on Earth. There are such unusual sensations that have been forged into marbles, and some incredibly imaginative ways of moulding the resin. While her father and brother might have done all they can to make trading in such goods an almost entirely profitless enterprise these days—primarily because of the *Sculptors'* alleged link to the *Stain* community—Eilish loves to collect such items and is thrilled that there are still some traders who try to make a living from them.

"G'mornin' yer Excellencies," bows the elderly lady who runs the stall. "What yer lookin' for this fine day?"

Eilish smiles at the lady, politely, trying to ignore the long straggly grey hairs that protrude from a scattering of contours across her leathery, wrinkled face. "I'm just interested to see the amazing variety of things you have here," she says.

"Yes, yes," the trader lady nods. "Come on in," she says, ushering them into the long, dark tent. "Real rare stuff with me today."

Chloe looks at Eilish, uncertain that going inside is a good idea, despite the security detail being all around them, ready to pounce if anything untoward were to happen. Eilish winks at her and steps confidently into the tent. Chloe stays outside.

A little oil lamp is lit in the corner of the velvet-lined tent, throwing a flickering light over the old lady while she rummages in a crate of marbles, muttering things under her breath. The noise of the festival outside has faded quickly, like a lost memory, and the heavy incense-filled air climbs into Eilish's nostrils. The tent feels both uncomfortably intimate and potently unusual.

"Ah yes," rasps the lady with glee. "Magician's Ruse. This is an extremely rare marble." She turns to Eilish, holding out her bony hand.

Eilish carefully accepts the marble, inspecting it. It is much heavier than a standard marble. The kind one finds in the marble cafes. And its spherical shape is imperfect. Other than that, its size and appearance—like a large blueberry—is much like other marbles.

"They're not made no more," says the lady, a little too close to Eilish's face. "This one's two hundred years old, give or take. Forged on the banks of the *Vergessen*; the river running through *Die Wiese*."

Eilish rolls the little sphere in her palm, inspecting the criss-cross of sparkling resin lines contained within it. "What sensations does it give?" she asks.

Now the lady is way too close, and she must be aware of it. Her sickly-sweet breath washes over Eilish. "Any consumer of a *Magician's Ruse* will believe that everything they see and hear is an illusion!" She elongates this last word, swirling her hands in front of her face like a conjurer. "A dangerous escape. But maybe a welcome relief for a trapped soul." She looks at Eilish as though she is somehow interrogating her soul.

Eilish, feeling awkward and uncomfortably encroached upon, steps back, returning the marble to the old lady. "And what are these?" she asks, pointing to a table of unusual jewels and artefacts, keen to shift the lady's attention.

"Ahh, a keen eye for the most precious items," smiles the lady. "Yes, these are *very* interesting." She picks up an item that looks a little like a half-burned candle—a stumpy little object, glass-like with a kaleidoscope of colour and a collar of solidified drips.

"When most of us arrive in the Meadow," she begins, holding the object up in the lamp light, "we go through some form of interrogation—usually at the palaces or workhouses. The place where our Interrogation Stone is created. The stone that holds the purest resin of memory from our lives on Earth. I am right, yes?"

Eilish nods. Of course, everyone in the Meadow knows this, and the pain from such an interrogation lives with them always.

"Well, not everyone who arrives gets interrogated… Some arrive in our realm in the most unexpected places, and they arrive alone. The *Stained!*" The old lady grins at her utterance of this title. She must know she is skating on thin ice talking about them with an official of the Distillery, but she seems to be energised by the risk.

"A *Stain* won't get interrogated… because there's no one to do it," she continues. "And so, in the weeks after they arrive, their tortured soul experiences the unexpected sensation of the resin of their memories of Earth starting to leech out of their skin." She pulls a face of disgust, as though imagining this happening to her own skin. "The sticky colourful resin we use to make marbles runs down their body… You'll remember when your Interrogation Stone was made, we innately know that our own resin is precious to us, right?"

Eilish nods.

"That's why we hold our Interrogation Stones so tight. Our eyes are the gateway to the soul on Earth. Our Interrogation Stone is the gateway to the soul in the Meadow. And so, a *Stain*, dripping with their own resin, will look to collect and save all the resin that they can. These items," she waves the candle-like object at the table of strange artefacts, "are all *Stained Identity Charms.*"

"Oh my," says Eilish, unnerved. "That's so sad."

"Do you want a lick?" says the lady, grinning.

"What?! No!" Eilish blurts. "Why would I do that?"

"Ah, the exposed resin of these Identity Charms—unlike the encased resin of a marble—means you simply have to lick them to get transported to a memory from the soul who made it. If you hold in your mind an idea like love, or hate, or fear, then you'll be taken to a memory like this."

"No, thank you," says Eilish, with certainty.

"It's ok," says the lady. "I won't charge you. A lick doesn't diminish the value of the Charm. They can be licked indefinitely; they don't run out."

"No, honestly, I'm ok, thanks," says Eilish, backing herself out of the tent. She's seen enough, and the old lady is a bit too weird and too pushy.

"Never mind," says the old lady. "You're not the only one afraid of the pain in resin."

"I'm not afraid," says Eilish defensively. But the old lady isn't listening.

Outside the tent, Chloe is waiting for Eilish. She holds an '*I knew it*' look on her face at seeing the shock and uneasiness in Eilish's eyes. Eilish smiles back at her but quickly ushers Chloe away from the stall and back amongst the crowds. She is too creeped out by the old lady and her 'charms' to linger there any longer.

As the day wears on, the crowds throng on the riverbank. Eilish and Chloe would struggle to make their way through the crowds were it not for their security detail closing ranks around them—half a dozen thugs, Ferrymen, employees of the governess' brother.

On the river beside the crowds, fishing boats of all shapes and sizes fill the channel. On the boats, the crews are dancing to the music playing from a riverside tavern. *The Angel's Whisper* hosts a band, *S.O.S*—the *Spirit of Shoreditch*. On the pontoon outside the pub, they are playing a popular shanty. Its chorus, sung in harmony up and down the river, goes like this:

> *Her loving rain is falling free,*
> *The soil thirsts, the raindrops sink into the sea.*

"Can you remember when your father tried to ban this song?" asks Chloe, shouting into Eilish's ear just to be heard.

Eilish frowns. "Not his only tone-deaf announcement this year!"

Up in front of them, there is a scuffle. An elderly lady in a heavy moth-ridden black cloak is attempting to squeeze past the Ferrymen to reach the governess.

"My son!" shouts the lady. "What has happened to my son?"

The lady is desperate. She strains against the burly security, frantically trying to be seen or heard by the governess. She wriggles and writhes. In her right arm, she clutches tight a wad of leaflets.

One of the Ferrymen, in an attempt to throw the lady to the ground, rips her cloak with his clumsy hand. The rags of the lady's cloak fall away, exposing a surprisingly elegant blue velvet ball gown she wears underneath. And, all of a sudden, she is free to run towards the governess.

Noticing the old lady hurtling in her direction, Eilish is struck–not by surprise, which would be expected–but instead by a curious familiarity. It's as if the lady's appearance is triggering a memory. Almost like a déjà vu, but different. Different in the fact that it feels like this is the first memory of a déjà vu. The memory that she knows will give her a déjà vu in the future—a *jamais vu*.

"My son!" the lady shouts at Eilish, thrusting a leaflet into Eilish's hand as one of the Ferrymen catches her again, slamming his weight into her midriff and throwing her to the ground. The rest of her leaflets explode into the air, catching the breeze and cascading over the astonished crowds.

"Be gentle!" shouts Eilish, dismissing her peculiar feeling. She is appalled as one of the Ferrymen lands a kick into the ribs of the old lady while another gags her using torn rags from her own cloak.

"Yes, your Excellency," responds the Ferry Man who has just landed his latest kick, without a hint of apology. He hauls the old lady from the ground and starts dragging her away back into the crowd.

As she is dragged away, the old lady stares, pleading at Eilish. Eilish looks back, ashamed by her association with the thugs. She looks down at the leaflet in her hand.

MISSING.
Eric van Koopler. Circus Performer from Sanger's Circus.
Age: 21.
Time in the Meadow: 10 years.

A picture of a young man with a sweep of blonde hair and piercing blue eyes looks out. He has model-like qualities. A sharp jawline and a shadow cast under his deep brow. The unsettling feeling of knowing she'll see this face again returns, the *jamais vu*. Beneath the picture, it says:

Nearly two hundred souls are now missing.
What is the Distillery doing about this?
We need answers!
The Horsemen are real.
They must not get away with this!

"Can you believe it is two hundred missing people now?" says Eilish, folding the leaflet and dropping it into her pocket.

"I know," says Chloe. "Always young men. All known for having perfectly clear resin. It's so strange. Have the Missing ever come up in the Council meetings? Do the Distillery know anything?"

"They've come up a few times… I've asked my father if I can look into it. But he thinks it's pointless. He is convinced, given the age of these young men, that they've 'gone on' through some misadventure of their own. He says the Distillery have bigger things to concern them than the careless antics of young boys."

"You don't think it has something to do with the bursting marbles, do you?"

"What's that?" asks the governess.

"I heard Andrew chatting to one of the workhouse guards. The consistency of marble production from the workhouses is at an all-time low. Naturally, your brother thinks that the *Sculptors* have something to do with it, being from the marble trade themselves. But Distillery-produced marbles are bursting unexpectedly, sending people 'on', all over the Meadow. There are an increasing number of cases being reported to the workhouses every day. The risk is so severe that even the guards are refusing to consume marbles produced in their workhouses."

"And you think bursting marbles could account for the missing men?"

"It could, couldn't it?"

"I don't know," says the governess.

"Young men tend to take the biggest risks with marbles," offers Chloe.

"I think the young girls take just as many risks," says the governess. "I think there is something else happening."

"You mean the *Horsemen?*"

"That's right."

"But they're just a myth... Aren't they?"

"Probably..." says the governess, looking at the note in her hand. "But not definitely."

"Hey, look," exclaims Chloe, unexpectedly looking forward, her eyes brightening.

A giant Indian elephant is being paraded down the riverbank. Beside it, circus performers are dancing, and street magicians are wandering amongst the crowds, impressing with their sleight of hand and showmanship.

"I know I shouldn't," starts the governess, her mood lightened by the spectacle, "but I do *love* the City Circus! It is the one thing from Earth that I miss... great shows and showmanship."

She watches as the acrobats flip over one another, casting each other effortlessly into the blue sky. Atop the Indian elephant, an elderly Asian lady sits, dressed in grand circus attire, with a long, gentle whip, keeping the elephant from inadvertently trampling its audience. The governess stares at the lady, impressed that a woman of such minuscule stature can command the leathery beast beneath her.

The elephant rider catches Eilish's eye. For a moment, the two women exchange a silent, visual interrogation. There is something warm and kind, and rather knowing, about the lady on the elephant, and Eilish can feel it. She smiles.

***

Chapter 11

Not just an observer

Earth - London

H ow was it, boss?"

"Windy!" says Marty, his eyes red and streaming.

"What about the chat?"

"Poor fella. He's grieving hard."

"Is he still blaming the ambulance driver?"

"Mr van Koopler is looking for answers," says Detective Fredrickson, leaning back on his chair on the top floor of Chiswick Police Station on Earth. "You can't blame him. Life can be really unfair. Have you got any good news for me, Jordan?"

DC Bates smiles smugly. "Your hunch about the newspaper was right, boss!"

"Not a *hunch*!" says Marty. "Just proper police work."

"Yeah, well, check this out…"

DC Bates opens his laptop, laying it on Marty's desk. A video clip is pre-loaded. It is from a petrol station, somewhere in central London. It is from the day of the crash.

"What am I looking for, Jordan?"

Jordan presses play, then scrolls the cursor to a key moment in the footage. "Watch when the ambulance crew go into the kiosk, boss," he says.

Marty leans in, looking at the grainy footage of the petrol station. He watches as the ambulance pulls up and the driver, unaware of what is to come later that day, nonchalantly starts filling up the fuel tank.

Jordan points to the corner of the screen. A female figure has just entered the frame. She is hobbling slowly towards the petrol station. Her hood is up, and she has a bag slung over her shoulder.

"Keep watching the hooded lady," says Jordan.

As the fatefully unaware young driver strides into the kiosk, Marty watches, intrigued. The hooded woman quickens her hobble and then, very intentionally, drops a newspaper from her bag into the open passenger window of the ambulance, before striding off without looking back.

"Why'd she do that?!" Marty blurts out. "Do we have other angles of her?"

"'Fraid not, boss," says Jordan, folding the screen closed.

"We need to follow back on this lady," says Marty. "We need to know who she is."

"She can't have had anything to do with the crash, though?" says Jordan. "What permissions do we have to track her?"

"Suspicion is permission," says Marty—an old-school policing cliché. "We need to understand who was at fault for the fatal crash, and this lady's behaviour is suspicious. I need to rule out her involvement. And I *need* to know what this symbol means…" he prods the newspaper that he has pinned to the corkboard beside his desk—the symbol of the water droplet with an encircling arrow.

There is a shrill ringing that cuts through the office. The internal phone relays a call to each desk in the room. Marty grasps his, silencing the others.

"Detective Fredrickson," he says, adopting his most official tone.

Marty recognises Constable Leslie's voice on the line immediately. "Detective, the response team have just had a callout to a motorcycle crash…"

"And…?"

"I ran the plates… I thought I should tell you… It's your boy's bike."

"When did this happen?" asks Marty, urgently.

"Five minutes ago," says the Constable. "They're up by the Grammar School. LAS are on the scene, as are our boys."

"OK. Thanks, Leslie." Marty drops the phone, not even thinking to put it back on its holder. He throws on his jacket.

"Find that lady, Jordan," he says, rushing out of the station and into the wind.

***

Marty ducks under the police tape cordoning off the street. The wind is wild, throwing his long blonde hair over his face and making the police tape slap against itself noisily.

In front of Marty is a scene of devastation. A scarlet double-decker London bus—an older model, the type that is soon to be retired—lies on its side, spanning the full width of the residential street, a juxtaposition to the quiet, wealthy lives of the people who live here in Chiswick.

Despite the proximate tragedy, the rattle of the city beyond the street goes on—taxis beeping their horns and distant sirens wailing. Even the tall Poplars that line the street, which are themselves untouched by the disaster, stand nonchalant to the carnage, though the smoke that coughs out from the felled bus still filters through their branches.

On first glance, it seems as though, miraculously, the crashed vehicle has avoided all other road users. Somehow, toppling in the one section of the street where parking restrictions create the widest opening. However, upon closer inspection, the picture isn't rosy.

In the middle of the street, sandwiched under the wheezing engine of the bus, the front wheel of a motorbike sticks out. Beside it, half a dozen paramedics, a couple of police officers from Marty's station, and some firefighters. They all surround the body of a motorcyclist who is trapped.

A tense grinding sound moans through the wind. Two firefighters wield an ungainly pneumatic spreader—the 'jaws of life', as they are known—bending and twisting the metal framework of the bus in an attempt to free the injured motorcyclist. The tool draws hungrily off a noisy generator, deafening the paramedics beside it.

Marty can guess who the paramedics are working on. But he needn't guess. He recognises his son's motorbike. There is a distinctive flash of green on the bodywork of the Kawasaki ZXR 750.

The firefighters' tool jams for a moment, and there is a brief moment of respite from the noise.

"He's still breathing," shouts one of the paramedics.

"Keep his head still," shouts another, aiming his instruction at a young police recruit who has been put in charge of keeping the young man's head, neck, and spine in line.

One of the police officers notices Marty.

"Detective?" he says. "CSIs are here a bit quick!"

Marty frowns. "That's my boy they're working on," he says, solemnly.

"Shit. Boss…I had no idea."

Marty shrugs. He carefully slides himself between the noisy equipment and the crashed bus, mindful not to knock it in any way, before crouching down beside the paramedics.

Everything from his son's waist up is free to the air. But he is unconscious, and his eyes are closed. He looks very calm. Calmer than Marty has seen him in a long time. Calm because those demons of self-loathing and guilt, the demons which have infected his fragile mind for years, have been silenced by the crash. His long, silky brown hair flows out from under his helmet and sways in the breeze.

Marty shuffles up beside the closest paramedic, who is busy scribbling notes about his son's condition. He reaches out to hold his son's hand.

"No touching the casualty," says a young paramedic, who is busy on his son's other arm, administering drugs to keep his organs stable.

"He's my boy," says Marty.

"Well…" the paramedic stutters.

The senior paramedic beside Marty stops writing in his notebook. "It's alright, you can hold his hand," he interjects, kindly.

"Is he going to make it, doc?" asks Marty.

"We're doing our best," says the paramedic, without commitment.

The pneumatic jaws screech into life again, and a shower of warm smoke belches out from the generator.

"Clear!" shouts a firefighter as a large, heavy portion of the bus's windscreen falls away from them, into the cabin.

"Ok, get ready for extraction," shouts the lead paramedic. "Police, Fire, can you lift the remaining obstructions?"

"Yeah, we got it, boss," shouts a firefighter. He's stacked—no doubt from hours in the station gym. He could probably lift the whole bus.

"Right, you stay on the head," the paramedic commands the young officer. "The rest of us, the moment he's free, we get him onto the stretcher and into the van. No messing around. Once the weight is off him, the internal bleeding becomes our biggest fight. We have to be quick."

Marty steps away. He will only complicate things by being among the rescuers.

On three the firefighters heave a tangle of bus and bike off Marty's son. Marty can't look. He has visions of crumpled bones, soaked in blood, under his son's tight jeans. He's seen that kind of thing before at other disaster scenes and doesn't want to see it again.

The well-drilled emergency crew from the ambulance slide Marty's son straight onto a stretcher and jog to the nearest ambulance, sliding him onto a trolley in the back. Two of the paramedics jump in after him. One of them holds a bag of fluids while the other monitors his pulse and breathing. The fact that they haven't leapt onto his chest to start compressions is an encouraging sign for Marty.

But just like that, the doors slam, the engine starts, the sirens scream, and the ambulance hurtles off towards St. Thomas' Hospital.

An officer throws his arms around Marty's shoulder. "You'll be ok, boss."

"Thanks," says Marty, recognising the Sergeant.

"Shall I take you to the hospital in the squad car?" he asks.

But Marty doesn't hear him. His attention has been stolen away. He has noticed something on the front of the bus. Scratched onto the license plate on the front is a symbol—the droplet with the encircling arrow.

***

Chapter 12

Hands in play

The Meadow - London

A group of a dozen prisoners, bound and gagged, are marched down a set of stone stairs into the underground Distillery workhouse. The air is heavy with the stench of sweat and decay. The guards, dressed head to toe in the purple uniforms of the Distillery, drag the captives past glowing kilns, where exhausted newcomers to the Meadow are pounding molten spheres into marbles—penance, the Distillery claims, owed to 'God'. A convenient claim that ensures the marble production lines operate at the highest capacity.

But the captives are not newcomers to the Meadow.

At the front of the line is a tall prisoner. A middle-aged man with a sweep of bedraggled grey and brown hair, and tiny bright, friendly eyes. He is pulled away from the group and dragged towards a confession chamber at the far end of the workhouse. The remaining prisoners, all much younger than he, watch him leave in terror.

Inside, the tall prisoner is made to sit, and a guard removes his gag. The stench of the guard's fusty uniform and the stale odour of his breath spew over the prisoner.

The prisoner stretches his mouth wide to use the muscles of his jaw for the first time in days; the gag had been on so long. He turns his head defiantly to acknowledge the guards standing behind him, smiling.

"Good risen," he says.

"Watch it!" the guard snaps, raising his hand.

Before he can strike the prisoner, the hatch in the wall slides open, revealing the Mineralist, seated on a throne, dressed in ceremonial robes.

"Professor Pelling," the Mineralist say, venomously. "Renowned astronomer, founding academic of Virgil College, and *agitator* with the Well-Wishing rebellion of ten years ago." He smiles filthily, stretching the sallow skin of his face and leans in towards the professor.

"*Aidan Elfman...* the *'Sand-Stealer'...* your reputation precedes you. What honour have I to be sitting in your presence?"

"Don't flirt with me! You scum!" shouts the Mineralist.

The professor grins. He has no respect for his captor. "So, what is this? Trial without a jury? Hard labour for your biggest critics? Even fascists on Earth eventually realised that you can't quell revolts that way. And on Earth, at least the prisoners would eventually age and die..."

It is the Mineralist's turn to grin.

"You're not familiar with the decree on executions, then, professor?"

Without a hint of fear in his voice, the professor stares back at the Mineralist. "Rebellions are happening all over the city. If you try to execute me publicly, you know the people will rise again. It wouldn't be worth your trouble executing me!"

"So, you don't know..."

The Mineralist's grin stretches his face so much that it opens sores around the corner of his mouth, dripping specs of blood into his chin.

"We picked you up in the Sculptor's enclave... the home of one particular type of vermin... I've seen your records... You took your own life on Earth, in London, hundreds of years ago... and that makes you one of those vermin... a *Stain.*"

"I will never understand," begins the Professor, a nervous sweat appearing on his brow. A dirty brown resin-filled sweat. "Why you hate us so much."

"It isn't just me," says the Mineralist. "The Lord Almighty despises your souls."

"The *'Lord Almighty'*?! What nonsense keeps you believing in *his* presence?"

The Mineralist clenches his hands around the edge of the hatch and spits in the professor's face. "You insult the Lord!" he cries, desperately.

"I insult no such thing, because there is no Lord!"

"There is!" shouts the Mineralist, losing his cool. "You might not know it, but the Distillery speak with His angels daily!"

The Mineralist expects the Professor to be silenced by this revelation, but he isn't.

"You're fools," says the Professor, ignoring the grimy sweat that pours down his face now. "You mistake visitors from another realm as divine messengers. *They* are not angels, as they profess. There is no 'Lord'. The stars alone hold truth."

"Enough!" snaps the Mineralist. "Your preaching ends here." He pauses and mops his brow with a handkerchief. "There's no hard labour or public execution for your kind. No. I reserve something special for a *Stain*—a special treatment only I can administer."

"And what is that?" the Professor asks, his voice wavering.

"You'd best hope that your stargazing is true. For when I am done, there will be nothing left of you, but the spark that goes up into the sky to join the stars."

"Extinction?" whispers the Professor desperately.

"Precisely."

"Yet the Distillery claim moral superiority?"

"Morality," says the Mineralist, standing up. He lifts his robe to reveal his bare chest. A chest burnt hideously, with blisters weeping and oozing, and callouses all over him. "For the past ten years, ever since the *Mighty Fire*, I have endured this physical pain. Pain, I suffered because I once naively believed in *morality*. But the truth is, Professor Pelling, the moral pendulum is swung by those wielding the power."

The professor's eyes narrow knowingly. "I'm intrigued… even in a moral vacuum, how do you justify the stains in your own resin?"

The Mineralist stares back at the Professor, a flicker of fear in his eyes.

"Why else does the Distillery carry dark handkerchiefs?"

"Take him to the furnace!" the Mineralist bellows.

"The people *will* revolt," the Professor continues defiantly. "The House of Sand will fall."

"Silence!" shouts the Mineralist. "No one will know of your fate. We will bury your memory deep in my sandpit. You will be lost in time and forgotten. Another grain of sand falling through the sand timer of the Meadow. A rebel with a futile cause. Goodnight, Professor Pelling. Shine bright!"

***

The bright, warm, sunny evening contrasts with the sombre mood in *The Angel's Whisper*. People restlessly mill around the pub garden, spilling out onto the pontoon that stretches out onto the River Lethe. A few members of the *Spirit of Shoreditch* play a melancholy song; a simple poem commemorating lives lost in the Meadow. Inside the pub, a group of rebels crowd the bar.

"All twelve of them, sentenced to public execution! And the Professor condemned to the workhouse!" groans the landlord behind the bar. "Where is the justice? They are just kids. They just lit a few fires. The punishment does not fit the crime!"

"We cannot accept it," Cyril Spate, the trawlerman, responds, bashing his fist against the bar. "We must fight them!"

"Fight? What good will that do?" the landlord responds. "It will just send more of our kids to the executioners' stall."

Kim-Joy steps forward, wrapping her arm around the landlord's tense shoulders. "The Distillery have been posturing like this for years, Carl," she says. "Don't worry, your son is safe."

"Safe? We can't keep them safe, that's the point. We have *Horsemen* snatching our boys from the streets. We have marbles bursting left, right, and centre. And I tell you, Kim-Joy, it won't be long before they start using Mist on all disrupters again."

"Carl, I don't think they will," says Kim-Joy. "They learnt their lesson ten years ago. The people would turn against them again."

"That may be," says Carl. "But more and more of their officers are carrying cannisters again. You know that. It doesn't have to be central policy for a few hot-headed Ferrymen to chuck their load!"

"Listen, Carl. I think the best we can do now is to hold firm. These new powers of execution show us one thing: the Distillery is scared. Scared of our rebels. And our numbers are only growing. A predator caught in a trap always lashes out."

"We'll send a team from the *Tide and Time Tavern* to the executions. If there's an opportunity to disrupt proceedings, it will happen. But in the meantime, hold your nerve."

Carl Farley grimaces and nods, picking up his cloth and ferociously cleaning the marble ramekins littering the bar.

"Kim-Joy, can I have a word?" asks Cyril, nodding to their usual quiet booth in the corner of the pub.

"Of course," says Kim-Joy, grabbing a handful of marbles.

"I'm with you on what you said to Carl," says Cyril, his voice hushed. "But you must acknowledge, things have changed. With these public executions, the Distillery are more dangerous than ever."

"I agree, Cyril. But there is no worth in worrying people, especially not loyal friends like Carl. You know, his boy was in the enclave the night of the raid? He was lucky; he had left Professor Pelling's house only a few hours earlier."

"Yes, I heard," says Cyril. "Listen, I think it's time I step things up with Governess Callaghan."

"What do you mean?"

"I think it is time I try and approach her…"

"Cyril, that is very brave, but that could be suicide for you. We don't know that she will be open to hearing us."

"I think she would… You saw her at the festival just like I did."

"Yes, I know," says Kim-Joy. "But having a kind heart is not the same as having a rebellious soul…"

"She has been to the bridge three times this week," says Cyril. "Her Arrival haunts her; I am sure of it. Telling her what I saw the night she arrived, I am certain she will, at the very least, want to know more."

"You think now is the right time to play your hand?" asks Kim-Joy.

"Better now, before it is too late."

Kim-Joy grasps Cyril's warm, leathery hand. Into it, she drops a small bronze locket containing a marble. "We made this together over a century ago," says Kim-Joy. "Please don't let this be all I have to remember you by."

Cyril leans forward and embraces the older woman. "You will always have more than a marble to remember me by," he says.

In a brief moment of intimate silence, an unseeable burden that both Cyril and Kim-Joy bear breaks to the surface. And in the shadows, also unseeable, the two of them hold each other's minds tight to their souls. This is *real* intimacy in the Meadow. An intimacy of two minds, equally dependent and independent of one another, entangled in a realm where time's mortal coil wraps itself round the mind rather than the body.

***

Chapter 13

The First Executions

The Meadow - London

Eilish shields her eyes from the cruel, bright sun. Beads of perspiration cling to the heavy makeup on her brow. She mops the resin nervously with her dark purple handkerchief. The glare of the crowd feels as prickly as the sun. Her hot skin itches under the elaborate regal dress she has been told to wear by her father. She has been dreading this day—the first public executions.

A huge crowd is gathered outside the palace. The sunshine is falling upon them mercilessly, mixing its harsh brilliance with their fear and fascination. There have been small pockets of resistance already this morning. Angry chants and soiled rags thrown at the presidential entourage. But the Ferry Man's ranks, whose riot shields cast severe shadows over the people, have quelled each moment aggressively and swiftly.

Chloe stands cautiously beside Eilish, wiping perspired resin from under her nose obsessively with a handkerchief; equally ashamed and afraid to be standing so prominent on such a dangerous and regrettable moment in Distillery rule. She feels like a tiny wren, perched on a post, desperate to flee at the slightest hint of danger.

The President and the Ferryman sit on grotesquely arrogant wooden thrones, elevated on a platform beside the stage. They casually ignore the crowds before them, chatting in hushed tones to one another, as though this is just another typical day in the Meadow. Their attention is drawn when a horn sounds from the palace gatehouse, followed by the emergence of eleven young prisoners, gagged and bound, being dragged towards the executioner's podium in front of the people.

The crowds wail and jeer in a stunned cacophony of chaos as they watch the prisoners stumble on the podium. President Callaghan grasps his son's hand, kisses him on the knuckles and nods. The Ferryman steps forward and raises his arms to silence the crowd.

"People of the Meadow," he begins, hollering out over the assembled mass. "Loving wives, honourable husbands, obedient citizens, and repentant sinners, all living as you should. Your conscience is clear. The resin that perspires from your skin is clear. Because you honour the divine being that gave you this second chance at life. And I hear you! I hear your calls for justice. For peace. For harmony. For a Meadow that has learnt from the errors of Earth and maintains an order to be proud of."

"There are some. A small, pathetic minority who try to wreak havoc on this order. They try to hide among us, dripping their dirty resin onto our streets. But we see them sweat… we see the stains on their clothes. My Ferrymen are charged with rounding up these sinners. Ferrying them back to the workhouses and palaces where they can be cleansed again. We are maintaining order for *you*, the good citizens of the Meadow. And we have tried leniency!"

At this statement, there are jeers from a small section of the crowd. The Ferryman looks at a group of his officers, standing along the front of the stage. He nods to them, then points with a long, condemning finger at the source of the jeering in the crowd.

Fearing repercussions, as a handful of officers in the crowd, those jeering go silent.

"But despite our leniency," the Ferryman continues, "there is still lawlessness from an arrogant and disruptive few!" He turns to face the podium. "Starting fires that threaten the lives of my men… distributing leaflets that spread lies to the young and vulnerable… littering the sacred ground of the Meadow with drips of their filthy resin… And we know they conspire with those troublemakers in the enclaves, the *Sculptors*. Wrecking the production of Distillery marbles. Wrecking the marble production so much that damaged marbles have left two hundred men missing. Men who have 'gone on' because you meddled in our production."

At this final charge, a number of the prisoners on the stage writhe in protest, and this time, the jeering in the crowd isn't isolated to a few pockets. Evidently, his attempt to land this accusation on the prisoners is not readily accepted by the people.

The Ferryman raises both hands to draw silence once more. "Disorder is how my leniency has been repaid. Well, no more! To all of you out there who think you can undermine the rightful rule of the Distillery... To those of you who have no shame in dripping dirty resin onto our streets, let today's punishment be a message. You are wrong!"

The Ferryman turns to the presidential party. "Governess," he gestures to his sister to stand up and make her way to the podium.

Chloe squeezes Eilish's hand, reassuringly. Eilish looks out at the crowds. This is the moment she has been fearing. Living it in her nightmares ever since the details of the public executions were shared with her. She reluctantly gets to her feet and makes her way, under the glare of sunlight and crowd, onto the podium, next to the prisoners.

"As defined by our laws," shouts the Ferryman to the crowd. "These prisoners are mercifully allowed to ask forgiveness for their crimes. The governess will hear these pleas and will, in due course, relay them to the Council of the Almighty. Their punishment is set, but they can trust that honest repentance to God can change their path into the afterlife." The Ferryman nods to the governess, who reverently steps towards the first prisoner.

Eilish's silhouette gives the prisoner momentary respite from the dazzling sun. The young girl, who is kneeling, must be in her early twenties. She has a freckled and kind face, plump with youth, and her eyes are red with tears.

Her hand shaking under the glare of the crowd, Eilish carefully removes the gag from the young woman's mouth. Then, from a clasp at her hip, she takes out a small gilt-edged journal to record the last words of the prisoner.

"Forgive me," whispers the young girl, quietly, so only the governess can hear. "If there is a divine being whose will I have betrayed, then I am sorry. But know that I have only ever acted out of love and care. I am sorry. I do truly love the life I have been given here in the Meadow, and I hope I can be granted mercy."

The young girl closes her eyes and misses a tear that tumbles down the governess's cheek.

"I'm sorry," whispers Eilish sincerely and privately, knowingly breaking the protocol of her role.

Writing the words of the young girl in her book, she moves down the line. Each of the young prisoners, none looking older than thirty, offers a similar plea. All clear in their commitment to love and peace, and regretful if what they have done has caused pain. As she closes her book for the penultimate time, the governess hates herself for the selfishness of her relief that there is just one prisoner left to hear.

Eilish steps up to the young man. His skin is as dark as night, but the scars on his wrists and arms, from toil at the marble workhouses in his past, are clear as day. In contrast to the other prisoners, the young man's eyes aren't red, but bright and clear. If anything, the man looks relieved and ready for what is coming his way.

The governess unties the gag, and the sweet aroma of the man's skin washes over her. The young man looks directly into her eyes. And as he does so, Eilish is struck by that awful feeling of not-quite familiarity she has had before—the *jamais vu*.

'*Not now,*' she thinks to herself, feeling her knees weaken with the familiarity. In her minds-eye an image flashes before her— a picture of the young man burning in an awful fire. Eilish's throat goes dry.

"I am ready for my fate," says the prisoner, calmly. "I have no regrets. And so, I offer no repentance. But I come with a secret message for you, Governess Callaghan... A friend and a rebel believes in your goodness," he says. "He knows of your pain, and he wants to offer you answers. He was there the night your plane crashed on the river in the storm twelve years ago..."

Eilish breathes in sharply but composes herself.

"Meet him at *The Angel's Whisper* the next time a storm hits London." The young man smiles at the governess, then closes his eyes obediently.

Stunned, Eilish whispers urgently. "Who is your friend?"

But the man stays silent, his message is delivered, and these aren't details he is willing to share.

"What should I write in my book?" she asks.

"Write '*Love is in the stars*'," says the young man, his eyes remaining closed.

Eilish's mind is racing as she steps down from the podium, passing the notebook to a waiting priest. She barely hears her brother's order for the Mineralist to take to the podium and begin the executions. She doesn't even see the shocked faces in the crowd as one by one the prisoners are brought forward, and the Mineralist releases the cannisters of Thermocline Mist into their mouths.

One spray of Thermocline Mist ends a person's life in the Meadow. It acts in an almost opposite way to the extraction of memories for marble-making. As it is drawn into the lungs and fizzles through the body, the mist dissolves a person's memories such that, without a single memory, their body doesn't have a conscious mind anymore and acts on impulse alone—the impulse to leave the Meadow.

Carrying Thermocline Mist had been common practice amongst the Ferrymen before the uprising a decade ago. But its use had always been sparing, acting primarily as a deterrent. Now, in front of a crowd of thousands, the Mineralist not only wields the Distillery's newly enforced power but uses it without hesitation.

It is only when the last prisoner steps forward, Eilish's secret messenger, that she regains her focus.

Standing in front of the Mineralist, the young man is the only one left on the stage. He stands, calm and resolute, looking out peacefully over the crowds. The Mineralist rolls up his sleeves for the last time and reaches into his belt for a final canister of Mist.

Stepping over the ten discarded cannisters around his feet, the Mineralist sniggers and turns to the crowd himself. A sick showman, enjoying his notorious moment in the sun. But in his arrogance, the Mineralist makes a mistake.

The prisoner, in one swift unexpected movement, grasps the cannister from the Mineralist's hand, and shouts out to the crowd, "Good risen!" as a final farewell, before releasing the cannister into his own mouth.

The crowd is stunned. The mist from the cannister engulfs the man's head, and he draws it into his lungs. Just like the prisoners before him, his eyes roll back as his head lolls, and his arms and torso go limp. When his eyes roll back, he stares, unfocused, into the distance. The man has 'gone on', as they say in the Meadow, and his body will now drift with his soul to the Source.

The Mineralist stands humiliated. The governess, like the crowd, is in shock. And the President and the Ferryman are furious that a suicide has upstaged their first public executions.

***

Chapter 14

Head case

Earth - London

How's it going, boss?" asks Detective Bates, looking anxiously at his senior. "I'm going to get another coffee; do you want one?"

Marty doesn't even look up from his laptop screen. "Yeah, go on," he says. "Black."

Marty's eyes are red from rubbing them. He is exhausted. He has been up all night looking over and over again at the CCTV footage from the bus. He is cycling through it all again now. He can only go back as far as a week before the incident. But he is sure, somewhere, there will be a clue.

How on earth did the hooded lady know his boy would let his intrusive thoughts win at *that* moment, making him swerve in front of the bus? There have been two similar accidents where the hooded lady has left her mark. And that's just two that he knows about.

Marty watches the pixelated footage from the cabin of the bus, scrolling forwards and backwards to inspect each passenger. But no one could possibly be her. No one stops by the number plate on the front of the bus or even looks at it. The bus only starts to become a 'key player' in that unexpected moment when his son swerves across the road. Marty never watches the conclusion of the CCTV footage. He will only watch the first few frames where his son's bike enters the shot, but he won't watch the impact, for his own sake.

Scattered around Marty's desk are pieces of a personal vendetta to find the hooded lady. He has gone back through years of crashes in the city, trawling through evidence and reviewing video recordings, desperate to see when and where she has made an appearance. Early inquiries had yielded some results. A handful of incidents where her symbol was recorded in the evidence—etched into road signs or car seats. But more recently, the searches have been futile. There hasn't been a suggestion of the lady anywhere else. Nonetheless, he can't help but suspect that there is a connection between the disasters. He might not see it now, but he will continue to dig.

A selection of grainy stills taken from CCTV footage is pinned to the wall beside Marty's desk. The haunting shadow of the lady has become his obsession.

"Can I have a word, Marty?"

He looks up. Detective Bates is there, holding a couple of mugs of coffee, but beside him is the Sergeant, Marty's boss. Jordan must have got him.

"What do you want a word about, sarge?" says Marty, not intending to sound disrespectful, blinking as he looks away from his screen for the first time in hours.

"A welfare chat," says the Sergeant, grabbing Marty's mug from Jordan and handing it to him, "in my office."

"Yes, sir," says Marty, reluctantly, standing up and stretching his stiff back.

*

Marty slouches in the sergeant's cluttered and claustrophobic office. The uncomfortably cheap plastic chair is determined to make this meeting brief. The air is stale with the odour of forgotten coffees, and the bright fluorescent light above him hums impatiently. The Sergeant leans back in his creaky chair, scrutinising Marty.

"Marty, you are one of the best I've got," he starts, his words loaded with the unsaid. "You've been with the force, what is it, twenty years now?"

"Nineteen, sir."

"You've seen *everything*. Your instinct is better than a dog's bark. But I'm losing you, Marty. Ever since your boy's crash, you haven't been the same. And I don't blame you. But, well, I think we might have to put you back on light duties."

"Sir! No!" says Marty, looking at his own shaking hands. He can't bear the thought of going on light duties again. It was 'prison' for those first three months while he visited his son every day in the hospital. He'd go to work but wasn't allowed to do anything. He just signed off on annual leave requests.

"Look at you, Marty," says the Sergeant. "You haven't shaved in weeks. You look, frankly... awful. You're living on coffee. Take a break, man!"

"I'm getting there, sir. I'm getting there."

"Getting where?"

"The hooded lady!"

"Listen, Marty. You might be onto something... and it's not for me to question your judgment. But think about it. Every case you're looking at... There are no crimes there. They're just terrible accidents."

"*Incidents*, sir."

"No, Marty. They're accidents. You are seeing coincidences because you are looking for them. It could be a different person each time. You never even see her face."

"It's *her*," says Marty, indignantly. "It is."

"Look, I'm telling you, Marty. Drop it. I know it's hard. But I need you to do your job again."

"But, sir..."

"No buts, Marty. Either drop it or drop out. I need you to work on other cases. We have unsolved homicides. We have gangs fighting. If you can't drop this, I'll have to act."

"Let me put Bates on it, sir?"

"What, the hooded lady 'case'?"

"Please, sir. I just want to know that someone is looking."

"Alright," the Sergeant concedes. "Bates is your inferior. You can put him on the case. Just make sure your focus is right."

"Yes, sir."

"So how is your boy doing?" asks the Sergeant, picking up his cup of tea and slurping it.

"Pretty much the same, sir."

"Still in a coma?"

"Yeah. They don't give him much chance. But I know my Elijah, he's a fighter. He's just working things out. He'll be back."

The Sergeant frowns, sad to see Marty so desperate and deluded.

"Well, my thoughts are with you both. Why don't you call it a day now? Come back in tomorrow. Fresh start. Visiting hours will be over in the hospital soon, won't they?"

"8 o'clock, sir."

"Then get over there now, Marty. And let me see an improvement in you tomorrow."

"Yes, sir."

"And, for god's sake, have a shower, Marty!"

***

Chapter 15

The Fisherman's Friend

The Meadow - London

An unexpected, but nonetheless possible, period of dry weather falls upon London in the Meadow. Unlike on Earth, in the Meadow, the weather is entirely unpredictable, changing only when an arrival from Earth brings its weather conditions with it. Without such an event, the weather remains constant.

The Arrivals coming into the cities are usually so frequent that changes in the weather here are chaotic and regular. The same can't be said for the rural areas, which, save for the edges of city weather systems, can remain constant climates for months, if not years. The Mynydd range, home of *The Mountain* and the Source, where all of the departing souls from the Meadow drift on to the next realm, has seen inclement weather for centuries already, even during the *Mighty Fire*.

Eilish is in the heart of London, with the most changeable climate in all of the Meadow. Only some peculiar circumstance on Earth can have meant that no souls have met misadventure, misfortune, or an untimely death in the city of London for the last two weeks and because of this, Eilish has had to mull over her mysterious invite to *The Angel's Whisper* for an unexpectedly long time. But this evening the dry spell has been broken. Heavy, cold rain washes through the city, punctuated by rumbles of thunder.

"You're not going to go, are you?!" asks Chloe, the only other soul Eilish has told of her invite. "You're too high profile, too important. If the rebels got hold of you, it would be a disaster. It's not safe."

Eilish pulls on a pair of loose jeans, tucking her ever-present marble pouch into her back pocket, and throws on a baggy green hoodie, plain clothes from a time before her family made a name for themselves. She hasn't worn them in years, but tonight she needs the anonymity they used to bring.

"I'm sick of being so safe, Chloe! My God, my father has been keeping me 'safe' my whole life. I am so trapped. They parade me around as 'The Governess' and I go wherever they tell me to go. I have to write the dying words of condemned prisoners for god's sake! We spend all our time out of sight, hiding the secret impurity of our own resin." She dabs her brow with a handkerchief. "Well, not anymore. I want to take this chance, Chloe. I want to know more about the night I arrived. I want to know why I am here. Why it still hurts so much. I want to know about Ciara's fate. I want to know more!"

"Then I'm coming with you," Chloe insists.

"Fine," snaps Eilish, unintentionally short. She knows there's no point arguing with Chloe. "I'll let Angus know we're off out…"

Eilish strides downstairs, starting to feel the scurry of excitement that the impending unknown brings.

In his extensive candle-lit study, Angus sits at his desk surrounded by a mess of star charts, deep in thought—a ponderous contrast to Eilish's energy. Behind him is a stack of bamboo poles—the hollow tubes he uses to store marbles extracted from his spies. Marbles that hold the names of citizens whose resin has clouded up. When he has reviewed these marbles, he'll pass on the names to the Ferrymen.

"I'm off out," Eilish calls in.

"Oh, ok," Angus acknowledges absently. He doesn't even look up. He doesn't care.

Eilish frowns. Her tingle of rebellious excitement is hit with the fatigued ache of reality. She knows she needs things to change.

Turning to leave, Eilish notices Angus's cannister of Thermocline Mist, resting on the mantlepiece on top of today's *Shipping Forecast*—what a scoop the paper would have if they knew the Governess was sneaking out tonight. Glancing at her husband, who has already dropped into his book again, Eilish grabs the canister and drops it into her pocket. *'There is no harm having a bit of extra protection'*, she thinks.

***

The dark cobbled street on the approach to *The Angel's Whisper* is deserted. As with all roads in the city, nature is a close companion to the built environment—a quirk of the built environment appearing in bits and pieces, in contrast to the steady consistency of nature. Tall, looming conifers cower over the cobbles, littering the floor with wet needles. High above them, the wind roars and rain sobs miserably through their branches, pattering onto the ground with a thumping percussion.

Rounding a bend, the swollen body of the River Lethe comes into view. The vast, dark expanse of water is rushing east, with the caps of waves collapsing into a fine spray in the air. It is just like the night that Eilish arrived.

The pontoon of *The Angel's Whisper* sways and splashes, its guide ropes creaking, but the pub itself is dark and quiet. All the curtains are drawn, and not a glimmer of light sneaks out.

Eilish approaches the entrance cautiously, giving the door a strong push with her shoulder. It won't budge. In soaked frustration, she bashes on the door with a wet fist, thumping the wood. Chloe joins her. Then, with a look of defeat, points to a notice plastered to one of the windows:

The pub is closed until further notice.

"No!"

Eilish isn't prepared to give up. She bashes the door again, willing it to open. Wishing it would open.

Chloe knows this isn't the time to bemoan the wasted, wet trip, but she isn't prepared to stand here getting soaked for long. She throws an arm around Eilish. "I'm sorry," she says.

But then, in the air of disappointment, there is a rattle, and the door in front of them creaks open.

"Come in," says a voice, emerging from a warm candle-lit doorway, "We've been expecting you!"

A languid marble mist hangs low to the floor of the pub. Despite looking closed and quiet on the outside, *The Angel's Whisper* is packed. Packed with people from all walks of life, all too busy to notice a pair of bedraggled strangers. They are full of cheer, chucking back marbles and chatting with mirth.

Before Eilish can place an order at the bar, a young server with sooty black hair and a great deal of perspiration on his brow stumbles over. Eilish can't help but notice the cloudiness of his resin, tinted blue. The man reaches deep into his apron and pulls out a handful of marbles, placing them into a dish in front of Eilish, smiling nervously.

"Courtesy of your friend," he says, avoiding eye contact. He gestures to a shadowy booth by the window, where a large, grizzled man sits, his back turned.

"Thank you," says Eilish, but the barman has already moved on.

She picks out a marble and slides the rattling ramekin in front of Chloe. "Stay here and enjoy these," she says. "Keep your head down, and we'll be fine."

"How will I know if there's trouble?" asks Chloe, leaning in nervously.

"If you see me reaching for my canister of Mist, run! Otherwise, don't worry."

Eilish pops a marble in her mouth—*Sailor's Mist*, a nerve calming luxury, a generous gift—and approaches the stranger cautiously.

The man shifts himself to one side of a small wobbly table, on which sit his two grubby hands and a deep ramekin, full of marbles. The mist of other discarded marbles, swim around the heavy leather boots on his feet. The dampness of his wet, heavy trench coat gives him and the booth a fusty odour.

Eilish recognises him immediately—the stranger from the bridge, weeks ago.

"How long have you been following me?" she asks suspiciously, not concerned to offer a polite introduction.

The man lifts his bushy eyebrows to look at the governess. He smiles warmly.

"I have known people to leap from that bridge," he says. "You looked very sad when I bumped into you… I wanted to make sure you were ok."

"And did you know who I was?"

He nods.

"And I know why you return to that bridge. I was here the night you Arrived. I understand why you are haunted…"

Eilish can feel the hairs on the back of her neck prickle. She is not ready to dive straight into this. Not without a few more answers first.

"If you knew who I was, then there are more conventional ways to contact me, you know," she says sarcastically.

"Yes, well, I don't exactly want to draw attention to myself in those places."

"You're a fugitive?"

"Not by choice," says the man.

"Who are you?" she asks.

"Cyril Spate."

"Spate…" says Eilish, considering the name. "The rebel leader? One of those pardoned for their involvement ten years ago?"

Cyril scoffs and bows his head.

"Your name has come up at council assemblies, you know? You are thought to be dead."

"Yes," he says, "and I have only managed to stay alive because I have kept a low profile. Exactly why your official channels have been closed to me!"

Eilish studies him warily. "You are taking a huge risk, talking with me."

"And so are you," says Cyril.

Eilish smiles nervously at him. "I still don't understand why you want to talk with me."

"Then let me tell you a story," says Cyril, leaning in close.

Eilish's body tenses, and she feels the cannister at her hip for reassurance, bracing for what comes next.

***

Chapter 16

Survivor's Guilt

The Meadow - London

I t was a cold night, and the city lights were twinkling over the Lethe," Cyril begins. "We had been weeks at sea on my boat, *The Guiding Star*, to the far reaches of the Meadow, and were returning with half a dozen crates of Resin Candies from the Americas. We approached London Bridge, and that's when you and your plane crashed into this realm—the single brightest and scariest thing I've ever seen."

Eilish shivers nervously as awful memories flood into her mind. The moment she had braced for death and then, in a chaos of noise, had found herself struggling in a sinking fuselage filling with water.

"We didn't realise it was a plane at first," Cyril admits. "The storm that arrived with you was so violent that all our attention was on keeping the *Guiding Star* afloat. When finally, I saw your plane, it was rolling over in the waves, the starboard wing thrown into the air like a desperate drowning soul, waving for help."

"We didn't hesitate. The oars came out, and we paddled frantically towards you. And as we splashed through the choppy waters, the bright light of the Opening faded, plunging the river into darkness. We lit a red flare. We weren't the only ones. Another boat, closer to you, did too."

Eilish blinks. She remembers the flares—red and blue lighting the chaos—and the confused shouting from nearby boats. Then a stab of pain hits her, shadows of memory of the faces of her family. Her father. He looked angry, fighting with the pilots at the front of the plane and scrabbling for the one life vest that remained. And Andrew, focused on himself, opened the fuselage door, making his escape, sending a torrent of cold water into the plane. And Ciara, Eilish's sister. She had been next to her before the crash, but had been thrown to the back of the aircraft. She looked dazed and resigned; her long copper hair plastered to her face.

The plane had rolled as the fuselage filled with water, and Eilish had tumbled onto the roof with the luggage. She lost sight of Ciara, and as the water rushed around her, she was sucked out through an open door into the chaos of the River Lethe, and away from the rapidly sinking plane.

"Please, go on," Eilish urges quietly.

Cyril nods.

"The other boat pulled you and two more passengers from the water, but we stayed with the wreckage, just in case. We wanted to see if there were any more survivors. But then some razor-sharp debris pierced our hull. We took on a lot of water and had to head for the bank. That's when I saw them. Two more survivors, splashing in the water."

Eilish's heart leaps in her chest. "More survivors?"

"Your pilots. Captain Mike Meadowcroft and First Officer Annabel Turner. They were in the water. And conscious."

Eilish gasps. Captain Meadowcroft had been a family friend for years—she had mourned him like she had mourned her sister. "They survived? Both of them?"

Cyril nods. "Captain Meadowcroft was only blessed with a few months in the Meadow before his mind succumbed. But, as far as I am aware, Miss Turner is still here in the Meadow."

"No! She can't be!" says Eilish. "She would have found me. She would have sought out my family, wouldn't she?"

"I'm not so sure. It seemed both pilots wanted nothing to do with their passengers."

Eilish recalls the heated argument between her father and Captain Meadowcroft. Her sister had overdosed mid-flight, prompting the dangerous order to 'land immediately'. Captain Meadowcroft had refused; the weather was too bad, and the visibility was dangerously low. But while Ciara was convulsing and vomiting in Eilish's arms, and the plane rocked violently in the turbulent weather, her father attempted to wrestle the controls from both pilots. It was minutes later that Eilish heard the warning alarms in the cockpit, and Captain Meadowcroft had shouted, 'Brace! Brace! Brace!'

She wasn't surprised that neither pilot wanted anything to do with her father in this new realm.

"So, where did they go?" she asks Cyril.

"We took them to the safest place we knew. A place to recover and adapt to their new life… a pub north of the river, now shrouded in notoriety… *The Tide and Time Tavern.*"

Eilish's eyes widen. "The rebel stronghold? Is Annabel still there?"

Cyril chuckles and shakes his head. "Miss Turner stayed maybe six months before journeying north and joining a rebel monastery... I'm sorry to say this, governess, but I think she rather readily adopted the path of a rebel."

Eilish grins sarcastically. "My father certainly wouldn't be her biggest fan! So, where is she now?"

"I'm not entirely sure," says Cyril. "She was involved in some 'star gazing' research, near the Source, last I heard… the sort written about by scholars like Professor Pelling. I haven't seen or heard of Miss Turner in ten years."

Eilish frowns, resigned. "So, she is gone, too."

Cyril shrugs. "It's strange," he says, sitting back, inspecting Eilish. "You remind me a lot of her."

"I do?"

Cyril rubs his eyes, looking at her with a new intensity. "Oh, you must know? You have the same kind, calm voice. The same determined presence. And of course, the same rusty, copper hair."

"What?" Eilish's chest tightens sharply. "Miss Turner had black hair. Short, black hair."

Cyril's eyes narrow. "No, she didn't. Coppery, wavey red hair, like yours. Freckled, pale skin. Pointy ferret-like features -"

"No!" says Eilish, her heart racing. "That wasn't Miss Turner." She holds on to the edge of the table to keep herself from fainting. Her knuckles are white.

"Who was it?" asks Cyril.

"It was my sister, Ciara."

***

Later, in the warmth of Angus's empty study, and safe from the rain that continues hammering the streets of London, Eilish recounts everything to Chloe.

"Can you be sure the trawlerman wasn't somehow tricking you?" asks Chloe, struggling to mirror Eilish's energy.

"Chloe," says Eilish. "No one in the Meadow, other than you, my father, and my brother, knows of Ciara. My father doesn't want people to know about her. He cannot reconcile that Ciara, his child, chose to end her own life... that his child was *stained*."

"But Eilish, you said it yourself... this Mr Spate thought it was the pilot of your plane he had rescued. Anyone could've guessed there was a pilot with an unknown fate."

"Yes, but he described Ciara exactly."

"Maybe he found your sister unconscious, drifting out of the Meadow?"

"It's possible," Eilish concedes. "But I don't know... I have to know more."

Chloe sighs reluctantly. "So, you're meeting him again?"

"Yes," Eilish nods.

"Same place?"

"No... I'm going with him to meet a lady who knows much more about Ciara. A lady who looked after her when she arrived in the Meadow. The landlady of the *Tide and Time Tavern*."

"Eilish?!" Chloe exclaims. "Don't be foolish! The Tide and Time Tavern is *the* rebel stronghold. Andrew's Ferrymen have that place watched around the clock. Anyone who comes and goes within half a kilometre of the *Tide and Time Tavern* is checked and searched."

A mischievous grin forms on Eilish's face. "The Trawlerman has agreed to take me through a secret rebel passage. Not a word to my brother!"

"This is crazy, Eilish," says Chloe. "If your father found out -"

"I have to do this, Chloe," Eilish interrupts. "Please, help cover for me—just once."

Chloe frowns. "I had a feeling you'd be bringing me into this!"

"It'd just be one day," says Eilish. "Pretend we're heading out of the city for a meditation or something. No one would even check."

"Ok," says Chloe, hesitating, "but nothing more. You might have Callaghan blood in you, but I don't!"

"I'd always vouch for you," says Eilish.

"I know," says Chloe. She looks out at the rain-soaked window. "But I can't vouch for myself."

Eilish looks at Chloe, sadly. There is a reason why Chloe can't vouch for herself. Why she knows so little of her life from Earth. The same reason why so many women feel so lost in the Meadow: she is a *Flicker* from the palace.

Men arriving in the Meadow are sent to the workhouses after being picked up by Distillery officials. Sent for hard labour making marbles, under the impression they are paying penitence. They get to leave when their resin runs clear.

But women, save for those who can buy a way out, like Eilish, are sent to the palaces. A place where women's resin is supposedly 'cleansed' from their sinful lives on Earth. A place where women's 'demons' are exorcised by *princes*—a band of men who Eilish knows from the council meetings—the cloaked observers from the House of Sand. Men whom her father holds in unnerving reverence. During the 'cleansing', some of the women in the palaces lose the connection to the part of their soul that remembers their past entirely.

Eilish has never asked Chloe for details of her time at the palace, nor what fragments of her old life she remembers. Her friend's past is a labyrinth of blocked memories. Loathsomely, all Eilish knows is that almost a decade ago, her brother picked Chloe as his wife from a line-up of palace girls. Chloe had had no say in the matter.

Chloe lets out a long, tired sigh, mopping her brow with a handkerchief. "I need marbles," she says, burying the moment of reflection—the silent screaming of her soul, as always, suffocated.

"I have too much on my mind. Can we put all of tonight's chaos to bed for now?"

"Sure," Eilish agrees, rubbing her own eyes.

She selects two calming amber marbles from a drawer in Angus's desk and settles down in a chair next to Chloe, beside the fading embers in the fireplace. The two women drop their marbles into their mouths and feel the warmth of sensation tingle through their bodies, dripping like honey through their veins.

Chloe closes her eyes.

Beside her, Eilish sleepily glances at the bookshelf next to the fire. *The Dance of the Sands* by Professor Pelling has been left lying open on the shelf. She pulls down the thick old thesis and rests it on her lap, intrigued by what the supposedly notorious academic wrote about. A sectioned entitled 'The Source Conundrum' seduces her drowsy interest.

Eilish starts to read, pleasantly resigned to the fact that she probably won't make it past the first page.

"As one who studies the stars and the properties of water in the Meadow, the Source has, for many years, been a particular interest of mine. The Source provides the purest water in the Meadow. A purity that has sparked many ideas in the Meadow, from the early development of the marble trade and the discovery of the industrial potential of the mountain's resin, through to the outlawed beliefs of the Well Wishers *and the connection between pure water and the supposed ability of a soul to return to Earth.*

The Source also has an intriguing link to the stars. Astronomers are unified in their agreement that the stars we see in the Meadow—likely the souls of those whose death on Earth did not send them to the Meadow—do ultimately drift northwards in a chaotic dance over the Source and off towards the Unknown. And we also observe that for every soul that drifts to the Source after death, a residue of themselves is left after their jump off the Perihelion precipice; a spark of light, their own star. A star that can be observed on a clear night near the Mountain, shooting up from its peak and joining the dance of the stars northwards. This spark, we have started to refer to as The Energy. The unifying force in the universe, the essence of the soul, the thing that makes us human.

This is where the conundrum lies. For the last one hundred years, I have monitored the number of Drifters venturing to the Source and the relationship to the quantity of sparks emanating from the mountain. The patterns, while imperfect, are nonetheless unnaturally similar. This tells me one of two things. Either my counting is off, or the pattern isn't always happening. I assumed the former.

I have revised my counting methodology and sent other researchers to work more closely with the Distillery Mining Teams at the Source. But the inconsistency remains (see Appendix for the method of counting). This has left me with one possibility—that not every soul that jumps from the cliffs loses its spark of life into the stars.

What does this mean? I don't know. It could mean, contrary to our beliefs, that not all souls in the Meadow contain The Energy. Or it could mean that the lives of some Drifting souls are not extinguished at the cliffs…"

Eilish's fingers slip gently off the page, sending the thesis tumbling to the floor. The amber marble has cocooned her into a deep and dreamless sleep.

***

Chapter 17

Anonymous Accusation

Earth - London

The warm summer air blows through Marty's thinning grey hair. He has a helmet swinging on the handlebars of his motorcycle, but unless the police stop him, he won't wear the sweaty casket.

Marty pulls up outside the hospital entrance, under the geometric shadow of its utilitarian façade, where listless patients loiter without intent. He rocks the heavy Kawasaki onto its stand and, looking up at the looming concrete mass, sighs. He's *here* again. He had got odd looks the first time he had turned up at the hospital riding the same motorbike his boy had crashed on. That was almost ten years ago. Now, after all these years, the doctors and nurses treating his son are well used to it. And well, as far as Marty is concerned, this bike has always been an extension of his son. It is the only part that is still there for him. Riding this bike is as close as he can feel to his boy.

The air outside the hospital tastes of the exhaust fumes spewing from the ranks of idling ambulances, and Marty feels no guilt lighting up a cigarette, despite the frowns. A few people tut. As though their desperation to preserve their own bodies should somehow affect the laissez-faire attitude he has to his own.

After a few long drags, he stubs it out on the metal lid of a bin and steps into the cold, clinical atrium of the hospital. The first few months he had visited, he couldn't help but notice the poor, desperate souls wandering around with ailments and worries. But he has been there so many times now, he doesn't see anyone. He just walks straight through to the lifts and presses the button that takes him to the fifth floor—the Long-Term Intensive Care ward. A ward where every room is filled with beeps, and every bed is permanently occupied, heavy with the weight of an agonising and desperate silence.

Everyone knows everyone in the ward, and everyone knows no one. Marty nods to the old lady visiting her husband and to the scared young couple visiting their grandmother. None of them has ever spoken to him. He is as much a part of the furniture as his son.

Elijah Fredrickson lies motionless on his bed. His eyes are closed and his breathing peaceful, as they have been for years.

Before tending to his son, Marty has got into a habit of straightening the bedsheets. They only move because of the breeze from the window, but it makes Marty feel like he is doing something for his boy, nonetheless.

He turns off the television set flickering above Elijah's bed; it's too distracting. Then, finally, he lets his eyes wander onto Elijah's peaceful, absent face. The nurses always try to keep on top of his long, flowing hair—hair that Elijah used to keep groomed, neat, and orderly. They never quite get it right, but nonetheless, his brown hair still resembles the gothic enigma that his son shaped himself to be. And the tattoos that sleeve his left arm still speak with the humour and free spirit of the boy he once knew.

Marty looks at the monitor beside Elijah's bed. Seventy beats per minute. Good oxygen saturation. Pretty much bang on the average. Marty has become a bit of a self-taught nurse. And yet every time he comes to the ward, he hopes that his presence will somehow change the monotonous pattern of his boy's vital signs, to show some signs of recognition, or even disruption.

"Hi Eli, kid," he says to his son, using the affectionate term he has always used. "Still riding that highway in your mind?"

He smiles. A superficial and desperate smile, and leans in. "I promise you, I'll get her, Eli—the lady who scratched your bike. She's the reason you're here; I know it…"

A nurse nearby rolls her eyes—she has heard Marty saying this to his son so many times before. It's tragic.

"I've taken my hunt online," he whispers. "There's plenty of vigilantes on there, wanting something strange to chase." He pauses. "I know what you'd probably say, *'you couldn't trust one of them as far as you could throw them'*. But, come on, we've waited long enough. And Sarge has closed the official case now—the fool. What harm can it do? I haven't said who I am. I've just said that there's a lady who's been scratching symbols onto tragedies, as though she knows they're going to happen before they do. And I've put that symbol out there. The encircled drop. Maybe someone can tell me what it means."

Marty twitches unconsciously. "I've put out a reward, too. Anyone with good information. A couple of thousand pounds. That shows I'm for real. I will get her, kid. I'll find out how she knew you would swerve into that bus. How she knew all those disasters were going to happen."

He squeezes his son's hand through the thin hospital sheets.

"I rode your 'metal pony' here again tonight," he says, changing the subject. That's how his son had always referred to the bike. "I'm still looking after her really well. The paint job is exquisite, and she rides better than ever. I'll keep her well fed and exercised for you. Ready for when you come back…"

He stops and looks intently at his son, and a tear sneaks out from the corner of his eye, tumbling down his cheek. This has been an awful ten years.

It is dark by the time Marty pulls up outside the knackered old town house in Finchley, north London, where he rents a tiny one-bed flat on the top floor. He leaves the bike in the shared garage and clambers up the mould-ridden, flea-bitten staircase. He swings open the old, paint-flaking door and, beside the growing pile of unopened post, he flops into his chair.

Marty lets out a long, relieved sigh and opens his laptop—a behaviour of habit.

The screen flashes into life, washing its cold blue light over his tired face. As the processor kicks in, a notification flashes up on the screen—a new mail responding to his blog.

Dear 'Curious Blogger',

I can help you find the hooded lady. But be careful. She is a murderer.

Do not approach her.

Sincerely,
A friend.

***

Chapter 18

Unrelated and uncomfortable

The Meadow - London

The Ferryman wades through a damp mess of household contents strewn across the decimated north London street. Fingers of splintered timber stick out from the rubble of buildings like broken bones, the weary remnants of homes that once stood firm. The King's Cross Enclave is reeling from the latest Ferrymen raid. Pockets of fire burn among the ruins, their glow casting flickering shadows that seem to whisper with memories, lingering in the silence, in the hush of a community that is being erased.

Chasing obediently and eagerly behind the Ferryman, apprentices of his security detail try to keep up. They gaze wide-eyed at the destruction and the line of around a hundred captured *Sculptors*. The men and women shiver in the dark. Many of them bruised and bloodied.

The Ferrymen guarding the captives draw their heels to attention and salute the presence of the Ferryman. He salutes back and approaches the senior officer.

"A good raid, Tommy?" he asks, shaking the officer's hand firmly.

"One hundred and twenty captives, all lined up ready to transport, sir."

"And any Drifters?"

"Just a handful, sir. I counted half a dozen."

"We need to get those numbers down," says the Ferryman with an air of disappointment. "We don't need the Source being clogged up with these vermin."

"What's going to happen to them then, sir?" asks the officer, confused about where they will be sent, if not the Source.

"They will be made use of," says the Ferryman cryptically. "Don't you worry about it." He pauses, looking down the line of sobbing captives.

"Yes, sir," says Tommy, understanding that he was not invited to know more. "So, how is Mrs Callaghan?" he asks, innocently, unexpectedly. "I hear she is away from the city?"

"She's fine," says the Ferryman, affronted to talk of his wife so candidly with an inferior officer. "She's away with my sister. Just a few days. Typical… leaving me to do the hard graft here."

"I hear that, sir," says Tommy, agreeing with his superior, even though he has no similar situation at home.

"Did you find any artefacts worth keeping in the raid?"

"Actually, yes," says Tommy. "Something very interesting."

"Go on…"

Tommy turns and whistles to a group of his officers standing beside a pile of ash-covered household belongings. Tommy makes an 'opening book' gesture towards them and beckons one of them over. The officer digs through the pile, pulls out a heavy book.

Instructing one of his apprentices to hold a lantern over his shoulder, the Ferryman inspects the artefact. It is a book containing page upon page of records; names, ages, date of Arrival, and 'details of demise'. He stops on a random page and glances at one of the rows.

Name: Sandra Pilkington.
Age: 42
Date of Arrival: March 1830
Details of demise: Mrs Pilkington met her demise after losing her daughter to Scarlet Fever. In her grief, and with an adulterous, abusive husband, she chose the rope and hung herself in her basement.

"What is this grizzly record?" asks the Ferryman, absent-mindedly scratching the scar on his cheek.

"We found it locked up in a secret chest, sir. It was in the nicest house at the end of the street," says the officer who had handed him the book.

The Ferryman looks to Tommy, the more senior officer, who confirms it with a nod.

"We think it is some kind of record of all the suicidal *Stained* in London," says Tommy. "We can't verify all the details, but have a look yourself, the records are all about people who met their demise by suicide on Earth!"

The Ferryman looks through the directory. Poisoning, gunshot, and drowning. Thousands upon thousands of suicides. He has never seen anything like this.

"This is an excellent find, Tommy," whispers the Ferryman. "This document could be vital in clearing the Meadow of permanently dirty resin."

Everyone's resin is dirty when they first arrive in the Meadow. That's what the palaces and the workhouses were set up for. Giving the Distillery time to interrogate new arrivals and in doing so, extract their dirty resin until the conscience of the arrival is clear, and so too, their resin. But it's different for the *Stained*. A tormented mind from Earth rarely, if ever, exhausts its trauma. And so, a *Stain's* resin never goes clear.

Another peculiar thing about Arrival in the Meadow by suicide is that the Distillery often misses such souls. Missed by the officers who patrol the streets and main points of entry, waiting to capture new arrivals. For, with suicide, it is almost impossible to predict the arrival location. Meaning undocumented, *Stained* and the dirty resin that leaks from their pores, exist outside of Distillery control.

Until now, there was no documentation or record held by the Distillery of those who have arrived in London by suicide. The Ferryman's recent purge of the *Sculptor Collectives* was designed to take many of them off the streets, but, save for a confession, only years of interrogation in the workhouses or palaces can produce a confident conclusion that someone's resin will *never* run clear—that a soul is no longer *stained*.

Looking at the large volume held in front of him, the Ferryman grimaces. If this book of records is correct, then the sheer scale of *Stained* in London far surpasses his expectations. He had assumed there were a few thousand, at most. However, this record appears to indicate that there are tens, if not hundreds of thousands.

"They're not just in the Sculptor enclaves," says Tommy. "I had a flick through earlier. There are high-profile names in there. A few big surprises."

In the flickering firelight, he looks straight into the Ferryman's eyes. "Some of them are a bit *too* close to home..."

Tommy turns the directory to a page with a recent fold on the corner, pointing the Ferryman to a specific record.

A quick glance, an intake of breath, and the Ferryman slams the directory shut.

"Not a word to anyone," he says abruptly, looking momentarily flustered. "If anything gets out, I'll know... There's only you and a few others with this knowledge... I'll make sure you regret ever opening your mouth!"

"Yes, sir," says Tommy, obediently, bowing his head, looking nervous.

The Ferryman fastens his coat and gazes around at the carnage in the street. "Take these vermin away," he shouts, pointing at the captives. Frustrated, he kicks a pile of ash on the ground.

"Come with me," he calls to his apprentices, aggressively striding away down the street.

***

Eilish paces, head down, her coat zipped up over her mouth. Her thick woolly hat is pulled down below her eyebrows. The frost is bitter, and her breath tumbles over her shoulder into the night. She feels strangely alone, as if the cold has dropped the rest of the city into hibernation.

Ahead of her, visible through the bare branches of the trees, stands the *Institute of Openings* at Virgil College. Not a college that often welcomes members of the Distillery.

She clambers the dozen steps to the entrance, clinging to the iron railings so she doesn't slip on the glistening ice, before hammering on the grand front door.

A hatch slides open, and from the darkness inside, a female voice whispers. "Can I help you?"

"I'm here to meet Mr Spate," says Eilish, leaning close so she isn't overheard. "He told me to say: *'May the seas warm, and the clouds form…'*"

To which the voice behind the door responds, "*…and may the rain fall, filling the rivers of Love.*"

Eilish waits as a series of bolts and latches are unfastened before the door swings open.

When Eilish steps into the building, there is no sign of the woman. She has scarpered. But standing at the end of a dark corridor is the unmistakable silhouette of the trawlerman, Cyril Spate.

"It is a privilege to make your acquaintance again," says Cyril, opening his arms in welcome. The heavy door slams shut behind Eilish. "I appreciate the great risk you are taking tonight, Governess. I hope our little trip into the rebel stronghold will be worth it for you."

Eilish nods nervously. The rebellion which her father and brother are working so hard to quash, and here she is, heading into the heart of the beast, betraying them.

"Is your cover story intact?" Cyril asks.

"Yes," says Eilish, thinking of Chloe, alone in a carriage, heading north for a weekend of meditation without her.

"Perfect," says Cyril. "Then follow me."

In the darkness of the deserted institute, Cyril leads Eilish through a maze of silent corridors, past offices, lecture theatres, and laboratories, before finally approaching the door of a cleaning closet.

"I hope you're not claustrophobic, Governess," he says, lighting a candle.

Eilish peers inside. A rough and primitive tunnel is exposed underneath a dirty tarpaulin on the fractured floor. Picks and shovels from the tunnel's excavation are discarded next to the hole.

"We'll be underground for a few miles," says Cyril. "I'll lead the way, but stay close behind."

***

Chapter 19

Secrets in the cellar

The Meadow - London

Rickety wooden boards creak underfoot as Cyril and Eilish pace steadily through the dark tunnel. Cyril's candle exposes the hurriedly worked earth and the precarious beams stopping the tunnel shaft from collapsing, but Eilish isn't given room to worry.

Cyril keeps them moving. Moving through the monotonous meandering path, where the sound of dripping echoes from somewhere unseen, becomes the rhythm of their progress.

Eilish loses herself in thought, watching the lumbering figure in front clambering over beams and rubble. She feels as though the walls of the tunnel are pressing in around her, like the sleeping city above can sense her treachery. Then she starts to feel a peculiar warmth pulsing from the walls of the tunnel.

"We're close to the marble workhouses," says Cyril, thumping his fist against the warm earth.

Soon, they reach a dead end, blocked by rubble.

Cyril smiles, clearing the stones to reveal a ladder. "After you, Governess."

Eilish climbs cautiously until she reaches a locked wooden door, bolted on both sides. Voices murmur beyond with the unmistakable clinking of marbles. Cyril instructs her to knock three times, pause, then knock again.

"Are the marbles still sparkling?" a woman's voice shouts back.

"Like the eyes of Albert Newman," Cyril responds, winking at Eilish, a broad grin stretching across his face. "Ok, Governess, you can unbolt the door now."

The panelled door groans as it opens, and the secret tunnel shaft is bathed in a warm orange glow. Standing in the doorway is a squat older woman, barely five feet tall. She has small, warm brown eyes and long grey hair. Around her neck hangs a silver necklace with almost a dozen lockets, and the sleeves of her heavy jute dress are rolled up over her sturdy forearms.

The lady offers Eilish a hand and pulls her up from the ladder.

"I recognise you," says Eilish. "You were at the Festival, riding the elephant."

The lady smiles. "My name is Kim-Joy," she replies warmly. "I am a landlady and a circus performer," she grins. "Welcome to my home... Welcome to the *Tide and Time Tavern.*"

The cellar of the *Tide and Time Tavern* is not like any old pub cellar. For a start, it is warm and snug—the sort of place where friendships are cemented in the reassuring glow of the firelight.

A log-burning stove sits under a broad chimney breast, emitting a throbbing orange heat infused with the sweet aroma of pine from the crackling timber inside. Nestled in front of the stove, two worn armchairs, deep and inviting, rest on a hand-woven rug, covered in scorch marks. Around the walls of the cellar, crates of marbles are stacked high to the ceiling. And in one corner, a pile of heavy sandbags sits beneath the loading trapdoor onto the street above.

Cyril leaves the two women alone, and Kim-Joy invites Eilish to take a seat by the fire.

She offers Eilish an icy-blue marble. "For clear thinking," she says. "To help you hear what I have to say, and so that you don't think later that I somehow duped you."

Eilish smiles gratefully and pops the marble into her mouth before sinking into the armchair.

Kim-Joy lifts a heavy, worn journal from the shelf. "First of all, Governess," she says, "I want to thank you, sincerely. It is no small deal that you have been willing to come here to the *Tide and Time*. I know you will have heard many things about this place. And I suspect they are not all glowing reviews."

Eilish smiles nervously.

"The *Tide and Time*, and I, have been here in the Meadow for over five hundred years," says Kim-Joy proudly. "And for more than four of those centuries, that is all that we have been; just a friendly community pub. And I hope you'll believe me when I say that is all I wish we were now. But alas… I am a lady of integrity. My pub has always been a refuge for those in need. For those without a home. By being such a place, sadly, my home has become a target."

"It's not just because you're a refuge," says Eilish, defensively.

"No, of course," Kim-Joy grins. "It is true that we held and housed fugitives. Including those souls who returned to Earth a decade ago. Of course, you know of those souls I am talking about, don't you?"

Eilish nods. She recalls the Mineralist listing them as the most dangerous souls to have ever existed in the Meadow: Gareth and Cerys Edwards, Ashley Arnold, and Hassan Dar.

"The two young men stayed with me when they first came to the Meadow," says Kim-Joy, grinning mischievously. "Naïve but honest lads. And the girls stayed here a bit too. Brave girls, both of them. They took risks and had good hearts. You remind me of them, Governess."

Eilish shuffles in the armchair. It wasn't as comfortable as it had looked in the firelight.

"But I haven't invited you here to defend my pub. And it isn't the reason you are here, is it, Governess?"

Kim-Joy lifts the journal onto her lap and starts flicking through the pages. "You know, I have kept a journal ever since I arrived in the Meadow. Every beautiful soul that has stayed with me is in here." She sighs and clasps the lockets on her necklace.

"Here they are," she says, lifting her eyes to Eilish. "Mike Meadowcroft and Annabel Turner… or rather Ciara Callaghan." She chuckles and hands the journal across to Eilish.

Eilish inhales sharply. On the page is a detailed sketch of a crashed plane sinking in a river, next to the portrait of a handsome young man—Captain Meadowcroft—and a nervous woman with long, thick, curly hair falling over her slight shoulders.

"Who drew this?"

"Me," says Kim-Joy. "I started as a bit of an amateur, but centuries of practice and I feel I can capture a real likeness now."

"It's perfect," says Eilish. "I haven't seen Ciara's face in more than ten years."

"Ciara was with me for six months when she first arrived. Naturally, she took some time to recover from the crash, but then she learnt about the Meadow and became very interested in the laws and nature that govern it. Though sadly, in the months she was here, Ciara's resin never ran clear. There was trauma deep within her that she never spoke of. We respected her silence but knew she could not live in a city with dark resin like hers. Not a city policed by the Distillery.

"We found her a safe passage north, to stay with a priory on the River Dee, not far from the Mountain. It was home to a community of Well Wishers who were involved in secret missions to the Source, attempting to understand the connection between the realms: Earth, the Meadow and the Beyond."

"Did you ever see her again?" asks Eilish, anxiously.

"Oh, yes," smiles Kim-Joy. "A few years later, when the rebellion erupted, word got round that my *Tide and Time Tavern* was going to be the staging post for an attempt to return to Earth.

"Your sister turned up here only a few nights before the Returners arrived from their expedition to the Mountain. She had learned a great deal in the years since I had last seen her. But she had the same youthful energy and the same kind heart."

"Was Ciara involved in the night of rebellion?!"

Kim-Joy smiles. "Yes," she says. "She was one of the first to storm the park. And one of the few to actually witness the four Returners step through the Opening."

"I can't believe it," says Eilish, staring at the glowing embers in the fire. "I remember that night. I was at a ball in Dante's College, on the Southbank. It was raining so heavily, but we mirthfully consumed our marbles under a rooftop canopy. But even despite the rain, we heard the commotion and saw the fires north of the river.

"And the fallout after. Thousands sent 'on', hundreds of Distillery guards injured, whole streets razed to the ground. The clear-up was immense. That was when my father and brother vowed to join the Ferrymen. I can't believe Ciara was so close that night, and so far. What happened next?"

Kim-Joy stands and places another log into the fire. "We lost many good and brave souls that night," she says. "But thankfully, your sister was not one of them. She came back to the *Tide and Time* for one night after the riot before heading north again with her comrades. Now the rebellion had begun, she told me she had a new and important calling…"

Kim-Joy sits down, letting the burst of heat from the burning log sting her face. "Well Wishers had been trying for decades to step through an Opening back to Earth. Every previous attempt had failed—ripping bodies apart, sending brave souls crawling as Drifters to the Source. But that night was different. The Returners did something new. Before stepping into the Opening, they had drunk pure water from the Source. I witnessed it, and so did Ciara. Something about the properties of pure water had allowed them to step back into a realm they once knew—back to Earth.

"Now there is another Opening in this realm that never closes… and Ciara had spent two years studying it…"

"The Source!" says Eilish.

Kim-Joy nods. "Ciara reasoned that if a conscious soul could step *back*, then maybe a conscious soul could also step *forth*, into the Beyond."

"But that's suicide!" exclaims Eilish.

"Not necessarily," says Kim-Joy. "You see, your sister held a belief, like I do, that this realm isn't just a passage from Earth, through death, to the Beyond. We believe we are part of a cycle of existence—a bit like the water cycle. As droplets in the vast ocean of existence, the realms are simply the different states through which we can inhabit. Realms into which we can travel *back* and *forth*. Realms which centre around each of our three essences—our mind, body, and soul. Earth is the realm of the body. The Meadow is the realm of the mind. And the Beyond, the realm of the soul.

"In contrast to the widely held beliefs of the Distillery, we believe we are not just here to cleanse our conscience, cleanse our resin, jump off the cliffs at the Source and go 'on'. The clarity of our resin is irrelevant to the journey. The journey is ours to choose."

"So, did Ciara do it? Did she jump off the cliffs at the Source?"

Kim-Joy inspects Eilish's face carefully. "I don't know," she replies calmly. "I know she went north after the rebellion. But after that night, security tightened exponentially around the Source. And of course, there was the *Mighty Fire*. There hasn't been word or sight of Ciara in ten years."

Eilish sits quietly. "Did she ever speak of me?"

Kim-Joy leans back in her chair, thinking for a moment. "Never in great detail," she admits. "Though I know it was she who sowed the seed in my mind that *you* could be a potential ally in the Distillery. I remember her saying, of all the Callaghan's, you had a kind heart. A heart, like your mother." Kim-Joy pauses for a moment. "Your mother, she wasn't with you on the plane, was she?"

"No," says Eilish. "No, mum died years before."

"I'm sorry."

"No, it's ok. I'm glad Ciara still spoke about her at least."

"Ciara spoke of your mother more than anyone else from Earth," smiles Kim-Joy. "She seemed to be something of an idol to Ciara. Though she spoke, of course, as though she were a close family friend."

"Mum *was* her idol," says Eilish, barely audibly.

She stares at the embers in the fire again, trying to suppress the memories that are now flooding back into her mind. Since she had arrived in the Meadow, she has tried to forget these memories. And for good reason. They are too painful. And too *dangerous*. Dangerous because they are the reason for a secret that Eilish, her brother, and her father share. The secret that, like a *Stain*, none of the Callaghan family can ever exude clear resin. The pain of losing both her mother and Ciara to suicide can never leave any of them.

And without knowing any different, Eilish had bought into the belief that the dirty resin they leak in the Meadow is an indelible stain etched into each of their souls. A residue that means the Callaghans are unfit to follow the path of other souls into the afterlife. That, after the Meadow, they are destined to be condemned to Hell. Could this belief be wrong?

Eilish loves her sister Ciara more deeply than any soul she has ever encountered on Earth, or here in the Meadow. If Ciara believed in a back and forth between the realms, where the clarity of resin is irrelevant, then she, Eilish, certainly could not rule it out.

"Can you teach me about Ciara's beliefs? About the beliefs of Well-Wishing?" Eilish asks Kim-Joy.

The old lady smiles. "I can certainly give you a start," she says. "Though there is a lot to learn, and it will likely be a journey you have to take yourself."

"I suspected that might be the case," smiles Eilish. "Well, I have until the morning, now. Let's see how much I can learn in that time."

Kim-Joy leans in, offering her hand. "You really are all your sister said you'd be." A smile grows across her warm and friendly face in the comforting glow of the fire.

***

Chapter 20

Spirit of Shoreditch

Earth - London

Dear 'Friend',

Thank you for your message. That is quite an accusation you make! Do you have evidence? If so, I need it.

I'm always careful. That's who I am.

Tell me, how can you help me find the hooded lady? I'm all ears.

Best,
The Curious Blogger

Marty presses send and leans back in his chair. Outside the window, past the condensation, the sky above London is angry and unsettled. It is another sticky summer evening. Billowing cumulonimbus tower into the sky, flexing their misty muscles, ready to spew precipitation over the city.

Tears of water drip down the cold bottle of beer and over Marty's dry, leathery hands. He allows himself to daydream for a moment. Imagining that this is like an old case he had, where the killer was desperate to see how his crime was being investigated, he inadvertently led Marty straight to him by pretending to be an innocent witness. He imagines that, right now, the hooded lady is crouched over a computer screen in some dark flat reading his message. He imagines her surrounded by photographs of disasters and an intricate plot that she has formulated, ready to orchestrate the next tragedy.

Marty is sleep-deprived. His usually clear mind would ignore this kind of fantasy thinking. Years as a detective taught him to expect the unexpected. Drawing a straight line between two points is rarely the right path.

Beep beep.

A notification flashes up on Marty's laptop. One unread message. Sender, unknown.

Marty opens it hurriedly. It hasn't even been a minute. He takes a swig of his beer before reading, throwing the empty bottle into the bin beside him. It clatters on top of the five bottles he has already consumed this evening.

Dear Curious,

Yes, I have evidence. But not to share. Not now. Not yet. Sorry.

If you want to find your hooded lady, go to the 'Spirit of Shoreditch' gig in Camden tonight. She'll be there.

Be careful,

A friend.

Marty does a quick search. The *Spirit of Shoreditch* are playing tonight. A small band he has never heard of. By the look of their website, they are some fusion of folk and punk. Tonight, they are playing in a pub basement in Camden. It is free entry.

A punk/folk fusion is not exactly Marty's cup of tea—he's more a rock music kind of guy. And neither is the Camden scene his scene. Marty doesn't know a single police detective who would be comfortable in Camden. Nonetheless, he knows he has to go. It's not a huge inconvenience, and if *she* is there, that would be massive.

Marty walks briskly from Finchley to Camden in the warm summer air. Travelling on foot is certainly preferable to taking the stuffy and sticky tube, and he still arrives with plenty of time, outside the *Knot of Three Ropes*, the hip pub in the heart of this bustling part of the city.

The pavements are awash with the people of Camden. Young people flounce around the street, like peacocks displaying their feathers. There are dozens of men looking like members of an American lumberjack community. There are women excited to imitate flappers of the 1930s, with floaty dresses tied by wide ribbons matching their hair, and lipstick that is the brightest red they can find. And then there's the Camden 'royalty'—those who are truly original, and truly bizarre. A man who looks like a technicoloured cookie monster sweats under a mass of chaotic fabric. At the same time, another androgenous attention grabber expresses themselves in an outfit consisting almost entirely of lacey lingerie. Their smooth, pale skin is held taut from every angle, exposing their bony frame, as if they are suffering from a Gothic famine. Marty feels a prickle of embarrassment run down his own sweaty back for them.

On the front door of the *Knot of Three Ropes,* the month's playlist is displayed. The *Spirit of Shoreditch* are highlighted. They are due to start in the next half hour. And while Marty had never heard of the group until today, they seem to have quite a following.

Marty wanders into the pub to get himself a lager, assuming a lager is a fuss-free drink to order. Not in Camden. There are fifteen different lagers on tap. Picking the only one he's heard of, he takes his drink to a seat by the door and sits down, ready to watch and wait for the hooded lady to make her appearance.

The pint finds its way, all too easily, into Marty's middle-aged belly, and the whole time, there is no hint of the lady. Other than an elderly lady who wandered into the pub with a much younger man on her arm—an age gap Marty couldn't help but notice—no one came in but young hipsters, eager to drink and dance. Maybe his 'friend' had been having him on? Perhaps this was just a trick? Or had he missed her? Was she down there in the basement venue already?

The opening number of the *Spirit of Shoreditch* begins. It's an unusual mix of scraping electronic sounds and floaty strings echoes up from the basement. As much as he doesn't want to go into the pit of sweat and pheromones, Marty knows he has to enter the basement and search for his suspect down there.

It is a narrow staircase which descends into the basement. Before he reaches the bottom, the pulse of the music has already crawled into Marty's chest, cloying to his heartbeat.

He steps, reluctantly, into the smoky darkness of the long, stretching room. The ceiling is claustrophobically low. Marty is no giant, reaching just over six feet, but he only has a few inches of clearance from the ceiling. Several others are having to stoop under the strip lights.

In front of the crowd, the *Spirit of Shoreditch* are playing. The lead singer is a young man with dark black skin and bright eyes. Flanking him are two women with bass guitars, a fiddle player, and a drummer lurking behind them, in the shadows.

Despite the proximity of adolescents, there is a sweet smell of fruit in the air. This is because every other person blows out temporary clouds from their Vapes, while the rest drink pints of deep stout.

'Whatever happened to pills and alcho-pops?' thinks Marty, reminiscing about his own youth.

He scans the room. It looks like it will be almost impossible to scout her out. That's if she is even in here. He leans against the back wall in thought, letting the damp condensation soak into the wet back of his chequered shirt. He starts methodically around the room.

'What if she is here without her hood up?' Would he even recognise her? Then, out of the corner of his eye, he spots a person on their own. His detective instinct instantly singles them out as an outsider, and they have their hood up.

It is a struggle to get through the crowd of young people, and Marty gets splashed with every other pint he passes, feeling his feet getting stickier and stickier the further he goes.

The band start a new song. A punky and upbeat number. It gets the people bouncing and makes it even harder for Marty to get through, but he keeps sight of the hood.

A few metres from his target, he treads carefully. After all, his 'friend' alleged this figure to be a murderer.

Marty shuffles forwards and alongside them, then turns, nonchalantly, hoping for a clear glance, which he gets. The hooded figure turns at the exact moment, facing straight at him. But it's a man—a man with a bushy moustache.

Marty turns away quickly, crestfallen. For a brief moment, he does wonder whether his hooded 'lady' was a man all along. But that was absurd. He had seen her body shape and posture in hours of video footage, and this tall fella certainly doesn't match the physique.

Marty starts shuffling away, heading back for the better vantage point from the wall. And that is when he *does* see her.

Coming down the stairs into the basement, out of sight and attention of the crowd, the hooded lady descends softly, like a ghost. She pulls something from her pocket and starts scratching something into the wall. But she is just too far away, and it is too dark and crowded to get a clear view.

Marty pushes young people out of his way, not caring about how cross he makes them. He has to get to her. But then he hears a scream. Multiple screams all at once. And the mass of people all around him surge.

Marty turns to see what is going on near the stage, and he is filled with fear. Flames are licking up the backdrop of the *Spirit of Shoreditch*'s set, billowing smoke like a stormy sea all across the low ceiling. Thousands of people are panicking, and there is a stampede towards the tiny, narrow staircase.

In less than a minute, there is only a few feet of clean air nearest the floor. Ideally, Marty should be crawling, keeping his head out of the smoke. But people are clambering over one another, and everyone knows they are in a race for their lives. Marty runs blindly towards the stairs.

He is fortunate. He reaches the steps before the smoke consumes him. He funnels up the steep steps with dozens of others crushed against his shoulders, tripping several times, but the wave of fear carries him with the others up and out, flooding into the pub above, the smoke chasing them all the way.

Marty takes in a lungful of acrid air as he piles out of the building and onto the street. People are shouting and screaming everywhere, stumbling and crawling with Marty to get as far from the fire as they can. A few others fight to go back in, desperate to find and save loved ones. But the smoke is thick and gets thicker and thicker. It starts to breathe in and out of the pub entrance. In and out. In and out. Like it is alive, and then, without warning, the smoke explodes in a fireball.

Marty stands in shock, just beyond the flames. There are dozens of people still in there. The *Spirit of Shoreditch* are in there too.

A few people attempt to shoot jets of fire extinguishers at the flames. They achieve nothing.

A moment later, fire engines roar into the street, and half a dozen firefighters in breathing apparatus drag hose reels from their vehicles, before charging at the flames. But Marty knows it must be too late for all of those who are still inside.

It had all happened so quickly. He looks around, suddenly aware of where he is and what he is doing. Where is the hooded lady? Did she escape? He has no idea. He has lost her again.

***

Chapter 21

A Desperate Gamble

The Meadow - London

Deep underground, in the hidden depths of London, in the Meadow, the tired and emaciated men in the workhouse gaze confused at two smartly uniformed men who stride past the kilns. The guards look almost as perplexed. They hurriedly stand to attention and salute, unsure where to look.

The President and the Ferryman haven't visited any of the workhouses in years. The Mineralist has governed the operations of these awful spaces, and they have happily left him to it. However, they have important work to do here today.

"You can see why I didn't invite Eilish," says the Ferryman, holding the extensive directory from the enclave under his arm.

"Yes, if it is true," says the President, in a harsh whisper, "she may be too close to think rationally."

"Do you think one of the captives will talk?"

"I think we have plenty to bargain."

"And the letter from the Princes?" asks the Ferryman. "Are they serious?"

"They said the Distillery has been, in their words, *'compromised'*. And until we get our house in order, our relationship is on hold."

"What do they mean, *'compromised'*?"

"It is ever since Samael's body disintegrated, and they went back."

"You don't think it's because of the number of Drifters we're creating from these raids?"

"Possibly," says the President, unconvinced. "But I wouldn't think they'd stop all cooperation, just because of that. No, I suspect something else is happening in the Beyond."

"What does this mean for the marbles? How long will the resin last if they aren't cooperating?"

"It's ok, I've spoken with the Mineralist already. He says we have weeks of supplies in reserve."

"And that's with the current proportions?" asks the Ferryman, looking apprehensive.

"That's what he says."

"It better be. We can't have him *tinkering* anymore. Workhouse marbles are already getting too unstable... Do you think you can sort things with Samael before the resin runs out?"

"I've already sent a delegation to the House of Sand. They'll get us more information and offer some new specimens for Samael to choose from. I'm sure we can iron things out and the princes will turn the taps back on at the Source, soon."

The Ferryman doesn't look convinced but forces a smile as they approach the Mineralist's office.

The Mineralist has seen them coming. He stands with his door wide open, beaming with a tortured grin. "Your excellencies," he says, dropping a minuscule bow. "What a pleasant surprise, down here in my little dungeon. I don't suppose you're hear for a social call?" He grins wildly, dropping a deep red crimson marble from his mouth. It smashes on the floor, hissing a sharp scarlet mist around his feet.

Inside the Mineralist's office, right in the middle and impossible to ignore, an emaciated workhouse slave is bound to a chair, gagged and cowering. The man's eyes are red with tears.

"I won't ask," says the President, glancing at the man.

"And I won't tell," says the Mineralist.

"We're here to interrogate one of your *Stained*," announces the President. "Are any of them still alive?"

The Mineralist looks quizzically at the President and the Ferryman. "That's intriguing," he says. "I do all my own interrogations. I didn't think you wanted anything to do with them. Don't you *trust* me?"

"Just this one time," says the President, ignoring the question. "Have you got any?"

"I have a couple," says the Mineralist. "When do you want them?"

"Immediately," says the President, unambiguously. "Alone."

"Alright, alright," says the Mineralist, sensing impatience. "And what's this book you have with you?"

"None of your business," says the Ferryman.

"I see… this is really not a social call," says the Mineralist, frowning. "Ok then. Go to the end of the corridor. On your right, you'll find a chamber. I call it the *Beach Hut*… you'll see why." He smirks to himself. "The two of them are in there."

The Mineralist reaches out, handing the President a brass key from around his neck. The President grasps it, without a word of thanks, and strides away, ushering his son to follow.

"He's a wrong'un," says the Ferryman to his father, as they wander down the corridor.

"No doubt," agrees the President. "But better to have him on our side."

They reach the *Beach Hut,* and it is clear why it has its name. Mounds of sand are piled high into mini dunes inside the vast chamber. Mounds of odorous sand, reeking of putrid decay. Reeking of fear and pain. Within the piles, many reaching head height, is a littering of trinkets and personal items; rings, necklaces, and religious pendants of one kind or another. It is like an ancient Egyptians tomb.

One of the dunes is particularly disturbing. While most of it is a fine shapeless dust, half is unmistakably the crumbling body of a person. A middle-aged man with wispy hair and small beady eyes; the eyes, like marbles, are the only part of the man not disintegrating into sand.

The President and the Ferryman pull out cloths from their pockets to cover their faces, eager not to inhale the loose particles in the room. They step through the piles of sand, wandering deeper into the chamber, towards the rear, where two men are asleep on the floor.

The men are gagged. Their hands and legs tied. One man is noticeably taller than the other, but both have horrific scars and scalds all over their bare torsos.

"I'll do the talking," says the President.

"Ok," agrees the Ferryman, handing his father the directory.

The prisoners stir and immediately stare in wide-eyed shock as they recognise their unexpected company.

"Today is your lucky day," says the President as a way of introduction. "I can see that you recognise me… and I am sure you are aware of the power I have to get you out of this little predicament, or, indeed, to send you deeper… My son and I are here with a few straightforward questions for you. Questions which, if you answer them correctly and honestly, you may well find that I am generous, and your fate can be unbound from the sands of time in this room." He pauses.

"I have with me a book," he continues, holding up the directory. "It was recovered from the raid of your enclave… Do you recognise it?" He looks at the prisoners accusingly. They still look stunned by his presence. "Come now," says the President, "I'm not a patient man."

The taller prisoner nods his head. The other follows suit.

"Good," says the President. "Then you will be able to answer my questions." He looks across to the Ferryman. "There were a couple of chairs out in the corridor, Andrew. Go grab them for us."

The Ferryman doesn't ask any questions. He wanders away, leaving his father alone with the prisoners.

"There is a wound," the President addresses the two men, leaning close. "A wound in my soul that is deep. And do you know why?"

Both prisoners shake their heads nervously.

"Because someone like you hurt me!" He lifts the shorter of the men's heads to inspect his neckline, grimacing with revulsion at the dirty grey resin which leaks from the man's skin. Then he looks at the man's wrists. Disappointed, he turns to the other man and does the same.

"Ah, yes," he says, holding the man's head up and inspecting the friction burns around the man's neck. "Yes, my wife was just like you," he rasps, squeezing the man's throat. Panic fills the prisoner's eyes before the President quickly lets go.

The President takes a deep breath. "There is a poison in the souls of people like you," he says. "A poison that rips into other souls."

He turns to look at the piles of sand around him and kicks the disintegrating torso that lies in one of them. The body crumbles. "I will squeeze this poison out of the Meadow."

He turns back to the two prisoners. "But I am a man of my word," he says with a sinister smile. "If you cooperate today, I will pardon one of you from your sentence. And you shan't be burned in the fire like your friends... but, only one of you will be pardoned... a little incentive to cooperate as much as you can..."

The Ferryman returns, dragging two wooden chairs behind him. The chair legs leaving wiggling trails of parallel lines in the disintegrated remains of the former prisoners.

The President wipes one of the seats with his hand, before sitting and laying the open directory on his lap.

"I'll do them one at a time, Andrew," he says to the Ferryman, "starting with the tall one," he says, pointing at the man with the reddened neckline. "Remove his gag."

The Ferryman steps up to the prisoner and aggressively rips the cloth bandage tied around his mouth.

The man coughs, his throat dry and rasping. "Please," he says. "Please, spare me." His voice wobbles desperately.

"Shut up," says the President. "You know the bargain..." He leans back in his chair. "So, my first question... What is this abominable book?!" He punches his forefinger onto the pages.

The prisoner sniffs and clears his throat. "We call it the *Chronicle of Sadness*. It is a directory of all the souls we know have arrived here in London through the centuries, who have taken their own lives on Earth. Because many of us never received any formal introduction into the Meadow. This record is our way of getting a sense of belonging here."

"And how has this Chronicle of Poison been compiled?"

"Much like the Distillery records," says the prisoner. "Each record is made through an interrogation. Though we don't create a new Identity stone. Our people already have their Identity Charms. The charms that they will protect for the rest of their life in the Meadow."

"That explains these, then," says the President, drawing his hand through the pile of sand next to him, sieving out three sparkling earrings containing colourful glass gems.

The prisoner winces, knowing the owners of the jewels.

"And are there copies of this book?" asks the President.

The man stays silent for a moment. He looks down at his feet and across at the piles of sand around him. "No, sir," he says. "No, that is the only one."

"Good," says the President. "That is what I wanted to hear... And one last question... what is *your* name?"

"Chester, sir. Chester Clay."

"And are you in this book?"

"Yes, sir. I am. Page 944."

The President flicks through the pages, then runs his finger down the records on page 944.

Name: Chester Clay
Age: 42
Arrived: July 1964
Demise: In a desperate attempt to better his family's lot, Chester gambled the family's possessions in a casino and lost. The shame and guilt consumed him. As his children were taken into care, he took a rope and ended his life.

"A gambling man," muses the President. "Let's hope, for your sake, that your luck is in today, Chester." He turns to his son. "Gag him again, Andrew, it's the next one's turn."

Turning the pages of the directory to where a bookmark has been placed, the President looks at the second prisoner.

"My name is Edward Hemsley, sir," he says eagerly. "I'm on page 372."

The President chuckles. "Hello '*Edward Hemsley*'," he says, sarcastically. "I'm not interested in finding your page!" He sniggers at his son. "First, I want to ask you, is what Chester said to me true? Is this called the Chronicle of Sadness?"

"Yes," says Edward, eagerly.

"Ok… And to your knowledge, are all of the records in it true?"

"Yes," he says, quickly. "Yes, they must be true. You can check by sampling the resin gems on the floor."

"I won't bother," says the President, looking disgusted by the very idea. "But what I need from you is to verify one of the records for me, please."

"Absolutely, yes. Whatever you want, sir."

The President steps forward, holding open the page where the bookmark had sat. The prisoner looks at it, his eyes widening as he reads the record under the President's thumb.

"Can you confirm this record is true and accurate?" the President asks impatiently.

Edward falters. He looks nervously at the President and the Ferrymen, and then back at the record.

"Your life depends on this," reminds the President.

Edward looks up. "Yes," he says nervously. "Yes, that record is true."

The President slams the directory shut and turns to his son. "We have work to do," he announces.

"There is one more thing," says Edward. "It's not true that there is just one copy of the Chronicle, sir. Every one of the Sculptor's enclaves has a copy."

The President turns slowly to look at Edward and Chester. "That's very interesting," he says. "Oh dear, Chester. It looks like you still have a fatal gambling problem!" He turns back to the Ferryman. "Andrew, we have some serious work to do."

"Yes, Father," he says, nervously itching the scar on his cheek, "We do."

*****

Chapter 22

Charred Suspicions

Earth - London

Detective Constable Bates looks around at the charred basement of the *Knot of Three Ropes* in Camden. He is a seasoned detective now.

"Honestly, boss, you were lucky you survived," he says into the mobile phone, held tight to his ear. "This place is utterly devastated."

Jordan's feet crunch on charcoal as he carefully navigates the crime scene. The bodies of the deceased have been removed, but their outlines remain, marked by plastic evidence tags, surrounding undamaged parts of the wooden floor that the bodies protected from the fire. There are blobs of congealed plastic everywhere, the remains of pint glasses now shrivelled into teardrops.

Jordan slips. The plastic elasticated covers on his shoes are not designed for this traipsing over wet ash. He manages to hold his balance, just about, as Marty's voice crackles on the other end of the phone line.

"No," Jordan responds. "I'm just making my way to the wall now. Just to the left of the stairs, right?"

Jordan carefully leans into the brickwork. He inspects the black ash, mixed with the dampness of the basement, which has dripped like Gothic tears. Around shoulder height, he sees what he is looking for. A scratched symbol. The encircled drop. The calling card of Marty's '*Hooded Lady*'.

"Ok, boss, I can see it… No, nothing that looks good for DNA… I'll call in the specialists. They might be able to find something."

He photographs the symbol on the wall and sighs. It'll join all the other images held in the cold case file he has been collating on the lady for years.

"Your lungs are sounding a bit better, boss? … Yeah, you think you will be back with us soon? … At least you can see your boy? … Ok, catch you later, boss." Jordan hangs up the phone, dropping it carefully into his back pocket.

"Was that *him*?" Asks the Sergeant, appearing from the staircase. Like Jordan, his feet are wrapped in plastic covers. He wears purple nitrile gloves and a tight dust mask that muffles his voice.

"Yes, it was, Sarge."

"So, what are you thinking? Do you think Marty was on to something when he started with this lady all those years ago?"

"It's hard to say, Sarge. I've looked at the tapes for this tragedy. There's no suggestion she was here any time except maybe the two minutes before the fire. She was in the basement for less than a minute and was never near the seat of the fire." He points towards the fractured black remains of the stage. "Another crazy coincidence is what it looks like, unbelievably."

"And have you followed up on her movements before and after?"

"Yes, Sarge. Dead ends everywhere I look. She travels by public transport. Her hood is always up, and she never looks towards a camera. She took the train from Euston on the day, out of the city, all the way to Shrewsbury, in the countryside. The camera coverage is poor from there, and she disappears."

The Sergeant ponders for a moment. "And what about Marty?" He asks. "How does he seem to be doing?"

"He sounds much better, Sarge."

"No, I mean, *mentally…*"

Jordan shrugs. "Hard to tell Sarge, it has been years like this, hasn't it. I still don't think he actually accepts he isn't a police detective anymore."

"It has been five years since we signed him off."

"I know," frowns Jordan.

"Do you have any suspicions about him?"

"Suspicions? About Marty?!"

"Why was he here, Jordan? You know Marty, as well as I do. This isn't the kind of pub that Marty comes to. And you've seen the footage. He was here alone. He was watching… waiting. As though he knew something. And he was supposed to think we closed this case years ago. I want you to be careful, Jordan. Keep an eye on Marty. I've seen what obsessions can do to detectives. Let's make sure he isn't becoming the kind of criminal he used to catch."

"Yes, boss," says Jordan, anxiously.

"This stays between me and you," says the Sergeant.

Jordan nods. He has no choice.

***

Hi 'friend',

What the hell? I nearly died! Did you know the fire was coming? How the hell did you know she would be there? I need answers, or I'm going to the authorities. At least tell me who you are and how you know about her. And consider my safety in future!

The Curious Blogger.

Marty coughs as he hits send. This is the first time back in his flat after a week in hospital. The damp has taken over again. Mould climbs up the walls and condensation drips down the windows, pooling on the sill while flies hover around the bin. He coughs again. A horrible hacking cough he has had since the basement fire.

He wanders over to the fridge. There's barely anything in date. The salad and vegetables in the bottom drawer are wilted or mouldy. A power cut a few days ago had gone unheeded. Nothing has survived well. He grabs the jar of gherkins from the top shelf; they could survive a nuclear winter.

Sitting down beside his laptop, Marty unscrews the tight lid of the jar and dips his grubby hands into the salty brine, picking out a fat, juicy pickle. He absent-mindedly scrolls news sites as his teeth crunch into the gherkin flesh. His scrolling habit is just as firmly established in his body as his mind, his fingers moving over the headlines while his mind ingests the facts, the spin, and the emotions they preach. There are still stories about the fire at the *Knot of Three Ropes*, speculation about the cause and more graphic details from survivors. But Marty is numb to these. That's all he has thought and read about for a week.

A notification pings up on his screen—a new message from an anonymous sender.

Dear Mr Fredrickson,

I know who you are. I know you are a detective for the Metropolitan Police. That is why I have been messaging you, and why I trust you with the information that I have.

I am sorry that you got so close to the fire. That was not my intention. I had no idea of the danger you were going into. I was unaware that a disaster was imminent. I just suspected that she had plans to be there. Did you see her? Did you find out more about her?

I'm sorry, I'm not in a position yet to tell you who I am. For my own safety. Nor can I think of a way of explaining my knowledge of her, without you thinking I'm crazy. So, for now, I hope you will let me stay anonymous and simply let me point you in the right direction.

Please take anymore tip-offs from me with extreme caution.

Sincerely, and apologetically,

A friend

Marty's heart beats fast. Being a detective, he expects to have the upper hand, knowing more about his subjects. He is uncomfortable being in the opposite position. This anonymous person knows who he is, and they know things he wants to know.

They hold the cards. They can play him and twist him how they want.

Marty reopens the search window on his laptop. Is there any way he can identify his anonymous sender without their knowing? Level up the playing field a bit. Maybe he could find an email address they were using? But he can't find anything. Everything he sees seems to lead back to himself. And the blog provider he uses encrypts any correspondence he receives. It's all part of the service he signed up for. The intention had been to encourage people to come forward. He never thought he'd have reason to seek contributors' details without their consent. His 'friend' solidly has the upper hand.

> Dear 'friend',
>
> OK. I accept your apology, but I still have many more questions than answers. How do you know who I am? Do I know you? Why don't we meet in person? Somewhere safe. Somewhere of your choosing.
>
> You don't need to warn me about taking your tips in future. Self-preservation will always come first.
>
> Awaiting your response,
>
> M.F.

Marty sends the message and waits expectantly. He throws another gherkin in his mouth, crunching it ravenously. But there is no response. And by the time he has finished the whole jar of gherkins, he gives up hope.

Marty closes his laptop lid, resigned, and wanders over to the vintage record player he has finally brought out from his son's empty room. He lifts the needle and drops the LP of *In the End* by Linkin Park onto the wheel. It's his son's favourite.

Marty sits back and lets the music and the angst wash over him.

***

Chapter 23

Rebel Talk

The Meadow - London

"Can you believe my father and brother?" says Eilish, blazing with passion. "Curfews passed for every inhabitant of London?! As though over-reaching with Distillery power will quash this rebellion. It'll be the socialites in the Paddock that they hit the most… they're the ones who are out at night filling the marble bars. *And* they're the only ones loyal to the Distillery now! And, as for marble-deprivation…" Eilish rolls her eyes. "What are they thinking? I thought they were committed to smashing the black-market trading of marbles? If the families and associates of convicted rebels are being starved of basic marbles, this will only exacerbate the problem, surely?!"

Eilish sighs and folds a letter in her hand, picking at the wax seal of the Distillery from its edge.

"And now they're not even talking to me! Just sending me letters! My father has, in his words, 'relaxed' my duties in the Distillery. In light of the rebellions, he feels it's 'too dangerous' for me to be travelling around the Meadow. He's such a control freak! I'm not even invited to council meetings anymore. I'm just a Governess in name! It's ridiculous. They have trapped me."

"You don't think they've found out about your visit to that pub?"

Eilish exhales.

"No. If they knew of *that,* my father would've confronted me… if not worse! I'm sure of it."

"You know, Andrew has been acting strangely towards me these last few days, too," says Chloe, dropping a rose marble from her mouth into a napkin and replacing it with a fresh one. "He's barely acknowledging me at the moment. I don't think he's even come into our bed since the weekend."

"I'm sorry, Chloe," says Eilish, frowning. "I really am. I wish I could have warned you about my brother before he married you."

"Eilish, he got me out of the palace and got me to meet you. That's more than most of the girls there ever got."

Eilish smiles politely and glances out of the window of the café. The river below is calm. A bright, warm sunshine bathes the banks, drawing people outside to relax and enjoy themselves before tonight's curfew comes into force. A fishing boat drifts by—its crew rowing it steadily upstream. Eilish thinks of Cyril Spate on his boat, the *Guiding Star*. He said he was off out into the Channel today, off to *La Prairie*—the French Meadow—to the port at *La Rochelle*—the home of many artisan marble makers who make some of the most unusual resin artefacts. Such a contrast to the café that Eilish finds herself in. Her secret visit to the *Tide and Time Tavern* feels a world away already.

Eilish realises Chloe is looking at her. "Sorry," she says, knowing she had drifted off. "I was daydreaming."

"About Ciara?" Chloe asks.

"Not exactly."

"So, this landlady... She said Ciara had joined the rebellion?!" says Chloe, looking sceptical.

"Yes," says Eilish, quietly.

"And she's on some *secret* mission?"

"Supposedly," says Eilish. "Though I don't fully understand what it is for. She was going to the Source and attempting to understand the leap from the Perihelion precipice into the Beyond."

"Do you think she's still there?" says Chloe.

Eilish smiles and shrugs. That thought had been lingering in her mind, but it seemed so unlikely. There hadn't been a word from Ciara in ten years.

"These beliefs about travelling between the realms, they have really caught my attention," says Eilish. "Do you think I'm crazy to be taking them seriously? That maybe the rebellion ten years ago was onto something?"

Chloe looks nervously over her shoulder and leans closer in. "Eilish, what has got into you?"

"We both know my family have done bad things here in the name of the Distillery. I always assumed my father had just misapplied the truth about the Meadow. Ultimately, I did still think we were the 'good guys'. But if Ciara saw it differently… She wasn't… isn't, a fool. She wouldn't get involved with a rebellion against us if she hadn't seen something worth fighting for."

Chloe shuffles nervously. "I was worried this would happen," she says. "The moment you took that invite, I could tell you were opening a door we couldn't close."

"Neither of us has been happy for years," says Eilish. "I need to find out more. I can't just let my life here waste away like this." She looks nervously at the handkerchief she has been using to wipe her mouth between marbles. There is a stain on it from the dirty resin that perspires from her upper lip. She carefully folds it over, hoping Chloe hasn't noticed anything.

"Eilish, we're so fortunate in what we have here. Look around us. Many people would love to have our lives. Bear in mind, you're lucky you haven't been caught. It's only a matter of time if you keep pushing at that door. Then what?"

Eilish frowns and waits a moment, thinking. "I am going to visit the *Tide and Time Tavern* again," she says. "I was hoping you might come with me this time?"

Chloe goes pale.

"Go with you?! I'm sorry, Eilish," she says. "I know you mean well, but I'm not a Callaghan like you… What you are talking about would be suicide for me. People on all sides might mistrust you if you are discovered, but you'd still have your father's protection. I dare not imagine what they'd think of me. No, I can't go with you… I can cover for you again if it would help, but that's all. Just please promise me you won't leave me here on my own?"

Eilish leans across and delicately grasps Chloe's palms. "I am so lucky to have you," she says. "I promise, I will always come back to you, Chloe. No matter what."

Chloe smiles and drops another marble into her mouth.

***

"So, you've honestly not been tempted to report us?"

Kim-Joy, lying back with her feet up on the table, shades her eyes from the sun in the garden of the *Tide and Time Tavern*, and smiles mischievously at Eilish. "I shouldn't be expecting Ferrymen to come bashing through our secret tunnel anytime soon?"

"Honestly, no," says Eilish. The thought of telling anyone in the Distillery wasn't even one she had considered. "You're not hurting anyone, as far as I can tell, and you are the only way I can learn more about Ciara. I more expected you to turn on me. Kidnapping a Callaghan would be quite a statement."

Kim-Joy chuckles. "Can you imagine… Me, a kidnapper?!"

Eilish sighs contentedly, leaning back to let the sun wash over her face. High up in the trees lining the pub garden, a small bird chirrups joyfully, and a gentle breeze rocks the branches back and forth in a happy dance.

"So, you want to know more about Well-Wishing and how we make sense of the realms?"

"Yes, please. I'm desperate to know about Ciara's religion…"

"Well, before we start," halts Kim-Joy. "Please understand, Well-Wishing is not a 'religion'. Nor is it some theological discipline. We are not an organised group. Well, some are… but I don't associate with them. I doubt many of us true believers actually think the same things at all. But I can give you a sense of the glue that binds us…"

"Yes, please. Anything," says Eilish eagerly.

"First things first, then… Let's start with 'water'. For it is indeed the Wishing Well around which we get our name."

Eilish leans forward, attentively.

"As you know, water in the Meadow holds its own unique properties. Unlike on Earth, our bodies in the Meadow don't need nutrition to sustain them. The Meadow is the realm of our mind. And it is our mind that requires sustenance. The mystery of water here provides this sustenance. The water, which is in the rain, and is in every marble that we suck, is driving every sensation that we feel. Water in the Meadow, intrinsically sustains, disrupts, and ultimately dissolves the mind."

"Now, Well-Wishing was founded on an ancient legend about this water… A legend that tells of some of the earliest settlers in the Meadow and how, knowing no better, they desperately sought water from the ground to sustain them. They dug wells. Deep wells. And, as they consumed the fruit of their labour, they rapidly dissolved their minds and went on to the Beyond.

But then, one day, a woman visited the settlers. Some say an Angel from the Beyond, or even the Creator herself. Whoever she was, she told them how water in the Meadow takes on two forms. One, a contaminated form as water travels through the ground, picking up sediment—the water that we use to make marbles. The water that can send you 'on'."

"And another water. A pure water. One that hasn't travelled through the ground but falls from the heavens. This pure water gives you no sensation at all, but it frees your mind. And this freedom allows you to see the Meadow for what it is: just another realm, like Earth, in which you can dwell or from which you can leave."

"The first Well Wishers stopped drinking from the wells and started dreaming of returning to Earth, of finding a way back. But this truth was soon lost. Stories of hope and the truths of water became contaminated as people got addicted to the sensations from the water that flowed through the ground. And soon, the idea of pure water was forgotten. Forgotten, but not lost. For in the fringes of the Meadow, there were still believers. People who treasured the truth. People who always believed in going back to Earth."

"I would never want to go back," muses Eilish. "Even if it was possible."

Kim-Joy smiles. "No," she says. "Me neither. And that is where the next foundation of our belief might be more interesting."

"For, while there have always been Well Wishers who were driven by a desire to go 'back'—believers who yearn for physical intimacy, often young people still in the bloom of becoming themselves—there are also those who have found their home in the Meadow and have no desire to move away from the realm of the mind—people like me and like Cyril. We have suffered the slow betrayal of ageing on Earth and have seen the fragility of the physical. But we found our home here, in the realm of the mind, and have no impulse to leave. And then, like your sister, there are also those whose life in their body on Earth, and life in their mind in the Meadow, are neither home... these believers are drawn to understand the other realm, the Beyond... The realm of the 'soul'."

"This is the triumvirate of Well-Wishing... the 'water cycle'. The three states—ice, water, and steam—all naturally occur as water moves through its cycle. Well-wishers think of themselves as water. Our three states—body, mind, and soul—are all co-present, yet in each realm, one dominates."

Eilish looks at Kim-Joy, bemused.

"Clear as mud, isn't it?!" Laughs Kim-Joy.

Eilish smiles. "Purgatory to cleanse the soul, and a simple journey through death... that's all I've been told before."

Kim-Joy frowns. "Yes... We all have had to tackle our own ignorance... *and* the stubborn ignorance of others."

"Forgive me," says Eilish, a little embarrassed. "But there is something that doesn't make sense to me..."

Kim-Joy smiles, knowingly. "Go on..." she says, rummaging through her pocket.

"If there are three realms," says Eilish, "and one person can travel back and forth between them, how do you account for..."

"...time!" Kim-Joy finishes Eilish's sentence. In her hand, she holds a delicate and peculiar brass sand timer. Rather than two chambers for the sand, joined by a pinch of glass in the middle, this sand timer has six chambers, making it work along three perpendicular axes.

"Beautiful, isn't it?" says Kim-Joy. "I had Cyril knock it up for me years ago... He had plenty of time back in the day."

"What is it?"

"A *Triaxial Vitaloscope* is its technical name. In a nutshell, it is a depiction of life across the realms."

Kim-Joy holds the instrument up for Eilish to inspect. "You see, while conventional wisdom has it that the Meadow exists in some kind of parallel or distinct dimension to Earth, we believe that the Meadow is actually existing in a *perpendicular* time-dimension. And a third realm—the 'Beyond'—traverses another final perpendicular axis."

"This means that, for each individual, depending on the realm that they find themselves in, their own sands of time will fall only for that dimension of themselves…"

"On Earth," Kim-Joy points her finger at the dark orange sand that fills one of the chambers, "your existence will run through the 'sand' of your body. But, when in the Meadow…" she tips the sand timer onto another axis, so that the orange sand stops falling, but white sand from another chamber starts to tumble, "you will start running down the clock of your mind… Now, it is hypothetical—but you must admit, *not* a giant leap—to consider what might happen if you were to leave the Meadow and enter the Beyond."

Kim-Joy tips the sand timer once again. This time, the white sand stops, the orange remains still, but now a fine black sand starts to fall. "Now, I believe that we are all given a finite amount of 'sand'. When one of these chambers is emptied, our access to that realm ends."

Eilish stares at the sand timer, struggling to get her head around it.

"Don't worry," smiles Kim-Joy. "Like I said last time, the beliefs of Well-Wishing might be something you need to learn in your own time."

Behind them, a door to the *Tide and Time Tavern* creaks open, drawing the two women's attention. Cyril strides over.

"Is everything ok?" asks Kim-Joy.

Cyril, shielding his eyes from the bright sunshine, acknowledges Eilish with a smile and bends down to whisper something in Kim-Joy's ear.

"She's here now?" asks Kim-Joy. "I didn't expect her back from *La Prairie* so soon,"

"Aye," Cyril responds. "Shall I keep her busy?"

Kim-Joy looks across at Eilish, and a thought occurs to her. A mischievous smile flickers across her face. "No, I think it could be good for Nailah to meet Eilish... and vice versa..."

"Nailah?" asks Eilish.

"A dear friend," says Kim-Joy. "A rebel leader, with a formidable strength, and, like you, governess, a kind heart."

"Are you sure?" asks Cyril, looking unconvinced.

"Oh yes," says Kim-Joy. "Bring her over."

Eilish inspects Kim-Joy suspiciously, but the old lady looks back without flinching and winks.

Cyril returns a moment later, flanked by the stolid figure of Nailah Hussain—a North African lady, with bright, gleaming eyes, and an air of unshakeable competence. She recognises Kim-Joy as she approaches.

"Kim-Joy!" she beams. "Good risen!"

"Good risen," the landlady responds, rising from her seat to embrace Nailah. "I wasn't expecting you back in London so soon!"

"No, me neither. The winds were favourable across the Channel this time."

The two women fold into an embrace of the closest friends. Nailah engulfs Kim-Joy, who is much shorter than her. Her jet-black curly hair covers Kim-Joy's face and shines in the sunlight.

As the two women disentangle, Kim-Joy introduces Eilish. "I assume you've never met my guest," she says.

Nailah's head snaps round, and the moment she realises whose presence she is in, her warmth turns icy cold. She pauses for a moment before her eyes narrow.

"What is *she* doing here?!" Nailah asks, her voice cutting like razors. "No Callaghan should ever set foot in the *Tide and Time Tavern*."

Eilish feels her heart rate rise and her body stiffen. "I beg your pardon," she says, facing up to Nailah, the fire in her spirit matching the vibrancy of her hair.

"I said, no Callaghan should set foot in this place... The damage your family is doing to the Meadow is *unforgivable!*"

Eilish feels the stab of judgement but brushes it off. She won't be spoken to like this. Not by someone who doesn't even know her.

"Nailah, please," Kim-Joy cuts in, grasping Nailah's arm and pulling her back.

"I know you're always willing to give people a chance, Kim-Joy, but this is too much. This is inviting the devil to the dance!"

"Nailah, you know we can't do everything from outside… having friends in the Distillery is *necessary* for our movement."

"Then we are to sell our souls, embracing *them*?!" asks Nailah, refusing to give Eilish a name or title. "Partnering with them, we become as bad as my ex-husband! Abandoning our standards… justifying any means to make our end…"

"This is different," says Kim-Joy. "Eilish here is not like her father or brother. She is not like Milton. In fact, I'd say she is more like you."

Nailah spits on the floor in disgust.

"You've not even given me a chance," Eilish says, standing up, confronting Nailah.

"Why should I?!… I know enough."

Eilish ignores this. "My father and brother can be vile… But they are family, so I have stood with them when I knew no better…"

"And what, you know better now?!"

"I'm starting to," says Eilish, holding Nailah's gaze. "I have always despised my father for his ignorance. But I'm now becoming enlightened to his lies."

"Please, both of you, sit down," says Kim-Joy, playing peacekeeper.

Nailah and Eilish maintain locked eyes but sit.

"And how are you starting to *enlighten* yourself?" Nailah asks Eilish sarcastically.

"I think it might be useful for me to reset the dial first," says Kim-Joy, butting herself into the confrontation. "For Nailah, as much as the name of Callaghan boils your blood, I regret to tell you that you have been working with a Callaghan for ten years already."

"I have not!" shouts Nailah.

"Do you remember when Annabel Turner came to join the expeditions?"

"The pilot?" asks Nailah, "the one who arrived with *her*... and wanted nothing to do with *them*?"

"That's the one," says Kim-Joy. "Well, she wasn't who she said she was."

"What do you mean?"

"She is my sister," says Eilish, folding her arms, looking satisfied. "Ciara Callaghan... she pretended to be one of the pilots to escape my father... I wish I had done the same."

"Annabel is a Callaghan?"

Kim-Joy smiles delicately.

"Have you met Ciara?" asks Eilish, her voice softening.

Nailah's eyes widen, and the tension in her body stumbles. "Many times," she says. "A friend of real integrity... or so I thought. A brave rebel soul."

Eilish smiles. "That sounds like my sister."

"The governess here has only just learnt that Ciara survived the crash."

Nailah stiffens again. She looks at Eilish. "Rebellion is not just about disliking your father, you know. It's about what you're willing to sacrifice."

"I wouldn't be here if I weren't willing," Eilish reacts.

"You've run away. That's not the same thing."

"You're right," agrees Eilish, resolutely. "But I hope it is a start."

She holds out her hand in front of Nailah.

Nailah stares at Eilish's palm, unmoved. Then she takes a deep breath and reaches out, shaking Eilish's hand. "You've made me soft, Kim-Joy," she says.

The landlady smiles. "I have started teaching Eilish here about our beliefs. About how the Well Wishers understand the realms... About the central role of water in our lives."

Nailah nods. "And what do you think?" she directs at Eilish.

"It is fascinating," says Eilish. "I don't think I am quite understanding it, yet. But I want to learn what I can."

"Well, just make sure you learn from the good ones," says Nailah. "There are bad eggs, even amongst the Well Wishers…"

"Sadly, that is true," Kim-Joy concurs. "Even though I told you I'm not part of an *organised* religion, that doesn't mean there aren't those who are…"

"And organised religion is always a problem," says Nailah, decisively. "Well-Wishing has been contaminated."

"Nailah has been trying to decontaminate the belief for the last ten years."

"Decontaminate?" asks Eilish.

"There are Well-Wishing priests who spout goodness from their mouths, but spurt evil with their deeds," says Nailah. "You no doubt know of the agreements made after the rebellion ten years ago… The sanctioning of Well-Wishing ideas in the Meadow, so long as the attempts to return to Earth were condemned… A rotten bargain, accepted by rotten priests."

Eilish nods.

"I came into the Meadow with a husband and a daughter. Two souls I loved unconditionally. But he changed from the man I knew on Earth. He became a High Councillor of the Well Wishers, and he was one of the rotten ones. His filthy thirst for power lost us our daughter… This is why I do not easily trust people."

Eilish nods, knowingly. "I understand."

"You are married, are you not, Governess?" asks Kim-Joy.

"Yes, I am," frowns Eilish.

"Don't look too happy!" smirks Nailah.

"You have loved and lost," says Eilish. "I have never loved at all."

"Go on," says Nailah.

"Like much of my life, my father arranged my marriage for me. A 'good' match… or should I say, a 'useful' match for him."

"Your husband… the Head of Distillery Intelligence?"

"That's him," says Eilish. "He is as good at his job as he is at being a husband," she frowns.

Nailah ponders for a moment. "Your husband isn't by any chance running a network of spies amongst the Well-Wishers, is he?"

"He is," she confirms, immediately realising just how relevant her husband's work is to Nailah and Kim-Joy. "He has many secret meetings with your priests."

"He does? What do they talk about?"

Eilish drops her eyes. "It's awful," she says.

"Please, tell me…" says Nailah, looking at Eilish sincerely.

"I've not seen it first hand," Eilish cautions. "But I understand that the priests are giving my husband names."

"Names?"

"Names of their congregation whose resin isn't running clear… names of people who have come to confession because they are in pain and vulnerable."

"Fucking hell," says Nailah, sitting down. "That's awful. People are trusting them. And that explains how the Ferrymen have become somewhat efficient in recent years, rounding up dirty resin… Is there a record of these meetings?"

Kim-Joy smiles opposite them. "It sounds like you are starting to see the value of having a Callaghan at the *Tide and Time Tavern*, Nailah!"

"The jury is still out," says Nailah, waiting for Eilish's response.

"There's definitely a record," says Eilish. "A marble record. But it doesn't do you any good knowing about it," she says.

"Why not?" asks Nailah. "A full record of names… we could save countless lives from being taken to the palaces and workhouses if we could smash those records!"

"All records are kept in the vaults under St. Paul's, and I do not have access."

"What do you mean you don't have access… you're the governess?!"

"The vaults are secret, even from me. They are somewhere in the cellars of the cathedral. But I have never been allowed down there."

"Could you find out how to get to them?" asks Kim-Joy.

Eilish thinks for a moment. She can vaguely recollect seeing blueprints for many Distillery buildings in Angus' study. The cathedral was likely one of them.

"I can try," she says, pausing and looking at Nailah. "But only if you can tell me more about Ciara... You are asking me to commit treason... I think it's only fair that I get something more in return. If I am to distance myself from my father and brother, I want to feel closer to Ciara."

Nailah nods. "Let's take a walk," she says, standing. "We can wander through the woods, down to the river. It's a lovely day."

***

Chapter 24

Choose your family

The Meadow - London

The walk through the woods behind the *Tide and Time Tavern* gives Eilish a fascinating insight into the goings-on at the rebel stronghold. If she weren't now becoming sympathetic to the cause, this would be valuable intelligence for her brother.

Dozens of rough, makeshift shelters are erected in the woodland. Crude temporary accommodation for hundreds of young people. Young people who talk in low, exhausted voices, with sooty resin stains down their faces. No doubt, these are the fire starters who have been wreaking havoc north of the river for months.

There are also kilns, many kilns scattered in the forest, around which artisan sculptors are making their own marbles. Eilish wonders if maybe some Stained have found refuge here.

And there are members of a circus troupe. Much to Eilish's delight, she spots the large Indian elephant she had seen Kim-Joy riding during the Festival of the Mind. The mighty animal is happily rolling logs in amongst the warm leaf litter.

"He's magnificent, isn't he?" says Nailah, looking up at the elephant. "His name is Pimlico. He was with Sanger's Circus before they relocated to *La Prairie*. I have just returned from visiting his old circus master..." Nailah holds up her hand, and the elephant delicately places his trunk onto her palm, sniffing the scent of her skin. "Pimlico was one of the bravest souls during the night of rebellion—I was riding him with Kim-Joy that night. You know, I also rode him with Ciara... not long after. Your sister was in a rush to get to the Source... and Pimlico needed to be out of the city before he was impounded. He was a wanted animal, and hard to hide!"

Eilish looks up at the elephant, imagining her sister sitting upon him, just like she had seen Kim-Joy doing. She imagines him rumbling out of the city in the dead of night, leaving the fires of rebellion burning in his midst.

"You were with Ciara after the rebellion?" asks Eilish. "You knew of her mission?"

Nailah looks at her. "I guess Kim-Joy has told you already, then? She really is too trusting. How much do you know?"

"Just that she had been studying the Source, and that she wanted to use this knowledge to understand the relationship between pure water and the opening at the Perihelion Cliffs…"

Nailah smiles. "That's right," she says. "You know, your sister was one of the first believers to seek me out when she heard I was cleansing the priesthood of contamination. She told me that she knew of high priests and councillors in her monastery who were selecting vulnerable believers for 'special' treatment… she didn't trust them, and so she gave me many names. This was a real boost to my work back then."

It's Eilish's turn to smile.

"Ciara always had integrity," she says. "Even if it would put herself at risk."

"Yes," says Nailah. "And that's true in this case, too, for there was something else Ciara revealed, which speaks to her mission now as well. She had heard rumours of holy beings—individuals with no history in the Meadow—who were somehow linked to the exploitation of the vulnerable at the monasteries. She had heard of some unusual beings with no obvious 'bodies' to speak of… like ghosts… who possessed angelic voices and hypnotic songs which the priests were employing to seduce the vulnerable. Your sister believed that these ghostly beings had come from the Beyond, somehow using the Opening at the Source to enter the Meadow…"

Eilish thinks of her angel on the bridge. She had never really *seen* her. Never really *heard* her, except for the intoxicating whisper of her song. Her music that travelled in the gentlest breeze, connecting with Eilish's ears and with her soul.

"Beyond simply a curiosity about the connection between the Meadow and the Beyond at the Source, Ciara had a calling: she could help us save Well-Wishing if she could understand and expose the 'holy ghosts'..." Nailah looks at Eilish, who looks bewildered. "Are you keeping up?" she asks.

Eilish smiles. "I'm trying," she says. "So, did you go with Ciara to the Source? Do you know what happened to her?"

"I took her as close as I could," says Nailah. "To the edge of the Distillery patrols on the border of the mountain. She left on foot from there. She planned to camp out in the foothills, learning the Distillery's movements, before finding an opening when their guard of the Source was down.

"That was ten years ago now," Nailah continues, "and we all know what happened at the Source ten years ago..."

"*The Mighty Fire?!*" says Eilish.

Nailah's gaze drops in sorrow. "Exactly."

"Few on the Mountain, or even in the surrounding foothills, are known to have survived the fire... and I left Ciara on the border of the Mountain itself."

Nailah leaves an awful gulf of silence in her recollection. Eilish feels her own heart pounding.

"I have heard nothing in ten years," Nailah goes on. "I fear either her attempt failed, or she burned alone in the fire..."

"Has no one been out to look for her?"

"The mountain range is vast, and the forests that survived the fire are wild and untamed," says Nailah, frowning. "It would be like looking for a lost earring on a beach. The Distillery's crackdown on expeditions to the Source has made it impossible for anyone to approach the area in recent years, and the chances that she was alive were so slim. And then, with your family's reign of terror, our priorities have shifted.

"These young people here," she gestures to the boys and girls sitting around the tents in the woodland. "They are the new frontier of our rebellion. Each of them has lost family and friends to your family's rule. Lost them to the bursting of increasingly fragile marbles. Lost them to cruel public executions for the most minor disruption. Or lost them to the latest travesty—marble starvation by association. They are all suffering—you can see how dark their resin has got—and all are committed to helping the cause. But we cannot go exploring other realms or attempting to go back to Earth anymore. Disrupting the fearful rule of your father, that is what we can do. Disrupt it so that the masses can at least see the fragility of the Distillery's power and be open to the idea that there could be something else."

"I didn't realise there was such hatred for my family," says Eilish.

Nailah scoffs.

"That doesn't surprise me. You live in the Paddock. Marbles are in plentiful supply over there, aren't they? You have warm homes and easy lives. The people north of the river, they are struggling. It is *their* scars that make the marbles that the Distillery feed them. And it is no secret that the marbles from the workhouses are becoming unstable. The people are scared. Their minds crave the sensations they get from marbles, and yet thousands are finding them bursting and sending them 'on'. Minds that shouldn't be leaving the Meadow are being extinguished. Naturally, people are cutting down. Choosing a life without joy or sensation. Tired and weary lives, filled with fear of the unknown. That is the Meadow that your Distillery has created. This is why we are happy to rebel."

Eilish feels awful, looking around at the conditions the young people are living in. But she can't help feeling a pinch of irritation from Nailah's glib dismissal of her own life, and the lives of the people in the Paddock. As though people of the Paddock don't have challenges. She doesn't know the *women* of the Paddock, living in the brutal patriarchal residue of Earth.

"Not all suffering comes from a marble hunger, you know? Not all rebellions are done on the street."

"I'd hardly call your life 'rebellious', governess!" says Nailah, arching her brow. "You might have silently endured some minor discomfort. But your silence and *real* sacrifice are worlds apart."

Eilish exhales, looking away, frustrated.

"Sometimes silent suffering is the biggest sacrifice of all," she whispers under her breath, "but I will find you the cathedral blueprints," she says aloud, decisively.

"Thank you," says Nailah, softening. "I don't mean to belittle you or your suffering. I just want you to open your eyes." She glances across at some of the young people. They are whispering suspiciously—no doubt realising that there is a Callaghan in their midst. "I think we should head back. I don't want you to outstay your welcome."

A young lady catches Eilish's eye. A confusing image flashes into Eilish's mind. A picture of the same young lady, bloodied and tied to a chair, sat in a hazy kitchen beside the naked flame of a candle—another *jamais vu*. But as soon as the image comes, it goes, and the young lady turns away.

"Come on, governess," says Nailah, grasping Eilish's hand.

Eilish isn't expecting the contact. Nailah's grip is firm, but warm. And an unexpected tingling tightens in Eilish's chest.

"Yes," says Eilish, unsettled by the feeling.

'Is this what it feels like to rebel?'

***

With her hood up, doing her best to conceal her identity, Eilish wanders back through the streets of London in a daze. She is wracked with shame as she walks past endless huddles of marble addicts, dark resin dripping down their faces, huddled around rubbish fires, consuming dangerously dark marbles, ripe to bursting, and pestering passers-by for their next sensation. And the groups of women, the Flickers from the palace, with no recollection of their lives on Earth, wandering aimlessly, trying to make sense of where they are, vulnerable to the attention of men with vile motivations. Then she sees the charred remains of a Distillery guard hut and the angry graffiti written all over it. And she sees the endless posters of missing men. North of the river is a world, stained by oversight and the negligence of her family's power. Eilish feels an overwhelming guilt tumble into the pit of her stomach.

Then Eilish wanders through the streets of the Paddock, south of the river. The wide, clean boulevards, observing strict curfews under the watchful eyes of the militarised police. She gazes in at the marble cafes, where people are carefree and lavishly indulging in any sensation they desire. The cafes she has enjoyed so much herself. And she notices the small purple flags, draped obediently in residential windows, showing fear and allegiance to the Distillery and her family.

Eilish's mind is racing. It feels like her eyes have been opened for the first time in the Meadow. She desperately wishes she could close them again.

Eilish's cover for going to the *Tide and Time Tavern* today had been a lie that she was out getting fresh air, walking the river path with Chloe. So, naturally, she heads to Chloe's house. There can be no loose ends if she is to keep up her treacherous behaviour.

Rounding the wide, poplar-lined street, Chloe's house comes into view. The grand mansion where Chloe lives unhappily with Eilish's brother.

The house looks different today. Eilish is taken aback by the sheer number of Ferrymen milling on the driveway. It was normal for a handful to be there, guarding the entrance for her brother, but there must be more than thirty this afternoon. All wearing the same guerrilla regalia: tight denim jeans and black bomber jackets.

A few of the Ferrymen draw their heels to attention when they see Eilish. Their black Doc Marten boots, snapping assertively like gunshots. They throw their hands over their mouths to salute the presence of the governess. A few don't notice Eilish and continue chatting. She isn't bothered. She sweeps up the stone steps past all of them, to the front door, under the stone eagle which stares down on her, its wingspan stretched over the entrance, resting on austere white stone columns.

Having seen the governess approaching, the porter opens the door, showing great reverence, bowing low as Eilish passes.

"Good day, Colin," she chirps to the porter. He is a familiar and kind face in an otherwise unfriendly home.

Colin keeps his head bowed, which is unusual as he is usually a chatty man. Eilish steps into the hallway and is surprised to see that, beneath the oil painting of her brother, the typically immaculate hallway is a chaotic mess. Chloe's clothes and dresses are strewn all over the floor. Chests of marbles have been turned over, many of them smashed leaving a multicoloured mist floating around the floor. And those marbles that haven't cracked are now a dangerous hazard to walk on.

Eilish feels her chest tighten. Something isn't right. She strides forward towards the lounge, where she can hear animated voices.

"Eilish!" shouts her brother. He stands with two of his officers in the centre of the lounge, surrounded by upturned furnishings. "Where the hell have you been?!

"What?" says Eilish, her brother's curt accusation taking her by surprise.

"I sent for you an hour ago!"

"Er, you don't *send* for me!" says Eilish, stiffening. "I'm your sister… You can either come and find me yourself or invite me over and wait. If you must know, I was out for a walk… can I not do that anymore?!"

"Angus said you were with my…" Andrew pauses. "Angus said you were with Chloe."

"Our plans changed," says Eilish, thinking on her feet, holding her brother's gaze without flinching.

"And you didn't think to inform your husband?"

"Please," says Eilish, exasperated. "I told Angus exactly where I was going, but you know Angus, he doesn't listen, even at the most critical of moments."

Andrew grunts, knowingly. Eilish feels the heat of her brother's glare drop away.

"What's been going on here?" she asks, flipping the conversation. "It looks a state. Where's Chloe?"

"Some privacy, please, gentlemen," says Andrew, turning to the officers beside him.

The two men cover their mouths in salute to the Ferryman and quickly leave the room.

"What is going on, Andrew?"

The Ferryman steps over to the dining table, flipping open a large book in front of Eilish; the *Chronicle of Sadness.*

"Read this," he instructs her.

She looks at the old directory on the table. Andrew's finger rests beside a record.

Name: Chloe Dolores Higgins
Age: 30
Arrival: 26th December 1999
Demise: Orphaned at birth, Chloe was adopted in London by Ms. Ashley Arnold, one of the Returners. *She learned of the Meadow and Well-Wishing while still on Earth in Ms. Arnold's care. In an attempt to support the imminent rebellion in the Meadow, she took her own life on Earth. Her arrival location is unknown, but thought to have been somewhere in the mountains near the Source.*

There is an asterisk beside the record containing a handwritten note:

*Chloe remembers none of her past. Chloe's attempt to infiltrate the palace and free Cerys Edwards, another of the Returners, *was a success, but her escape was not. She became a Flicker in the palace. The Stained will never forget her sacrifice.*

Eilish reads the record twice before she looks away from the page. She hardly believes what she is reading. Chloe's lack of memory from her time at the palace had meant she never knew where she came from. But Eilish had assumed that Chloe was newer to the Meadow than her. Instead, Chloe had a long history in the Meadow. A forgotten but rebellious history.

"Where is she?" asks Eilish, suddenly concerned by her friend's absence.

"Did you know about this?" asks Andrew.

Eilish turns to her brother. His face is contorted and furious.

"What have you done with Chloe?" repeats Eilish, stepping away, towards the door.

Andrew grabs her arm. "Did you know about this?" he growls aggressively.

"Let go of me!" shouts Eilish, trying to wriggle free of her brother's tight grip.

Andrew grabs Eilish with both arms now, pulling her face up towards his own. "DID...YOU...KNOW?!" he shouts. Flecks of his saliva splatter all over her.

In a frenzy, Eilish wriggles and kicks her brother, breaking free. She ducks around the sofa, hurtling out of Andrew's reach.

"She has been taken care of... like all *Stained* should be dealt with!" Andrew shouts.

Eilish looks at her brother, horrified, turns, and runs out of the room.

"Chloe!" Eilish shouts, striding into the hallway. "Chloe!" Her voice is sharp and panicky.

Colin, the porter, is still sitting in his usual chair by the front door. He looks at Eilish. His eyes sad and forlorn.

"Chloe!" shouts Eilish again, kicking the clothes and dresses that litter the room. She tramples on one of the hard marbles, sending pain shooting up through the soles of her feet. She runs up the stairs.

"Eilish!" shouts Andrew, entering the hallway. "She's not here!"

Eilish stops and leans over the bannister. "Where is she?"

"She's a *Stain*," says Andrew. "She is a liar. She is filth. She is with the Mineralist and will be sentenced tomorrow."

"You heartless, evil bastard!" shouts Eilish, tears now streaming down her face. She storms down the stairs, throwing whatever she can at her brother. "What is wrong with you!? What is wrong with this family?!"

Hearing the commotion, two Ferrymen step out from the kitchen. Andrew holds up his hand to stop them from approaching Eilish.

"Let her vent," he says. "She needs time."

"Does dad know what you have done?!" shouts Eilish, spitting rage at her brother.

"Yes, he knows," Andrew confirms.

"Arghh! I hate you both!" shouts Eilish. "I HATE THIS FAMILY!" She kicks a pile of marbles on the floor beside her. They smash into the doorframe and wall, hissing and oozing mist.

But Eilish doesn't stop for breath. She marches to the front door and barges it open angrily. Then she glances back at her brother. He just stands there, watching her like a statue. Unmoved and uncaring. She slams the door and runs into the street.

***

Chapter 25

A broken home

The Meadow - London

Crashing into the kitchen, Eilish barely notices she is home. She is out of breath. Her hair a tangle of wires all over her face. She rifles through the drawers, knocking a copy of today's *Shipping Forecast* onto the floor, finding the small velvet pouch of Sailor's Mist that Cyril Spate had given to her. She needs a calm mind now.

She plops a marble into her mouth and leans both hands on the kitchen surface, exhaling sharply. Her heart is thumping, and her shoulders heave up and down. Her mind is a race of tumbling chaos.

The marble gets to work quickly. The oozing sensation of a calm sea and a gentle breeze fizzes through her body, and her breathing calms. She needs to find Chloe. She needs to get to the Mineralist's quarters and stop this madness.

Eilish wanders into Angus' study, trying to remember where she had seen him put the maps and blueprints. She doesn't even think to knock before entering. She doesn't even think whether Angus is home. Her objective is too clear for such distractions.

"Eilish?!" Angus's shocked voice cuts through the air.

Eilish looks up, dropping the marble from her mouth in surprise. Angus is standing near the window. His hair is a mess. His forehead is dripping with a passionate sweat—a clammy, unclear resin. All around him, the floor is littered with a scattering of bamboo poles and numerous cracked scarlet marbles. A lustful red mist of desire floats up around his ankles.

"Angus! What in the Meadow are you..."

Before Eilish can finish her sentence, another man emerges from the mist. A priestly-looking man. His hair is ruffled, sticking to the sweat of his brow, like his words stick to the back of his throat.

"Eilish, I can... I can explain," Angus stammers, pathetically.

"I think I understand well enough," says Eilish, avoiding the gaze of either man.

"I thought you were with Chloe?"

"Yes, well... things changed," says Eilish, stepping back to the door, pulling it open. She waits.

Angus hurriedly sweeps up the marbles littering the floor, dropping them into the fireplace, dissolving the incriminating evidence with a hiss. He tries to mop his brow, to hide the dirty marks of his resin, and flattens his hair. The other man just cowers behind him.

"I'm waiting," says Eilish.

"I'm sorry," says Angus. "Please..."

"I'm waiting," says Eilish, again, her tone threatening. "I'm waiting for you to go and take a walk. It's a beautiful evening. I need peace and quiet."

Angus looks at Eilish, afraid. It is the first time he has concentrated on her and her wishes with such intensity in years. He doesn't say another word as he leaves the office with his friend.

Eilish waits. Listening as the footsteps of the two men meander down the hallway, before the front door opens and closes gently.

Eilish plops the *Sailor's Mist* back into her mouth. She can already feel her heart rate starting to rise. A calmness returns almost immediately. She fastens the latch in Angus' study and approaches his desk.

In a long, thin drawer, he keeps the rolled parchments of star-charts and the portfolios of maps and building plans. She slides it open delicately and pulls out the contents, scattering them over the desk. A few star-charts fall onto the floor.

The first maps are just street maps of London. One overlays the streets and buildings of the Meadow with those of Earth. The parallels and contrasts would usually fascinate Eilish, but not right now. She rifles through the pile and comes across a map of a mountain range. The concentric contours spin like spirographs across the parchment. The map is of the *Mynydd* mountain range. In the centre of the map is *Mynydd Aaru* (this is its name on Earth)—the mountain of the Source.

Eilish gazes at the map for a moment, thinking of Ciara and wondering if Chloe arrived in the Meadow somewhere on there. The south face of the mountain has the Perihelion precipice marked, and there is a spider's web of little black lines wriggling near it. These are the mining tracks and the location of the Distillery resin mines. The most valuable source of resin in the Meadow. Without it, Distillery production of marbles would stop. And hidden amongst the mining tracks is the grand and mysterious *House of Sand*—the home of the Council of the Almighty, the secretive branch of Distillery power. A branch that supposedly keeps 'order' at the Source and connects the Meadow to the Beyond.

Eilish traces her finger along a dotted red line circling the Mountain. The resin fields and the *House of Sand* require this fortified boundary all around the Mountain. The resources of the Mountain are too valuable to risk. Along the eastern boundary, a bridge does cross the boundary line—*Pont Fawr Bridge*. This is the way to the Mountain for the Drifters on their final journey out of the Meadow via a jump off the *Perihelion* precipice. But Pont Fawr bridge has its own garrison to ensure that only Drifters can enter the Mountain. And similarly, dotted around the fortified boundary, are half a dozen similar Distillery garrisons—there is no trespassing on the Mountain.

Eilish folds the map and places it in her pocket. If she can look for Ciara one day, it won't hurt to have a map.

Near the bottom of the pile, Eilish finds what she came for. The portfolios of building blueprints belonging to her husband's *Bureau of Distillery Intelligence*. In particular, the blueprints for St. Paul's Cathedral. There is a bundle of pages fastened together. Each page contains detailed drawings of the rooms and layout of the building, floor by floor.

Eilish flicks through the blueprints of the top floors. The bell tower, the altar, and the nave are all there, as she recognises from the Council meetings. But by the fourth page, from the basement level down, a darker, hidden side of the Cathedral emerges. A side that she is not familiar with. Interrogation rooms, exorcising vaults, and solitary confinement cells. Below these rooms are dozens of units simply labelled 'Purification Chambers'. Finally, three stories underground, Eilish locates the marble vaults.

The vaults are laid out like a vast underground library. Aisles of Interrogation Stones—the marble created when a soul first arrives and is interrogated in the Meadow—fill much of the first floor of the vaults. Below these, the next floor down contains the Criminal Record Stones and the Distillery's Intelligence Stones. This is where the lists of names from the treacherous Well-Wishing priests must be kept.

Eilish carefully rolls up the Cathedral blueprints, fastening them with a band from her hair. She pauses, looking around at the familiar mess of her husband's office. Angus must never know anything is amiss. She calmly collects up the remaining maps and rolls of parchment and places them back into the long, thin drawer. She will hide her plunder for the time being, until she commits treason by taking these secrets to Nailah Hussain, and before, in all likelihood, she abandons this house and her husband. But first, she must find Chloe.

***

The only way to reach the Mineralist, outside of Council meetings, is via his London workhouse: the underground marble production site where new arrivals work all hours of the day by the light of their kilns. These confused and oppressed men hammer away at molten glass for months, sometimes years, making marbles that will ultimately feed their minds when they graduate, having purified the resin that drips from their pores and 'paid their penitence' to an unseen god.

There is only one way into the workhouse, via underground carriages that shuttle to and from Euston train station. It is highly unusual for a woman to take one of the carriages. This is made all the stranger when that woman is a governess of the Distillery. Nonetheless, the officers in charge of the carriages know better than to question the activities of such a senior statesperson when she asks to be taken to see the Mineralist.

A solitary officer escorts Eilish underground.

"My apologies, Your Excellency," says the officer. "If we had known you were coming, we would have laid on a special carriage for you. The Mineralist never mentioned you had an appointment."

"I don't have an appointment," says Eilish calmly.

Eilish follows closely behind the officer as they meander through a maze of marble-making kilns. The presence of a woman is far too distracting for the hundreds of tired, bruised men working there. Some stand, open-mouthed, as though a firework of sensations is exploding in their minds. Minds that haven't seen a woman for years. Their sticks of molten glass droop flaccidly, dripping wastefully on the floor.

The workhouse guards are equally distracted. Many of them have never seen the governess before. They salute meekly, staring. The officer escorting her swells with undeserved self-importance. When they reach the Mineralist's office, he knocks firmly on the closed door.

"Not now!" the Mineralist's voice shouts back, indignantly.

The officer looks at Eilish, hoping for direction. She strides forward, nudging him aside and tries the door handle. It is locked.

"I said not now!" shouts the Mineralist.

"You will see me now," Eilish shouts back. "It is urgent, Mr Elfmann."

The door unlocks.

"Governess!" the Mineralist smiles. "What a pleasant surprise." He opens the door fully, ushering Eilish into the room.

"Father!" says Eilish, noticing him sitting opposite, in an armchair.

"I thought you'd be here, sooner or later," says her father. "You're here about Chloe, I presume?"

"Dad, what the hell is going on?! This is ridiculous!"

The President puts a finger to his lips. "It's ok, Eilish. Calm down."

"Calm down?!" Eilish storms forward. The impact of her last *Sailor's Mist* has long since passed. Her father doesn't get out of his chair.

"Eilish, it's ok," he says. "It is why I'm here… to sort out this little misunderstanding."

"Misunderstanding?" says Eilish, confused.

"Just a little *misunderstanding*," repeats the President. "The wrong name in the book… a false record… I'll talk to Chloe. I'm sure she can correct things… I'm sure she can show us all that she isn't a *Stain* and wasn't a rebel. Then things can go back to how they were."

"Andrew said…"

"Andrew is impetuous," says the President. "He was furious when he found out. Naturally. Give your brother some slack."

Her father's composure takes Eilish aback.

"Where is she?" asks Eilish. "Can I see her?"

The President glances at the Mineralist. He shrugs.

"I don't see why not," says her father.

"She's in a cell at the end of the hall," says the Mineralist.

"Just a precaution," confirms the President, before Eilish can respond. "We'll hopefully have her out and home before the day is done."

The Mineralist lifts the key chain from his neck and unfastens one, handing it to Eilish.

"Just be careful, Eilish," says the President as she goes to leave. "There is still a chance that this is all true… and she has manipulated us all."

"You have ten minutes, governess," says the Mineralist, lifting an hourglass on his desk, starting the grains tumbling into the chamber.

"I'll have as long as I want," says Eilish, curtly.

"No, Eilish," says her father. "The Mineralist is right. Ten minutes is plenty. It is strange enough having a woman in the workhouse… this place is not fit for a governess."

"First door on your right," says the Mineralist with a twisted grin. "Cell Four."

All the eyes of the kilns are on Eilish again as she walks to the cells.

"No," she says, "I don't need an escort anymore," as the officer tries to follow her.

His self-importance is shaken, but he knows better than to challenge a governess.

The cells are quiet in the dark stone corridor. There are dozens of them, illuminated by a scattering of lanterns hanging from the damp stone walls. The floor crunches under Eilish's feet. There is a wet, silty sand congealed all over the cobblestones. And it stinks. Stinks of decay.

Eilish reaches Cell Four. She places a cool-blue marble into her mouth, and hurriedly unlocks the door, wriggling the rusty iron bolt, and throwing her body weight against it.

The cell is bare. A small lantern burns beside a little iron bedframe. On the bed lies Chloe, unconscious. Some dirty white sheets are pulled over the lower half of her body. She is fully clothed, wearing the same vest and jeans that Eilish saw her in this morning. Her face and eyes are puffy; her hair is damp and ruffled.

Eilish rushes over. Chloe is temporarily unconscious because of a marble sedative she has been given. Eilish scoops the marble from Chloe's lolling mouth, throwing it to the floor. It smashes and hisses, cloaking the cobbles with a grey mist.

Chloe's eyes lift into focus. "Eilish?" she says.

"Chloe!"

Eilish lifts her friend upright and hugs her tightly.

"Oh, Eilish. I'm so sorry," says Chloe. Her voice muffled against Eilish's shoulder.

"You have nothing to be sorry for," says Eilish. "I should never have left you today. If we had been together, like we said we would, I could have stopped this straight away."

"You couldn't have stopped Andrew," says Chloe. "Not when he is like that. You've said it yourself; he's a monster!"

"It's going to be ok," says Eilish. "I've spoken with my father. He's going to get you out of this."

"You think?" says Chloe, unconvinced.

"He promised me. He said he'll show that the *Stain's* record isn't you... set it straight... get you home."

"Oh, Eilish, I'm sorry!" says Chloe, looking down at her feet, guiltily. "The record won't change."

"I haven't been completely honest with you, Eilish... I'm sorry... You see, ever since I can remember, the truth is my resin hasn't ever been clear. At first, I thought it was a residue from my experiences at the palace... so I hid it. But in all these years, it just won't clear..."

"Oh, Chloe," says Eilish.

"And I have this memory," she continues. "I think it is from Earth... I'm not sure. I am standing on a cliff edge in a storm, and I know that I am going to jump off and end my life..."

"But Chloe, if it's true, you'll be... executed! I cannot lose you... *Please!*"

"I'm sorry, Eilish, but what can I do...?"

"Lie!" says Eilish, her mind becoming clear. "Lie. Say that you cannot remember anything. Say that you had a different name."

"But they'll interrogate me, Eilish. They'll find out."

"Not straight away, they won't."

"What good is that?"

"We will... run away... together," says Eilish. "Run away to the *Tide and Time Tavern*."

"Run away?" says Chloe, incredulously. "That's madness."

"Is it?!" Eilish exclaims.

"You'd be running from this easy and safe life we have. You'd be running from your family. You'd be running away from Angus."

"My *real* family has already run," says Eilish. "And as for Angus... he'll be just fine without me."

"You can't *really* be serious about running away?"

"I'm absolutely serious," says Eilish. "I am already in too deep. I'm helping the rebels conduct a raid... I am going to help them to rob the intelligence vaults..."

"Eilish!"

"... It will help the rebels to keep thousands of their tormented friends out of the workhouses... And in return, they are going to give me a way to find Ciara. Come with me, Chloe, let's get away from this hell together!"

"I'm not sure, Eilish..."

"Look, there is a secret tunnel at Virgil College that can take you straight to the *Tide and Time Tavern*. We just need to get you out of this cell and secure half an hour alone together. We can get to Virgil College in that time. And when we get to the tavern, I just know that they will protect you. Nailah will protect you."

"Who's Nailah?"

"Oh, gosh," says Eilish, feeling her chest tighten with rebellious excitement. "She's one of the rebel leaders. I met her this morning. She's a formidable woman. Blunt, rude, and intimidating."

"And she will *protect* us?"

"Oh yes," says Eilish, without hesitation. "She is harsh, but I can tell she is a woman of integrity. She's rather..."

Eilish pauses.

"Well... Magnificent."

"Sounds like she made an impression!" Chloe teases.

Eilish's cheeks flush. She doesn't know where that word, 'magnificent', even came from.

"So, how do you propose we get me out of this cell?"

Eilish checks that no one is listening at the door before crouching next to Chloe. "Lie to my father when he visits later. Tell him that you had a different name than the one in the record... say you have a fleeting memory of a car crash on Earth, but that is all. Say nothing more. This will buy us time while your claims are verified at the archives. You're my brother's wife. My father would hate the shame of the truth. He would hate to reveal this in front of the people."

"When you get home, don't say anything to Andrew. Go straight to your room. I'll meet you there in the morning to accompany you for a 'walk'."

"Will I need anything?"

"No," says Eilish. "We are disappearing… We take as little from our lives here as we can."

Chloe grasps Eilish's hand. "If this doesn't work," she says, an almost tangible fear and sadness flickering in her fingertips.

"Don't worry… It will… It must."

***

Chapter 26

Bonfire at the Palace

The Meadow - London

Eilish ambles up the steps to Chloe's house. Today's *Shipping Forecast* lies uncollected on the mat—the paperboy always does his rounds at dawn. It is a dull and overcast morning, and Eilish is wearing the most boring, most ordinary clothes she could find in her closet—the kind of clothes to blend in with the average person on the street, which isn't as easy as it sounds when the roads are filled with people from all eras of history. She has decided to wear a straight-cut olive woollen suit, the kind a lady might wear amongst the city workers of London in the 1950s.

In contrast to the weather and her clothes, Eilish feels as though the sun is shining down on her. There are no Ferrymen in sight today, and she is pleased to see that her brother's house, except for the uncollected paper, looks much like it always does. Neat, ordered, and unwelcoming. It seems that the chaos of yesterday has been put right.

Eilish rearranges the canister of Thermocline Mist against her hip. She can't be too careful today. She can feel the weight of her pouch of marbles tied around her waist, too, and grasps her shoulder bag to reassure herself that she hasn't forgotten the secret parchments—the blueprints of the Cathedral vaults. She feels everything and sees everything. Her whole body, mind, and soul are on alert. She rolls her tongue over the last of the *Sailor's Mist* marbles in her mouth. How else would she be feeling calm when the stakes are so high?

Eilish knocks gently on the front door and waits.

A moment later, Colin, the porter, opens it. His eyes are bloodshot, and his usually smart uniform is crumpled, as though he hasn't slept all night.

"Governess?" he says in an unusually questioning tone. "What are you doing here? Why aren't you with the others?"

"What do you mean?" asks Eilish, confused.

"Your brother and father left hours ago," he says.

"Where? What for?"

Colin drops his gaze. "I haven't been told exactly. But I suspect it's for Miss Chloe's sentencing," he says solemnly.

The marble drops from Eilish's mouth, cracking on the floor and rolling down the steps behind her.

"Sentencing?!"

"Yes," he says, passing Eilish a note.

F.A.O. Staff at the Ferryman's Residence,

I wish to inform you of my separation from Miss Chloe Callaghan with immediate effect. Miss Callaghan has betrayed her oath of marriage to me as well as her oath of obedience to the Distillery. I am devastated.

Miss Callaghan will be sentenced this morning. She will not be returning to this residence.

Your grateful master,
Andrew Callaghan

Her father lied! Eilish thrusts the note back into Colin's hand, wishing she had never seen it.

"Where is the sentencing?" asks Eilish, her voice shaking with panic.

"At the Palace of London, your Excellency," says Colin. "In front of the Palace gates."

Eilish spins on her heels and shoots down the steps, crumpling the copy of the *Shipping Forecast* and crushing the Sailor's Mist as she hurtles into the street. Colin doesn't have a chance to say anything else or wish her well. He watches helplessly as Eilish disappears, off on her way to the Palace.

***

"ROLL UP! ROLL UP! BIG NEWS! MEADOW EXCLUSIVE!" yells a young boy, flogging the morning's paper. "Ferryman's wife exposed! Rebel leader! *Stain*! She's being executed today at the Palace gates. Roll up! Roll up! See history in the making!"

Eilish, who has fashioned a shawl into a face scarf, concealing her face, snatches a newspaper from the boy's hand as she rushes past.

"Steady on, Miss," shouts the boy.

Eilish ignores him. She bundles into the crowds that are thronging towards the Palace.

On the front page of the newspaper is a rough sketch of Chloe, her hands bound, being dragged out from her cell, in the middle of the night.

"Fast-paced night operation shows that the Ferryman puts the people before himself", reads the subtitle. Eilish throws the paper down in disgust and quickens her pace to try and get in front of the crowds. She runs as fast as she can and rounds the corner onto the Mall.

The Palace gates are only a few hundred metres away, but already thousands of Meadow citizens have congregated. Despite the short notice, the biggest news for years has quickly mobilised the baying mob, and the square is already a roaring sea of faces, surging together in feverish waves of morbid eagerness, hungry for the imminent spectacle to begin.

Eilish looks desperately for a way through. She could probably get fifty metres or so without much trouble, but then the people are packed too tight. Even if people did recognise her and tried to make a way through, she'd still struggle.

She spots some Ferrymen on horseback, marshalling the crowds. "Excuse me!" she shouts. "Excuse me!"

One of the Ferrymen, on his horse, pulls on the reins and looks down at her face. "Can I help you?" he asks, not recognising the governess.

"Yes," she says. "Do you not know who I am?"

The officer looks at her more closely. "Governess Callaghan?"

"Yes!" she says, "and I need your horse."

The Ferry Man hesitates.

"Well…," she says. "Are you going to ignore an order from me?"

Another, higher-ranking officer trots over. "Governess Callaghan," he says. "The Ferryman said we should keep an eye out for you today."

"Did he?" says Eilish. "Well, I'll pick that up with him myself. Now, I need a horse…" She holds out her hand to grab the reins.

"Sorry, Governess," says the senior officer, pulling his horse away from her. "Ferryman's orders… We are to keep an eye out for you and, if we see you, we are to escort you back to the Presidential residence."

"You're kidding me!" Eilish blurts.

The officer jumps down from his horse, stepping up to Eilish. "Your Excellency, we have been advised to use necessary coercion, and were warned you might put up a fight." He pulls out a truncheon.

"This is outrageous!" shouts Eilish. In a flurry of rage, she grasps the horse's bridle, yanking it down sharply. The horse whinnies and throws its rider to the ground.

With both men momentarily distracted, Eilish dashes into the crowd, pulling her scarf up so only her eyes are visible. She must get to the front. She must try and get to Chloe. If Chloe is being charged for being part of the rebellion and for being a *Stain*, there is only one sentence she will receive. Death. If Eilish can just get within earshot, maybe she can disrupt proceedings. Perhaps she can change Chloe's fate. She has to hope.

Eilish ducks and barges, knocking countless people, checking that the Ferrymen haven't managed to follow her, until she is only a hundred metres from the front and can see the stage. The same stage she has been on for the previous public executions.

A sordid warm-up act is already performing to the crowd, like a medieval hanging. Ferrymen pretending to spray thermocline mist over one another. Eilish is sickened by the cheers, boos, and jeers from the mindless mob around her.

When Eilish is around twenty rows from the front, the crowd goes silent. She stops. Upon the stage, she is surprised to see that her brother and father are absent from the presidential box. The only person she recognises is Aidan Elfmann, the *Mineralist*. He has just stepped onto centre stage, raising his arms.

It is only now that Eilish notices the unusual platform for this public execution. Behind the Mineralist stands a tall, unlit bonfire. On top sits a solitary, unoccupied chair.

"Thank you, people of the Meadow!" shouts the Mineralist, his slimy voice echoing out over the crowd. "Are you ready to witness history!?"

The mob cheers.

The Mineralist ushers silence again. "I am humbled by the number of you who have turned out today. Thank you! And thank you, friends at the *Forecast*, who have so diligently printed and reported this trial in such a timely fashion this morning."

"You will no doubt have heard that today we sentence a *traitor*!" There are some cheers and boos at this announcement. "A traitor to the rule of the Distillery... and a *blasphemer* against the Lord!" There are hollers across the crowd.

"You will no doubt appreciate the great speed at which our President and the Ferryman have acted upon discovering this traitor. And you will, of course, respect their absence today... for the Distillery can NEVER accept blasphemy. Today's *criminal* is an unrepentant *Stain*! She leaks dirty resin without shame. And more... she is a rebel! She has dishonoured her family. She has dishonoured her husband. And she has dishonoured the Lord!!!"

The crowd stirs into a chaotic frenzy. People shout and whistle, cheer, and scream. The Mineralist knows how to boil the mob. Eilish will listen no longer. She drops all politeness as she scratches and scrabbles, pushing and pulling people side to side, forcing her way to the front of the crowd.

"Bring out the prisoner!" the Mineralist screams.

A cheer from the mob tells Eilish all she needs to know. Chloe has entered the stage.

Eilish is just half a dozen rows from the front when she catches a glimpse of Chloe. She has been dressed up in an elaborate ball gown, but her hair is messy and her face puffy and bruised. Looking into her eyes, Eilish can see that she wears a veil of melancholy, an almost visible cloak of sadness. And this breaks her heart.

Chloe is dragged onto the stage by a handful of Ferrymen, pulling her bound wrists up a step ladder concealed within the pile of logs and kindling, and onto the chair at the top. Her arms and legs are fastened tightly to the chair.

The Mineralist quietens the crowd once more.

"A criminal of this magnitude," he begins, "does not deserve the honour of execution by mist. A criminal of this magnitude must be... *EXTINGUISHED!* Let anyone know, if you wish to defile the Lord, the Distillery has *no fear!* Watch as this criminal burns! She will not drift to the Source. Let her spark go out. For she is not worthy to receive the privilege of the Beyond!"

The crowd are silent, processing what the Mineralist has just announced. This is beyond the punishment any of them has ever witnessed, even before the rebellion. Everyone has seen a Drifter in the Meadow, but most people have only ever heard rumours of the terror of an extinction.

"Stop this madness!" shouts Eilish at the top of her lungs. "This is evil!"

A few heads near Eilish turn, surprised by her outburst. Soon the whole crowd are shouting. Some, trying to silence people like Eilish. But others are on her side. They are disgusted by the sentence that has just been announced. Undeterred, the Mineralist continues. He strides to the side of the stage and lights a torch.

"Goodbye Satan!" he shouts at the top of his lungs, plunging the torch into the base of the bonfire.

The crowd gasps as one, horrified as the flames lick up the logs towards Chloe.

Eilish throws herself forward, using every sinew in her body to scrabble to the front. She gets there and feels the warmth of the flames on the stage. A metal barrier keeps the crowd back, marshalled by a line of Ferrymen.

Eilish doesn't think twice. She hurdles the barrier and darts for the stage, taking the Ferrymen by surprise. She breaks through the ranks of guards momentarily and scampers up the steps towards the stage. The heat of the fire is intense. The orange flames obscure her view of anything.

A Ferry Man catches Eilish in her moment of hesitation. He grasps her ankle and throws her down onto the steps. But she isn't his only concern. Her race toward the stage has sparked a reaction from the crowd. Dozens of others are crashing through the barriers behind her, scrabbling up the steps.

There is frantic shouting from everywhere. Ferrymen shouting desperately to try to regain order. And citizens screaming, horrified by the fire on the stage, and ready to rise up.

Eilish tries to get to her feet. But the officer is still beside her. He lands a heavy blow with his fist against the side of her head. She falls to the ground again, in agony, holding her face in her hands. Brushing past her, the scuffed trainers of another disgruntled citizen pound forward, making it onto the stage. The Ferry Man beside her shouts, careening after them. Now Eilish *can* get up.

She looks up desperately at the bright and horrific fire burning on the stage. The needles of flame rage chaotically. Like a sea of yellow arms, surrendering in pain. Chloe is completely engulfed. The silhouette of her body is distinguishable, just, but she is silent and unmoved. Then there is a fizzling of colour in the fire, and a super-bright orb of light grows from where Chloe is sitting. It is in this ball of light that Chloe's life in the Meadow is extinguished. Her Energy lingers for a moment before shooting up into the sky to join the stars that head north.

The back of Eilish's head is struck violently, but in her shock, she doesn't register the pain. She stumbles, her consciousness wavering. Then she falls, but it feels like slow motion, the ground crawling up towards her. Someone has caught her, stopping her from hitting the ground. It is a young girl. A teenager. Her hair matted with soot, her fingernails black with grime, and her faced stained with dirty resin. Before Eilish can thank the girl, the two of them are set upon by more Ferrymen.

There is no chance of escape. The stage steps are too narrow, and the Ferrymen come at them from above and below.

The woman and the girl are struck with truncheons before being man-handled to the floor, face down. Eilish feels her wrists yanked up sharply behind her back, pulled together painfully, and cable ties zipped tightly to immobilise her. Her face scarf is still in place. The officers have no idea who they are handling. But she has no energy or intention of telling them either, not yet.

Incapacitated, Eilish and the young girl are dragged from the stage, escorted with dozens of other captured citizens along the barriers in front of the remaining crowd, towards a dozen vehicles parked up in a nearby street.

Even as they are dragged up the street, the chaos outside the palace is deafening. There are thousands of people thronging in the crowd, and their screams and shouts continue, no matter how much the Ferrymen and the Mineralist on the stage try to wrestle back control.

Eilish is kicked into one of the parked vehicles with half a dozen other captives. It is some kind of old transport wagon. Its dark, olive-green exterior is tinny. Where once stood a bright red cross on a white background, the emblem of the Distillery, the Speared Drop, has been painted over the top. This old hospital truck is now a Ferryman's wagon—a mobile jail to detain disruptors.

There is barely room for the half dozen captives. The guards struggle to close the back door, squashing the prisoners into uncomfortable contortions before squeezing the door shut and bolting it. The other people trapped with Eilish are bruised and disgruntled. It's dark, so she can't make out their faces, and neither can they make out hers. The young girl is somewhere nearby. She can feel her frightened breathing against her back, pressing against her tied wrists.

A few of the captives, wriggling inches of space for themselves, start kicking and bashing the sides of the wagon. But it is futile. They might make the most minor dents to the metal, but they certainly aren't breaking free.

Outside, Eilish can hear other wagons being filled. She is sure that they are just one of dozens now loaded with captives. She grits her teeth. She can't wait to see the Ferrymen's faces when they see who they have arrested.

"Did they get your stones?" the young girl whispers urgently beside her. "I felt them grab my pouch."

"Oh god!" exclaims Eilish, wriggling her hands up to her hip, discovering that her precious pouch of marbles has gone. '*Of course. To stop captives from fleeing, the Ferrymen seize identity stones.*' Eilish feels horrifically exposed. They have her passport to life in the Meadow. They hold the gateway to her soul. It is what gives her identity, citizenship, and status. In the twelve years she has been in the Meadow, she has never been without it.

'*It's ok,*' she thinks to herself. '*I'll get it back. As soon as we get to the station. As soon as they realise who they've arrested, they'll give it back.*'

But then a horrifying realisation hits her, knocking the air from her lungs. Her captors won't be protecting the stones they have seized. Maybe if the Distillery Police had captured her, they would have kept hold of the marbles as a bail condition. But she was captured by the Ferrymen. Their standard practice is to destroy any identity stones they seize.

"Let them beg for a new interrogation!" Andrew had said at the council meeting where he introduced the practice.

Outside the wagon right now, the Ferrymen will have lit a fire and, after weighing the seized marbles, each Interrogation Stone—the stone which weighs precisely a fifth of an ounce—will be poured into the flames, shattering them. As for the other marbles, they will be impounded. Held for intelligence gathering.

Eilish had hated the marble-burning practice when the Council approved it. But now, experiencing it first-hand, she feels a visceral outrage. The stone containing her freshest and purest memories of her life before the Meadow. The stone that can never be recreated as perfectly and purely as when she first arrived will be crackling in a fire right now, and soon lost forever.

Out of nowhere, Eilish's wagon is struck by something huge, throwing the vehicle over on its side. The captives, caught unaware, crash on top of one another. A man beside Eilish screams out in pain, and she feels the cable ties on her wrists bite tightly into her skin. Outside, there is the unexpected sound of trumpeting—the call of an elephant.

Before Eilish can make any sense of what's happening, the back door of the wagon flies open.

"Get out! Get out!" shouts a man, dragging the captives free from the cabin.

In the daylight, Eilish's pupils dilate. It's still chaos in the streets, and the air is alive with the fury of rebellion. Dozens of people, faces covered by balaclavas, are fighting violently with Ferrymen, fearless under the anonymity of their masks. There is a fire, hissing with the colours of crackling marbles. A few balaclava-clad rebels are dousing the flames with buckets of water, trying to salvage any unbroken Interrogation Stones.

"Eilish!" shouts a voice. Standing in the shadow of a great elephant is the unmistakable Cyril Spate—an image of dauntless and unflinching courage.

He paces over to Eilish, pulling out a pocketknife and slashing the cable ties on her wrists, freeing her hands. "We've got to get you out of here!" he growls.

"My marbles?!" she cries, desperately.

"Too late!" he responds, dragging her under the belly of the elephant to where two saddled horses stand waiting. "Can you ride?" he asks her.

"Yes!" she calls back.

He throws her some reins and leaps onto one of the horses. A giant of a man, already, on the back of the sturdy shire horse, Cyril is an indomitable force of nature. He doesn't leave Eilish room to think or ask questions. In a flash, he heads off at a canter down the street.

Eilish throws herself over the other horse's back, and before she is even seated upright, the beast sets off, trying to catch up with Cyril.

Eilish glances at the devastation she is leaving behind. Rebels and Ferrymen are fighting hand-to-hand. She spots a Ferrymen release his thermocline cannister into the face of one of the rebels—the young girl who had been captured with her. The mist surrounds the girl's face, it's purple fog curling around her throat like grasping fingers, and as she inhales it, her body goes limp. She is now a Drifter, heading out of the Meadow.

In less than a minute, Eilish is alongside Cyril, and the two of them are hurtling through the streets, northwards, heading away from the Palace and towards the slums where Distillery control is fragile.

Eventually, and only when there are no Ferrymen or Distillery Police in sight, Cyril slows his horse to a trot.

"Thank you for rescuing me," says Eilish.

"More for us than you," says Cyril.

"Come again?"

"We can't have you being held and interrogated by the Ferrymen. You know too much about us and the Tide and Time Tavern. We thought we were safe bringing you in. I thought there was no chance that a Governess would do something reckless enough to get captured by the Ferrymen!"

"Sorry," says Eilish, blushing. She hadn't even considered how, without an Identity Stone, she would have been forced to face a fresh interrogation like all the other captives. The kind of interrogation where your memories are eked out. You cannot lie in one of those meetings. Everything from the last few weeks would have been there for the Ferrymen to see. The treachery, the plans for the palace raid, her intention to run away, and the secrets of the *Tide and Time Tavern*. She feels awful. How could she have risked all this?

"It's ok," Cyril growls, his grizzled face offering a sympathetic smile. "I just hope there's nothing else you were carrying that might expose us?"

Eilish stops. In her shock and confusion, she had completely forgotten about the other marbles that were confiscated from her pouch. The precious and rare marbles she had collected over the last twelve years. Most of them posed no risk to her, to Cyril, or to the others at the *Tide and Time Tavern*. They were just intriguing artefacts she had collected. But there was one marble. A marble she had dropped in there absent-mindedly after she saw Chloe in the cell last night. The thought of this moment right now shoots pain right through her heart. It contained her last memory with Chloe. The problem is that memory also details every element of her treason, including the plot to raid St. Paul's.

"What is it, Eilish?" asks Cyril, inspecting her worried face.

"There is a marble that exposes all of us. And it's now in the Ferrymen's hands!"

"Right," says Cyril, unflinching. "Let's get to the *Tide and Time*... We'll figure out a plan with Kim-Joy.

***

Chapter 27

Find Her

The Meadow - London

What do you mean, she's 'missing'? You're Head of Intelligence, you fool. Find her!" shouts the President.

"When did you last see her?" asks the Ferryman, addressing the cowering Angus on his doorstep.

"Last night," he says, from the shadow of the two men before him.

"Had she been to visit Chloe?"

"I don't think so… she never said anything."

"Well, was she out all night? Did she leave a note?"

"For fuck's sake!" shouts the President. "The Mineralist does a hash job of an execution, we nearly have a rebellion on our hands outside the Palace, and now my daughter goes missing?!"

"She'll be back," says Andrew, trying to calm his father.

"You think?!" says the President. "She seemed pretty *pissed* last night to me!"

"Well, who else can she go to?" asks Andrew, defensively. "She doesn't know anyone well enough in the Paddock… And she's not going to go north of the river… they'd hang her!"

"We should never have let her out of our sight," the President grumbles. "What if she's been taken by the rebels?!"

Andrew places his hand on his father's shoulder. "Let's not jump to conclusions. The most likely explanation is that she has gone for a stroll this morning to gather her thoughts. Most likely, she'll come bursting in here later today, ready to give us both barrels about how my ex-wife should have been spared… but we can handle her hysteria. We have done for years." Andrew smirks at Angus.

"I'm not prepared to wait," says the President decisively. "I want to mobilise the police and your Ferrymen, Andrew.

Anyone who finds her will be instructed to bring her in. I'm not worried about handling her hysteria when we have her. It's her cavalier attitude to her own safety that I won't tolerate anymore."

"Agreed," says Andrew.

"Angus, go home. Do not utter a word to anyone that Eilish is missing. Let us know immediately if she turns up. Otherwise, stay put and wait."

"Ok," says Angus, obediently, relieved to have escaped any blame for Eilish's disappearance.

"Before we do anything, though, Andrew," says the President, turning to his son, and flicking his hand, telling Angus to leave. "I need a moment in private."

***

"I've had word from the House of Sand," says the President, once they are alone inside the house.

"And?"

"The taps are still off."

"Fuck! Our supplies won't last much longer. What's happening up at the Source? Is there a backlog of Drifters filling the Mountain? People will notice something is wrong soon."

"No, they are letting the Drifters through still," says the President. "But the resin is absent from the river."

"What do they want?"

"Help."

"Help? With what?"

"Catching a fugitive."

Andrew smiles, relaxing a little. "Well, that's my speciality, isn't it? Who is it?"

The President pauses.

"Do you remember Eilish telling the council of an uprising in La Prairie—*Les Mariées Bleues?* The Blue Brides?"

"Yes," says Andrew, souring. "My Ferrymen have started detaining some of them here in London, too. Is the fugitive one of them?"

"The original one," confirms the President. "The Blue Bride herself."

"And who is that, exactly?"

The President frowns. "Samael wasn't clear. He said she isn't from The Meadow originally, but she's operating here now, recruiting conspirators."

"Women from the palaces?"

"Not exclusively."

"Well Wishers?"

"Maybe. Either way, Samael explained that her conspirators are leading a rebellion in his realm, and to stop them, he needs her captured."

"Sounds like his problem, not ours."

The president frowns at his son. "Because she is operating out of The Meadow, Samael says the Almighty and his angels are losing faith in our ability to govern The Meadow. The name of Callaghan is being tarnished. Samael told my delegation that, unless we catch their fugitive or clear the Meadow of conspirators, the taps will stay closed."

"That will only fuel rebellion," says the Ferryman. "What good will that do?"

"Samael also says, if we can't keep our own house in order, then a change of leadership will be ushered in the Meadow."

"Bastards," says the Ferryman, looking desperate. "Did the princes give us anything more about this fugitive or her conspirators? Anything at all?"

"You're not going to like it," says the President.

"Well Wishers?" says the Ferryman, pre-emptively. "But we already have their priests under our control."

"No... not the Well Wishers directly... There's an establishment in the city," says the President. "An establishment you have been trying to shut down for years..."

"Oh, for fuck's sake," exhales the Ferryman. "The *Tide and Time Tavern!*"

"That's right," says the President. "The beating heart of the rebellion ten years ago is connected to this fugitive and her band of conspirators."

"But we're watching that place around the clock. We've never seen anything."

"Someone there knows something," says the President. "We should start with the landlady."

"But you know if we bring *her* in, there will be trouble," says Andrew.

"There already *is* trouble!"

***

Chapter 28

Trapped by coincidence

Earth - London

He's on foot, heading east," DC Bates whispers into the microphone concealed in the collar of his jacket. "I'll keep him in sight, Sarge."

A few hundred metres ahead of Jordan, Marty strides into a run-down terraced street in Dagenham on Earth. A street where houses are leaning into each other like they've lost the will to keep standing, and where even the weeds that sprout through the stained pavement are dying of neglect.

The cold afternoon signals a definitive end to the summer. If there were trees in this part of London, their leaves would be turning orange and brown about now. But instead, the leaf litter here is actual litter that blows across the pavement, under Jordan's feet.

He passes a crowded bus station and feels everyone staring at him. This isn't his neck of the woods, and everyone can see that. But he keeps going. Wherever Marty goes, he'll go.

"He's turned down Steele Street... he's looking at the numbers... Yeah, I reckon he's meeting someone. Can you run the addresses on this street? Let me know if there's anyone that I should be aware of... Thanks boss. I'm going to get closer."

Ahead of Jordan, Marty wanders up to one of the terraces. Number 22. He knocks, and a moment later, he is buzzed into the building.

"Who's at number 22, boss? ... I'm going to hang back till you have something." Jordan slinks past the house and tries to glance in, but the curtains downstairs are all closed. Something secret is going on.

He continues up the street, waiting for an update in his ear. The wall outside number 40 is low and dry, so he perches himself on it for a moment, and looks up and down the road, taking it all in.

"Fucking hell, Sarge," he says. "This street reeks. Rotten eggs, or something. It's disgusting! People need to have more pride in their homes around here… for fuck's sake!"

A few doors away, at number 29, directly opposite Marty's location, an anxious-looking man steps out, checking up and down the street. He doesn't spot Jordan, who is good at blending in. He locks his front door, checks his watch, pulls up his hood and strides away down the street.

"Say that again, boss," says Jordan, adjusting his earpiece. "It's what? A bereavement counsellor? Shit! So that's what Marty's doing? He's getting support to prepare him for Elijah's death. Didn't you hear? They're making plans to turn off his life support. Fuck me, boss. I shouldn't be here. I knew he was clean… Yeah, I'm heading back now before he sees me… I need to get away from this awful smell."

Suddenly, there is an explosion that rattles through the street. Inside the kitchen of the house at number 29, a gas hob had been left on, and its noxious fumes just met the lit candle in the living room. The entire terraced property blows to pieces in a violent fireball, collapsing itself and the two houses on either side into a dusty cloud of rubble.

The shockwave throws DC Bates to the ground, knocking him unconscious. The Sergeant, on the other end of the line, hears the explosion, followed by white noise. He is the first to mobilise the emergency services, and he gives the order for the arrest of his former colleague, Marty Fredrickson.

Outside number twenty-two, unaware of his imminent arrest, Marty wanders out, shocked and confused by the dust cloud, unable to compute the entirely missing house.

A dozen police cars, fire engines, and ambulances scream into the street, bringing more chaos. A squad of officers spots

Marty immediately and, without hesitation, rushes to apprehend him.

"I'm one of you!" shouts Marty. "Don't you recognise me? I'm a badged detective. Check my record!"

"You have the right to remain silent," shouts the arresting officer. "I don't know you from Adam." He twists Marty's wrists and fastens the handcuffs tight, bundling him forwards toward a waiting police van.

Marty looks about horrified. Why have they grabbed him? It makes no sense. And then he sees *her*. The hooded lady is here.

She stands up the street, beyond the carnage and debris. Beyond the crumbling shell of number 29. Beyond the flashing lights and sirens. But she is there, on her own with her hood up, watching.

Marty stares back. He can't see her well enough to make out her features, but he can feel her, and he knows that right now, right over there, she holds all the answers.

He struggles and tries to make a run for it. If only he could just get to her, he could explain his way out of this nonsense. But he is out of luck, and he knows the drill. Anyone who tries to flee arrest gets taken down with any necessary force.

A truncheon smashes Marty on the back of his head. The pain sears through his eyes, and he crumples to the floor. He tries to keep his eye on the hooded lady. But it is in vain. She is gone.

***

Things are moving fast and out of control. Panicked, Marty looks around the interview room on the ground floor of the custody suite in Farringdon. He had used this suite many times before to interview suspects. But he had never been on this side of the table and never with his hands cuffed.

It is a small room. Oppressively so. Dominated by necessity. There is a table and two chairs, each scarred by years of nerves and sweat. The walls are colourless, and the scratchy carpet is a tired metropolitan blue. Everything about the suite is designed to sap the will and blunt the energy of the interrogated.

Marty's old Sergeant walks in. He should be a friendly face, but the red light is on. Anything said when the red light is on is being recorded as evidence. So, this is not a social call or a bailout. This is part of his interrogation.

"Marty," exhales the Sergeant. "Marty, what is going on?!"

Marty takes a deep breath. He is going to have to careful what he says. It is so easy to implicate yourself when you don't know what's going on. When you don't know, you're out of control.

"I've been brought in, sir. They think I had something to do with the explosion in Dagenham. But I just happened to be there. Seriously, it was bad timing. Bad luck."

The Sergeant nods, slowly. "In the same way you just happened to be at the *Knot of Three Ropes* last year?" he says, with an air of sarcasm.

"Come on, Sarge!"

"No Marty… grief is a peculiar thing. It makes us act in the most unusual ways. You were a good detective, Marty. You know, as well as anyone, *coincidences* are rare."

"I know, but you've got to trust me, Sarge. I had nothing to do with these tragedies. How could I?"

"How are you going to prove it, Marty? That's what you need to be thinking. Because all the arrows point to you right now."

"If I can just get hold of my laptop, boss, I can prove my innocence. I can show you why I was in Camden and why I went to Dagenham today… There's this guy… he reached out to me, online. He said he could point me to her… the hooded lady. He arranged my therapy today. He must have known those tragedies were imminent. He's where the investigation needs to turn. He should be sat here."

"Who is this guy?"

"I don't know, Sarge. But I'm sure the digital forensics teams can hunt him down."

"I don't know, Marty."

"I know it sounds fishy, boss. But it's the truth. I would never lie to you. Please, bail me out of here now. I will go straight back to my flat and get my laptop. I can be back here in less than an hour. I can show you all the correspondence with this guy. You can have it as evidence. I have nothing to hide."

The Sergeant looks at Marty. It is so sad to see Marty like this. He used to be the sharpest tool in the shed. Now he's a grieving, rusty, blunt implement.

"Ok, Marty," sighs the sergeant. "You have an hour. But if you're not straight back here, that's tantamount to admission of guilt."

"Yes, Sarge. Thank you, Sarge," says Marty as his hand is uncuffed. "I owe you."

"Just don't make me look a fool, Marty."

***

Chapter 29

No time to lose

The Meadow - London

W e're going to need something stronger," shouts Cyril
leaning forward, holding Eilish's heaving shoulders. Her
breathing is frantic, a mixture of panic and anger. Since
getting to the *Tide and Time Tavern* it has started to take control of
her fragile mind.

Cyril scoops the *Sailor's Mist* from Eilish's mouth, flinging
it to the ground. The anxiety has got so intense that even a stable
marble such as this has quickly intensified its colour putting it at
risk of bursting and sending her 'on' at any moment.

"Here," calls Kim-Joy, throwing a pouch to Cyril. "*Earth
Marbles* from Carl. They are about as centring as a marble can
possibly be."

Cyril places a single marble under Eilish's nose. Amidst her
tears, she leans forward and sucks the marble into her mouth.

The intense earthly oozing squeezes itself through every
pore of her body. It works a trick. Her heart rate and breathing
slow, and she looks up at Cyril.

"That's better," she says to the trawlerman, whose heavy
palm is resting tenderly on her shoulder. "I'm sorry."

She blinks. She can just about remember the ride through
the cobbled streets towards the Tide and Time Tavern, holding
tightly to her horse's reins and following close behind Cyril. She
vaguely remembers being met at the pub's entrance by Kim-Joy.
Then, before she can recall what happened next, Chloe's face
flashes in front of her eyes again and her breath quickens, tears
welling up in her eyes.

"It's ok," says Kim-Joy. "Let it out. Say what you are
feeling."

"How could they?" Eilish wails. "How could they?!"

Kim-Joy and Cyril rub Eilish's arms gently, crouching down beside her.

"Chloe is gone, isn't she?" Eilish pleads to Kim-Joy.

"Yes... She has left the Meadow," confirms Kim-Joy.

"No!" Eilish screams. "No! She's gone... Gone forever. Extinct!" She writhes at the thought and the memory.

Kim-Joy squeezes Eilish's hand. "We don't believe in extinction here," she says calmly. "I watched Chloe's spark dance up into the heavens. She has joined all the other souls that have ever existed... Joined them in the flow of Energy around the realms. She is looking down from there now, but she is not gone."

Eilish sniffs. She's not sure if Kim-Joy's belief is a comforting one or not. She can tell it is supposed to be. She grasps her chest and feels the sharp pain of losing Chloe ripping through her heart. A pain, the sort she has felt before. The pain she felt on the night she arrived, the night she had held Ciara in her arms as she convulsed and writhed on the floor of the plane. Writhing from the pain of her overdose. Eilish knows how this pain works. She can hold it inside, and eventually, its throbbing will align with her heartbeat. But the pain will always be there; it will just become part of who she is.

Kim-Joy and Cyril hold on to Eilish in the silence of the cellar, holding her like parents. Holding her like the warmth of a pleasant marble. Slowly, Eilish feels her mind find composure, and the details of the room become clear.

In the hearth, the fire is lit. Its burning embers beat a metronomic warmth. Beside the fire, incense sticks send smoke dancing up to the ceiling. And in one of the armchairs, sits Nailah, facing the glow of the fire. Seeing Nailah sat there, so strong and composed, as always, Eilish feels an additional warmth, deeper and more intimate than the fire. A burning mix of awe and joy that she is there with them. On Nailah's lap sits a copy of the *Chronicle of Sadness*.

"I've seen that book before," says Eilish, composing herself. "How did you get it?"

"This copy has always been at the Tide and Time," says Nailah.

"My brother had a copy."

"Yes," says Nailah. "We figured that was how the Distillery found out about Chloe."

"You knew?"

"We've all known for years," says Kim-Joy. "Chloe was so brave, but when she re-emerged from the Palace as a Flicker, betrothed to your brother, we knew that her memory of her former life was gone. We thought maybe this new life was a reprieve for her. A reprieve from sneaking around in the shadows. And we knew, if any of us so much as hinted at her true identity, her life would be in danger."

"I wish I had known," says Eilish. "I could have done something."

"You did," says Kim-Joy. "By being a friend, you protected the last remaining fragments of her mind. You gave Chloe, as a Flicker, what she needed most: friendship and love. Not many women from the palaces ever get this again in the Meadow."

"So, you knew her before the palace?" Eilish says to Nailah, wiping her eyes.

Nailah nods, staring into the fire. "But I have mourned her once, already." She lifts a locket from around her neck. It is much like the lockets hanging from Kim-Joy's necklace. Nailah opens the clasp and shows Eilish a cracked marble inside.

"This was an *Inseparable Stone* once," she says, holding it close enough to Eilish's face that she can smell the sweetness of her skin. Then opens another locket, and a glowing orb fills the room with light. "Until this morning, it was like this. There is nothing in this marble anymore... But I am keeping it to remind me of her."

"What was she like... Before the palace?" asks Eilish.

"The kindest and bravest woman you'd ever meet," says Nailah. "She took risks, much like you did today."

"I wish I could have met the old Chloe," says Eilish.

"There was no difference to the old Chloe," says Kim-Joy. "You might have met her at a different time, but you met the same Chloe that we did—the same soul, fired by the same spark of Energy. I showed you this last time, didn't I?" she says, reaching onto a shelf and lifting off the old brass contraption—the *Triaxial Vitaloscope.*

Eilish nods.

"For any of the grains of sand to tumble, an external force must topple the timer," says Kim-Joy, rocking it to alter the orientation of the sand timer. "*The Energy* exists outside of our perpendicular realms of time. You should not worry about when and where you meet another soul. Whenever we meet, it is the alignment of the Energy that binds us. An alignment of energy that is infused into the memory of resin… infused into the memory of our marbles."

A vision flashes in front of Eilish's eyes. A foreboding vision of Ferrymen gathered around a hoard of confiscated marbles. Her marbles. The marbles that could expose them all. "Oh my god… The marble!" says Eilish, feeling a pit in her stomach, her mouth dry and tight.

"It's ok, don't panic," says Cyril, gruffly.

"What happened?" asks Kim-Joy.

"After the Governess here, instigated the storming of the execution platform this morning…" he says, purposefully elevating Eilish's role in the fight. "The Ferrymen took her captive, smashing her Interrogation Stone and confiscating the other marbles she held."

"And am I to assume," says Kim-Joy, "one of these other marbles might contain details that could compromise us?"

"Exactly," says Cyril.

"What exactly does the marble memory hold?" asks Kim-Joy, looking at Eilish.

Eilish closes her eyes for a moment, ignoring the pain of recalling the memory and focusing on what she had said to Chloe in the cell. "I can't remember perfectly," she says. "I know I mentioned the plan to raid St. Paul's and destroy the intelligence stones, and I know I discussed running away to join you here at the Tide and Time Tavern… I definitely mentioned the location of the secret tunnel."

All eyes turn to the old cellar door concealing the entrance to the tunnel.

"Then we have no choice…" says Nailah.

"No choice?" asks Eilish, confused.

"We have to find that marble and destroy it before anyone sees its resin," says Nailah.

"But how?" asks Kim-Joy.

"Eilish, you've already told us about the marble vaults under the cathedral. I assume this marble will be taken there?"

"Yes, but…"

"Then," says Nailah, looking oddly triumphant, "we now have more than one incentive to conduct a raid… and soon."

Eilish bends down and picks up her bag. She pulls out the crumpled portfolio of cathedral blueprints. "I was hoping to use this as a bargaining chip for Chloe's protection, too," she says. "Maybe it is protection for all of us now."

Nailah grabs the blueprints gratefully. "Good work," she says, her eyes beaming at Eilish. "Finally, the tide might be turning on this awful day…" She keeps looking at Eilish, who sees a softness in her eyes for the first time. "I assume Eilish can stay here now, at the Tide and Time, right, Kim-Joy?"

Eilish turns, hopefully. But Kim-Joy looks worried. "If Eilish goes missing, I think we can assume her father will use everything the Distillery has to find her… Intelligence from recently seized marbles would be one place to start, right?"

Eilish nods.

"Then I think the safest place you can be right now is back at home."

"Back with her brother and father?! After what they've done?" Nailah exclaims.

"If you think you can lie, Eilish, then being back in your own home will not raise suspicion and may buy us time."

Eilish hangs her head. She knows Kim-Joy is right.

"Eilish, this is not permanent," says Kim-Joy. "But while our secrets are vulnerable, we must keep our heads down."

"And what if they look at the marble before we can destroy it?!" says Nailah.

"Then we are all in very urgent danger," says Kim-Joy.

Cyril stands.

"The trawler folk are ready if we need to flee," he announces.

"Yes," starts Nailah, "but is Sanger's Circus ready to receive us yet?"

"I'll send word to Kathleen straight away," says Kim-Joy. "There's a crew crossing the Channel tonight. How quickly can you mobilise your people to raid the cathedral vaults?"

"I have a team… They are ready."

"Good, then start your preparations right away. We cannot delay."

Kim-Joy turns to Eilish. "If you can keep your head down for a few days, Eilish, great," she says, decisively. "Once you get wind of our raid, you can flee your home—if you still wish to—and use the tunnel to meet us here."

"Got it," says Eilish.

"Just make sure you are not followed," says Cyril, looking nervous.

"Of course."

"In that case, governess," says Kim-Joy, getting to her feet. "We gain nothing by dallying. You can take these marbles to help you through the next few days." She passes a full pouch of *Sailor's Mist* to Eilish. "Good luck," she says, holding Eilish's gaze.

"Thank you," says Eilish. "And good luck to you," she says, looking at Nailah, who is already studying the cathedral blueprints intently.

Nailah nods appreciatively. "Good risen, governess," she says, absent-mindedly.

Eilish pauses and smiles. "Good risen," she responds, for the first time in her life.

***

Chapter 30

Voices in the air

The Meadow - House of Sand

Two young men stand in the shadow of *The Mountain*, on the veranda of an old mansion—the *House of Sand*—overlooking the shores of the lake below. The air is still, and the light from the sun fails to penetrate the blanket of mist that rests below the *Perihelion Cliffs* of the south face. Both men are lean and muscular. Their bodies, pillars of perfection. One dark and brooding, the other pale and fair.

"Do you really think they can help us find her?" asks the brooding man.

He doesn't pose this question to his companion. Instead, he utters it in the direction of the lake. And, though no physical being stands there, a presence hovering over the lake responds with a hypnotic voice that dances over the stillness of the water.

"We know she has been travelling back and forth between this realm and Earth," says the presence. "We've listened to the Returners back on Earth… She has been here on the mountain numerous times. Ten years ago, she was here, helping them in their quest."

"What is she up to?" asks the fair-haired man.

The lake responds. "She is mocking us… she is mocking Him, for she knows better than any of us how He desperately seeks her. Ever since He fell, she has been driving all this chaos."

"Is she still interfering on Earth?"

"For now, yes… but I have a friend closing in on her. She'll abandon Earth soon."

"Excellent. But even if we do trap her here, what can the Distillery really do? We've seen them through the years… utterly incompetent… utterly *human!*"

"I know," the other man agrees. "They have strong bodies, but weak minds. They are no match for *her.*"

"Maybe not," says the lake. "But she has found sanctuary in their realms. Realms where only humans move freely. And we know some of them are protecting her. President Callaghan and his son may be fallible and human, but their souls are brutal. A brutality that we have harnessed for years. It is this brutality, unleashed, that I think could help."

"What about the resin?" asks the darker man on the shore. "Their marbles are vital to their control of the Meadow."

"They have bought our lie that we turned off the taps," says the lake.

"That may be so," responds the man. "But at what cost? When their production ceases, they won't be able to hold back any rebellion that will surely follow."

"No," agrees the lake. "But threatening to install the governors of *La Prairie* to rule the Meadow is unleashing a more potent brutality in our friends at the Distillery. They are proud men... predictably so. Working with them in such a heightened rage is our best hope of disrupting her."

"And you're convinced that she is behind the floods in our realm?"

After a moment of silence, the presence on the lake responds. "I have pieces of a puzzle," it says. "And some of them point to her. I have sent angels upstream to unblock the channels and see what they can find..."

A breeze whips across the lake, accompanying the ponderance of the two men, sending ripples across the water.

"Are you still there, Samael?" asks the fair-haired man.

There is no response; the presence on the lake is gone.

***

The Meadow - London

Eilish knows she can't go straight home. She would only lash out. That would gain her nothing and could risk *everything*. She can feel anger bubbling in her veins, and not even *Sailor's Mist* is calming enough for her now. So, she is wandering around the city, taking in its sights. The everyday people, going about their everyday tasks. An every-day that feels so alien. And amidst it all, she can't help sniffing the acrid smell of smoke that clings to her clothes—and, if not her clothes, her mind.

With her experiences and knowledge of the last few weeks, Eilish finds that the city of London has taken on a whole new, pained, and sinister atmosphere. She looks with guilt at the marble addicts crowding the street corners. She feels shame when she sees Flickers, women like Chloe, sitting alone on benches. Confused and waiting for something to make sense.

Out of habit, Eilish eventually finds herself on London Bridge. She stops over the river and gazes across the familiar water. The sky above gives the Lethe a cool, grey tone, but there isn't a whisper of wind on the surface. And, in the stillness of the river, she feels her approaching—her angel.

As is always the case, Eilish can't exactly see the angel approaching with her eyes, but she knows she is there. Her hypnotic song whispers in the silence, drifting over the river, heading downstream towards her. Kind, loving, and listening. Always listening.

Eilish wouldn't usually wait for her angel during daylight hours. She is too conscious of looking 'unhinged', standing on a bridge and talking to herself. But not today.

"Who are you?" she calls out towards the water.

The presence makes no sound, as always.

"I'm leaving London," Eilish says. "I'm going to find Ciara."

Hearing this—if *hearing* is even the right way to describe it—the presence seems concerned, and though she remains silent, Eilish senses her pleading. Pleading with Eilish to stay in London.

"Why?" Eilish asks. "Why? I can't stay here anymore."

Eilish waits. But the sense of pleading ceases.

"Speak to me, please!" Eilish calls blindly over the river.

And, for the first time, she does—just a whisper, but definitely a voice.

"Go back, Eilish. Go back before you go forth!"

"Go back?" she calls. "Back where?"

But her angel is gone. She waits, hoping she is wrong. But she feels the euphoria of hearing a voice tingle and fade, and she knows she's not coming back. From the tone of her angel's voice, whoever she was, she was clearly taking a huge risk just making a sound.

Go back before you go forth.

"No loitering on the bridges, Miss!" A Distillery officer shouts across the bridge.

"Sorry," Eilish calls back, composing herself and not looking up, at risk of exposing who she is. She turns away and strides off.

"Hold up a minute!" shouts the officer.

Eilish pretends she hasn't heard.

"Stop right there!" shouts the officer, his rubber boots thudding against the cobblestones.

"I need a word with you, miss!"

"What do you want a word with me about?" asks Eilish, still not turning her head.

"I'm collecting statements… I need to know where you've been today, Miss, and what you've been doing."

"That's none of your business," says Eilish, stopping.

The officer catches up with Eilish and puts his hand on her shoulder. She bats it away and turns to face him, finally.

"Listen, miss," says the officer. "Distillery officers have been injured at the palace this morning. I'm tasked with gathering a bit of information, especially from people acting *suspiciously*."

"And what's suspicious about standing on a bridge?" asks Eilish, obstinately.

The officer is momentarily perplexed, before reacting, "I don't need to justify myself," he says petulantly. "You either tell me what you've been doing, or I take you in… 'obstructing a Distillery officer'—that's a week in the palace at least."

Eilish decides to play her trump card. "If you must know," she begins. "I was meeting my brother. You might have heard of him: Andrew Callaghan, the Ferryman?"

The officer stops and stares at Eilish. Only now does he see who is standing in front of him.

"Governess?" he stutters. "I'm begging your pardon, your excellency. I didn't recognise you." He clicks his heels to attention, awkwardly feeling the need to salute her now that he knows who she is.

"Oh, give over!" says Eilish, exasperated by the show of obedience. "Just leave me alone."

"I'm sorry, your excellency," the officer continues. "I can't do that neither. President's direction, Your Excellency… We're to bring you in."

"I think I can bring myself 'in'!"

"I'm sorry, your excellency, we've been explicitly told to keep hold of you if we find you."

Eilish glances over the officer's shoulder and makes a split-second decision. She thrusts both of her hands into his chest, knocking him off his feet. He falls to the ground, and Eilish runs.

She hurtles into the street, her head down, not sure where she is going.

"Governess!" the officer shouts, chasing after her. Then he starts blowing a shrill whistle, drawing as much attention as he can to the chase.

Before Eilish has even escaped into a side street, half a dozen more officers appear. She doesn't stand a chance of evading them, but the fury that is bubbling inside her gives her the desire to try. Even if she just gets to kick and scratch a few of her brother's men.

"It's the Governess!" shouts the officer from the bridge. "Go lightly!"

'Go lightly?' thinks Eilish. *'Fuck you!'* Instead of running from the officers, she turns and throws herself towards them. Growing up with a brother on Earth, she knows how to scrap. And one thing she knows about turning the odds in your favour is the element of surprise.

The first officer that Eilish meets is a victim of this knowledge, as Eilish launches herself shoulder-first into his midriff, knocking him flat. She bounces off him and stumbles chaotically into the next officer. He gets a scratch on the face. The third, a kick to the shins.

Eilish starts to think, she might just get out of this mess. Then two of them hit her, around her waist, tackling her to the ground.

"Get off me!" she shouts, kicking out as violently as she can. "You know who I am!"

"Yes, Governess," says an officer's voice, right by her ear. "And I'm not letting you out of my sight. Not this time!"

Eilish turns. It is the officer who confronted her outside the palace. She stares at him, trying to work out what he has seen. Does he know she stormed the stage?

The officers pull Eilish off the floor, twisting her arms behind her back, making her stoop.

"To the station, boys," says the officer. "That bonus is ours!"

***

Chapter 31

Captivating Predicament

The Meadow - London

Eilish paces up and down the interrogation room. The officers haven't dared to put her in a cell. But this room isn't much better. A chair lies on the floor. She had kicked it over in frustration when they brought her in a few hours ago. Now her voice is hoarse from shouting, but no one is listening. She is locked in here until her brother comes.

A small dish of marbles has been left on the interrogation table—warm, golden marbles; calming marbles. Well, Eilish doesn't want to calm down. She is furious.

"Eilish?" says a voice at the door.

She can't tell if it is Andrew or not.

"What?" She shouts back.

"We need to talk." It is Andrew.

Eilish charges to the door and grabs the handle, hoping Andrew has unlocked it. He hasn't. She rattles it furiously.

"Open this fucking door, Andrew!" she shouts. "Let me out!" She rattles the door again, angrily. "Andrew?!"

It is quiet outside. Eilish's chest heaves.

"Andrew?!"

"Listen, Eilish," comes back her brother's voice, eventually. "I'm not coming in unless you're going to be reasonable."

"Reasonable?! Fuck you!" She kicks the door. "Fuck you!" She hammers the door with her fist, sending pain shooting through her arm. Her rage is on fire, but it is also tiring. As she kicks the door one more time, her shouts become sobs. "Why? Why Andrew?! You piece of shit! Why?!"

There is silence on the other side of the door. Eilish tries the handle again, but it is still locked. She waits. Andrew can break the silence this time, she thinks. But as she waits, she realises he's gone.

Eilish shouts out furiously, but the echo of her voice is all the response she gets. She grits her teeth and kicks the door again. She has never felt this powerless.

She steps over to the chair, grasping it with both hands, about to throw it angrily at the door, when she stops herself. From nowhere, an extraordinary clear logic floods into her body, calming her rage, and a trickle of clarity forms in her mind. Andrew doesn't deserve her rage. Her father doesn't deserve her rage. Not yet. She needs to get out of this interrogation cell. She won't avenge Chloe by thrashing about with anger in a Ferryman's station where no one can see her. And she won't find Ciara by shouting and screaming in the dark.

Eilish puts the chair down and slides it up beside the table, sitting on it and crossing her legs. She lies her head back and closes her eyes, letting out a long, deep breath.

'I've made up my mind,' she thinks. *'I'm in the rebellion now.'*

Amidst the chaotic and unpredictable shifting sands all around her, Eilish starts to feel like a bedrock is forming beneath her feet, ready to withstand a storm.

An hour or so passes before Eilish hears the familiar clicking of her brother's heels marching down the corridor.

"Eilish?" comes Andrew's sickeningly calm voice.

"Yes, Andrew," says Eilish, sarcastically.

"Are you going to be calm now?"

Andrew's condescension falls nonchalantly to the floor, washing off Eilish harmlessly.

"Yes," she says. "As long as you are, too."

Andrew doesn't bite, but Eilish hears him rattling the key in the lock before the door opens.

The first thing to scratch Eilish's fragile self-control as her brother steps into the room is when she notices the bare wedding ring finger on his left hand. She holds it in.

"You know why we had to bring you in, don't you?" asks Andrew.

"Let me guess," says Eilish. "My 'safety'?"

"Don't be so flippant," says Andrew. "If it were up to me, I'd leave you to fight your own battles. But father won't have it."

"So, why lock me up?" asks Eilish.

"We didn't want you doing anything stupid!" says Andrew.

Eilish's jaw clenches, and she digs her toes into the sole of her shoes to relieve some tension. "Right," she says calmly. "And now what?"

"Now you should go home," he says. "It has been an emotional day."

"Has it?" she asks, fixing her eyes on her brother, looking right into his dark, unflinching, brown eyes. "You don't look like you've shed a tear."

"There are other ways of showing emotion," says Andrew dismissively.

Eilish stands up. She can't hold it in.

"How could you do this to her?!" she shouts in Andrew's face. "My best friend! Your wife! You heartless piece of shit!" She goes to strike Andrew, but he catches her wrist.

"You don't think I *wanted* to do this, do you?! You don't think it hurt me as much as you?! You don't think it haunts me, putting the People before myself?"

"You fucking liar!" shouts Eilish. "Your life has always been about you! No, I don't think this is what you *wanted* to happen. But do you know what's worse? At least if your actions had been somehow vindictive against Chloe, it would have shown that her life affected yours. But I think you couldn't care less either way. You treated her just like you treated Ciara!"

Andrew's head snaps upright with this final accusation. His jaw clenches so tight his teeth grind together.

"Fuck you!" he shouts at Eilish. "You have no idea what's in my head, you stupid, naive little girl!"

Eilish spits in her brother's face.

"Like I said," says Andrew, carelessly. "You can't know what's going on in my head, Eilish. So, I don't need to apologise to you."

Eilish spits in her brother's face again. He has gone too far. Andrew wipes it away. "Go home, Eilish."

Eilish stares at her brother, considering spitting in his face again.

"You're free, Eilish. Go home."

"Fine."

She strides away from her brother, not looking at him, and wanders out into the corridor where a group of Ferrymen have been standing guard, listening. Eilish scowls at them as they all stand to attention. Such mindless obedience to their rank and role. She intentionally scuffs their shiny boots with her heel as she marches past them, out of the station.

"Thugs!" She says, under her breath.

It is a ten-minute walk back to her house, and Eilish knows there's no point trying to go anywhere else. She knows Andrew will have a number of his men following her all the way. She doesn't care. She *wants* to go straight home. She wants to start preparing the most destructive escape from this life as a governess that she possibly can.

***

Chapter 32

When the innocent run

Earth - London

A wind blows aggressively in Finchley in north London on Earth, as Marty strides up the steps to his flat. The blustery gale is just like the day of his son's crash all those years ago. He fumbles with his keys at the front door. His hands are shaking.

Inside his flat, Marty is straight onto his laptop. If it is going to be impounded as evidence, he might as well check that he is up-to-date on correspondence from his 'friend'.

There's a new email in his inbox. It's from a name he doesn't recognise, *Anthony Singleton*. There is just a short subject line: *'Now what?'*. Intrigued and confused, Marty reads on.

Hi Marty,

Thanks for the advice. I did everything as you instructed. Wow, what an explosion!

You said you'd help me hide. I'm heading to City Airport. I've got my passport. Are you meeting me there?

Don't be long. I feel very exposed right now.

I've transferred the money, so I've upheld my end of the bargain.

Anthony.

Marty rereads the email. It makes no sense, but it is part of a chain, so he reads backwards. In horror, he sees that the previous email is from him. He cannot remember sending this. Certainly not, given it was sent last night.

Hi Anthony,

OK, here's what you need to do…

First, you need a candle. Steal it. A church is a good option—they never have CCTV. Place the candle in your living room, but don't light it. Not yet.

Next, dismantle every electronic gadget you own—phone, laptops, tablets. Remove the hard drives and break them. Lay these directly around the candle. Still don't light it. Not yet.

Next, shred all the documents that have anything related to your crimes. This includes all your receipts. Scatter the shredding around the whole house.

Finally, you can light your candle and say a prayer (if you're so inclined). Turn on the hob in your kitchen and leave <u>immediately</u>.

Make sure you get out of the vicinity, and quickly. Don't look back. Don't look suspicious.

Meet me at City Airport. Bring your passport. If you're all paid up, I'll help you disappear.

In confidence,
Marty.

The real Marty Fredrickson stares at his screen, panicked. '*Have I been hacked?!*' he wonders. '*Is someone pretending to be me?*'

He goes back into his Sent folder. There are dozens of emails over the last fortnight with Anthony Singleton.

'*Shit.*'

Marty scrolls frantically. What about the emails with his 'friend'? '*I bet the bastard hacked my account!*' But the emails to his 'friend' are gone.

And then there are other emails. Emails to a disgruntled bartender in Camden. A bartender from the pub where the *Spirit of Shoreditch* were playing.

Marty's brow bristles with sweat. He is being set up! This is the evidence he was supposed to be using to clear his name. Not to implicate himself.

Marty bundles himself into his bathroom and splashes his face. He needs to be sharper. He stares into the mirror. '*Come on, Marty,*' he says to himself, gritting his teeth. '*Find a way out!*' He slaps himself in the face.

Outside the bathroom, he hears the laptop ping. He scampers out, his face and hands dripping, crashing down next to the screen. A new message, from an anonymous sender.

Marty,

You've been compromised. Get out.

Run!

Your friend.

Marty writes a quick response.

Run? Where?

And a message comes straight back.

Shrewsbury Train Station

Marty responds.

How can I trust you?

The response.

You have no choice.

At that moment, Marty's phone rings in his pocket. He almost jumps out of his skin. It's Jordan.

"Jordan! Something's wrong. I'm being framed!... What do you mean you're on your way here?! A man? Who?... Shit! I didn't send those emails, I swear! No, I won't run. But you need to trust me... I'm being framed!"

Marty hangs up the phone. He is fucked. A man called Anthony Singleton has handed himself in and gone on record to say Marty helped him destroy his house. What can he do? Jordan didn't sound convinced that he believed Marty.

Shit!

He's going to jail, and there is nothing he can do. Whoever has framed him has played him perfectly. It's checkmate.

Marty drops his phone to the floor and feels the blood drain from his face. Things are falling apart and falling apart fast. But he doesn't have time to think. He can't think. It's like his mind and his soul are desperately abandoning his body. He grabs the bunch of keys for his son's motorbike and runs out the door.

***

Chapter 33

The power of memories

The Meadow - London

The lights are on upstairs. Angus must be home.

'He's going to want to talk,' thinks Eilish, dreading the idea. She has had enough of *men* and their opinions today. With any luck, Angus will be in bed—the familiar statuesque figure of their unhappy marriage.

Today's events are taking their toll on Eilish. She is spent of tears. She aches from rage. Yet her mind is clear. Life as a 'governess' is done. She is a fugitive now. A fugitive with a vendetta. She will bring this house down, and then she will find Ciara.

Eilish strides down the corridor to Angus' office. She is intrigued to know what Distillery secrets might be lying hidden in there. Secrets that might help her undo the monopoly of power held by her family.

The fine art on her corridor's walls feels like a stuffy reminder of her undeserved privilege in the Meadow. Rare and priceless antiques that clutter her mantles and cabinets cruelly parade the craftsmanship from Earth, locked up in her dark, private home.

Mindful not to wake Angus, Eilish opens his office door as carefully and quietly as she can. Becoming a rebel has made her sneakier than she has ever been.

"Looking for something?"

Eilish stops. Sat by his desk, in the dark, beyond the embers in the fireplace, reclined beside an almost empty ramekin of marbles—many of them cracked and emanating mist on the floor—is Angus.

"You've got a nerve!" she says, lighting a lantern. "Yes, I am looking for something. Actually, no... not 'looking'... *waiting*...waiting for an apology from you!" She folds her arms and tilts onto her hip, staring at Angus.

"Yes," says Angus. "Yes, I have to admit, it was an apology that I thought I'd be giving too. But while I've been waiting for you, I've been told something that rather changes things... Changes things such that we are somewhat, even!"

"Even?!" Eilish exclaims.

'*What does he know?*' she thinks desperately. She can't help it; she glances down at Angus' desk drawer, where she had stolen the cathedral blueprints. Does he know they are missing?

"Part of my job as Head of Intelligence," starts Angus, fiddling with the marbles in the ramekin, "is to understand what is going on with this rebellion. I have informants all over the city, keeping their eyes and ears peeled for suspicious activity. One of my closest informants... a Well-Wishing priest... You had the pleasure of meeting here the other day..."

"I think it was you who had the *pleasure*," says Eilish sarcastically.

"Yes, well," says Angus, coyly. "Paul is a trusted informant. Like many of my informants, he frequents some of the more rebellious establishments in the city, keeping an ear out for me. Have you heard of a place called *The Angel's Whisper*?"

Eilish feels herself wobble, but she nods carefully.

"I've heard of it."

"Yes, I thought so," smiles Angus. "Another priest in my *confidence*, was there the other night when two women came visiting. A horrid, stormy night. You might remember the storm?" he asks rhetorically. "Well, I've seen the priest's marble memory from that night. Indeed, it was not a night for a casual marble with a friend. The weather was awful! And these women who came to the pub weren't there casually at all. One of them, she was there for a secret meeting... a secret meeting with a wanted criminal called Cyril Spate..."

Angus looks at Eilish, trying to read her expression.

"Cyril Spate is a man we thought was dead. Indeed, he was one of the most notorious rebel leaders who went missing after the failed rebellion a decade ago! Well, if this woman is meeting with him, that is bad news. Bad news that he is alive. But worse news for her! Fraternising with a wanted criminal... a terrorist... 'public execution' is written all over it. And then I discover the most shocking detail... she isn't just any ordinary citizen. The lady visiting Cyril Spate is a governess of the Distillery... my wife!"

Eilish is unnerved by her husband's unusual confidence and his arrogant tone. She has never felt frightened by him before.

"And...?" asks Eilish, trying to call Angus' bluff.

"And?!" Angus blurts out. "You know what I've seen!"

"*You* don't even know what you've seen!" cries Eilish.

"Treachery!" Angus shouts. "I have seen you committing treason!"

Eilish looks at Angus. "What do you want?" she asks, bluntly.

Angus leans forward. "You would like me to stay quiet about this, wouldn't you?" She pauses, then nods. "Well, I would like you to keep my little secret quiet, too."

"Your little secret?" asks Eilish.

"Yes," winks Angus. "I want to continue to see Paul with your blessing, so we shan't have to hide in our own home."

"And what about *us*?" asks Eilish.

"Oh, come on, Eilish! There has been no *us* for years... there has *never* been an 'us'. This was a marriage of convenience from the start. Let's just agree not to make it *inconvenient!*"

Eilish folds her arms. Annoyingly, Angus is right. Ever since her father selected Angus as a bright academic suitor for her, she has only ever found him to be *interesting*. Nothing more. And he's right. Now that he knows about her meeting with Cyril Spate, his silence serves as her protection.

"I've made up the guest bedroom for you," says Angus, showing just how well this conversation is going to his plan.

"I'm sorry, Eilish," he says, standing and stepping past her. "I'm not a bad person. I never wanted to be like this."

"It's ok," says Eilish. "I'm not a bad person either."

"I know," says Angus.

The two of them stand in silence for a moment, looking at each other. It is a weirdly and ironically intimate moment.

"Oh, by the way," says Angus, breaking the spell. "Colin, the porter from your brother's house… has left you something."

"What is it?" Eilish asks.

"I've no idea," Angus responds, pointing to a small parcel on his desk. "He said that Chloe wanted you to have it." He looks at Eilish, as though trying to tell if she was expecting such a gift. "I'll let you open it in private," he says, going to leave.

Eilish holds out her hand to shake Angus's hand—an accord between two neutral parties. But Angus steps forward and embraces her. It is the first time in the years of their marriage that Eilish feels some real connection with him. Like her, he is desperately unhappy and trapped in a lie.

"Thank you, Eilish," he says, giving her a resigned smile. He ends their embrace and steps past Eilish, leaving her alone in the room.

Eilish stands, stationary, perplexed. She listens to Angus' footsteps heading up the stairs. No doubt Paul is up there, waiting and listening.

She wanders over to Angus' desk and picks up the parcel left for her. It is only a small item, wrapped carefully in parchment. She recognises Colin's scrawl on a note beside it.

Miss Eilish,

Words cannot convey my pain. A pain which I know you share.

We, the staff, have been told to vacate your brother's house. He has 'no need' for us anymore. I'm told there is work at Dante's College, though I suspect it won't have half the glamour of working here.

Please forgive my behaviour this morning. I haven't slept. The maids have been told to burn anything belonging to the late Mrs Callaghan.

What a vile request! I knew she would have wanted you to have this, so I've saved it for you.

Please, for my sake, do not tell anyone that I have done this.

Yours, in secrecy,
Colin

Eilish looks at the little parcel. It is the size of a matchbox and looks entirely unremarkable. She delicately unfolds the wrapping and unfastens the box inside. Inside, swaddled in velvet, is a delicately crafted glass charm. It clinks as it rocks onto the desk. On first inspection, the watch-face sized broach seems to contain the emblem of the Distillery; the Speared Drop. But then Eilish realises it is something much more interesting. The symbol depicts a water droplet with an encircling arrow. The forbidden emblem of the Well Wishers. A very unusual item for Chloe to own.

Eilish picks up the glass charm to inspect it more closely. It isn't made of glass at all. The charm leaves a sticky residue on her fingers. There is only one substance with this property in the Meadow: resin.

'*Oh my god!*'

It is Chloe's *Identity Charm*. The precious artefact that she will have made in the weeks after she first arrived in the Meadow. The weeks following her suicide on Earth. It is the most intimate artefact of her life. The thing that, in polite society, you would avert your eyes from. Avert your eyes, so you don't gaze, uninvited, into another's soul. The same reason you avoid the gaze of strangers' eyes on Earth.

Absent-mindedly, Eilish licks the sticky resin off her finger. And in the beautiful moment of the resin touching her saliva, she is filled with a feeling that Chloe is right there in the room with her. She licks her finger a second time, intentionally, indulging another fleeting sense of Chloe's presence. Then she stops, a realisation striking her.

She scrabbles over to the bookshelf beside the glowing embers of the fireplace and runs her fingers along the spines. There is one book in particular she is looking for. *The Art of the Marble* by Professor Pelling.

Before his arrest, Professor Pelling had been known all around the Meadow for *The Art of the Marble*. Indeed, it is a text that all new arrivals in the Meadow, those under Distillery jurisdiction at least, have to study during their assimilation programmes. It details the realities of the marble and marble-time. Marble Past—the memory captured and contained within a marble. Marble Present—the sensation you get from sucking it. And Marble Future—the fact that a sucked marble can become so full of memories that they risk bursting and, if bursting in someone's mouth, will send that person 'on'.

Eilish flicks through the little textbook to the chapter titled *'Interrogation Stones'* and reads the opening paragraph.

> *The Interrogation Stone is the most critical marble in the Meadow. It captures the essence of the soul, preserving the clearest and freshest memories of Earth. It has become synonymous with a passport for all who enter the Meadow and should never be exchanged or traded. The resins contained within these stones are potent and won't dissipate as other marbles do. The memories contained in its resin, in contrast to all other marbles, can be visited over and over again, without erasure. Indeed, save for being incinerated in flame, an Interrogation Stone— or other Identity Resin artefact—will outlive its creator.*

Eilish looks at the charm, sticking to her fingers, wondering what memories it holds. She quickly, quietly, and carefully locks the door to Angus' office and slides into the old armchair beside the fire. She had spent so many happy evenings in this very spot with Chloe. She places Chloe's charm into her mouth.

***

Chapter 34

What Chloe knew

Earth - Mynydd Aaru

E ilish blinks. She finds herself standing in the bright morning sun, surrounded by mountains. Droplets of dew glisten in flashes of silver around her, shining off wildflowers that tremble gently in the soft breath of wind. There are birds singing joyfully from the trees, their voices mixing with the sweet perfume of blossom and mountain air. Towering high above her is the mountain, *Mynydd Aaru*—the highest peak in the British Isles on Earth.

Eilish turns at the sound of footsteps behind her. Chloe stands there. She is in a much younger body. She is maybe sixteen or seventeen and looks bright and full of life. Beside her is an older lady. Her mother, maybe? The old lady is skinny. She has square-ish shoulders and dazzling, bright green eyes.

As with any resin memory witnessed, Eilish's presence in the memory is completely unseen to the two women on the mountainside.

"I can't believe I'm finally going to meet her!" says the young Chloe.

"She won't *definitely* be here," says her mum.

"I know, I know," says Chloe, energetically. "But if she is… I've never met an angel! How will I know it's her?!"

"You'll know," says her mum. "You won't see her with your eyes, or hear her with your ears, but you'll feel her in your heart. I told her I'd bring you here one day. And today is perfect for her to appear."

"What do you mean?"

"I don't know the ins and outs of it," says the lady. "But she has told me that for a spiritual presence to appear on Earth, they need one fundamental condition. The stillness of the air. Without this, they cannot appear."

"Why not? What would happen if the wind blew?"

"Well, she blows away," says her mum. "She would usually come back again if it's just a gust, but she has told me that the Earth is not a stable place for spirits."

"Where is it stable for spirits? The Meadow?" asks Chloe, her eyes brightening expectantly.

"No, somewhere beyond the Meadow," says her mum. "Somewhere I've never been."

"But you met her in the Meadow as well, right?" asks Chloe.

"Yes, in some ways. Although I didn't know it was her at the time. I know Gareth met her too."

Chloe chuckles.

"Stop laughing every time I mention Gareth," her mum responds, irritated.

"I can't help it," sniggers Chloe. "It's just *too* weird that you supposedly meet him in another world and fall in love with him. He's just a little boy!"

"He isn't when I meet him," her mother defends herself. "And he is *very* important. Not just for me. But for everyone who has ever, and will ever, live."

"That's the mountain, isn't it?" says Chloe, pointing to the peak of *Mynydd Aaru*. "That's where you and Gareth climbed the mountain and went to the Source, before your return from the Meadow?"

The lady looks up at the mountain reverently and pauses, smiling. "It is indeed!"

"Will you ever go back, Mum?" asks Chloe.

"If I can," she says. "But I've told you before, we can never guarantee a passage through to the Meadow. And anyway, I'm waiting for Gareth to come back here first. I want to spend time with him where we're not on the run."

"Do you think he's going to want to live with you as an old lady?" Chloe asks. "He'll only be like twenty and you'll be nearly seventy."

"We'll see," says her mum, smiling. "Ok, let's sit ourselves down here."

Just in front of the two women, a small stream tumbles into a cool, clear pool. Around the pool, the branches of a Willow tree hang softly in the water. The two women clamber onto a large boulder which sits beside the falling water, facing the pool.

"What do we do?" asks Chloe.

"We sit, and we wait," says her mum. She reaches across to Chloe, grasps her hand and smiles.

As they wait, Eilish watches the Goldfinches and Blue Tits skipping and fluttering around the Willow. And she watches the Water Boatmen skidding over the surface of the pool. She doesn't think she has ever witnessed such a calm and peaceful setting. It reminds her of the times she has met with her angel on the River Lethe.

In a moment, the animals go quiet, and the hairs on Eilish's neck stand on end.

"*Ashley!*" the air whispers. "*Ashley!*"

Eilish can't really hear or see where the voice is coming from. But equally, she *can* 'hear'. She can sense the presence of someone new, and she can feel the melodic pulse of a familiar angelic song.

"This is my girl," says the old lady. "Chloe, say hello."

Chloe looks around her. "Hello?" she questions.

"*Chloe!*" whispers the air. "*How lovely to meet you. Finally. Your mother has told me so much about you.*"

Chloe smiles. "It feels like we have met before. But I know we haven't."

The air seems to chuckle. "*We have met before. But not yet. Somewhere in the future.*"

The air pauses, while Chloe tries to make sense of this.

"*And how have these last years been for you, Ashley?*"

"I am blessed to have adopted Chloe," smiles Ashley. "She has brought light into what felt like a very tedious wait."

"*I saw you outside his school, a few months back,*" says the air.

"You were there?" asks Ashley.

"*Yes. We have just as much interest in Gareth as you do. But be careful. You know he must not recognise you before the crash... Does Chloe know all about your time in the Meadow?*"

"I do!" beams Chloe. "It sounds amazing!"

"*Your mother is courageous. She has given hope where hope was lost.*"

"I want to go there," says Chloe. "I want to see it. The circus, the elephants. I want to fight the Distillery."

The air chuckles, and the branches of the Willow tree quiver.

"*Have you told Chloe of her mission?*" asks the air.

Ashley grasps her daughter's hand tight. She looks sick with nerves. "I haven't said anything... not yet."

"What? What is it?" asks Chloe.

"*Oh, beautiful and innocent soul,*" begins the air, "*there is a journey you must take. One that will put you at the heart of your mother's story, and the heart of Gareth's story. Into the story of victory over the Distillery. A victory of love over fear in the universe.*"

"What journey?" asks Chloe.

"Please, she's too young," says Ashley, pulling her daughter tight to her. "She's only sixteen."

"*Chloe needs all the time we can give her,*" says the air. "*She must make her choice to go on the journey as informed as she can be. She must not take it on a whim of emotion, for such a journey can fail.*"

"Um, hello?" says Chloe. "I am still here! What is this journey?"

Ashley puts her head in her hands as the air speaks.

"*Chloe, your mother only succeeded in returning to Earth from the Meadow and becoming your adopted mother because the stars have happened to align in one version of time.*"

"What do you mean?" asks Chloe.

"*I mean, without the right interventions in the different realms at the right time, the likelihood of your mother following the path that leads to here and now is small. It is just one of many paths. And if she takes a different path, well, then everything changes... this conversation doesn't happen... Your mother never returns... You are never adopted... and the battle against fear in the realms rages again.*"

"I don't understand," says Chloe. "You are here now. Mum *did* adopt me. She remembers the Meadow. It must happen, no?!"

"If only it were so simple," sighs the air. *"If only the present proved the future, and the past. But, alas, across the realms, the present is just a possibility. The past and the future, just a memory or a dream. And so, it is only in the present moment, in whichever realm that you find yourself, that you can act… that you can change things. Change things or sustain things, prevent things, or pursue things."*

"So, do I need to do something to make sure that all this… that it actually *is*?!" Chloe looks towards her mum, desperately.

"Exactly," says the air. *"But what you need to do to make this happen is not easy."*

"Please," says Ashley. "Tell her gently."

"It's ok, mum. I'm not a little girl."

The air seems to breath down gently onto Chloe's head, encouraging her to sit again, ready to take on an important message.

"Chloe," starts the air. *"In the Meadow your mother joined a whole group of brave souls who ventured into the mountains to a cliff face where they collected pure water falling from a spring, enabling them to break the stranglehold of destiny, and allowing them to show all the souls in the Meadow that they weren't only destined to follow a path through that realm to death, but had an opportunity to choose their own fate, even return to Earth."*

"Now, your mother's mission into the mountain was riddled with danger. The Source that sends water cascading off the Perihelion precipice creates an almost permanent mist around the mountain. A mist that is slowly dissolving all the minds lingering there. The mission could not succumb to this mist. Their chances of success were tiny. But your mother is a testament to the fact that success is possible. At least in one version of the future and the past."

"Ashley, perhaps you can tell Chloe about the lady on the mountain?"

Chloe looks at Ashley, who lifts her head but looks straight forward, as though in a dream.

"When I was on the Mountain, I nearly chose to 'go on' from the Meadow," says Ashley. "And Gareth told me that he fell on the snowy slopes and almost tumbled to his death. But that night on the Mountain, there was a lady… a lady that none of us knew. And she saved us. She lifted Gareth from his fall. And she convinced me not to jump."

"Who was she?" asks Chloe.

"Someone from the future, from another realm," says the air. *"She was... she is... you, Chloe."*

"I don't understand?"

"In the version of the future that we live now, there is a lady with knowledge of the Meadow who will take her own life on Mynydd Aaru ten years from now. She will pass through an opening in the Meadow, arriving on the Mountain at the precise place and time to protect both Gareth and Ashley. She can ensure that the expedition to the Mountain and the mission of the Returners succeed."

"For everything that you know to be true right now, Chloe, your fate is already entangled in the future," says the air. *"Ten years from now, at a date and time you must figure out, you will have to come up here, past this very spot, and up the Mountain on your own. And you will need to take your own life. A sacrifice to save Gareth's life, your mother's life...to save your own life right now."*

"I'm sorry," says Ashley. "When I adopted you, Chloe, I had no idea that this would become your fate."

"It's ok," says Chloe. "I am part of your life."

"I have also learned more," says the air. *"More about your journey, Chloe, than I have ever been able to share with you, Ashley. Your journey won't end in the Mountain. For it seems that it is not only journeys back to Earth that you are destined to aid... but also journeys forth into my realm."*

"What does that mean?" asks Ashley.

"Your journey, the return to Earth, will unsettle the norms in the Meadow," says the air. *"But, sadly, I have gleaned that it will not change the prevailing wind either... No, the Distillery and their power in the Meadow will survive the rebellion you begin. The sinews of fear across all the realms will continue to cling to power. Only when the rebellion sends ripples across all the realms will we unsettle this. Only when we flood the realms can we change the winds of fear."*

"I don't know how your journey will play out, Chloe, but whispers from the future tell me that you have a big part to play in flooding the Beyond."

The air seems to drop like a blanket over the two women on the rock by the pool. Even Eilish can feel it, witnessing it in a memory. And as the air drops, the surface of the pool begins to ripple, and the willow branches start to sway.

"Take your time," whispers the air. *"Ask Ashley anything you need. We have ten years to get ready. There is no rush."*

Then Eilish feels the wind blowing on her face, and she watches as Chloe and Ashley embrace. The presence over the pool fades away, the birds start to tweet again, and the flies begin buzzing over the ground. The memory fades, and Eilish finds herself returning to Angus' study with the sticky broach in her hand.

She rolls the broach across her palm, feeling its resin cling to her skin. She inspects the jewel, amazed at how it can hold the vast catalogue of memories of Chloe's life on Earth. She tells herself that she won't view *that* memory. The final memory contained in the resin, the memory of the moment that brought Chloe to the Meadow. It would be horrific, and it feels morbid to want to know. To see her suicide. But the more Eilish stares at the broach, the more she realises that she *needs* to see this memory.

Eilish shuffles into a more comfortable position, then rocks her head back and, concentrating on the idea of suicide in her mind, she places the broach back onto her tongue.

***

In front of Eilish, as before, the mountain appears. The weather is markedly different. A heavy storm pounds the Mynydd range at dusk. Snowflakes dance chaotically, tumbling in the gale-force winds, and there is not a hint of the animals that graced the slopes before. No birds or bugs. They are all sheltered away from this winter storm. But amidst the chaos, Eilish spots Chloe.

Chloe is wrapped head to toe in layers of clothes. Her top layer consists of a long leather trench coat, which drags along the dirty ground. On her head, a bright headtorch beams out searchingly into the fog. She carries a heavy backpack with her. She trudges alone through the snow, up the mountain.

Eilish draws in closer to Chloe, looking at her face, hidden under her hood. She looks older, just as Eilish remembers her from the Meadow. Her face is determined, and her cheeks are rosy from the cold, biting wind.

High up on the mountain face, Chloe strides purposefully toward a cluster of rocks and boulders. Her confidence on this treacherous route suggests that she has been here many times before. She clambers up the rocks, holding tightly so that she doesn't slip on the ice. Eilish follows calmly. When witnessing a memory, the challenge of negotiating obstacles is non-existent. One can simply drift with the memory weightlessly.

After a short scramble up the rocks, Chloe comes across a sharp precipice, protruding out into the swirling fog and snow. In the shelter under this protrusion, Chloe kneels on the dry ground and removes her backpack, spreading out its contents onto the dry slates that have been protected from the wind and snow. The beam on Chloe's headtorch gives Eilish a chance to see what she has been carrying.

There is a map, obviously. Though as Chloe inspects it, Eilish sees that it is a map for the Meadow. There is a dotted line along the contours, showing the location of a mine shaft labelled 'Beatrice's Cave' and a route to the Perihelion Cliffs. Placed on top of the map, Chloe has put a Stanley knife and a ruler. Next to these items, there is a medical-grade face mask and a first aid kit full of pain killers—even a syringe of morphine. There are also some binoculars and a book. A blue leather-bound first edition of Through the Looking-Glass by Lewis Carroll from 1872—a book that Eilish knows very well. But it's not the memory of the story that Eilish recalls that well; it's the actual print edition that she is familiar with. Indeed, it appears to be the exact book from her childhood. The book that her, Ciara, Andrew, and their mother had curled up together in bed to read. What are the chances? That edition was long out of print when she owned it, it being passed down through her mother's family for generations. Eilish remembers their copy, a visceral memory from her childhood. She even remembers the coffee stain that circled the back cover.

Chloe turns over the book, and to Eilish's surprise, she spots the same stain. This book is *her* book. While Eilish stares, Chloe turns to a page where a photograph falls out, catching her by surprise. Eilish leans in beside Chloe as she picks it up to get a look at the picture. What she sees almost wakes her from the memory. It is a photograph of Eilish and Ciara.

Eilish stares at the picture. Did Chloe know them? Did she, Eilish, know Chloe on Earth but had forgotten her? No. She definitely never met her. But why does she have this photo?

Before Eilish can make sense of what she is seeing, Chloe repacks the sack and then, rather unusually, she throws off the trench coat that was keeping her dry, to reveal a beautiful long blue ball gown that she is wearing underneath. She wraps a blue silk scarf around her face and slings the backpack over her shoulder. She mutters something into the wind and waits, just in case the air responds. But it doesn't.

Eilish watches as Chloe steps back into the storm. She clambers up onto the precipice of rock and teeters carefully towards its sharp protruding edge. The dance of snow and fog swirls all around her, thrown about by the gale. The hem of Chloe's dress flaps in a rage of its own. Then, as she planned, and as Eilish reluctantly expects, Chloe closes her eyes and leaps off the precipice, headfirst, to her death.

***

Chapter 35

In sickness and in stealth

The Meadow - London

Eilish stares at the broach in her hand. Chloe had come to the Meadow with one thing in mind: to fight the Distillery. And somehow, she had ended up as part of this very same institution with no memory of her past. The realisation is cruel. Unless it had all been part of her plan? The photo sticks in Eilish's mind. Why did Chloe have it? How did she get it? And the book?

Eilish feels out of sorts. More so than ever. It is like her fate is a puzzle, and a mess of pieces are only starting to come together. If Chloe had joined the rebellion, and known Nailah, and if Chloe's mission had been to help Ciara, then Eilish knows she has to speak to Nailah again. And soon.

But how? She is basically under house arrest. There are Ferrymen outside right now, guarding her escape. And even if they weren't, she couldn't just run off and talk to Nailah. Angus has made it clear he is trapping her here, too, and he knows too much. Somehow, she'll need his silence before she can run off anywhere.

Eilish gets up from her chair and wanders to the window, drawn to see the freedom of the streets. Outside, the sky is clear as dusk falls over London. The cool light of the stars on their journey north twinkle over the empty curfewed streets, and shimmer on the Lethe that can be glimpsed between two distant town houses. Away on the horizon, north of the river, fires of rebellion are burning again.

'*At least some of the Ferrymen are occupied tonight,*' she thinks. A few less thugs to keep watch over her.

But what does it matter? Eilish feels powerless. She had accepted Kim-Joy's plan to wait here in 'safety'. But that was before. Things have changed now, and she can't bear the thought of biding her time, out of control and trapped, just left to hope things will change. Hope that Nailah manages to get to the vaults under the cathedral. Hope that no Distillery official decides to look at her confiscated marbles. And all the time, at risk of being betrayed by Angus.

No, Eilish knows she needs to do something now. She needs to take back control.

Eilish muses on Angus and Paul, and she smiles desperately. What an awfully twisted situation she is in. Her husband is happily and knowingly sharing their bed with another soul. At the same time, she stands here on her own, lost, with her identity in tatters (literally, with her Interrogation Stone gone), and her fate spiralling out of control.

'*It's time I put myself first*,' Eilish says to herself, gritting her teeth. She strides over to the marble drawer in Angus' desk and turns over the smooth tray of tiny spheres, the whole kaleidoscope of colour. She is looking for the best marble for blackmail. A small icy-blue marble should do it. She remembers what Kim-Joy had said about them—they provide a clarity of mind and imprint a clarity of memory.

Eilish delicately places a little blue sphere into her mouth and quietly steps out of the office.

The marble rattles around Eilish's teeth as she sneaks upstairs and into earshot of the master bedroom. She can already hear its occupants. Their muffled voices are passionate, and there is a rampant creaking of bedposts, vibrating the floorboards under her feet. Eilish smiles to herself. The marble in her mouth is undoubtedly going to shift the odds with Angus. It won't be her word against his anymore. It will be her undeniable marble memory against his fallible human memory.

Eilish pauses for a moment. The groans and moans from inside are neither subtle nor discreet. And while she feels ashamed for standing there, listening, she knows this is necessary for her plan. She takes a deep breath, then knocks firmly on the door.

The noises stop. Eilish knocks again.

"Eilish?" calls out Angus, surprised.

Eilish pushes open the door carefully, making sure to catch a glimpse of the infidelity in action.

"Sorry," says Eilish, feigning naivety. "I need a word, Angus."

"Can't it wait?!"

"Actually, no," she responds.

Angus leaps from the bed, throwing a robe around him. His friend, Paul, looking like a rabbit in the headlights, pulls the bedsheets up and over his naked torso, all the while staring towards Eilish in the doorway.

"Seriously, Eilish," says Angus, reaching her and pulling the door closed to give Paul some privacy. "This is a very unwelcome interruption."

Eilish ignores his condemnation. "I've decided I need to go away," she says firmly. "Just for a few days. I need some space."

"Well, yes, of course, I understand that's what you want, Eilish… I want that too. But you can't. Your father's orders are to keep you here. The Ferrymen are guarding the house. I've been told to keep you close. So, there's no way you can go away."

"I'm just asking for a few days," says Eilish, dropping the marble from her mouth and pocketing it. "Come on, Angus. You can't want me to be here."

Angus, overlooking the pocketed marble, glances over his shoulder. It's true. He would much rather have the house and his time with Paul absent from Eilish rattling around, prying inadvertently into his private affairs.

"Where do you want to go?" he asks.

"I can't tell you that," says Eilish.

"But you promise it'd just be for a few days?"

"I promise," Eilish lies.

"And what if you don't come back?"

"Then you can expose me to defend yourself."

Angus ponders Eilish's plan for a moment. The temptation to sneak her out of the house yet stay blameless for her disappearance is tempting. But then he has a change of heart.

"No," he says, lowering his gaze. "I can't let you go. It's too risky."

"I'm not asking you to *let* me go," she says. "I'm telling you, I'm going."

"But…"

"You'll have to figure out how to cover for me."

"Eilish. We had a deal. If you run out and leave me at the mercy of your father, then I'm sorry, but I'm going to have to tell him about your secret meeting at the *Angel's Whisper.*"

"That would be foolish, Angus," Eilish responds. "I'll deny it. I'll say you're just trying to frame me because I know about your affair."

Angus straightens up, bullishly. "Well, I'll deny the affair," he says triumphantly.

Eilish lifts the marble back out from her pocket. "But I now have evidence to condemn you," she smiles. "The marble never lies. You just have a story from a priest who is spying on his congregation. I think I know who I'd believe."

Angus looks at her, stumped.

"I will come back, I promise," says Eilish, with a condescending tap on Angus' shoulder. "And when I do, I expect my secret to be safe."

Angus stares at Eilish and nods. "Ok," he concedes. "I will cover for you as best I can. But I can only do my best. The longer you're gone, the harder it will be."

"So long as you do your best, your secret will be safe with me," says Eilish.

Angus smiles, ironically. "It seems we've never needed each other more."

Eilish smiles back and shrugs her shoulders.

"So, this is goodbye?" says Angus.

"Yes… Goodbye, my Angus," says Eilish, winking at the small man in the doorway.

"Goodbye, Eilish… and good luck."

Angus closes the door quietly.

Eilish stands for a moment before wandering back downstairs. Now she just has to figure out how to get past the Ferrymen.

She wanders into the porch. She has no intention of running. That would be foolish. But she wants to know how many Ferrymen are guarding the house. Guarding her.

She pushes open the door, feeling the cool night air blow on her face. On the street corner, four Ferrymen stand, chatting. They look cold. It's certainly not a night to be standing around in jeans and bomber jackets.

One of the Ferrymen notices Eilish peeking out at them. He throws his hand over his mouth and snaps his heels together, saluting her.

"Evening gents!" Eilish calls out politely. "Fresh evening, no?"

"Aye, Your Excellency," the Ferry Man calls back. "Is all well, Ma'am?"

"Yes, excellently well," she says, smiling sarcastically. "Can I interest you young men in a whiskey marble?" she asks, flirtatiously. It can't hurt to have them on her side.

"That's very kind, Ma'am. But we can't be having them while we're on duty."

"Very well," she says, smiling, and she closes the door.

So, four men are guarding her. She'd stand no chance if she made a dash for it. And save for burning the house down, it'd be hard to distract them from their duties.

Stepping back into the house, Eilish inadvertently kicks today's *Shipping Forecast*, which lies on the floor. '*He never picks these up!*' she thinks, frustrated at Angus' lazy tendencies. She bends down and picks up the paper, carrying it through with her to the kitchen.

Eilish slumps down at the kitchen table, wondering how on Earth she can get out of the house unnoticed. The front page of the *Shipping Forecast* stares at her. Her brother's cruel self-congratulatory condemnation of Chloe, and the haunting sketch of her friend, hands bound, being dragged out from her cell in the middle of the night.

Eilish wonders what tomorrow's *Forecast* will say. Whether her brother and father are, right now, concocting their opinion pieces to condemn Chloe further, and peddle more propaganda in favour of a compliant society. '*Such a fallacy!*' She heard the resentment in the crowd today. She felt their wave of support as she tried to storm the stage. Who is her father kidding? Himself. There is a reason that rebellions are happening again in the Meadow.

Then a thought occurs to Eilish. The paper boy at dawn. He'll be dragging his trolley full of tomorrow's papers right up to the front door. A trolley big enough to hide someone inside? How much would it take to bribe the paper boy to sneak her out? A handful of marbles, maybe? She'd be willing to pay more.

'*What's the worst that could happen?*' she thinks. If they catch her, they'll just send her back into the house.

She folds today's Forecast and leans back in her chair.

'*That's a plan!*'

***

Chapter 36

Under a looming shadow

Earth - Near Mynydd Aaru

Tucked into the winding country lanes and falling under the evening shadow of the Mynydd hills, the town of Shrewsbury has a quintessentially rural English feel about it. The stone houses are quaint and mismatched. The shops sell tat and afternoon tea. And nobody looks remotely interested in a stranger who rides a bright green motorbike through their town. Unlike the city Marty has left, everyone dawdles in Shrewsbury, and nobody stares.

Pulling into the train station car park, Marty clocks the CCTV camera high above. The one pointing towards the station exit. The one where he has seen numerous captures of the hooded lady. The last camera footage before she disappears.

Marty remembers just where the field of view of the camera ends, and so he parks his son's bike out of shot. There's no point in making life easy for the Sergeant to find him. The hour has long passed since he left the custody suite, and they'll be looking for him now.

Marty throws up the hood of his jacket and heads into the station.

As a detective, he had always assumed that when someone runs, they must be guilty. That's what the Sarge will be thinking right now. But the reality is, you don't know why people run until you run. Marty is running because he is trapped. He is being framed, and he doesn't trust anyone but himself to clear his name.

It is deathly quiet on the platforms. There is no train for the next two hours, coming or going. Not unusual for such a remote station. A station devoid of rush or urgency. A station whose pace is driven by the rhythms of the countryside and not the anxiety of the commuter. Such a contrast to the city. There are even posters along the station wall advertising shows in the city that have long since run their course. Such is the provision of public transport outside the cities.

The ticket booth is shuttered, and a handwritten sign suggests it hasn't been open in six months. Beside it, a gleaming metal ticket machine stands. It is the only modern thing on the station. Though it has already been graffitied. '*Fuck the machines*' it says. Marty sniggers. How the rural folk are still fighting for their quaint jobs. Jobs that machines have long since replaced in the city.

Marty doesn't know where to start. He had built a fantasy on his ride here that the hooded lady would just be sitting there on the station, waiting for the next train. Of course, she isn't.

Marty's phone vibrates in his pocket. '*That'll be the Sarge,*' he thinks. '*There's no way I can answer.*'

He pulls the phone out, intending to turn it off, but he notices a strange error. His phone screen suggests that the incoming call is coming from himself. Against his better judgment, he answers.

"Marty?" he says, grinning at the idea of talking to himself.

"*Hello Marty,*" whispers a voice on the end of the line.

"Who's this?" says Marty.

There's a long, silent pause.

"It's you, isn't it?!" asks Marty, his mouth going dry. "So much for being a 'friend'."

"*You wanted help to find her… I'm helping you.*"

"You're not fucking helping! What are you trying to do?! Ruin me?! Why are you setting me up?"

"*I'm setting you free!*"

"What the fuck are you talking about? Because of you, I'm a wanted fugitive. I have had to flee my home, and the police are after me. What the fuck!... WHO ARE YOU?!"

Marty ducks his head into his hands, hearing his own voice bounce off the tracks. So much for being discreet.

There is silence, as though the voice on the end of the phone is thinking.

"*I'm... a friend.*"

Marty bites his lip to stop himself from screaming down the phone.

"Listen," says Marty, a stab of threat in his voice. "I will hunt you to the end of the Earth. Don't you fucking play with me!"

"*I'm not playing Marty,*" says the voice, seriously. "*The lady you are chasing is extremely dangerous. She is a threat to much more than you can possibly comprehend. I will help you find her. And I will help you stop her. I need you to stop her. But you have to march to my tune first.*"

"Look, buddy. Just come straight with me... Tell me who you are? Or tell me who she is. I'm not chasing shadows anymore."

"*What's the weather like today?*" asks the voice.

"What?!" Marty blurts out, taken by surprise.

"*Do you have a clear sky?*"

"What? Err... Yeah?" says Marty, answering out of instinct.

"*Look west... You can see a peak, right? A tall mountain peak?*"

"Well, yeah... of course I can," says Marty, peering at the ominous horizon beyond the station. "I can see the peak of *Mynydd Aaru.*"

"*Yes... precisely,*" whispers the voice. "*She is very familiar with that mountain... In fact, I have reason to believe she* lives *on the mountain...*"

"She lives up there?"

"*I believe so...*"

"Why?"

"*Because on the mountain she can disappear...*"

"Are you suggesting that I hunt for her on *Mynydd Aaru?*" says Marty, feeling overwhelmed by the towering peak staring down at him.

"*Not yet,*" says the voice. "*The mountain is treacherous, and you are not a mountaineer, are you, Marty?*"

"Ha!" Marty blurts, spontaneously. "No, I am not!"

"*There is a café at the base of* Mynydd Aaru... *Go there. Ask around and see what you can find. Lie low for a while and wait for me.*"

232

"You're going to meet me?" asks Marty.
"*Yes… when the time is right.*"

***

Chapter 37

Treasure in the sand

The Meadow - London

Inside the *Tide and Time Tavern*, raucous music tumbles through the jubilant energy of the night's crowd, misting the windows with the breath of camaraderie. Outside, it is a cold, crisp night, approaching dawn. But inside, the body heat of a thousand revellers, dancing to the beat of the band, makes it a sweltering refuge of laughter and joy.

The singer of the *General Electrics* starts a chorus again, and everyone joins in, smashing marbles onto the floor and filling the bar with a rainbow of mist. It is hard to believe that it could have been like this all night, and despite the approaching dawn, there's no sign of things quieting down.

> *Her loving rain is falling free,*
> *The soils thirsts, the raindrops sink into the sea.*

Nailah holds a sentimental smile, looking around at her friends and fellow citizens, acknowledging her handpicked crew for tonight's raid. This will be the last song before they set off.

Nailah leans across the bar to embrace Kim-Joy. The two women squeeze tight and, as they let go, Nailah throws out her hand, clasping Kim-Joy into a masculine handshake.

"Good risen!" says Nailah.

"Good risen, and good luck!" smiles Kim-Joy.

Around the bar, the members of Nailah's crew start saying their farewells to friends and loved ones—those who know of their impending and dangerous mission. But most of the people in the pub tonight have no idea of the secret raid that is about to set off. That general ignorance is the way that it needs to remain.

Kim-Joy unlocks the door to the cellar and props it open with an old marble crate. Before her, one by one, Nailah counts the members of her crew as they descend the stairs, patting them on the back as they go.

The *General Electrics* pick up the beat for their next song, as Nailah gives Kim-Joy a last wink and steps into the cellar herself, closing the door behind.

The half dozen members of Nailah's crew have already donned their black hooded robes for the raid when she reaches them. Beaming, she ushers them close and hands out a *Sailor's Mist* to each of them. They will need steady heads this morning.

Two of the raiders, a couple of young women, carry a handful of fuel-filled jerry-cans and, on their backs, sacks full of corked glass spheres and plenty of rags. These are all the ingredients for the Molotov Marbles—exploding balls of fire and resin. The two women, form the *'Distraction Crew'*—raiders who will enter the Cathedral first and will hurl their Molotov Marbles at strategic locations to cause fires and sensations of mist, engaging the Ferrymen and Distillery Officers to keep their attention away from the vaults.

The four remaining raiders are called the *'Treasure Hunt'*. Led by Nailah, this group will be going into the heart of the cathedral to find the Distillery's marble vaults. Once they can confirm the location of the intelligence archives on the Well Wishers and find the marbles collected during the Palace disturbances, they will destroy them and wreak as much havoc as they can before the Distillery can regain control.

There's no realistic chance that the six of them can cause such destruction that the Cathedral and its workings will be disrupted for long. And it is almost certain that not all of them will return. Such is the danger of the mission, and such is the bravery of the six souls.

Nailah pulls out the blueprints of the cathedral vaults to inspect them one last time in the candlelight. The others lean in.

"Ok, we all know our roles," says Nailah. "Kelly and Robyn, get in, do your damage, get out. No unnecessary heroics. Cause as much destruction as you can, but don't harm a soul." She looks at the two girls who nod their heads, shaded under their heavy hoods.

Nailah lifts a sack onto the table and opens it. Inside are half a dozen thermocline mist cannisters—the kind that the Ferrymen carry and the Distillery guarding the cathedral will hold. It is illegal for any citizen in the Meadow to carry their own. "One each," she says. "Worst case… and remember, only use it on yourself. Suicide can be noble. Murder cannot."

Each of the raiders reaches forward and grabs a canister, clipping it to their belt.

"Right, my team," says Nailah. "We'll go in through the Postal Door," she prods her finger to a small rear entrance of the Cathedral on the blueprints. This is the place where the Distillery correspondence and daily newspapers get dispatched and received. "Fires from the *Distraction Crew* should keep our path clear down to the East Stairway. We'll take the first two flights of stairs down from here, then, avoiding the security checkpoint, we'll make our way down this corridor, past the *Purification Chambers*." She looks nervously at the group.

"We don't know what we'll find down that corridor. There's no record of its existence anywhere. Even our informant was unaware of it." Nailah doesn't say anything more about Eilish, their informant. Her identity needs to be kept secret until the governess is no longer in danger.

"Hector and Edmond," Nailah addresses two men from her crew. "You will be our eyes and ears down this corridor. We need the two of you to get us through to the Sand Chute."

"Of course, darling!" says Hector, from behind his hood. His voice is camp and lilting. "We are always ready to make a scene!"

Nailah grins. Hector's cavalier and nonchalant attitude helps bring her back into the moment, as it has on many occasions before. "The blueprint suggests this chute will be big enough to abseil down," she continues. "It'll bring us out on the vault floor, two storeys below."

"Cyril," says Nailah, turning to the prominent, robed figure beside her, "have you got the abseiling gear?"

He nods. Under his robes, he carries a thick climbing rope, rattling with attachments for making a belay.

"Ok," says Nailah. "If all goes to plan, the Criminal Records and Intelligence Vaults will be there in front of us. We'll need to find the marbles collated by Angus Callaghan-Crawford—the Head of Distillery Intelligence. Our informant tells us that Angus' marbles records—the ones detailing Well Wishers with dirty resin—should be easy to spot. They are stored and transported inside hollow Bamboo poles. The rest of the marbles will be loose or in pouches, probably archived in some way, like a library. Amongst the pouches, we need to find and destroy the most recent marbles—those collected from the palace disturbances yesterday. Hector and Edmond, you will focus on those marbles. Cyril and I will focus on finding the Bamboo Poles. We destroy what we can. Then, we get out!"

"Ok," Nailah breathes in and out slowly and intentionally. "Are we ready?"

Everyone nods.

Nailah packs the blueprints into her bag and throws on her own long black hooded robe.

"*May the seas warm, and the clouds form…*" she says.

To which the rest of the crew respond, "*…and may the rain fall, filling the rivers of Love.*"

"Good risen, crew!" says Nailah, opening the door to the secret tunnel under the *Tide and Time Tavern*.

The *Distraction Crew* go first, followed by Nailah and the *Treasure Hunt*. The raid has begun.

***

Tied to a chair at the end of a dark, low-ceilinged chamber sits the dying body of a young man. His head lolls as dark resin drips from a wound above his eye. His arms and legs are bound, tight. There are fresh scars beside old ones, on his torso and arms. His breathing is laboured, rasping and dribbly. His saliva drips onto the floor. Between his legs is a large glass bowl, into which a dance of colourful resin sloshes about. Resin that has dripped from his forehead because of the most cruel and intense interrogation of his life.

Bending down in front of the man, the Mineralist looks into the bowl, swilling the sticky resin with his long, bony finger.

"This is exactly what we needed. Thank you, Edward Hemsley. You have again proven that, despite being a *Stain*, you have value to the Distillery. Now, before our conversation ends, I must press you for one final confirmation... The lady we have spoken of... are you sure she will be there tonight?"

Edward nods.

"Good. Very good..."

The Mineralist stares into the bowl, inspecting the fruits of his interrogation. "Sadly, Edward, this is to be our last 'conversation'.... I'm afraid with this last confirmation, your value to the Distillery has now expired. We're a bit crowded here in my little workhouse, you see. And I don't like it when a lodger outstays their welcome. It is time for you to... join your friends."

Edward tries to protest. His head rocks over, and he manages to open one bruised eye to look at the Mineralist. He lets out a bubbling, mumbling groan, but no words come out.

"I hope, for your sake, Mr Hemsley," starts the Mineralist again. "That your final acts in the Meadow here have softened the heart of the Almighty. For, when your Energy now enters his presence, the pain you are about to feel will be nothing compared to His wrath."

Edward coughs, spluttering globules of congealed resin onto the floor. He strains with every ounce of energy that he has to speak. "You... gave me... your word!"

The Mineralist smiles—a small and evil smile.

"Yes... But my word is worth... well, nothing. Maybe, where you are going, words will have more value... but here, they have none."

The Mineralist bends down and lifts an old leather wineskin from the floor. It sloshes noisily.

Raising the wineskin over Edward, the Mineralist pours its clear contents over Edward's head, and immediately, the fumes of the paraffin are overwhelming. The Mineralist continues to douse the young man, all the way down to his bare and bloodied toes, before dribbling a trail across the floor.

"Please," Edward rasps, paraffin dripping into his mouth, mixing with the congealed resin. "Please?"

The Mineralist doesn't respond. He pulls out a box of matches and strikes one without hesitation, dropping its pathetic little pinch of flame into the paraffin.

In an instant, Edward Hemsley's body is engulfed in flame. He writhes and screams, but only for a few seconds. His body burns, and his mind gives in to the severe pain, and he loses consciousness.

The Mineralist stands and watches. A cruel and sick observer of his own private crime. He watches with morbid pleasure as the young man passes away, and his body starts to disintegrate like sand in the flames. Then, a sparkle of light, the young man's pocket of Energy, squeezes out from his inert body and shoots up through the ceiling and away.

Edward Hemsley is now extinct.

The Mineralist bends down and picks up the bowl of resin from under the crumbling remains of the dead man, before he walks out of the chamber with it, not once looking back.

In the atrium of the Cathedral, many floors above the Purification rooms, three ranks of Ferrymen stand to attention, obediently silent for their leader. The Ferryman turns when he hears the Mineralist enter.

"Were you successful?" he asks, plainly.

"Of course," smiles the Mineralist, raising the bowl of resin high above his head.

"Good."

The Mineralist strides over to an altar-like table beside the Ferryman. He gently places the bowl of resin beside the prepared ladles and cloths before taking his place beside the Ferryman.

"Right, men," shouts Andrew. "One row at a time, come forward to the table. The Mineralist and I will offer you one ladle each. Do not swallow until you are back in your ranks and sitting on the floor. Is that clear?"

"Yes, sir!" shout the rows of men.

"Good. Then, first rank, come forward."

One by one, the Ferryman and the Mineralist administer the resin. Each man obediently did as instructed, returning to the floor and sitting in an orderly row before swallowing his mouthful of resin. And as each man swallows, he is transported into the extracted memory of the late Edward Hemsley.

"Did your interrogation confirm that she will be there this morning?"

"Oh yes," says the Mineralist. "And I think you'll be very pleased with the level of detail I extracted. We have a way in! Chin chin!" He dips the ladle into the resin and offers it to Andrew.

The Ferryman steps forward, reverently, his mouth open. The Mineralist delicately pours the resin into his master's mouth, then takes him by the arm and gently lowers him to the floor.

"Sweet dreams," he says.

***

Chapter 38

Cathedral Bells

The Meadow - London

With the pale fingers of the dawn light just starting to climb the dome of St. Paul's Cathedral, the cover of darkness is still sufficient for Nailah and her crew of *Treasure Hunters* to sneak in the shadows towards the quiet and hidden postal entrance. At this early hour, there is no one on the street and not a single curtain twitches.

From the other side of the cathedral, by the grand entrance of the monumental building, the first signs filter through that Kelly and Robyn—the *Destruction Crew*—have set to work. Frantic and panicked shouts can be heard, and a few wisps of dark smoke can be seen and smelled. The raid is on!

Stooping with their hoods up, and their robes brushing the cobbled street, the four members of the *Treasure Hunt* scamper down the alley.

The small door to the post entrance is unremarkable and unguarded. It is locked, of course. They get quickly to work. Hector slides a wedge through a crack in the door, beside the handle, while Cyril takes a step back and throws his great bodyweight into the door.

Crash!

The break-in works surprisingly easily. Cyril's impact jolts the door past its latch and throws it open, into the adjacent wall where it crashes loudly against the masonry. The raiders pause, cautious that the noise could alert the guards. But the silence lingers, they are clear.

The unoccupied Postal Room is full of empty post sacks. The day's *Shipping Forecast* will likely be delivered in the next hour or so before being distributed around the chambers of the cathedral. But, for now, there's no activity in this part of the building—just as they hoped.

Nailah cracks open the next door, peering through before swinging it open silently. One by one, the *Treasure Hunters* enter the main corridor of the cathedral building. There's no turning back now.

In front of them, a wide corridor opens out on either side. It is one of the main passageways in the body of the cathedral, designed, when it was on Earth, to allow choirs, priests, and other members of the church hierarchy to filter in and out during the big services. It is used here for the Distillery councilmen to do deals before entering the nave, and for them to chat and consume marbles. The floor of the corridor is littered with discarded old marble fragments and sheets of paper with various itineraries and agendas dropped by absent-minded councillors.

The raiders rush left down the corridor, knowing the route they must take. Their footsteps are light and silent, the only noise being the unavoidable jangling of the abseiling gear slung over Cyril's shoulder. They head straight for the east stairway. From here, they can hear noises high above. Panicked shouting and calls for water and reinforcements. The Distillery officers are evidently struggling to subdue the fires set by the *Destruction Crew* to the west.

Nailah points downwards into the darkness, where the east stairway descends below ground level. Peering over the stone bannister, she can see flaming torches illuminating the landing of each floor. But no one is on the steps.

The stairs between the floors are haunting in the darkness. Religious carvings within the bannister flicker their silhouettes against the walls, where tall paintings of former Distillery ministers loom over the raiding group as they descend the stairs.

Approaching the landing of the floor two stories below ground, Nailah stops them. "Ok," she whispers. "We're approaching the Purification floor. There could be security. Hector, I want you to lead the way with me. Have your distractions primed."

Hector steps up beside Nailah, releasing a Molotov Marble from his belt, holding it tight in his hand.

Two tall stone statues of angels guard the corridor of the Purification Chambers. Mean and angry-looking angels whose wings are outstretched, producing an archway over the entrance doors. In the hands of the statues are flaming torches, casting flickering shadows on the angels' faces, giving them lifelike qualities.

Together, Nailah and Hector push the brass handles on the heavy oak doors, unveiling the corridor. In darkness, the corridor stretches away. It is wide and cold. The floor, walls and ceiling are covered with glazed burgundy tiles that reflect the light they have poured in. The security checkpoint on this floor has recently been abandoned. A torch flickers inside, but a call to support the crews battling the fires in the West has pulled the normal occupants away from their posts—a stroke of luck.

The *Treasure Hunters* walk cautiously past the checkpoint and through the corridor, peering into the Purification Chambers that peel off on each side. They are acutely aware that at any time, they could be confronted by whoever, or whatever, inhabits these chambers.

Most of the chambers, however, are unoccupied, giving little information as to what the purpose of these rooms even is. Ominous furniture inside each room disturbs the imagination. The chambers, mottled by the light of the corridor, each contain a bed frame or a chair with straps for hands, necks, and feet. Besides these are bowls for resin collection and implements that look like they would be at home in a field surgeons operating kit. On the scorched floor of every room are ripped and bloodied rags, marble fragments, small piles of sand, and the unmistakable smell of paraffin.

Towards the end of the corridor, there is a vault that stands out from the rest. The door to the vault is closed, but the light inside pours out of a window, drawing their attention. Peering in, they can see that the chamber has been converted for a different activity.

Inside the vault, there is still a bed at the centre. But this bed is occupied. A young, handsome man is asleep. A deep sleep, sustained by a drip of sedatives that are connected by cannulas to his arms. All around the man, on display boards that butt up to the bed, are images. It is like a police investigation board. There are images of people, places, and things, all connected somehow.

An image of a man appears multiple times in the pictures—a middle-aged man with long blonde hair and bright blue eyes. There are also pictures from Earth of a grand old police station, a small country train station, a wealthy London street, and a tall, looming mountain. And on a table beside the sleeping figure is an assortment of strange objects. Telephone wires, modems, and all sorts of superfluous technology from Earth. No such technologies work in the Meadow.

"Have you seen his hands?" whispers Cyril.

Nailah looks closer. The man's hands have disintegrated. Piles of sand have formed on the floor beneath where his hands should be, and his arms conclude in rough, sandy stumps. It is as though the man is disintegrating while he sleeps.

"What the hell is this?" asks Edmond.

"It doesn't look right," says Hector.

"Come on," says Nailah, ushering them away. "Let's stick to our mission."

At the end of the corridor, a low cupboard door reveals the entrance to the sand chute. Beside it stand a couple of rusty spades.

Nailah pulls open the door. The wide chute is certainly wide enough for two people, but it descends into pitch black darkness.

"You sure about this?" Hector whispers. "It's a long way down!"

"The blueprints show the chute to be winding and shallow," says Cyril, tying the end of the rope around a heating pipe running along the floor. He yanks it roughly, and it doesn't budge. "Just hold these and take your time," he says, passing out descenders—small hand-held devices for abseiling down the rope.

"Who's going first?" asks Nailah, looking around the group—no one volunteers. "Ok... I'll call when I get to the bottom," she says, crouching down and clambering into the chute.

She looks back at the rest of her raiding party and winks. "See you in the sand pit!" she says, smiling, before pushing off and disappearing into the darkness.

The sounds of Nailah clattering through the chute echo back up. At one point, it sounds like she is gaining speed, whizzing, and zipping, as though she has lost control of her descent. Then it goes quiet.

The silence lingers for a moment before Nailah's voice climbs back up. "All good!" she calls. "It's a soft landing!"

One by one, the raiding party jump into the chute, trusting Nailah's judgement and Cyril's rope. Cyril himself is the last to descend. He appears in the room, now four stories under the cathedral beside the others, landing on his backside with a thump on the mound of sand on the floor.

The room is dark, save for a delicate light glimmering from Nailah's lantern—one of many essentials she carries in her backpack. Its orange glow casts her shadow against the ceiling.

"This sand," whispers Edmond, his fingers pinching the bridge of his nose, as Cyril clumsily gets to his feet and dusts himself off. "This isn't...?"

Nailah nods. "Kim-Joy warned me that extinctions may not be a new thing for the Distillery," she whispers. "There has been concern that this has been an unsaid Distillery punishment for years. So many souls have disappeared from the Meadow without a trace. The public extinction of Chloe a few days ago only confirmed our fears. There is no longer a depth where the Distillery won't stoop.

"*This* sand," she says, running her fingers through the odorous mound. "I guess it is the sand of extinction. The disintegrated remains of Meadow-bound bodies. The remains of people whose spark has left."

Edmond coughs, retching. "I think I've inhaled some!" His whisper breaks into voice.

"We've all inhaled extinction sand," says Nailah, shh-ing him. "It is the same sand that forms the glass in the marbles we suck. It is the same silt that is deposited in our rivers. We cannot avoid it. Ultimately, it is how our bodies are connected."

"Still," whispers Edmond, wiping his mouth on his sleeve. "I don't want fresh sand!"

Piled up in neat rows around the edges of the room are full sandbags.

"Why are they collecting the sand?" asks Cyril.

Nailah ponders for a moment. She doesn't have an answer.

"Maybe they are collecting it for the marble workhouses?" offers Hector, wandering over to the bags and inspecting one.

"Unlikely," says Cyril. "Resin is scarce, but sand isn't. And they need tonnes of it each day in the workhouses."

"*Stained Sand*," reads Hector from the side of one of the bags. "What does that mean?"

Nailah frowns. "I suspect it means that this sand has only one origin. It means the *Stained* are not being put to work in the workhouses at all. They are being exterminated!"

"How could they do that?!" exclaims Edmond, in shock. "That's inhuman!"

Nailah carefully replaces the sandbag on the pile, then puts her hand on Edmond's shoulder. "Come on," she says. "Let's do what we came here to do."

With her lantern held high, Nailah wanders over to the door, pushes it open and steps into the pitch-black marble vaults. Hector, Edmond, and Cyril follow, lighting their own lanterns as they go.

Aisle upon aisle of Criminal Record Stones are illuminated by their lanterns—the marbles that have been recorded over centuries of Distillery rule. The marbles used to condemn people for their crimes—even 'crimes' as unavoidable as producing dirty resin—and sentence them to time in the palaces or workhouses. Hundreds of thousands of marbles have been collected and recorded by the Distillery Police. They are gathered up in pouches, one pouch of marbles per crime recorded, ordered by date. But these aren't the only marbles that the raiding party are looking for.

"Keep your eyes peeled," whispers Nailah. "There could be patrols down here. Hector and Edmond, you're looking for marbles from yesterday's disturbance at the palace. Cyril, we're looking for the Intelligence Stones."

"In the bamboo poles, right?" asks Cyril, looking overwhelmed by the size of the vaults.

"That's right," says Nailah. "They should be easy to spot… I hope!"

"Ok, let's split up," she says. "We'll be quicker if we're in two groups. Just remember the protocol… Whistle if you find your *treasure*. Clap if there's trouble."

Nailah and Cyril take a right turn while Edmond and Hector head left.

Peering down the aisles, Nailah is looking for any sign of the bamboo stack. She assumes there will be hundreds of them. But all the aisles look the same—tray upon tray of marble pouches and nothing else. Then, as they approach the right edge of the vast vault, she hears a clearly audible clap. Hector and Edmond have immediately run into trouble.

Nailah and Cyril quickly extinguish their lanterns and drop to the floor, staying silent, waiting to hear what is happening.

In the pitch-black silence, it is frightening. They are deep in the heart of the Distillery's secrets and if any of them are caught here, there's no defence that will stand up.

From the opposite side of the vault, they hear the main doors open and the sound of Distillery officers pacing in. Despite the vastness of the vaults, the relative silence allows the voices of the officers to drift all the way to them.

"The vaults are secure," announces an officer. "These fucking rebels. So long as they don't get down here, our jobs should be safe."

"I fucking hope so!" another officer responds, sounding worried. "Do you think they know the Ferrymen were mobilising from here?"

The doors slam closed behind them, before the officer responds, the noise echoing harshly through the vaults. With it, a gust of air filters up through the aisles setting off an unmistakeable cacophony of clinking and clonking from the ceiling. The sound of bamboo windchimes clattering about their heads.

'*Of course*,' Nailah looks up. She re-lights her lantern and holds it high above her head. There, dangling gracefully, are hundreds of bamboo poles containing the Distillery Intelligence Stones.

Nailah reaches up, grasping the nearest pole. The attachment appears to be elasticated, making it easy to pull the pole down to eye-level where Nailah can read along its shaft '*Operation Stackpole*'.

"Eilish said that we should be looking for *Operation Jack and Jill*—they're the intelligence from Well Wishers," whispers Nailah. She releases the pole in her hand, allowing it to shoot back towards the ceiling and rattles amongst the others.

High above them, many storeys above the ground, in the darkness over London, they can just about hear the clanging of the cathedral bell.

"What time is it?" Nailah asks.

"Dunno," says Cyril. "We can't have been here long… no more than a half hour."

Cyril, being much taller than Nailah, doesn't need to reach far to check the labelling on the bamboo poles. He grabs a handful and yanks them down. There are a few more *Operation Stackpole,* but also *Operation Bluebottle* and *Operation Asphodel Flower.* He releases the bundle and reaches up for more. And as he does so, high above, the cathedral bells clang once more. A discordant and chaotic symphony.

The penny drops as Cyril releases a second handful of poles. There is a failsafe in the Intelligence Vaults. Pulling and releasing the bamboo poles are causing the bells of St. Paul's Cathedral to ring.

"Cyril! Stop!" shouts Nailah, sharply.

"Who's ringing the bells?" calls Hector, careening round the corner with Edmond, their arms laden with pouches of stolen marbles.

"Us!" says Nailah, her voice quaking. "We found the bamboo… but I think the Distillery now know we're here."

She points up to the dangling bamboo poles above them. "They're connected to the bell-ringer's ropes."

"How long do you think we have?" asks Edmonds.

"Minutes… maybe?" says Nailah.

"Then, quick, get on my shoulders," Cyril barks at Edmond. "Let's make this worthwhile."

He hoists Edmond and his lantern high into the air, then clatters him through the bamboo, starting the haunting wooden chiming once again. *"Operation Jack and Jill...* that's what we're looking for," he barks.

"They're here!" calls Edmond. "Dozens of them!"

"Grab what you can," shouts Nailah, urgently.

As Edmond drops to the floor with a bundle of poles grasped to his torso, Cyril whips out a pocketknife and slices the ropes, setting off another chaotic clanging of the bells above.

"Let's get out of here!" shouts Nailah, just as the doors at the opposite end of the marble vaults crash open.

"We know you're in here!" shouts a distant Distillery officer. A glow from his flaming torch visible over the aisles of marbles.

"We'll distract them," says Hector, pushing Nailah towards the sand room. "You and Cyril need to get away."

"We can all escape," says Nailah.

"No," urges Edmond. "We knew when we joined this raid that this was our role." He pulls from his belt a Molotov marble. Lighting one end, he hurls it over the marble shelves beside them. There is a smash and a hiss before a bright flame ignites on the floor where it landed.

Hector starts to climb the shelf of marbles. "Get out now," he barks, rocking the shelf dangerously above them.

As Nailah and Cyril tumble into the sand room, they hear a tremendous crash as Hector manages to topple the entire aisle of shelving. Thousands of marbles shatter instantly, hissing loudly and spewing great clouds of colour into the growing flames beyond them. Not only does Hector's aisle topple, but a domino effect ripples through the vault. Aisle upon aisle of marbles rock and fall. Thousands of Criminal Record Stones are being destroyed in minutes, engulfing the marble vaults in mist and flame.

Nailah slams the door shut. "Don't breathe in," she shouts to Cyril, terrified of being consumed by the mist herself.

Cyril pulls out two ascending devices and attaches them quickly to the rope that still dangles from the chute above.

"We have to be quick!" He ties the heavy bamboo poles around his waist and starts to ascend.

Alone in the sand room Nailah listens for a moment, hearing the desperate shouts echoing from within the vaults. She knows Hector and Edmond have little chance of surviving in the mist and fire. Nonetheless, she cannot condemn them herself. Nor accept their fate. She leaves two ascenders attached to the rope below hers, just in case they make it to the sand room. Then she ascends the dark chute as quickly as she can.

***

Chapter 39

The Last Café

Earth - Mynydd Aaru

amp, dull, and desperately poor'. That is how the most recent of a long series of 1-star reviews describes the lodgings above the Mountain View Café at *Mynydd Aaru*. It had been the last thing Marty read on his phone before he disassembled and disposed of it piece by piece in public bins all around Shrewsbury. Standard practice for a criminal trying to leave no trail. He'd since ridden Elijah's Kawasaki down an abandoned country lane, overgrown with nettles, and hidden it inside a crumbling old shepherd's hut. It wouldn't be impossible for someone to find it, but it would certainly delay them.

Standing alone in his private bedroom, in the failing evening light that falls behind the looming shadow of *Mynydd Aaru*, Marty concurs with the dire reviews. Black mould climbs up the walls, and the single bedside lamp that still has a bulb flickers as though it is about to die. The mattress on his bed is lumpy and dips in the middle where slats are broken or missing. But Marty doesn't care.

He catches a glimpse of his profile, reflected in the window. His long grey hair has been shaved off completely. A cheap, no-frills, no-booking-required barber had given him the closest wet shave imaginable, completely altering his appearance. That, alongside the worry that has shrivelled his aura these last few years, makes him almost unrecognisable to anyone who knew him back in the day, and indeed a contrast to any 'Wanted' images that will soon be circulating for him. He is a gaunt shadow of that man.

A pile of smart new mountaineering gear lies on the bed. He purchased them on his way here. They are almost as imposing to Marty as the mountain outside. They claim to withstand negative temperatures up to -19 degrees Celsius, storm-force winds, torrential rain, and extreme solar radiation. Marty doesn't do *torrential* anything. He doesn't do *extreme* anything. *Slack, loose, relaxed.* Those are the words that used to describe him and his clothing. Not anymore, it seems. His world is different now. He is alone and fighting. Fighting to survive.

He hadn't mentioned the hooded lady when he arrived at the café and booked his stay. Best not to draw any unnecessary attention until he knows the lie of the land. Anyhow, lodging comes with an optional evening meal with the café owner. Not something he'd usually go for, but today he is hungry. Hungry for food and hungry for information about *her*. If she were to come up in conversation, he would certainly be ready to talk.

The bedside lamp gives up, plunging the room into an eerie indigo from the fading light outside. Marty stares up at *Mynydd Aaru*. One doesn't have to be a mountaineer to feel its magnitude or sense its danger.

The tallest mountain in Wales, *Mynydd Aaru,* claims the lives of dozens of people every year. Neither mountain thrill-seeker nor naïve tourist can feel safe on its slopes. Marty knows of the mountain from the stories. There are semi-frequent news cycles of tragedy and the occasional TV drama that recreates the disasters on its face.

Staring at the great mountain, Marty inspects its silhouette cutting into the sky. He knows the face that is hidden in its shadow. It is notorious. The *Asphodel Face.* A site of pilgrimage amidst the country's current mental health crisis. A crisis hitting the rich and poor, young, and old. A crisis that has brought countless souls to this Mountain in recent years, to *that* face, to take their own lives. The *Asphodel Fall* now rivals Beechey Head for lives lost each year.

Of its own volition, the bedside lamp flickers back on, illuminating the walls of Marty's room again. He had looked past the graffiti all over them when he came in. All hostels he's ever stayed at are covered in such mindless daubing. But now he notices them. He notices them because they are different.

There's no '*Anton 4 Shaznay 4 Eva*', or anything like that. The graffiti messages all over these walls say '*goodbye*', '*sorry*', and '*remember me*'.

'*Parting words?*' wonders Marty.

The realisation makes the room feel cold and even less welcome. It even makes the 1-star reviews seem unreasonably generous. He senses the agony of the people who had stayed here before him. He had never felt an affinity to people sinking to such depths before. But now he feels an acute camaraderie with anyone who feels they have nothing left to lose.

There is a knock at the door.

"Hello?" says Marty, his voice wavering.

"Mr Jamieson," says the voice. "I'm cracking open a bottle of red, if you want to join me?"

"Oh great," says Marty. "Yes. I'll be down soon."

*

"So, you're from the city?" asks the café owner, filling another deep glass of crimson wine an hour or so later.

"How'd you guess?" smiles Marty, sniffing his glass before swilling it, watching the residue cling to the walls of the vessel.

"I've never seen anyone faff with their wine so much before taking a sip! Just drink it, man!" says the café owner, his glass held to his lips.

Marty grins. "The little details," he says.

"So, which city is it? London?"

"Brighton," lies Marty, knowing it does him no harm to disguise the truth.

"All one and the same to me," says the owner. "I used to live in the city myself, years ago. I don't miss it! Competition and corruption, that's all I found."

"Mmm," Marty frowns.

"I heard something on the radio this morning. They've got an ex-policeman on the run for helping blow up a house that killed two people. That's why I stay away from the city. You don't know anyone and can't trust anyone. Not like out here. You've got to be able to trust people out here. We rely on each other. That's how it should be." He looks at Marty, who sips his wine. "So, what brings you here?"

"Escaping the competition and corruption," he winks. "You're lucky. You've found a way out. Most of us in the cities are trapped."

"No, nobody is *really* trapped. You just need a leap of faith."

"Yes... I've heard that about this mountain."

"That's not what I meant! But sadly, you're right. It is the leap that most people come here for these days." The café owner frowns. "It never used to be like this. Ten years ago, we had not had anyone perish on the mountain deliberately. Plenty of accidents. But what a state we're in now, eh?"

"I've seen the graffiti on the walls in my room," says Marty.

The café owner drops his gaze. "Mmm..." he says, frowning. "Sorry about that. I would remove them. But it seems... insensitive. It's not mindless graffiti. It's desperate. The last mark of many of those poor souls."

"Can you tell when they stay here that that is what they're going to do?"

The café owner inspects Marty quizzically.

"That's not my plan... I promise," adds Marty quickly.

The owner doesn't look convinced. "I used to invite mental health workers here. Nurses, therapists... all sorts. They used to have their own table, over there," he gestures towards the window. "They used to talk to anyone and everyone. They were listening ears and helping hands. But they don't exist anymore... cuts! Government cuts! It's as if Westminster thinks people never find themselves needing help... what a fucking 'society' we live in. Careless and broken!"

"I do my best, though," the owner continues. "If I see someone going out there unprepared, I give them tips, try and help them out. I have loads of spare gear as well... free to anyone. But... well often, these guys, their mind is made up. As though another force is pulling them up the mountain. As though they've already left this world and their body is trying to catch up."

There is a moment of silence between the two men as Marty digests the café owners' words.

"So that's not why you're here then?"

"No," says Marty. "No… not exactly."

"Not exactly?"

"I have a friend… a lady…" The café owner raises his eyebrows. "Not like that," frowns Marty, the lie forming rapidly in his mind. "She's just a friend. Like a… like a step-sister, I guess. I'm worried that she has been coming here because she plans to take the leap…"

"What's her name?"

"Sorry, she wouldn't want me to say," says Marty, a convenient lie.

"Well, what does she look like?"

"She's an introvert… she conceals herself as best she can at all times, keeps herself to herself. She never wants to draw attention to herself and never gives anything away. But she has this injury… a chronic problem that gives her a distinctive limp…"

The café owner leans in, placing his glass down on the table. "I know who you're talking about," he declares. "She's the most unusual lodger I've ever had."

"Has she been here recently?" asks Marty, eagerly.

"Oh, I thought you would have known?" says the owner.

"Go on…"

"She was here last night. Same room as you're in tonight… She saw those two friends of hers again."

"Friends?"

"The couple… the lady who's… well, much older than her man."

"Is she still here?" asks Marty, eagerly.

"Oh no. It's always the same these days. She only stays one night. Then it can be weeks, months, or even years before we see her again. Same pattern every time."

"Do you know where she goes?" asks Marty.

The owner turns to the window, where the darkness has set in outside, but they both know the mountain still looms over them. "Up there," he says to Marty. "You know, the first time she went up onto the face, I thought I'd never see her again… but she always comes back."

"So, you're not worried about her?"

"Well," says the owner, "after what you've said… I don't know. But she's been doing this for years. I call her the *Lady of the Mountain*."

Marty grins. That beats his 'hooded lady' shorthand. "*Lady of the Mountain*," he muses. "So, you don't think she'll be back for a while?" asks Marty.

"Probably not… though sometimes she is back in a few days. I can pass her a message if you want?"

"No!" says Marty, a little too quickly, making the café owner squint suspiciously. "No, I'll wait here for her," he corrects himself. "At least a few days."

"Well, I saw you have all the gear… You don't fancy climbing *Mynydd Aaru* while you're waiting?"

"Yeah, right," chuckles Marty, "All the gear and no idea!" He enjoys completing the phrase that he'd heard so many times in a policing context.

"Well, the weather is meant to be nicer tomorrow."

"No, I'm ok," says Marty. "Anyhow, I've got another friend who's meant to be coming over here too. To help me find her. I won't be venturing out until he gets here."

"In that case, you'll be up for another drink then?" smiles the café owner, pouring a very generous top-up into Marty's glass.

"Thanks!" says Marty, swigging without swilling.

***

Chapter 40

Special Delivery

The Meadow - London

Elijah Fredrickson—the young man delivering the Shipping Forecast to the Callaghan residence this morning—is full of contradiction. His youthful face is bright and smiley, his air breezy and cheerful, and he holds himself with an entertainer's confidence. But look closely and you can see his fingernails are nervously short, bitten beyond the threshold of pain, and his eyes, behind the smile, are deep and lost, wells of long forgotten agony.

"Morning, Ferrymen," Elijah chirrups, throwing out an arm theatrically and bowing low. "Can I interest you in a scroll of today's finest journalism?"

One of the Ferryman guarding the Callaghan house grunts, "I'll have one."

Elijah, mid-bow, tilts his head up and cups his ear expectantly. "Do I hear a 'please'?" he teases with a wink.

"No, you don't. And you won't get one, you clown."

Elijah responds with a strained smile and passes a copy of the Forecast to the man. He didn't expect a warm welcome on this street anyway. There was never a *'good morning'* or a *'how are you?'* from anyone who lived here. Most of the time, he would be leaving today's paper on top of yesterday's, such was the wasteful life of the rich who inhabit the Paddock. Anyway, it isn't long now before he can have a rest. His shift started hours ago, and he is down to his last fifty papers.

He pushes the trolley up to the dark porch of the grand Callaghan House, where the blinds are lowered, and, for the first time that he can remember, the front door creaks open.

Appearing in the doorway, in her dressing gown, with a towel tied around her head, is Governess Callaghan.

"Governess Callaghan! What an honour. An honour beyond words. A privilege. A blessing from the universe. Good morning, Your Excellency," Elijah declares, back in character, bowing flamboyantly.

His bombastic flair could easily have crash-landed as disrespectful sarcasm, but Eilish chuckles, her face prickling scarlet. "Good morning!" she exclaims back, feeling unexpectedly uplifted. "And good morning to you, Ferrymen! Did you have a good night?"

The Ferrymen stand up. "Fine, your excellency."

"Good… So, young man," Eilish addresses Elijah. "I don't think we've met…"

She holds out a hand, and Elijah respectfully shakes it, lowering his gaze.

"We have not, Your Excellency."

"Have you been working this street for long?"

He looks up at her before answering, catching her eye. "A few years, miss," he smiles, but curiously notices a flicker of recognition.

Indeed, as Elijah's marble-like eyes meet hers for the first time, Eilish is struck by a barrage of images, almost memories, which crash through her mind. Sparks bouncing off tarmac. Swirling snow. A noisy flash of green. She thought the *jamai vu* had stopped. Clearly not.

Eilish composes herself and tries to settle into the present moment naturally again. "A few years… wow!" she says, a little too enthusiastically. "That's longer than many people have been in the Meadow. I think that deserves a reward!"

"A reward?" Elijah chuckles flirtatiously. "Your presence is reward enough."

But now it's Eilish's turn to catch Elijah by surprise.

"Why don't you come inside with me?" she says. "Have a rest and share a marble? I could do with some company… I'm a bit *housebound*, you see." She flicks her eyes over at the Ferrymen. "If that's ok with you, gents?" she hollers, accusingly, clipping the end of her sentence.

The most senior Ferryman shrugs. "Can't do any harm," he says.

"What do you say, then?" Eilish looks at Elijah.

"How could I say 'no'?" he smiles. "If you're sure?"

"Absolutely. Come on in. Let's keep your trolley in the porch... so it doesn't get wet."

Eilish holds open the door and ushers Elijah, flummoxed by this unexpected invitation, into the porch. She glances inside his trolley. '*There's plenty of room in there,*' she confirms to herself.

"What would you like then?" she asks, leading Elijah into the kitchen and throwing opening a chest of marbles taken from Angus' office.

Elijah's eyes widen. He has never seen so many different and exquisite marbles. He barely manages to live on one solitary marble a week at the moment. That's all he can get access to. He doesn't know what to say when confronted with such abundance.

"Any of them?" he asks, bewildered, tucking a strand of his long hair behind his ear, nervously.

"Yes, any," she confirms. "But I do recommend these." She points to a couple of *Sailor's Mist* that she had saved from Kim-Joy. It would do her good if the lad had a clear mind for what she was going to ask him to do.

"Yes, please," he says, accepting the light blue marble in his palm and carefully dropping it into his mouth.

Eilish smiles as she too takes a *Sailor's Mist.*

After a brief, awkward silence, Elijah speaks up, but with none of the showmanship he displayed on the street. "I'm sorry for your loss," he says.

"My loss?"

"Miss Chloe Callaghan," he says, handing her today's paper. On it is Chloe's face, plastered to the front page, beside the headline '*DISGRACE AT THE TOP: Questions Raised About Friendship with Governess Callaghan*'.

"Don't believe all you read about her," pleads Eilish.

"No, I don't. I don't believe anything from the *Forecast.* Worst journalism in the Meadow!"

"You mean that?" asks Eilish. "Then you are a good judge of character."

"Why, thank you," Elijah grins.

"Can you keep a secret?"

Elijah looks at Eilish suspiciously. "Yes…?"

"I am locked here in my house," she begins, holding unwavering eye contact with Elijah. "And I need a way out."

Elijah doesn't know what to say or where to look. This isn't the moment to respond comically.

"You cannot say a word about this," she continues.

"I won't."

"But *you* can help me."

"I can?"

"Your trolley," she begins. "It is big enough for me to fit inside, wouldn't you say?"

Elijah looks at her, perplexed.

"I need a way out without being seen by those thugs outside," she says. "Do you think I could get inside your paper trolley and be wheeled out past them?"

He chuckles, then realises she's serious.

"I just need you to take me a few streets… that's all." Eilish slides the chest of marbles towards him. "These are all yours if you help me," she says. "There are enough marbles there for you and your family for years. You won't need to sell the *Forecast* anymore."

Now Elijah really can't talk.

"I'm telling the truth," says Eilish. "I promise. And you can hold me to it with that marble in your mouth. It holds this moment in its memory. Keep it as your insurance."

Elijah is dumbstruck.

"Two streets, that's all," Eilish repeats.

"For *all* these marbles?"

"They're all yours," says Eilish, carefully closing the case. "Do we have a deal?" Eilish holds out her hand.

Elijah reaches forward and seals the deal. His palm is sweaty from nerves, making Eilish grin.

"You'll be fine," she says to him. "Trust me."

Eilish unwraps her hair from the towel around her head. It is dry. It was never wet. And under her dressing gown, she already wears a complete outfit of plain clothes: a rough knitted jumper, some loose jeans, and a pair of tatty trainers. And tucked into her belt, not visible to Elijah, a single canister of Thermocline. As always, just in case. A very un-governess look.

At the front door, Eilish grabs hold of a pre-packed rucksack. Some clothes, a bag of marbles for herself, and a whole bundle of blueprints for Distillery-run offices and buildings are stuffed into it. If she is going to commit treason, she might as well do it properly.

Carefully opening the door into the porch, the blinds still concealing it to the outside, Eilish crouches and slides herself gingerly into the trolley.

"Are you comfortable, your excellency?" asks Elijah, grinning at the ridiculousness of the situation.

"Yes, comfortable enough," says Eilish, resting on the remaining copies of the *Forecast*.

Elijah slides the case of marbles into the trolley beside Eilish and fastens the cover, concealing everything inside.

"Just two streets then," he says, breathing in.

"Perfect. Thank you."

Eilish holds her breath as they rattle slowly down the driveway. She hears the porch door drop onto its latch and recognises the bumps of the paving stones along the drive.

"A marble with the governess, eh?" she hears a Ferryman say. "That'll be one to tell the folks back home, won't it?"

"It was more than a marble," smirks Elijah, enjoying his modicum of power over the Ferrymen.

There is a slap on top of the trolley, and it stops. Eilish freezes. "You've still got to do Poppyfield Avenue, haven't you?"

"I have, indeed," says Elijah, confidently.

"There'll be a couple of my colleagues working there," says the Ferryman. "Tell them to hurry up! Tell 'em Mick has been waiting an hour now, and he's not happy."

"You want me to give him a kick up the backside too?" chuckles Elijah, then immediately realises he's overstepped.

"Don't be cheeky now," hisses the Ferryman.

"No, sorry. You're right," mutters Elijah, overly apologetically.

The trolley starts to trundle forward again, and Eilish breathes once more.

She can't gauge distance from her hiding place. But eventually, they stop again, and Eilish hears the young man unfastening the fabric of the trolley cover.

"Is this ok, miss?" he whispers.

They have stopped in a little alley, just off the South Bank of the Lethe. Over on the other side, Eilish can see St. Paul's Cathedral towering high into the sky. The day is just about dawning, and the early sunlight silhouettes the city to the east.

Eilish stretches her back as she clambers out of the trolley. "Thank you," she says, beaming at the lad. "Thank you so much... Have you got a name?"

"Elijah Fredrickson."

"Well, thank you, Elijah. You have saved me today," she smiles.

Elijah drops the *Sailor's Mist* into his palm. "Would it help you if I erased this memory?" he asks.

"Of course," says Eilish. "But that is your insurance. You don't have to."

Ignoring Eilish's warning, Elijah throws the marble down onto the street, smashing it. A blue mist fizzes and dissipates.

"Thank you," says Eilish, looking at the young man with the most profound appreciation.

Elijah grins. "I think I'm going to finish my shift here today," he says, pulling out the case of marbles and pushing the trolley into the shadows of the alleyway.

"A good idea," says Eilish. "Where are you going?"

"North... Well, north of the river, at least."

"Me too," says Eilish. "Fancy some company?"

Elijah nods, a grin stretching like a Cheshire Cat across his face.

There is a gentle breeze as Eilish and Elijah cross Southwark Bridge together. Eilish feels an exhilaration trickling through her body. She is heading to the *Tide and Time Tavern*. She is heading back to the formidable, but magnificent, Nailah, to start a new life right here, right now.

Up ahead of them, the bells of St. Paul's Cathedral ring out.

"The bells are early!" says Elijah.

"What do you mean?"

"They shouldn't be ringing for another half hour, at least. They're my guide every morning, you see, and I'm usually much further on my round when they ring like this."

A moment later, the bells clang again, discordantly. Eilish looks at Elijah, puzzled.

"Now, I've never heard that," he says.

Somewhere behind them, south of the river, they hear whistles and shouts.

"There's smoke coming from the cathedral!" exclaims Elijah.

Eilish looks forward. He is right. Whisps of smoke are rising from the roof of the cathedral.

Then the bells clang loudly again.

"What's going on?" asks Elijah.

Eilish thinks she knows. Nailah's raid must be happening right now!

Stepping off the bridge, Eilish turns back and can make out the distant figures of Distillery officers and Ferrymen hurtling along the South bank. They are shouting and blowing their whistles frantically. They must know something is wrong at St. Paul's.

'Do they know about me, already?' wonders Eilish. *'Surely not!'*

"The cathedral!" a Distillery officer shouts from Southwark Bridge. "Get to the cathedral!" he instructs his colleagues, who run alongside him.

'So, there is a raid. And the Distillery are mobilising to stop it!'

"I've got to get going," says Eilish. "You don't happen to know shortcuts to Virgil College, do you?" she asks Elijah. "I need to get there quick!"

"Oh yes, that's easy," he smiles. "Follow me!"

Elijah crosses the street and sneaks into a barely visible alley.

Eilish follows, but squirms as she sees the path is crawling with rats and marble addicts.

"Are you ok with this?" asks Elijah, realising where he has just led the governess of the Distillery.

"Yes," she says, looking away from the rats. "This is perfect."

***

Chapter 41

Delusional Spirits

Earth - Mynydd Aaru

Marty stumbles drunkenly down the landing in the dark. The café owner certainly knew how to drink, probably how he flitted away long winter months in the mountains, but Marty hadn't meant to drink so much.

Marty pushes open the door. His room is just how he left it. A neat pile of clothes on the bed and the windows wide open, letting the warm evening air clear out the cobwebs and dry the damp from the walls.

It is well past midnight, and outside it is dead calm. Not a creature stirs.

Marty collapses onto his bed, his legs tired and weary. He rubs his face, trying to force a keener alertness to his exhausted mind. But his head is throbbing from alcohol and dehydration, and his forehead is sticky with perspiration.

'*So, she has been here,*' he thinks to himself. '*Only yesterday. I am so close.*'

Marty feels a breath of air dance through the room. He looks up towards the window, considering closing it, when a strange feeling engulfs him. As though with the wind, someone has stepped into his room beside him.

Marty sits up, blinking, trying to focus on the darkness. The room is spinning.

"Hello?" he says, swaying. "Who's there?"

The room is silent and still.

Marty's eyes adjust to the light, and he peers into the darkest corner of the room. It is in that corner that he has the strongest feeling that someone is watching him.

"Who is it?" says Marty, his voice wobbling. "Is there somebody there?"

"*Marty*," says a voice, though Marty is not sure he hears it with his ears. "*Have you been drinking?*"

Marty rubs his eyes desperately.

"Who is it?" he says again, urgently. "Show yourself."

"*It is me, Marty… I said I would come.*"

Marty stops.

"It's *you*?"

"*Yes… The friend you need to get you out of your little pickle…*"

Marty feels his jaw clench. A 'pickle'?! How fucking glib.

"Step into the light, you coward!"

"*No.*"

"No?!" Marty blurts. "I'll fucking make you!"

He stumbles clumsily towards the dark corner, swiping his drunken arms all around, hoping to grasp the man he can't see.

There's no one there.

"Where the fuck are you?"

"*I'm here,*" says the voice, now somewhere behind him.

Marty swivels. Still no one.

"Where?!"

"*It doesn't matter.*"

"It matters to me!" Marty throws his head around, sure he'll catch a glimpse of his intruder somewhere.

"*That's not my concern… Right now, I need you to listen very carefully…*"

"Not until to show yourself."

"*You're in no position to tell* me *what to do, Marty,*" says the voice, rising angrily.

Marty feels dizzy. He leans against the wall.

"Look mate. You might think you can keep playing me. But I've lost fucking *everything*—and that's thanks to you! I don't have anything else to lose. So actually, I *am* in a position to tell *you* what to do!"

"*You're an idiot, Marty… Without my help, you have lost everything… lost it all forever…*" Marty's head twitches angrily. His fists and jaw clench. "*But do as I say, and I can help you find it all again, and more.*"

"Find what? My job? My life?" says Marty, sarcastically.

"Your son."

"I haven't lost my son," says Marty, his voice wavering.

"Yes, you have. And without me, you will lose him forever," says the voice, an air of threat in his tone. *"But I can also bring him back to you."*

"What do you mean?"

"I can raise him from his coma."

"That's impossible."

"Not for me."

"I don't believe you."

"Fine. Then Elijah dies."

Marty drops to the floor. He hasn't heard another soul utter his son's name in years.

"What do you need me to do?" he asks, resigned, as a breeze whispers through the open window, drawing his gaze to the looming mountain hidden in the darkness outside.

"She's up there, Marty. If you can find her and bring her to me, then I will bring your son back to you."

"That's it?"

"That's it."

"Why is this happening to me?" Marty asks desperately.

"That's something to ask her."

***

Chapter 42

Chasing Horsemen

The Meadow - London

B y the time Eilish and Elijah emerge from the dingy alleys, the acrid smoke from St. Paul's fills the air. The chaotic clanging of the cathedral bells has mobilised every Distillery officer within ten miles. Their whistles and shouts have, in turn, woken most residents north of the Lethe. And, despite the curfews and the early hour, there are groups of people in every street, chatting earnestly, looking at the billowing clouds of smoke that climb high into the bright morning sky. Some people even run past, carrying buckets of water, fearing a repeat of 1666—the year that they entered the Meadow.

Eilish and Elijah cling to the shadows, jogging down the street, weaving behind the scattered congregations of people, avoiding any Distillery officers they see.

In a doorway, a couple of shadowy figures are huddled. They wear long hooded cloaks, pulled up over their heads, like they don't want to be seen. Eilish and Elijah tuck in beside them, keeping their heads down also.

"Virgil is the next street," they hear the hooded figure whisper.

"*Nailah!*" exclaims Eilish. She can't help herself.

The two figures turn.

"Eilish?!" stutters Nailah, surprised. "But, but… you're supposed to be in your home… You're supposed to be where you are *safe!*"

"I don't care about being 'safe' anymore," starts Eilish. "You were right when we first met. Silent suffering and sacrifice are different things."

Nailah peers through her hood at Eilish, and a flicker of admiration twitches across her lips. She squashes it quickly.

"Yes, and *recklessness* is a different thing altogether," she frowns.

Eilish clenches her jaw.

"This isn't recklessness. I'm here to join you," she says. "Have you done the raid?"

The burly frame of Cyril Spate turns beside Nailah. Smiling infectiously, he opens a fold in his cloak, showing Eilish the bundle of marble-filled bamboo poles. The poles labelled *Jack and Jill*.

"Great!" says Eilish, punching her fist in celebration. "How did it go?"

"As well as could be expected," says Nailah, dropping her gaze mournfully. "And we're not home and dry. Not yet."

"Did *you* set the fire at St. Paul's?" Elijah butts in, staring up at the smoke-filled sky.

"And who might you be?" asks Nailah, cautiously.

"My apologies," says Eilish, quickly. "This is Elijah. He delivers for the *Forecast*—or *did*. He helped me escape."

Nailah smiles at the young man. "Yes," she says. "We set the fires. A necessary act of destruction to cover a much more important task."

"Did you find *my* marbles?" asks Eilish earnestly.

"Yes, they're destroyed," Nailah confirms, smiling warmly at Eilish. "You're in the clear."

Eilish feels a weight of worry lifting from her shoulders. Now she is just a *missing* governess. Not a *wanted* one.

"So, lad... You helped smuggle out our friend Eilish, here?" asks Cyril.

Elijah sniggers. "If chucking a governess in a paper trolley counts, then yeah... sure!"

Cyril laughs. "Good man." He holds out his hand. "Name's Cyril Spate. Trawlerman by trade. Spent half my life at sea. Where is it you call home? You got family here?"

Elijah's playful smile drops to a grimace. "No home, nor family, I'm afraid... I just live... well, anywhere I can."

"Oh gosh, I'm sorry," says Eilish, guiltily. "I just assumed..."

"It's no bother," says the young man. "Plenty of us live from marble to marble on the streets these days."

"Have you heard of the *Tide and Time Tavern*?" asks Cyril.

"Of course," says Elijah. "Why?"

"*The Tide and Time* is a beacon of hope in this dire city," says Cyril. "Especially for homeless lads like you. Kim-Joy, who runs the place, is always taking in newcomers. Helping them find their feet and get out of the city." An infectious smile forms across Cyril's face, beaming at Elijah as though he were already family. "I can introduce you, if you like? I know Kim-Joy would love to have your company."

"That sounds grand," says Elijah.

"And besides, the street is no home for a governess-smuggler," Cyril winks with a grin.

Elijah beams.

"As heart-warming as this little invitation is," starts Nailah, frowning, "I feel obliged to point out, we're cowering in a doorway, surrounded by Distillery officers, with condemning ash on our clothes and a smuggled governess in our midst. We need to get moving. Virgil College is around the corner—that's our only way to the *Tide and Time*."

Keeping tight to the shadows under the canopy of conifers that line the street, Nailah leads them away, her eyes peeled for signs of trouble.

When she reaches the corner, she stops and recoils. Turning to the others, she puts her finger to her lips and beckons them to peer into the next street.

Virgil College stands before them, majestic as always. Its entrance cut out from the conifers, with its great oak doors a symbol of its standing in the Meadow. But it doesn't look like the last time Eilish visited. Today, ranks of Distillery officers surround the building, forming a barrier in front of the college, blocking the entrance.

"Why are *they* here?" asks Eilish.

Nailah shrugs.

"Look," says Cyril, pointing to four horses waiting in the shadows.

"Are they…" starts Elijah, but before he can finish, the doors to Virgil College open and their attention is drawn.

A senior Distillery officer steps out confidently, snapping his heels to attention. "About face!" he shouts to the ranks in front of him.

The ranks turn away from the college entrance and drop to one knee, lowering their eyes so that they are unable to see what is going on around them. In doing so, they create a discrete path from the college steps to the horses in the shadows.

"Eyes shut!" shouts the officer, dropping to one knee himself and closing his eyes. The ranks beyond him obediently do as commanded.

In the privacy of the obedient ranks, a procession emerges from the entrance of Virgil College. Two pairs of hooded, cloaked figures and a prisoner. A diminutive prisoner, hands bound, with a hessian bag draped over their head. They descend the steps slowly and carefully, keeping their faces covered and the prisoner moving forward, ignoring the ranks of kneeling officers.

As the procession proceeds, Nailah can glimpse the prisoner more clearly.

"Kim-Joy!" she whispers.

"Let me at 'em!" says Cyril, rolling up his sleeves, dauntless in the face of peril.

"No! There's too many," whispers Nailah, blocking Cyril from doing anything rash.

Another figure emerges in the doorway of Virgil College—the Mineralist. There is a cruel and satisfied grin stretching across his sallow face, enjoying the privilege of watching the prisoner's escort while the ranks of Distillery officers avert their eyes.

The procession stops just short of the horses. One of the hooded figures steps into the shadow and begins unfastening the animals. The remaining figures converge around Kim-Joy. One pulls out a little black box, which they offer to another. A syringe is removed from the box and stabbed into Kim-Joy's thigh. She is given no warning.

Kim-Joy falls limp, caught from hitting the ground by two of the hooded figures.

"Have they…?" Eilish stutters, her voice fragile and scared.

"No," says Cyril. "That looks like a sedative. Those kinds of medicines from Earth are rare."

"Who are they?" asks Elijah.

It's a reasonable guess. The figures are evidently in the employ of the Distillery, but do not clearly identify themselves as Distillery officers.

"I don't think so," says Eilish. "If they were, I would have known of this kind of operation. The Ferrymen work for my brother, and I've never seen or heard of them taking prisoners like this."

"Then who are they?!" asks Cyril.

Stepping out of the shadows, the figures lead the horses into the light. A white stallion, a rusty reddish colt, a jet-black mare and finally a pale grey draft horse.

"The four *Horses of the Apocalypse!*" exclaims Elijah, his whisper breaking out into voice and wavering nervously.

"The horsemen are not real," says Cyril. "Are they?" He sounds uncertain.

"I hoped not," says Nailah.

They stare as the four horsemen lay Kim-Joy's unconscious body over the back of the jet-black mare before mounting the horses themselves. There is barely a moment to comprehend what is happening before the horsemen with their prisoner kick the flanks of their animals and set off at a canter, away and out of sight into the coniferous streets of the city.

"We need to follow them!" says Cyril, not worrying about staying quiet now.

"On foot?!" says Nailah. "No chance!"

"We have to try!"

"No," says Nailah, grasping Cyril's shoulder. "We mustn't be reckless. Now is the time for clear heads. Someone has betrayed us. Someone who has told the secrets of the *Tide and Time Tavern*. Secrets that have held for over a decade."

She turns to Eilish, her warmth gone. Now there is a sharp accusation in her eyes.

"What?!" says Eilish. "You think I've said something?!"

"Well, have you?" asks Nailah, harshly.

"Of course not!"

"Well, someone has!"

"They're getting away," interrupts Cyril, sounding panicked. "They have Kim-Joy and they're getting away!"

"Be calm, Cyril," says Nailah, trying to stay calm herself. "We can catch up with them."

"How?!"

"They will be heading to Dover," she says.

"Dover? How do you know that?"

"I've been hearing rumours from the southern monasteries for months. The priests have been telling me stories of a shady posse, galloping past their chapels towards Dover in the middle of the night. I had been dismissing these as hysterical nonsense—priests caught up in the furore of the *Four Horsemen*. Clearly, I was wrong."

"So, we head to Dover?" asks Cyril.

"First, let's go to the *Tide and Time*. I need to see what damage has been done," says Nailah.

"Agreed," nods Cyril.

"In that case, you two are free to go your own way… There's danger ahead with us," says Nailah.

"Danger?" smiles Elijah. "Danger trumps flogging the *Forecast* any day!"

Nailah smiles and turns to Eilish.

"Oh, I'm coming with you, don't you worry about that," Eilish grins triumphantly.

"Alright!"

***

For years, entry into the *Tide and Time Tavern* via any of the multitude of streets surrounding it has been guarded by the Distillery. Officially, the pub is 'open for business', but in reality, to get to the Tide and Time, customers are searched on the way in and on the way out. The only way into the pub without a search, until today, has been via the secret tunnel from Virgil College. The only way by land, at least. Like many of the establishments along the riverbank, the *Tide and Time* receives their marbles by shipments on the river.

The trawlers that sail up the Lethe, delivering marbles to the taverns, are searched by Distillery officials at the Port at London Bridge. Meaning that, by the time they reach the beer garden of the *Tide and Time Tavern,* it is assumed they are clean. This is how rebels have, for years, snuck into the tavern, and how it has been possible for their encampment in the forest to grow. An encampment which, right now, is mobilised against a Distillery force who have brazenly kidnapped the landlady and are carrying out a hostile search of the whole building.

As Nailah, Cyril, Eilish, and Elijah approach the vicinity of the *Tide and Time Tavern,* the confrontation between the Distillery and the rebels is in full swing. Broken marbles hiss, and frightened voices shout out from both sides. Thankfully, no smoke is rising from the tavern—the Distillery seems to want to keep any condemning evidence intact. But there is a huge mass of Distillery ranks on the adjacent streets, meaning there is no way for them to approach safely.

"I think we can assume it's only a matter of time before the *Tide and Time* falls," says Nailah, frowning.

"Indeed," sighs Cyril, looking mournfully towards the commotion. "Kim-Joy knew this day was coming."

"Is there nothing we can do?" asks Eilish.

"There is…," says Nailah. "But first, we need to rescue Kim-Joy. Then we regroup, plan our return, and banish the Distillery from the *Tide and Time* for good!"

"I love it!" says Cyril, emphatically, before pausing. "But *how* exactly do you propose that we rescue Kim-Joy?"

"Oh, come on," teases Nailah. "I can take you to water, Cyril. Do I have to make you drink as well…"

"*The Guiding Star!*" he chuckles, a proud grin forming across his face. "Aye. She's moored off the tavern's jetty. Her and dozens of others. We've had them ready all week."

"Ready? For what?" asks Eilish.

"Migration!" says Cyril. "Kim-Joy knew the *Tide and Time* was under threat. Once the executions started, she knew it was only a matter of time. We started making plans to move Well-Wishing out of the Meadow altogether. To migrate to *La Prairie*."

"So, the *Guiding Star,* is she sea-worthy now?" asks Nailah.

"Of course," says Cyril. "She can be off in minutes."

"Then are we going to *La Prairie*?" asks Eilish, confused.

"Dover, first," says Cyril. "And beyond, if needed. I hope you've got your sea legs!"

Eilish grimaces. She's taken countless voyages out from the Meadow before. But every time she had got sick in the rolling waves and the yawing horizon. She doesn't relish another voyage anytime soon.

"Come on then," says Nailah. "We haven't got a moment to lose."

She leads them south towards the riverbank where the thick conifers reach the water's edge. The reeds in the shallows have been flattened, evidently from the regular comings and goings of small craft to the tavern.

They stride a few hundred metres up the river, hugging the river's edge, before the boundary of the beer garden to the *Tide and Time Tavern* comes into view. Distillery officers, huddled in pairs, swarm around. On their belts, they clutch cannisters of Thermocline Mist. Somewhere, out of view, is the rebel encampment. Even from where Eilish is crouched, she can hear the shouts of rebels, hiding in the trees.

"Ok," whispers Nailah. "The water is shallow enough for us to sneak around the river's edge. We can be around the rocks and out of sight in a few minutes. Just wait for my signal."

"What signal?"

She pulls a small glass globe from her bag—a Molotov marble. "We'll need a distraction to get the guards away from the riverbank. When you hear this smash, get going. I'll be right behind you."

With the flick of a lighter, the fuse of the Molotov marble is lit, and Nailah shoots off into the trees and away from the rivers' edge.

There's no time to question Nailah's plan. Moments later, they hear the smash, her Molotov Marble exploding into a shower of mist and flame a few metres from the Distillery officers guarding the bank.

"Ok," says Cyril. "Let's go."

They scurry over rocky ground before setting foot on the cobblestone ramp where the guards had been moments earlier. Fifty metres up this path, around the corner, is the entrance to the *Tide and Time Tavern.*

Following Cyril's lead, Eilish and Elijah remove their shoes and roll their trousers to their knees.

Eilish has never set foot in the Lethe before. She knows that the folk north of the river regularly bathe in it, believing in its cleansing properties. But being from the Paddock, the river has always been portrayed as dangerous and dirty.

Eilish is delighted, therefore, when a calming sensation pulses through her as the smooth water laps against her ankles. But there is no time to indulge. Clinging to the waters' edge, Cyril cajoles them quickly towards the rocks, jutting out from the bank, a stone's throw away.

The rocks are both sharp and slippery, but with cautious urgency, the three of them traverse the outcrop and, to their great relief, round the bend and out of sight of the cobble-stone boat ramp.

In less than a minute, Nailah has rejoined them, and they emerge beside the jetty of the *Tide and Time Tavern.* Nestled amongst dozens of other boats, its mooring rope tightening and slackening, sits *The Guiding Star*—Cyril's ship.

The Guiding Star is just as Eilish had imagined it. A great steel fishing vessel with cabins, a large deck, and the machinery of a fishing trawler. On Earth, equipped with a giant fuel-guzzling engine, *The Guiding Star* would have impressively chugged her way in and out of harbours all around the world. Here in the Meadow, where the oar and sail are the only means of propulsion, such an engine is redundant. Instead, two sets of oars lie on the deck beside the captain's cabin. They'll have to use these to head out on the Lethe.

"Hello, girl!" grins Cyril, walking confidently to the end of the jetty and grabbing onto a stanchion. "She's been waiting for an adventure like this!"

The Guiding Star rocks as they step aboard one by one. When Cyril, last to board, lunges onto the deck, the hull rocks so much that river water is squeezed between the hull and the jetty, spraying up over them all.

"You'll have to get used to that!" chuckles Cyril, watching Eilish wipe the spray off her face. "Just keep your mouth closed when we're in the waves... You don't want to be taking on too much seawater during the voyage."

This is true. Consumption of sea water in the Meadow is a sure way to send a soul 'on' to the Beyond. Not all water holds the same level of danger. Rainwater is the least potent and is usually safe. River water, however, which has travelled through the ground picking up sediment, is more dangerous (especially near the river mouth). A pint of river water consumed can send a soul 'on'. But the sea water, flush with salt and sediment that has been absorbed throughout the history of the Meadow, is highly potent. A cupful of sea water would send anyone 'on', maybe even half a cup.

Eilish notices a bundle of cloth face masks hanging on the cabin door.

"Yes," says Cyril, striding to the stern and untying the tiller. "We'll be wearing those when the weather is bad!"

"Right, Elijah... you come and helm with me... that'll get your sea legs settled. Nailah, can you release the mooring rope?"

"No problem," shouts Nailah, already whipping a loop of the rope over the cleat and releasing them.

"What about me?" asks Eilish.

"Main thing with you, Eilish, with respect, is you mustn't be seen! If someone spots Governess Callaghan heading out to sea on my boat, you can bet we'll have every vessel in this land heading out into the Channel after us... You should be fine to take one of the oars—I mean, we're going to need everyone on the oars eventually, but I need you to stay on the southside and keep your head down until we're past London Bridge."

"Ok," says Eilish reluctantly, taking up her position.

Cyril leans over the side of the boat and plunges an oar into the silty riverbed, manoeuvring *The Guiding Star* away from the jetty and into the main channel. In no time, the current takes hold of the hull, and they start drifting downstream and away from the *Tide and Time Tavern.*

"Right, Eilish and Nailah," Cyril calls, "Get rowing! We're a bit unsteady in the current. Elijah and I will keep us close to the north bank, but we won't be stopping until we're past London Bridge. Until we're out into the Channel."

"How long will that take?" asks Eilish.

"With the current today, not long… an hour or two."

"And how long till we get to Dover?" she asks.

"To Kim-Joy?" says Cyril, looking worried. "I'm not sure. We'll be heading for a safe mooring tucked away, out of sight of the main port. We should be there by nightfall. Sooner, if the wind is favourable. I'll get the sails up as soon as we're clear of the headland."

Eilish glances with admiration at Cyril. He is a grizzled veteran of the sea, and his courage is as boundless as the horizon. It's true what they say about sailors and fisherfolk. Someone who looks cumbersome and uncomfortable on land can be in their element on the water.

***

Chapter 43

Lessons and Lighthouses

The Meadow - The English Channel

Looking out from the deck of the rusty old fishing boat into the endless expanse of wide-open sea, Eilish feels a wave of calm wash over her, which is ironic, given she is fleeing house arrest with two of the most wanted fugitives in the Meadow.

As Cyril had expected, travelling down the Lethe and out into the Channel was painless. It is only the vessels entering London that concern the Distillery Port Authority. A regular ship like *The Guiding Star* is barely noticed leaving the city.

After rounding the headland at Margate, Cyril has set *The Guiding Star* on a course due south, where, to the west and east, beyond the visible horizons, is landfall in the two nations. But *The Guiding Star* is in the middle of a deep blue sea, and there is not a soul in sight.

On the deck, the peeling paint is hot to the touch in the bright afternoon sun, and despite the shade of the sail that Cyril has rigged, Eilish feels temptation wrapping itself around her, nudging her to cool off in the vast and lethal crystal blue water beneath and around them.

Cyril stands at the helm, humming convivially to himself. Nailah has her eyes closed, relaxed on the bow. Elijah, however, is in the cabin on his own. He had managed to keep a semi-cheerful face on the Lethe, but as soon as they had entered the open water, and swells had begun to roll the boat, he had taken himself away to his hammock, giving the occasional disgruntled moan. "Better to get the sea sickness out early," Cyril had said. "Better in calm seas than a storm."

The cloth face masks hang unused on the cabin door. There is minimal risk of any seawater splashing anyone's face.

"You see them boats, over there?" says Cyril, pointing to a row of black dots peppering the horizon far off the bow to the south.

"Er, just about," says Eilish. "Are they trouble?"

"No, no… not for us anyway. Have a look," he says passing a pair of binoculars to Eilish.

Eilish rests her elbows on the warm gunnel and peers through the eyepieces. The dots on the horizon are barges. Large wooden paddle steamers packed with people. The passengers are working hard, and Eilish frowns. She has seen these kinds of boats before, in the docks of *La Prairie*. They are powered by Drifters and Founderers from continental Europe—the unconscious and semi-conscious souls heading to the Source. The Founderers used to come to the shores of the Meadow and were put to work to support the needs of conscious inhabitants. But now they all head to Holyhead, to the port off North Wales closest to the Mountain and the Source.

"I remember my father talking of the challenge of overseas Founderers," says Eilish.

"Yes, well," says Cyril. "Since the World Wars each state in this realm has been inundated with Drifters. You see the same problems everywhere. Even in the Americas."

Despite travelling as a Distillery envoy in her former governess role, Eilish had never travelled beyond Europe.

"I've never seen any Drifters coming from the Americas," says Eilish.

"Well, that's because they have their own 'Source'," says Cyril. "High up in the Rockies. A similar set up to our Mountain."

"What other openings are there?" asks Eilish.

"There's half a dozen I know of," says Cyril. "They're scattered all around the Meadow lands. Most of them are like ours… a spring of water spewing from a mountain peak. But they are not all like that. In *Charaah-gaah*—somewhere in South Asia— it is in the River Delta where you find their connection to the Beyond. An unusual tidal current creates a whirlpool from a deep-sea fissure which injects pure water into the sea. It's a nightmare to navigate! Worse even than the *Tysilio* whirlpool off North Wales. And then there's the opening in *Dong Co*—in East Asia—a spring that has formed deep in an underground cave. It's a beautiful and unmissable place. There are crystals and stalagmites all around the cave before a drop into the unknown in the misty cave."

Eilish looks at Cyril. What a life he leads in the Meadow!

"Oh, hello!" Says Cyril, looking into the far distance off the starboard bow.

Eilish shifts her gaze. There is a bright white shaft of light, unmistakable on the horizon, reaching from the sky down to the water—an Opening from Earth.

"This could get interesting," says Cyril. "Facemasks on everyone! The weather could be about to change. Eilish, go and wake Elijah."

As Cyril anticipates, within half an hour, *The Guiding Star* is hit by the raging storm that emerges from the Opening. Indeed, many Openings at sea lead to this kind of treacherous weather. For a disaster on Earth in the ocean is, nine times out of ten, the result of bad weather. The storm is the residue of Earth brought through with the souls lost to the Meadow.

Elijah looks awful. He retches desperately often and clings to the marble crates on the deck, his head between his knees. The rest of them fight with the rigging, trying to keep *The Guiding Star* level.

Mercifully, despite the storm, the wind is in the right direction, and they make rapid progress towards Dover. Eilish, now at the helm, does her best, on Cyril's instruction, to keep the compass pointing Southwest. All of the crew are looking out for other vessels and for a Lighthouse that will jut out from the land just before Dover. That's where they are heading.

Despite being uncomfortable in a face mask, Eilish is very grateful that she has one. Spray from the sea splashes over the deck every few minutes as the bow of *the Guiding Star* smashes into wave after wave. This is why it is so dangerous to travel in the seas of the Meadow. Without a mask, it would be almost impossible to avoid consuming seawater. Even the most diligent of souls wouldn't last more than a few days before the cumulative potency of the consumed water would send them 'on'.

Eilish wonders what must happen to those souls who go 'on' at sea. Can they drift over the ocean like they do on the shore? Do they swim? Can they swim? A disturbing image forms in Eilish's mind. Dozens of emaciated and unconscious bodies splashing desperately towards the shore, struggling for days on end.

Starting to feel a little queasy, Eilish looks to the horizon, hoping to see an end to the weather. But the weather will only change with an Opening. And an Opening at sea could take a while. Then she sees something else. An arc of light flashing on the horizon. Just a few degrees off the bow. A lighthouse.

Eilish shouts to Cyril and Nailah, but neither hears her over the wind. She tries to wave, but before they notice, she slips. *The Guiding Star* has pitched and rolled on a wave, catching Eilish by surprise. She slams onto the deck with a thud, and the helm slips from her hand.

The Guiding Star immediately starts to careen uncontrollably downwind. Nailah, near the bow, throws her arms up and grasps tightly to the mainsheet, trying to stop the boat from capsizing. Elijah, fearing for his life, flattens himself on the deck beside Eilish. But Cyril doesn't panic. Holding tight to the stanchions, he drags himself across the boat, clambers over Eilish, ducking under the boom that whips over his head, and grasps tightly to the helm. He pulls with all his might and turns *The Guiding Star* back on course.

With the deck levelling off again, Eilish gets back to her feet, peering apologetically at the trawlerman.

Cyril looks back at her and winks. His weatherworn face is etched with joy and determination. 'Are you alright?' he mouths.

She nods and gestures out to the southwest.

Cyril leans in towards her.

"The lighthouse!" She screams. "I've seen it!"

Cyril looks up and spots the arcing beam of the Lighthouse. He pats Eilish on the back and smiles.

"Just an hour to go!" He shouts, laughing heartily in the din of crashing waves. "It might be rough getting to the mooring!"

Sure enough, the chaos of the storm sustains all the way to the lighthouse. And, as with all lighthouses, it sits where it does to try and warn ships *not* to get too close. But that is precisely what they are doing. For it is from this lighthouse that Cyril knows they will have a clear sight of Dover. And Cyril is a good friend of the lighthouse keeper. She will be able to provide a useful update on the comings and goings from the port.

Scooting close to the headland, Cyril grips tight to the helm and trains his eyes firmly on the surface of the water, looking for dark patches indicating the presence of submerged rocks. He knows the coast here well, but in this choppy water, a slight miscalculation and a lost heading could be catastrophic.

Nailah holds tight to the mainsheet, keeping the speed of *the Guiding Star* in check. She loosens and tightens the line, making the sail flap noisily, keeping just enough forward momentum against the chaotic water.

Eilish and Elijah are glued to the deck.

"It'll be calm, soon," shouts Cyril. "Just around this headland!"

The lighthouse is nearly in reach. Peering up at the grand and stoic tower, Eilish catches a glimpse of the solitary lighthouse keeper, standing below the lamp, observing them through a telescope. Cyril throws an arm up and waves.

Then, suddenly, Cyril rolls the wheel, and they lurch to port. Looking over the side, Eilish spots a dangerous jagged rock, peeking out from the waves. A close call! But Cyril doesn't seem concerned. He grips the wheel tightly and weaves a new course through the shallow and dangerous waters, like a snake stalking its prey.

Eventually, when the base of the lighthouse feels almost close enough to touch, Cyril pitches them towards the land, and the lighthouse blocks them from the wind, and the water goes calm.

"Throw the anchor here!" Cyril shouts to Nailah.

Nailah, ready with the chain, launches the heavy iron anchor into the sea. In a few seconds, they feel the yank as the anchor bites into the sea floor, and *The Guiding Star* comes to a settled and stable stop. Though the storm continues all around them, in the shadow of the lighthouse, it is peaceful and calm.

"Well, that was fun!" grins Cyril, wringing drips from his beard and removing his face mask.

Before anyone can disagree, Elijah leans over the side and hurls.

"You'll have your sea legs soon," chuckles Cyril. "That was a baptism of fire, I'll give you that!"

Elijah offers a weak smile in return.

***

Right at the centre of the top storey of the lighthouse is a vast clay kiln. Throbbing white-hot embers glow emphatically inside, positioned under an elaborate contraption of turning cogs and mirrors, which cast bright white light out over the ocean. But this is only one of the mechanical wonders in the expansive circular room. Strewn all around are the most wonderfully elaborate dials and contraptions imaginable. It is like an emporium of brass antiques. There are telescopes, sun dials, hourglasses, sextants and quadrants, brass lenses, and cartographic instruments of the type and complexity Galileo would envy.

"What's most incredible," says Cyril, running his hand over the brass eyepiece of a telescope trained on the horizon, "is Orphelia here knows how to use each and every instrument in this room." He casts a broad smile at the Lighthouse keeper.

Orphelia is a long, bony old lady. Her features are pointy and sharp, and she towers head and shoulders over everyone, even Cyril, though she certainly doesn't 'loom'. She is much like her lighthouse—a jutting figure with a brightness that sparkles behind thick rimmed spectacles. And she is very old. Older than Kim-Joy. But like Kim-Joy, she has an energy and a vibrancy of spirit that belies her years on Earth and in the Meadow.

"If you had the time, I'd happily talk you through each and every instrument," Orphelia smiles. "I am always delighted to impart knowledge from my menagerie of measurement."

Elijah, who looks much more himself now he's on solid ground, wanders amongst the instruments, beaming in wonder. "You're not just looking for boats, are you?" he asks, peering down at a star chart stretched across a table.

"No… barely at all," chuckles Orphelia. "I mean… I do my *job*… I'd have the authorities on me if I didn't!" This sparks a realisation in Orphelia, and she scampers over to the kiln. "I do get distracted!" she giggles, turning a sand timer beside the brass handle above the kiln.

As she winds the handle slowly through three full turns, the cogs above her start spinning, and the mirrors projecting the light onto the sea start their arc. The light that Eilish had seen on the horizon a few hours earlier had been triggered by this same simple movement.

"Do you have to do that every time the light shines?" asks Eilish.

"Every time," smiles Orphelia. "The life of a Lighthouse keeper in the Meadow! But it doesn't matter if I'm a few minutes out of sync here or there. Which gives me plenty of time to study… and you're right, young man," she says, looking at Elijah, "I don't really tend to study the comings and goings of boats. No, my interest is more *celestial.*"

"You're a star-gazer!" says Elijah. "My Meadow Guardian was a Star-gazer too."

"Oh, yes?" says Orphelia.

"Yes," says Elijah, holding Orphelia's gaze resolutely.

"Then I presume you are a…" she looks at him quizzically.

"I am," says Elijah proudly.

"What?" asks Eilish.

"A *Stain*," says Elijah. "Sorry, Eilish… I didn't think you'd want to know."

"It's not something to be hidden!" Orphelia snorts. "I'm a *Stain,* too!" She shows them the scars around her neck. "We all have our reasons why we're in the Meadow," she smiles. "What happened to your Meadow Guardian? Have they gone 'on' now?"

"I lived with him in one of the enclaves," says Elijah, avoiding Eilish's eyes. "But the enclave isn't there anymore, is it? And neither is he."

Eilish feels sickeningly guilty.

"I see," says Orphelia, looking from Elijah to Eilish, and across at Nailah and Cyril, trying to unpick the tension. "Well, either way, star-gazing is a common and ancient skill of our people. Such a valuable exploit, seeking knowledge, truth, and understanding of our realm. Of course, others hate us… they are scared of what we might find. You know, many notable Well Wishers have been *Stained*?"

"Very true," says Nailah proudly. "Many great discoveries of our belief have come from the *Stained*."

"Yes," says Orphelia. "An opportunity from amidst a pained soul. Pain can often free the mind to think in different ways."

"I guess you can see the stars very well from here," says Cyril.

"Oh, yes. The most perfect vantage point when the sky is clear."

"But aren't the stars and their trajectories already mapped?" asks Eilish.

"Oh, no," says Orphelia. "There are many anomalies still unaccounted for. Beautiful unexplained patterns in the night sky. And the Energy that surrounds this realm and gives spark to every life, it is still a beautiful mystery… And it's not only the stars in the sky that we see in abundance from here… no, I witness the fleeing sparks of many poor souls that have been lost at sea. Their souls are cast up into the sky, becoming stars on their demise."

"Their bodies don't go to the Source?" asks Elijah.

"If they could, they would… but, alas, many souls that fall into the sea will never manage to swim against the currents. Those poor souls are extinguished in the depths, leaving just their spark to go 'on' without them."

"It is all part of life and death here in the Meadow," reasons Nailah. "You know, Eilish's sister was at the Source studying the journey of sparks?"

"Oh, yes?" says Orphelia, smiling at Eilish. "So much credit is owed to you and your community of Well Wishers, Nailah... It was your followers at the Source who found the anomaly, was it not?" she looks inquisitively at Eilish.

Eilish, perplexed, turns to Nailah.

"It was indeed," says Nailah, proudly. "The imbalance between drifters jumping from the Perihelion precipice and the sparks that followed," she explains for Eilish. "The discovery really ruffled feathers. The simple idea that all Drifters heading to the Source and their stars all heading north to the Beyond, doesn't hold true... There are other paths."

"And it is another of these paths that we witness here, on the seas," says Orphelia. "Not a path that all souls take, but another beautiful anomaly taken by some. The sparks of lost sailors that stay with their crafts. Sparks that become guiding stars for the ships of this realm."

"A guiding star?" asks Eilish, curiously.

Orphelia looks at Cyril.

"Yes," Cyril confirms. "We lost a boy, once..." He pauses. "He is still up there now... shining down on us whenever we sail."

Foundering in a rolling sea of memories, Cyril gazes out over the horizon and fiddles with a leather bracelet on his wrist. A bracelet containing a marble locket.

Eilish looks at Cyril, hoping he will divulge, but he doesn't. Nailah wraps an arm around his broad shoulders.

"There are many people lost at sea whose souls stays with their boats," says Orphelia. "They shine over and guide their loved ones in this realm."

"So, they *never* head north, towards the Beyond?" asks Eilish.

"No, dear," says Orphelia. "They don't have to, and so, they don't. If you were here at night, you could witness the fabulous dance of the stars... The stars are *alive*! They choose their own paths through the sky."

"You keep watch of the port from here, as well, don't you?" asks Nailah.

"Yes, of course," says Orphelia, sensing that the moment for theological introspection isn't now. "Though the Authorities are not aware that I do."

"That's why we're here, Orphelia," says Cyril. "You know Kim-Joy, don't you?"

"Of course," smiles Orphelia.

"Well, she's in trouble," says Cyril. "*The Tide and Time Tavern* has fallen, and she has been snatched."

"Snatched?"

"You've heard the rumours of the *Horsemen*?"

Orphelia's face falls. "I have. And they're *not* rumours," she whispers, sorrowfully. "They operate out of the port here... plying their evil trade. So, *they* have snatched Kim-Joy?"

Cyril nods.

"Then they will be bringing her to Dover."

"Yes," says Nailah. "But where she'll go from there... that's where our knowledge stops..." She looks at Orphelia, hopefully.

"There's a boat," says the lighthouse keeper. "*Charybdis*. An old wooden galleon."

"I've heard of that ship," says Cyril. "But only from the lips of fisherfolk, drunk on marbles. I never paid them any worth... Mad tales. Tales of an old galleon captained by Death himself with a secret morbid manifest of missing souls... a galleon that sails under no flag from this realm."

Orphelia runs her hand through her fine, grey hair thoughtfully. "Well, I don't think she's captained by Death," she muses. "But maybe by your *horsemen*... and by some of the men they have snatched. It is guarded whenever she is in port, and no one—save for the horsemen and the men they have snatched— ever sets foot on her deck. But it's true of her manifest... the contents of her hull are never shared... though I suspect there are more of the missing men in there."

"How long does she stay in port?" asks Cyril.

"Never more than two or three nights... the horsemen are never inland longer than that... She's in the dock right now."

"How long has she been there?"

"Long enough," says Orphelia. "I've seen them making ready all day. I suspect they plan to leave tonight… Have a look for yourselves." She gestures towards a telescope trained on the port.

Eilish steps forward, then hesitates to let Nailah or Cyril go first.

"No, after you, Governess," winks Cyril.

Through the eyepiece, Eilish can see that the port of Dover is feeling the full force of the storm. Boats' rigging flaps aggressively, and the flag of the Distillery flying above the town hall is rapidly losing its downwind thread. On the streets, Eilish can see trawlermen and sailors, all fighting with the elements, unloading, or reloading their ships and dragging crates across the harbour. Some are cajoling their nervous colleagues back onto the boats, ready to head into the storm. And, of course, there are the Distillery's Drifter barges.

Herds of unconscious and semi-conscious souls are already crammed on the decks of one barge, and some are still shackled to the harbour wall, their bodies trying to pull them inland, north, towards the Source. In the wind and the rain, the metal chains around their necks whip and crack. Many of them have bruised and bloodied faces.

"Which is the *Charybdis*?" asks Eilish, keeping her eye on the harbour.

"It's the wooden, square rigger at the far end of the harbour."

"The one with three masts?" asks Eilish, adjusting the lens to focus on the ship.

"That's her… she's quite astonishing, isn't she?"

Eilish agrees. The *Charybdis* is by far the grandest ship in the port.

"They're unfurling one of the sails."

"They are?" asks Orphelia. "Then their departure is imminent."

"In this?" asks Nailah, astonished. "They must be mad!"

"Wait!" shouts Eilish. "There's a group of people approaching." She squints. With the spray and the cloud cover, the clarity of what she can see isn't perfect. "It's them!" she calls. "The *Horsemen!*"

"Is Kim-Joy with them?" asks Cyril, eagerly.

Eilish steadies the telescope, trying to pick out the landlady.

"Yes, she's there," says Eilish, noticing a small, squat figure being aggressively cajoled towards the ship, but there is a wobble in her voice.

"What's wrong, Eilish?" asks Nailah.

"My brother is with them too," she says quietly. "Andrew is with the *Horsemen!*"

"Ah ha," says Cyril, triumphantly. "So, the Distillery *are* behind the disappearances… I knew they were."

Eilish pulls her eyes from the telescope, gesturing for Cyril to verify what she has seen. He peers through the eyepiece, only very briefly, before turning to address them.

"Right, crew," he says. "There's no time to lose. *The Guiding Star* will have no trouble keeping pace with a square rigger, and we can handle the storm. But we mustn't let her out of our sight."

"Do we know where she's headed?" asks Nailah, looking to Orphelia for answers.

"Not for certain… She always heads out west first, towards the Atlantic… but naturally, she could change course once out of sight, and we wouldn't know it…"

"Great, so it's decided, is it? We're going back into the storm," grins Elijah, sarcastically. "I was just starting to miss that acidic burning sensation in my throat!"

Cyril smiles and pats him on the back.

"Good lad! So, we're agreed then, are we? The voyage continues!"

Elijah grimaces and nods.

"Let's go chase a galleon!"

***

Mercifully, the storm over Dover is short-lived. A car crash on a coastal road on Earth creates an Opening just outside the town a few hours after *The Guiding Star* sets off. A bright, calm sunshine spreads itself out from the Opening and over the Channel. And soon, white fluffy clouds are stretching from horizon to horizon. Slices of light catch onto the gentle rolls of the ocean in patches all around *The Guiding Star,* and a steady blow keeps the hull inclined and the crew concentrating, while the fishing boat cuts a smooth parabolic path through the sea.

"You still got the *Charybdis* in sight?" shouts Cyril from the helm.

Eilish, her legs dangling over the bow, splashing in the cool sea, lifts the binoculars. A nautical mile or so westwards, the square rigs of the *Charybdis* are clear. It is hard to miss the great galleon that has maintained a westward heading since it broke out of the controlled waters around Dover.

In the warm southerly breeze, both the galleon and the fishing trawler are making good headway. *The Guiding Star* has plenty more sail speed if she wants it.

"She's still there!" shouts Eilish through her facemask, throwing up her thumb.

"Excellent!" Cyril calls back. "Time to swap places with Elijah then?"

The young man nods eagerly. His sea sickness evaporated with the storm, and now the joy of the ocean has captivated him.

"The lad's a natural," chuckles Nailah, as Eilish clambers back onto the deck with her and Cyril.

Eilish catches Nailah's eye and smiles. Nailah's skin seems to radiate in the warm sea air, and her thick curly hair shines in the sun.

Nailah nods to the bow where Elijah is already lying prone, watching the *Charybdis* through the binoculars and dragging his hand through the sea spray. She smiles.

"Incoming!" shouts Cyril, unexpectedly.

Eilish turns, but too late. She gets caught in the face with a heavy, slapping splash of sea water. It is only a ripple across the great expanse of sea, but its collision with the hull throws enough water to drench them all. Eilish is grateful she has her mask on.

"You were supposed to duck!" grins Cyril, looking at Eilish, her deep red hair dripping.

"Oh, really?" says Eilish, sarcastically, ringing the water out.

Nailah laughs.

"Have you always been a trawlerman?" Eilish asks Cyril, sitting down on the deck, hoping the sun will dry her out.

"Depends on what you mean by 'always'…"

"In the Meadow," she clarifies.

"Well, I have, as long as I can remember…"

"As long as you can remember? Can't you remember your Arrival?"

Cyril glances across at Nailah. "No… no, not really," he admits cautiously. "And that's a risk, of course. You know as well as I do. When those memories start fading, it only means one thing: the Beyond is beckoning. But still, I have two hundred years of Meadow memories… that's enough!"

"Wow," says Eilish. "Two hundred years… and those memories aren't fading?"

"Not yet," grins Cyril. "Memories from here are like our bodies, though, aren't they—they don't seem to fade. They go on as long as the mind wants them to. As for my memories of life on Earth… well, they have almost all gone now."

Cyril looks mournfully out over the sea. "You know Kim-Joy has been here more than five hundred years."

"Five hundred?! That's incredible," says Eilish. "She must be one of the longest inhabitants of the Meadow?"

"If not *the longest*," smiles Cyril. "You know she was here before the Source appeared."

Eilish stops. "*Before* the Source? I didn't know there was such a time?"

"Oh yes. The Source is younger than Kim-Joy."

"How can that be? What happened to people if there was no Source?"

"You mean, what happened when they went 'on'?"

Eilish nods.

"Well, they didn't," says Cyril. "It didn't used to be the case that when you died in the Meadow you wandered north to the Source. No, it used to be much more like... extinction, I suppose. People were here much longer then. Centurions weren't rare, and well, I guess, people only left the Meadow when their minds got too old. Like I know Kim-Joy has told you, when the mind ends in this realm, the person can no longer exist here."

"So, what happened to people back then?"

"When the mind ended, I am led to believe, people just disintegrated. Like sandcastles. Their bodies just collapsed, and their spark of light shot up into the sky to join the stars."

Cyril glances up into the clear, bright and vast sky above them. "Sounds nice, doesn't it?"

"Then why did the Source appear?"

Cyril glances nervously at Nailah.

"Hundreds of years ago, we weren't the only souls in the Meadow," starts Nailah. "We shared the Meadow with spirits. Spirits from another realm—the Beyond. They claimed to be 'Angels'. They had no bodies, but on still days they dwelt amongst the people of the Meadow. They were the same spirits that the ancient's talked about on Earth. You know of the Angel Gabriel from the Christmas story? Gabriel was here as well."

"For real?" asks Eilish, her mind racing to her angel on the Lethe.

"Yes. But then, sometime around five hundred years ago, the angels all left, and a darkness fell over the land. No one saw it coming, and there had been no whisper of its approach from the angels, but there was suddenly an anger in the atmosphere that consumed the Meadow for months. People thought it was the end times. The apocalypse.

"It wasn't.

"As quickly as it arrived, the terrible storm cleared. But in its wake, all over the Meadow strange openings had emerged. Breaks and fractures in the fabric of the Meadow. Openings into the Beyond. But the angels did not return.

"The Source was one of the fractures. And from that day, death in the Meadow changed. People no longer left this realm as a spark, travelling into the sky. Instead, they became brain-dead bodies—Drifters—that wandered into the new openings, never to be seen again."

"Life in the Meadow changed after that. What was once a beautifully long life in a disordered realm was lost. Thanks to the awful new circumstances and the emergence of groups like the Distillery, this second life has been herded into bureaucratic order, sold to newcomers as Purgatory, and destined to end in an awful march to death at the Source. That's the Meadow we live in now, isn't it?"

Eilish frowns guiltily.

"But I guess your life has rather moved away from the Distillery now, hasn't it, Governess?"

"Moved?" says Eilish. "Just a bit. I used to feel comfortable when I believed the Meadow was Purgatory. I used to like the control and order."

"Yeah… those are two words that are greatly overrated," says Nailah, smiling.

"Over-rated?!" Cyril snorts. "They're words I've banned on this boat. As well as 'planning', 'perfection', and 'discipline'."

"But you need control and order to sail the seas, surely?" says Eilish, looking at Cyril.

"Less than you'd think," he says. "One can be blinded by a desire for control… and a *fool* chases it. Embracing the unexpected and being flexible to chaos… that's really how to operate at sea."

"And it's how the Well Wishers operate," says Nailah. "You see, Eilish, I believe that's the root of the problems we have here… the way *control* has taken over the Meadow. Don't get me wrong, a desire for control and order can come from a good place—or at least a good heart—but it is, more often than not, driven by *fear*. Fear of disorder. Fear of being out of control. And this *fear* is the problem."

Eilish stares at Nailah, captivated by the clarity of her mind.

"If a little bit of control is captured… control of the self, for example—like control of the body on Earth or control of the mind in the Meadow—then a fear of losing that little bit of control grows, becoming deadly. Becoming destructive."

Eilish nods. She knows Nailah has her brother and father in mind.

"The Distillery itself began after people found the connection between life and water in the Meadow. It came about because that little bit of understanding offered a sense of control, and people were afraid of losing it. It drove fear in each and every person and led us to where we are now… a place where the power of the Distillery, the power of your father, is so afraid of losing control that it destroys more souls, more bodies, more minds, than the free consumption of water ever could."

Eilish drops her gaze guiltily, but Nailah reaches out and lifts her chin gently.

"We've seen the same amongst the Well Wishers…" she concedes. "Even though we were built on the idea of disruption and the ability to choose our journeys through the realms, the temptation to control the belief, to control Well-Wishing, has been too great for some. And with control comes corruption… Like Cyril says, control can never be the right way."

"So, the *right way*… is to relinquish control, and let go? Just to 'go with the flow'?" asks Eilish.

"Nearly, but no," smiles Nailah. "Learning to embrace chaos and relinquish control does not mean *'going with the flow'*. It means choosing *your* flow. You made a brave choice to join us, Eilish."

Eilish smiles, but drops Nailah's gaze coyly.

"You went against the flow of your life as a governess. But your choices are not done. The true way of the Well Wisher… the true way of freedom… is not simply 'choice'. It is *making* choices. Making them over and over again. It is active. This is what we have learnt from *Her*."

"Her? The lady who the angel loved?"

Cyril clears his throat, making both Eilish and Nailah turn. He looks at Nailah. There is a mixture of fear and caution in his eyes.

"I trust her, Cyril," says Nailah, confidently.

Cyril looks at Eilish, interrogating her with every sinew of his conscious mind.

"Don't you trust her?" asks Nailah.

Eilish holds her breath. She knows that Cyril's word is significant.

"If we were to be captured," Cyril asks Eilish. "If the *Guiding Star* were to founder, and you found yourself in the hands of your father and brother again… how far would you go to protect the biggest secret in the Meadow? A secret that Kim Joy, Nailah and I have vowed to hold over death. A secret that binds us."

"A secret," Nailah interjects, "that Ciara holds."

Eilish looks at them both, feeling her heart racing. "I have no allegiance to my father and brother anymore. The only family I have is Ciara. If she can be trusted, so can I."

Nailah beams.

"Then you will need to prove it," says Cyril.

"Prove it?"

"Yes," says Nailah, her smile dropping. She pulls out a crate from under her. The crate is packed with boxes of marbles. Dark, potent marbles, near to bursting. The type of marbles that no one should attempt to suck. Nailah slides them in front of Eilish, then pulls out the chain of marbles from around her neck. The same chain she wore at the *Tide and Time*. The one with Chloe's cracked marble.

"Many of these marbles are *Inseparable Stones*," says Nailah. "Cementing a forever bond between two minds… Some of these are *Trauma Stones*." Nailah runs the chain through her fingers past a couple of dark black lockets. "You know of *Trauma Stones*?" she asks.

Eilish nods. These are marbles made from the most painful memories an individual holds in the Meadow and are often used for blackmail by predatory individuals and abusers. Not the kind of marble Eilish would expect to see around the neck of someone like Nailah.

"Not all *Trauma Stones* are surrendered through abuse," says Nailah, reading the concern on Eilish's face. "They can be given voluntarily, to someone you trust with your deepest, darkest secrets."

"Are you wanting to traumatise me? To make a stone?" asks Eilish.

"No!" Nailah exclaims, horrified. "No, that would be awful. No, we need you to create another stone... one you've already made once... an *Identity Stone*."

"That's ok," says Eilish, relieved. "I need a new one anyway. Mine was taken after the rebellion at the Palace. I need to remake it sooner or later."

"I'm not talking about *remaking* your Identity Stone," says Nailah, frowning. "No. I am talking about building one around a new identity altogether..."

"A new identity... how can you do that? Surely the marble never lies?"

"Exactly," says Nailah. "That is, of course, why the *Identity Stone* is so important. No, what I am actually asking is to break the bond you have between your past and your life here in the Meadow."

"Break the bond?"

"You know how the palace girls—the Flickers—lose that part of themselves that remembers life before the Meadow?"

"Of course," says Eilish, remembering the tearful nights with Chloe where that gap in her mind caused her such pain. "Do you need to erase my past?" asks Eilish.

"No, not everything," says Nailah. "Just the memory of your Arrival... We need to erase it and implant a new arrival story. Implant an arrival story that does not align with the truth of your arrival. A story that your father and brother could not accept."

Eilish looks at Nailah, confused.

"Cyril and I, Kim-Joy, Ciara... we have all done this. As have all who know the deepest secret of Well-Wishing."

"You have? Why?"

"Our *Identity Stones*—should they ever be extracted—they will not tell of how we *actually* came to the Meadow... They will not betray who we really are. Indeed, we no longer know, or at least remember, that truth. And so, the result of any future interrogation will be either a failure to extract anything at all, or the conclusion that you are not who you say you are, and your resin is corrupted. It's stained."

"Stained?"

"Yes. Because implanted in our new arrival stories is... suicide."

"Suicide?"

"Yes... suicide is etched into each new arrival story. If your brother or father were to find you and interrogate you with such an identity, they would conclude that you were not the daughter they remember from the Meadow... They would gaze into your soul and not find familiarity... they would conclude that your memory is false..."

"Why suicide?"

"Suicide is a deeply personal end to life on Earth... and as such, it won't meet contradiction to any other life in the Meadow—that's the most important thing."

"So, how do you do it? How do you change what forms in your *Identity Stone*?" asks Eilish.

Nailah looks at Cyril.

"It is a most unpleasant thing," says Cyril. "For you, and for us making the stone... You see, we will need to ply you with marbles... lots of marbles... get you deep into a marble haze... not a nice one but one of dark and depressing thoughts. And in this haze, you will have to tell us of a place that only you remember from Earth. Knowing this place, we will then need to discuss the finer details of your sadness and pain. And ultimately, we will need to retell the end of your life on Earth in that place, through suicide.

"This will be such a strong, emotional, and affecting experience of recollection that infusing it in a marble will make it become *the* defining memory of your Arrival. And it will haunt your dreams... Your mind will have been changed forever, and your resin will never run clear... And only having made such a change can we know, without doubt, that we can trust you with our secret."

Nailah lifts the dark black stones from around her neck. "These," she says, "These are not *Trauma Stones*. This is what an old *Identity Stone* looks like when it expires…"

"I thought they couldn't expire?" says Eilish.

"No, generally they can't… Only when the story of beginning is retold, can an identity stone expire."

"Then whose stones are those?" asks Eilish.

"This was mine," says Nailah, thumbing the first. "And this was Kim-Joy's…"

Eilish turns to Cyril. "Do you still have yours?" she asks him.

"No," he says, "Mine is out there on the *Charybdis*," he nods past the bow. "Kim-Joy holds it. But I do hold another." He pulls up his sleeve to reveal the leather band on his wrist. On it, a single marble is encased in a locket. "The owner of this marble gave our boat her name," he says. "A young man… precious and devoted… Kim-Joy's son… Sachi."

"Kim-Joy had a son?" asks Eilish.

"Yes. Sachi crewed for me when I first joined the Well Wishers centuries ago," says Cyril. "He was a skilled sailor and a beautiful soul, just like his mother. And one day he saved my life… He saved my life at the expense of his own." Cyril looks up to the sky. "Sachi became the guiding star that hangs above us always. On the next clear night, I will point him out to you…"

"So, Eilish," asks Nailah. "Are you willing to change your story?"

"And make a new *Identity Stone*?" asks Eilish.

"It won't be a stone," says Nailah. "You are to become a *Stain*…"

"…and will make a *Stained Charm*," finishes Eilish.

"Charm?" says Cyril, ironically. "Nothing could be less charming."

"Do you know of how resin falls from the pores of a *Stain* on Arrival?" asks Nailah.

Eilish nods.

"It is *not* a pain-free experience. If you are to commit to this process, not only will we depress you into a marble haze and change your story, but for the coming few days, resin will squeeze from your forehead, falling as agonising drips, like a part of your soul is being flushed out of your pores."

"You've been through this?" asks Eilish.

Nailah reaches into her pocket.

"You don't need to show her," says Cyril, concerned.

"I do," says Nailah.

She pulls out her own *Stained Charm*. It has been roughly fashioned into the shape of two figures embracing: a mother and daughter. "This is the most precious thing I own," says Nailah. "And it hurt immensely to create it."

"And, if I do this… If I change my story and make my own charm, will you be able to trust me?"

"Completely," says Cyril. "And don't worry about helping out on the boat," he grins. "If Elijah thought his sea-sickness was bad, you have a much worse voyage ahead of you."

Eilish feels her throat go dry. She knows she has only one real option. If she chooses to stay in the dark, she is choosing to remain tied to her father and brother. Her choice now, as it has always been, is to follow Ciara.

"Ok," says Cyril. "Let's start pleasantly… the first marble can be of your own choosing. Nailah, I think half a dozen dark marbles should be sufficient for later on?"

"Agreed," says Nailah. "And what do we tell Elijah, if he asks?"

"I'll fill him in on what he needs to know," says Cyril.

***

Chapter 44

Mountains and Mind Games

Earth - Mynydd Aaru

void the Asphodel Face', that is the only thing that has stuck in Marty's mind from the two-hour briefing with the café owner this morning, fuelled by multiple cups of strong back coffee. That, and *'Steer clear of the old mine, it is liable to collapse at any time'*, and *'Don't even think of going above the snow line'*.

The café owner seemed somewhat too cautious when it came to blessing Marty's intention to head up the mountain. How could it be that dangerous? He was hardly likely to go poking about in a disused mine, nor was he going to try and scale the treacherous routes. There was a tourist train that went to the summit after all! Anyway, Marty took the advice in good spirit and enjoyed the free refills. But now, with the sun beating down on the crown of his head and the breeze around the mountain pass dying, Marty looks wearily up at the mountain. The whole peak, including the snow-covered summit, is bathed in baking sun. All except for one sharp, craggy face—the *Asphodel Face*.

The cliffs of the *Asphodel Face* are infamous for the countless deaths and the danger of trying to scale them. But on such an unexpectedly roasting day like today, the shade is inviting, even if the sheer rock isn't.

The lead-in to *Mynydd Aaru* from the café is a six-hour hike, and that's before you even start ascending across gravelly sandstone paths, worn into the valley from decades of rock-climbing and sheep farming. The latter forged the paths, the former eroded them into deep, firm grooves.

Marty's new waterproof boots are too new. The ball of his left foot and his heel rub, forming angry blisters, and his right sole aches, giving him a limp. He tries desperately to scrunch his toes to stop the blisters getting worse and worse, to no avail.

Marty pulls out a handkerchief and mops his brow. Sweat is pouring off him. '*Stay hydrated*' was another useful, but relatively obvious, tip from the café owner. Beside Marty, a gentle stream trickles alongside the path. But Marty knows better than to fill his bottle from such a stream. He had been a Scout once and remembers the lesson about the sheep that died upstream of a freshwater pool, poisoning what looked like fresh water. Marty knows he is relying on the metal water bottle that clinks as it dangles from his backpack. It is still half full, for now.

A cluster of hawthorns and cherry trees offers shade up ahead—the perfect place for a rest. A rest where Marty can eat a few sweets and have another look at the map.

The café owner had helped Marty identify some possible locations where someone could shelter from the elements and survive on the mountain. Marty never explained that he was interested in such places because he actually believed—or at least, had been told—that the lady was living on the mountain. If he had admitted this, the café owner would have thought him mad. No, he implied his 'friend' probably took shelter on the mountain, on her way to distant towns and villages, and he was interested to see if she'd left any clues of where she is staying now.

The peaceful shade of the cherry and hawthorn forms a perfect little idyll. The stream's trickle of water plunges as a tiny, delicate waterfall into a perfectly crystal-clear pool beside the bushes.

Sitting in the cool blanket of shade, Marty leans back against a gnarled nook of Hawthorn. Up, beyond him, in the scorching sun, stands the majestic *Mynydd Aaru*. It's perfect reflection flickers in the pool.

Marty gratefully unties the laces of his boots, flicking each loop off the hooks around his ankles and feeling the immediate release as his heat-swollen feet push free. He delicately peels off his long walking socks, mindful not to rip a blister off his soft soles. His feet are grateful for the cool air.

The blister on Marty's left foot is red and angry. He can feel the layer of skin of the blister trying desperately to detach and expose the stinging bare flesh below.

He places his feet carefully down onto the cool rock and allows them to slide gently into the cold pool of water. It is the most pleasant and appreciated sensation he could possibly imagine. As though the cooling pure water on his feet sends a shiver of happy tingles up his legs and into his body, washing away the tension of the morning's climb.

For a moment, Marty simply appreciates the beauty of his surroundings and allows his troubled mind to forget, or ignore, everything. Just for a moment to be *in the moment*. His heart rate slows, and his breathing relaxes, long and steady. A whisper of air tickles across the water and soothes him, as though telling him *'everything is going to be alright'*.

Not the kind of man to indulge for too long, Marty's brain soon clicks back into action. He rummages through his backpack and pulls out a large, detailed map of the mountain. Circled in red pen are the two likely locations where the Lady could be seeking refuge. One location is a Shepherd's Hut halfway up the west face—it is out of reasonable bounds today, given the treacherous snow cover and deadly sunshine on the face—but the other is a little cave at the base of the *Asphodel Face*. This is possible to reach.

Marty desperately hopes to strike gold in the cave. Otherwise, it'll be a long and frustrating wait before it is safe to attempt to reach the Shepherd's Hut. And even then, it might still be an unlikely goal. It is a full day's climb with complex conditions to contend with, even for an experienced mountaineer. For a novice climber like Marty, well, it might not be possible at all—at least that is the café owner's opinion. But what does he really know?

Marty traces his forefinger across the gridlines of the map, triangulating his position. The mountain is directly north, and this little pool, although small, is big enough to appear on the map. Following directly south from the mountain, running his fingers over the tightly packed brown contours, Marty pinpoints where he is sitting. The pool is marked—a perfect blue circle, like a punctuation mark before the shadow of the mountain.

He runs his finger from the pool to the cave at the bottom of the *Asphodel Face*. It stretches from his thumb to the end of his little finger, a full handspan—about 5 or 6 miles. At the rate he has been travelling in the heat today, that's probably another two hours' trek. He sighs.

Attempting to plot his route, Marty inadvertently knocks over his water bottle. The lid bounces off, and all his remaining water trickles hurriedly down into the pool.

"Shit!" he exclaims, as the bottle itself rolls down the rock and splashes into the pool.

He leans down to fish out the bottle from the ankle-deep pool. But he notices something else nestled amongst the pebbles— some kind of charm, a glass charm, resting on the bottom. Algae has made the charm almost the same colour as the pebbles, and had he not dropped his bottle, he would never have noticed it. He fishes it out.

The little charm is delicately made from an unusual translucent, glass-like substance. It is peculiarly sticky to touch and, holding it close to his eyes, Marty can see it is shaped like a water droplet with a spinning tail that encircles it.

'*My god!*' thinks Marty. '*That symbol! She has been here!*'

Energised by his find, Marty hurriedly packs his bag, pulls on his socks and boots, wincing as he catches the blister with his fingernail. He looks over at the sun-scorched path ahead of him, at the towering mountain face above him, and then at his empty water bottle.

'*This is going to be crap*' he thinks, feeling a scratchy thirst already starting to itch his throat. '*But I have to push on!*'

The *Asphodel Face* towers over Marty. An imposing skyscraper of sheer rock. Dark purple veins of sediment wriggle through the slice of slate—varicose incisions besides sharp freeze-thawed fractures. The face reaches hundreds of feet from the base of *Mynydd Aaru*. Bright sun shines over every other part of the mountain, but the *Asphodel Face* is draped in dark, icy shade.

Staring towards the peak, even on a bright day like today, Marty can just see haze. Droplets from a stream at the summit dissipate into a fine mist, creating a lingering cloud where the top of the face disappears.

In the shaded base of the mountain, a tumbled cascade of slate slabs and cracked rocks lie together, making Marty's navigation to the cave challenging. Specs and flecks of colour wilt in piles, here and there. Bunches of flowers left in memory of the jumpers; the dozens of suicides that end at the base of the mountain.

The creaking ice and rock from the face high above, almost sound like the pained groans of a mountain that has witnessed too much pain and tragedy. A sharp crack interrupts the groans, and a pebble bounces into the ground from somewhere high above. Each staccato crack makes Marty flinch. He can't help but expect to hear the crash of the latest victim of *Mynydd Aaru*.

Where the largest dark vein of purple sediment cuts up from the base of the mountain, Marty sees the entrance to the cave. It is small and discreet and extremely exposed to rockfall.

Marty steps carefully over the scree, needing to use both hands on the cold rock to help heave himself to the cave's entrance. It is barely big enough for a single person to enter.

"Hello?!" Marty calls in. "Anybody... home?"

His voice echoes abruptly, indicating just how small it is inside.

He ducks his head into the entrance, tensing, expecting to find himself face-to-face with a stranger. But it is too dark to see anything inside. He pulls out his torch and clicks the stem, lighting his palm first, before throwing the beam into the cave. The bright light reflects back off the wet slate that is all around him.

It is only about as big as a garden shed inside the cave, with the ceiling making it too low to stand. There's no one inside, that is clear, which allows Marty to relax a little. He glances back out of the cave, feeling vulnerable with his back turned, but he is alone.

There are some markings on the far wall of the cave to investigate.

Shuffling on his hands and knees, Marty crawls up to inspect them. It is a commemoration to a suicide from the mountain. But there is also that symbol again. Of course, he half expected that. And there is a name beside a statement—the first lead.

Chloe Dolores Higgins.
Too brave for this world. And too brave for the next.
You give us all hope.

Marty scribbles down the name, feeling the thrill that the first piece of evidence always used to give him in a case. If he doesn't find anything else today, at least he can spend the evening trawling the internet at the café, finding out about Chloe Dolores Higgins.

He looks around. There really is nothing else in the cave. He inspects every inch of the rock and turns over every stone, just in case, but the memorial scratchings are all the secrets the cave holds.

Nonetheless, the buzz of discovery is like a drug to Marty. As the adrenaline trickles away, he can't help but crave more. The cave, while holding a small but valuable secret, certainly isn't the hooded lady's permanent refuge on the mountain. And it is her refuge, which is the *real* prize. *She* is the prize.

Marty pulls out his map, flashing the torchlight over the intricate details of his own scribblings and onto the little black square amongst the contours. The shepherd's hut, high up on *Mynydd Aaru's* face, beyond the disused and collapsing mine. The café owner had told him it was out of reach. Out of reach for a novice climber like him. But was it? Surely this *had* to be where the lady was hiding. She wouldn't be in the mine unless she had a death wish. If he could just get to the hut, all his torment could end. It could end today. This thought teases another shot of adrenaline to course through his mind.

It might be inadvisable to seek the hut on the treacherous snow-covered slope in the oppressive sunshine, but Marty feels that he could certainly try. And in his naivety, the mountain's dangers suddenly seem to pose less concern. Especially compared to the teasing thrill of finding the lady today. And, like the peak of *Mynydd Aaru,* his judgement becomes devastatingly clouded.

The hot needles of bright sunlight sear into Marty's skin. The back of his neck, his exposed forearms, and the tips of his ears singe in the heat, but the path to the Shepherd's Hut has no alternative, and no respite from the afternoon sun.

Marty has never sweated this much before. And he has sweated plenty, riding motorcycles in the summer. The front of his shirt is wet through, creating a sticky psychiatrist's butterfly across his chest. His eyebrows glisten and drip metronomically between his knees as he struggles to pull one foot in front of the other up the steep western slope of *Mynydd Aaru.*

The dead weight of sausages and black pudding—this morning's over-indulgent breakfast—congeal and drag in Marty's stomach, while his throat sticks with a dry rasping and his lips peel themselves off one another every few seconds. If only he had some water, contaminated or not.

Heat and exhaustion throw Marty's mind into a kaleidoscopic delirium, countered by his determination to reach the hut. He starts to hallucinate. And his hallucinations are disturbingly real. Each, like a déjà vu. Like a memory. Half a dozen times, when passing a pile of rocks or a drift of snow, his mind's eye shows him another way this climb could have ended. He sees himself stumbling on rocks, gasping for water, feeling his body and brain frying in the sun, giving up and succumbing to death on the snow and rocky debris. It is as though his unsettled mind is projecting a plethora of alternative realities, whereby this solo walk up the mountain is his last. He even imagines newspaper stories: '*Crooked Cop Cooks on Mountain Top'.*

But these projections aren't real. Not here. Not this time. Not yet. Marty grits his teeth. He won't give in. And sure enough, with this attitude and despite dropping to a sluggish crawl and feeling the skin on his neck blistering, Marty gets close enough to spot it up ahead: the Shepherd's Hut.

It is nothing to write home about. Half a kilometre away from him, over rough, snowy ground, it stands; barely more than a semi-ordered pile of weathered rock, covered with corrugated iron. But irrespective of what it is, the pile of rocks offers shade. It would take away the brunt of the harsh, condemning sunlight and would give refuge for his desperately tired body.

Marty's mind is determined to make it. Stubborn, even. But, as with all minds on Earth, this is no match for his body. A body that cannot fight anymore will stop the mind, no matter how determined. And Marty has pushed his too far.

An innocuous stone juts out into Marty's path. It catches a lazy step from his blistered left foot. He stumbles and falls, cracking his head hard on the rattling slate. His tired limbs barely soften the impact.

In the seconds after his fall, Marty doesn't move. He barely utters a moan. He just stares down at his body, crumpled in the snow and rock. There's no getting back up, and he knows it. He tries to instruct his body, but he can't. His mind is tumbling into a new chaos. His body just lies there in the baking sun, desperate, as a wound oozes from his temple and the blood congeals on the hot slate around his face.

If only he could will himself out of the sun, he'd give himself a chance.

'How the hell did I get myself into this situation?' he thinks, desperately. He feels incredulous. He feels devastated. Why take such an unnecessary risk? And now he will pay for it. Bowing out of Earth, and there is nothing he can do. He has been beaten by the mountain, by the sun, by the stress of the last few months, and by the fear of losing everything.

Marty closes his eyes one last time and listens to the farewell sounds of the mountain.

***

Chapter 45

Gazing at the stars

The Meadow - The English Channel

Eilish shivers uncontrollably. Her skin is pale and clammy, and her head lolls. She retches again and again, filling the bucket by her feet with acidic vomit.

"You poor thing," says Nailah, rubbing Eilish's sweaty back and holding her thick auburn hair away from her face. "This won't last forever, I promise."

Eilish lets out a quiet moan and tries to focus her eyes on Nailah, but can't. Her mind has gone into a spasm. It takes every bit of energy just to keep breathing and keep upright.

"I'll go and empty the bucket," says Nailah, squeezing Eilish's shoulder.

Eilish lets out a desperate moan and tries to hold Nailah's arm, but she can't coordinate herself.

"I'm sorry," says Nailah. "I won't be long."

A tear drips down Eilish's face. A clear droplet of water. A contrast to the dark beads of resin that have started to squeeze themselves out of her pores.

On a table beside Eilish is a metal tray. She has captured every drop of resin that eked out of her skin. It's a deep, earthy green resin with the occasional fleck of colour. She had started to mould the resin. A semi-circular curve, like a C for Callaghan. Or maybe for Ciara.

As Eilish feels the latest drop of resin coagulate on her chin, she leans over the tray and lets the heavy, sticky sphere fall.

"Hold in there, my love," says Nailah, straining under the weight of the bucket.

Nailah, carrying the heavy bucket, steps up onto the moonlit deck of *The Guiding Star* and into Cyril's shadow. The trawlerman stands at the helm, gazing up at the clear night sky, mesmerised by the dance of the stars.

"How's she doing?" he asks, alerted to Nailah's presence by the invasion of a stench into his nostrils. He pinches his nose as Nailah plunges the bucket overboard.

"As well as she can," says Nailah, grimacing. "It has been two days. The resin is coming through quite steadily now, and the vomiting is less frequent. Hopefully she'll be speaking tomorrow."

"Poor girl," says Cyril. "But a good one. We can certainly trust her now."

Nailah glances out beyond the bow, where the dark stretch of ocean reflects the stars above. In the distance flickers another source of light. The *Charybdis*, like them, sits stationary in the flat calm sea.

"You have any more thoughts about how we rescue her?" asks Nailah.

"We haven't got much choice," says Cyril. "Unless we can find out where she's going and beat them there... Otherwise, we'll have to launch a raid."

"What do you think they're doing?" asks Nailah, looking concerned.

"What they always do... interrogating... interrogating the fibres of this realm... the fibres of her mind."

"She won't give anything away."

"Of course she won't," says Cyril, smiling. "But that'll certainly make the whole experience worse for her."

"You don't think they'll..." Nailah stutters and stops. "Are you sure she's still alive?"

Cyril feels the bracelet on his wrist. "Yes," he says.

"I hope you're right," says Nailah. "Kim-Joy is the resin that holds us all together."

"We'll get her back," says Cyril, looking up at the stars.

"Is that him?" asks Nailah, pointing to a stationary star that hovers millions of light years above them."

"That's him," says Cyril. "That's how I know Kim-Joy is still here with us."

Nailah dips the empty bucket overboard, swilling it clean. "I'll stay with Eilish for now," she says. "If the weather changes, I'll head straight back up."

"No problem," says Cyril. "Send the lad up, will you? I know he likes to star gaze."

Nailah rubs Cyril affectionately on the back, like she would a brother. The affection is for Cyril's benefit and her own. It's always nice to know you have friends close by.

A few minutes after Nailah departs, Elijah's head pokes up from the cabin.

"Still got your sea legs, I hope?" Cyril asks Elijah, who clutches a rattling ramekin of *Sailor's Mist*.

"These are helping," he smiles.

"That's good," says Cyril. "We have plenty."

"Nailah said you wanted to see me?"

"Yes. Come up here," says Cyril. "You'll like what you see."

Elijah steps up onto the deck and is bathed in the perfect sparkling light of the night that stretches from horizon to horizon. The cloudless, uninterrupted sky dances with stars.

"Beautiful, isn't it?" smiles Cyril, enjoying Elijah's wide-eyed wonderment.

"I've read about the night skies at sea," says Elijah.

"And can you see the patterns they talk about?"

"A few of them," says Elijah. "Up there, that's the *Northern Drift*, right?"

"Indeed," says Cyril, confirming the identification of the belt of stars above them that all drift northwards towards the Source. A steady drift that is visible even inland and has led to the widely held belief that *all* stars head north to the Source.

"And that must be our Guiding Star," says Elijah, pointing.

"Good lad," says Cyril, grinning.

"Oh wow, over there... is that the *Cluster of Origins*?!"

"You do know your stuff," says Cyril. "Yes, that's them. The sparks from the first days of the Meadow, or so they say. Yeah, you can usually see them at sea... And can you see that flickering star... the stationary one in the middle of the Northern Drift?"

Elijah stares carefully. "Where?"

"Up from the horizon to the north, about forty-five degrees up. Right in the middle of the band of drifting stars."

Elijah looks carefully. "Ah yes, I can see it twinkling… like a star from…" he pauses.

Cyril grins. "You've guessed it, haven't you?"

"The sun?!"

"The very same," says Cyril. "Or so we believe… a tiny speck of light that we have seen and known before. A speck of light that is shining on Earth at this very moment, as well as on this realm."

Elijah stands, stunned. He gazes in awe at the sky.

"I don't miss Earth," he begins, mournfully. "But I do miss my father. I never said goodbye properly. It's my fault, of course. I just left… I guess that's why we're called the *Stained*. Stained by our decision to leave… our decision to leave people behind. I look at that little speck of light now, and you know what, pathetic as it sounds, it comforts me…"

"Not pathetic," says Cyril, putting his arm over Elijah's shoulders. "It'll be shining on him now, too."

***

Chapter 46

Lost and Found

Earth - Mynydd Aaru

In a vast and empty nothingness, there is a quiet fizzing. Then the edges of the darkness flicker, like shadows, and Marty Fredrickson starts to feel, again.

His first sensation is tightness. A tightness in his breathing. But he *is* breathing. And then he senses a searing heat that scorches his eyelids, threatening his mind to keep his eyes closed.

The fizzing becomes a buzz. A buzz followed by a tap, tap, then a buzzing again. Then a few more sporadic taps punctuating the incessant buzz. A fly, trapped.

And then, smell. Dampness. Cool, stuffy air. And tea. The smell of brewing English Breakfast Tea.

A burning pain shoots up Marty's leg, and a cold scratch of a broken blister scrapes through his left sole.

'*I'm alive,*' thinks Marty. He goes to open his eyes. His sore, burning eyes. But the slightest opening floods his mind with a bright and burning redness. The pain is excruciating, so he scrunches his eyes closed again.

He shuffles his body, expecting to hear the scraping of rocks. But there are no rocks beneath him. Instead, there is a rough fabric and some cushioning, similar to a bed.

Marty tries his eyes again, and this time, though the pain is awful, he lets in a little more light. Enough light to realise that he is no longer lying in the direct sun. Something is shading him. But he can't look for long enough to figure out what. An unbearable, nauseating sickness accompanies this brief engagement of his retinas.

Marty grits his teeth and tries one more time. This time, he opens his eyes fully. Angry light floods in, but not cleanly. He has some kind of scratchy material covering him. A blindfold. But he can't move his hands to remove it. His arms are being crushed tight to his body. Crushed *by* his body. He is lying on his front, but this realisation doesn't help. He hasn't got the strength to roll over.

Somewhere, not far from Marty, there is the sound of knocking. Knocking followed by bleating. There must be a sheep, or many sheep, nearby. Then Marty hears a creaking like a door opening. And, through his blindfold, his sanctuary is bathed with a harsh, oppressive sunlight.

Marty recoils, scrunching his eyes tightly closed, shielding himself by furrowing his brow, and feeling a violent, sharp, throbbing pain fill his mind.

There is a commotion. Some creature seems to be rattling against the door, trying to get to him. Marty knows he cannot keep his eyes closed; he could be in imminent danger, but the pain is so intense. The light, too bright. Even through his eyelids, he can see it burning red.

The commotion stops, and darkness is restored.

"Are you ok?" says a woman, her voice dancing like a song into Marty's mind.

Marty squints, despite the pain. Through the fabric, he can see, silhouetted against a small square of light, the shape of a woman. The shape of *her*. The hooded lady? The Lady of the Mountain?

"I've found you," he whispers, his voice dry and rasping.

"Come again?" says the woman.

"I've found you!" Marty says, louder, his voice cracking.

"Found me?... I found you!" she says, incredulously.

Marty frowns. His tongue feels heavy, and his lips are painfully cracked. "You... found me?"

"That's right," she says, moving across the room. "You are lucky I did... You were barely clinging to life, freezing to death and blinded by the sun. What on earth were you doing so high on the mountain?! And on your own?!"

Marty tries to sit up, but the pain that bursts through his body strangles his senses, and he slumps back, breathing out heavily.

"Stay still," says the lady firmly. "Don't make the pain worse. You need time to recover. I've given you painkillers. The strongest I have. And water… well, tea. But you need proper help. Medical help."

Marty swallows painfully and gives up trying to respond.

"When you have enough strength, I will help you down the mountain. But my hut is the safest place for you now. We can't have more souls losing their lives unnecessarily on this mountain." The lady tucks a blanket under Marty's hip. "Far too many have been lost already."

Marty cautiously lifts his hand, hoping to feel what is covering his face and, if possible, remove it.

"Leave it," the lady instructs him. "You're not ready for the light."

Marty takes a deep breath and braces for the pain of speaking again.

"I need to see you," he pleads.

"You can't," says the woman. "Your eyes and eyelids are burnt awfully. You have terrible snow blindness. I'm sorry. But it is necessary to keep your eyes covered… necessary if you ever want to see again."

Marty drops his hand onto the prickly mattress next to his chest and grits his teeth once more. "Then at least tell me who you are?" he demands, feeling his lower lip splitting and a sore oozing of blood bursting out. He groans in agony.

"Who am I?" says the lady, carefully dabbing Marty's lip with a soft cloth. "I'm nobody. Nobody important."

Marty can't believe it; he's going to have to speak again. He can't leave her answer at that.

"Tell me. Please," he hisses desperately.

"I can't," she says.

He grimaces in silent agony, feeling his whole body throbbing with pain. And the pain doesn't relent. In the silence between them, the pain screams through his body, clawing at Marty's mind. Telling him to let go. Telling him to give up.

Then Marty feels himself falling away. Tumbling into an absence of sensation. Losing all consciousness and care. He feels himself dying. He wants to hold on, but he can't.

He feels his mouth being prised open and, numb to the pain, hears something rattle against his teeth. Something that gives his mind just enough energy to hold on.

"You are not meant to die here," says the lady. "Not yet."

***

Chapter 47

The Doldrums

The Meadow - Near The Irish Sea

Igh in the sky, the stars twinkle bright, and the air is biting cold. But there is not a breath. A dozen nautical miles west of *The Guiding Star*, where the Channel starts to mingle with the Irish Sea and the furthest reaches of the Atlantic Ocean, sits the *Charybdis*.

The old, creaking decks of the *Charybdis* are deserted, save for two solitary figures. One on the starboard deck. One on port. Lookouts. Dark, hooded figures who silently survey the horizon.

Deep in the hull of the galleon are the prisoners' quarters. Through a tiny porthole, starlight beams into one of these cabins. A cabin where a small, squat lady in dirty robes, with her arms and legs bound to a wooden chair, is beginning to regain her consciousness. Since being taken unceremoniously from her pub on the north bank of the Lethe, she hasn't seen natural light in days.

Sat opposite Kim-Joy, looming in the shadows, watching her come around, is a man whom she has never met, but a man who has been hunting her for years. Governor Andrew Callaghan. The Ferryman.

"I bet you thought we'd never get you? Thought your little tavern was impenetrable! Well, you're a fool!"

Kim-Joy shuffles uncomfortably, and her eyes open, needing some time to adjust to the dim, blue starlight. Her body aches, and her mind races. Before looking at the man, she tries to make sense of where she is and what has happened.

She remembers a commotion in the cellar at the *Tide and Time*. She remembers the shouts— '*The Distillery are here!*'. And The Mineralist. He was there. Holding an injection needle, approaching her at pace. Ready to sedate her. *'Sweet dreams!'* That was the last rasping voice she remembers.

Kim-Joy turns her head to the porthole. *'I'm on a boat, at sea,'* she deduces, her mind filling with the possibilities of where.

"Well?" says the Ferryman, impatiently.

Kim-Joy turns to face him, finally.

"Andrew Callaghan," she says, like a headteacher talking to a troublesome pupil. "I thought you might be involved."

"It's *The Ferryman,* to you!" he growls.

"Oh, but Andrew is such a lovely name. I'm sure your mother would rather you used it more."

The Ferryman spits in Kim-Joy's direction.

"Don't you fucking speak of my mother!" he shouts. "You know nothing of her!"

As his phlegm drips down her forehead, Kim-Joy stares back unmoved.

"I know more about her than you imagine," she says.

The Ferryman grits his teeth, straightens his jacket, and sits upright. Altering his physical stance, he tries to regain control. That's his intention, at least.

"You know why you're here?" he asks menacingly.

"I don't even know where *here* is!" says Kim-Joy.

"We're on a voyage," says the Ferryman. "Taking you to... shall we say... your Final Choice... A little jump into the Beyond or a fire to Nowhere!"

Kim-Joy grins sarcastically. "Sounds exotic!"

The Ferryman gets up and strikes Kim-Joy across the face. It leaves her cheek red and stinging. Though she doesn't flinch. She blinks a few times before returning her stare, resolutely, at the coward in front of her.

"Do you want to know why we are taking you there?" asks the Ferryman, unsettled by the lack of reaction from the old woman.

"I think I know," says Kim-Joy, running her tongue over her bruised gums.

"Yeah?!" says the Ferryman. "And why is that?"

"Maybe *you* don't know?" Kim-Joy teases.

The Ferryman doesn't respond. It's true, he doesn't know precisely why the *Horsemen* wanted her. Or at least, why they wanted to take her alive. But he also doesn't want her to know that.

"I guess it's the same reason you've been after my *Tide and Time* for years," starts Kim-Joy. "Because you're scared of me! Scared of us! Clinging to control in your impotent Distillery, but knowing the truth… the truth that you are completely and utterly out of control, and nothing makes sense!"

The Ferryman steps forward again, towering over the old woman tied to the chair. He can't ignore such obvious goading. Even when he has the clear physical advantage. He puts both of his hands around Kim-Joy's neck and squeezes.

"I should end your life here in the Meadow right here, right now!" he says, his voice grating into Kim-Joy's ears.

Yet, still, she stares right back at him. And as she stares, Kim-Joy looks deep into the Ferryman's eyes and knows she is right. He is a terrified little boy. Afraid of her and terrified of how little he understands of the world around him. Scared because he has no idea what to do.

The Ferryman can't hold her gaze. His eyes jump from her face to the window, to the door, and back. And his grasp doesn't tighten. He is not trying to kill her. He is trying to scare her.

Footsteps coming down the corridor towards the prisoners' quarters make both of them turn. Andrew loosens his grip and steps away.

And, even though no hands are blocking her airway, it is now that Kim-Joy holds her breath. She knows, whoever is about to come through that door, they are someone that even the Ferryman is afraid of.

The cabin door opens with an agonising yawn, and a lantern light, clutched in the hand of a tall, hooded man, pours in. He is flanked by others just like him—the *Horsemen*.

"Ah, good. You've come around," whispers the lantern-bearer.

"Your dosage was precise, Samael," says one of his colleagues.

"Of course," says Samael, the lantern-bearer. "I don't leave things to chance."

Samael steps forward and places his lantern on the floor before stepping up to Kim-Joy and removing his hood.

Kim-Joy stares in surprise at the familiar face in front of her. A young man, Eric van Koopler. He had been with the City Circus before he went missing a year ago. Kim-Joy had been supporting his mother at the *Tide and Time* since.

But there is no recognition in Eric's eyes. In fact, as Kim-Joy stares at the young man, something peculiar hits her. Eric's face is perfect and smooth, as it always was. His features are crisp and attractive. But around the edges of his mouth, and in the pinch of his eyes, grains of sand have formed. And she can't help but notice that the tip of his nose appears smooth and grainy, as though it is eroding away.

Eric doesn't say a word as he inspects her. Then he places a hand on her forehead, moving her backwards so that he can look at her neckline.

"You have interfered with the prisoner," he rasps, accusingly, turning his head towards Andrew.

"I... I barely touched her, your lordship," he responds sheepishly.

"You weren't supposed to touch her *at all!* We told you how important it was that you deliver the goods intact."

Kim-Joy can't take her eyes off Eric, who they are calling Samael. As he speaks in the lantern light, she notices showery grains of sand emanating from his mouth, as though his lungs are producing them instead of the usual condensation of breath.

"Is she damaged, Samael?" asks a hooded man who has stayed in the shadows by the door.

Samael turns back to inspect Kim-Joy. He leans in close to her face. So close that she can smell the sweet scent of his breath. She is utterly unprepared for what he does next.

Without warning or consent, he pulls his lips against hers, drawing her into a passionate kiss. She doesn't have time to react, and the man's grip on the back of her head is tight, so she can't pull away.

In this awful moment, Kim-Joy's mind fizzles with confusion, fear, and fury, and she feels a feeling she hasn't felt in centuries. An oozing of resin squeezing out of the elderly pores of her forehead.

Sensing this, the man pulls away, wiping his finger across her forehead.

"No damage," he declares, without looking at Kim-Joy. "You're lucky, Callaghan."

Kim-Joy's mind returns to a sharp and bewildered focus. Her silence can last no longer.

"Who are you?!" she asks, her voice quaking. "What do you want with me?"

"Ah… the *devil* speaks," smiles Samael, turning back to his victim. "You know of us, surely? Your people have reified our legend, plenty enough!" He chuckles. "I am… we are… the *Horsemen*. Horsemen of the Apocalypse."

"Don't patronise me," says Kim-Joy, defiantly. "Those pious fairy tales have never washed with me. I know you're not from the Meadow. Well… at least part of you isn't from here… Are you from the Beyond?"

Samael sniggers. "It's hard not to patronise," he says. "When speaking to such an infantile mind… the 'Beyond'… come on! Surely you know its real name… *Elysian*. We… I… hail from Elysian… We are angels of *His*. We are guardians of the truth. The protectors of order. If *She* hasn't told you that, well, then *She* obviously doesn't trust you."

Kim-Joy stares at Samael. "But you're not *all* angel right now, are you?"

"I beg your pardon?"

"Your body. I know your body from another life."

Samael's gaze shifts to his colleagues by the door, as though this is a revelation he had not anticipated.

"The body is a temporary vehicle… in this realm. A vehicle to take me from A to B, as you earth-folk say. And it stinks. Stinks of the vile human who wore it first…"

"So, it is you," says Kim-Joy carefully. "One of the homeless souls that are connecting us to Elysian… the souls bringing a darkness that plagues this realm. A darkness that holds the Distillery in its palm." She casts an angry look at the Ferryman.

"Ah, so you *do* know about me! But how blinded you are by *Her* lies. We are not darkness, we are light. You... She... Her... that is darkness. Chaos! But not for long! We know you are close to Her and know you have been hiding Her while She protects you. Well, no more! Your tavern is in ruins. Your stronghold in the Meadow is decimated. Indeed, *you* are no more if you don't cooperate."

"Then, what is it you want me to cooperate about?" asks Kim-Joy calmly. "Can't you speak to Her yourself?"

"Don't insult me," rasps Samael. "We are closing in on Her. She thought she could hide here in the Meadow. She thought she could hide on Earth. But her sanctuaries are collapsing... and we will have her soon. But that is beside the point... It is the unnatural witchcraft that she has instilled in your rebellious movement of Well-Wishing... the vile practice of going against His Will... of going against the natural order, that you are charged with. You started it with your Returns to Earth. That was bad enough. But now, She has helped you to traverse consciously onwards to Elysian, flooding our realm with Her chaos."

"We know *She* has a sanctuary here in the Meadow... She must have. She is being protected in the realm of the mind. But we have looked far and wide. We have scoured every inch of the Meadow... even your beloved *Tide and Time Tavern*. And still there is no trace.

"Tell me, where is she hiding? You know where we can find her... You can tell all and end this *madness!* Else, your extinction and the extinction of all your rebels await! He is merciful. But He is also vengeful."

"Are you going to cooperate?"

Samael leans in close to Kim-Joy once more. She winces, bracing for another assault. But it doesn't come.

"We have ways of making this easier, or harder?" he says, pulling a pouch of marbles from his pocket. "Each marble lubricates the path to truth," he says, rolling the marbles in his palm. "Truth can come from torture, or trust." He holds a single marble between each thumb and forefinger. "It's your choice."

Kim-Joy stares at the two marbles, resting in the young man's palms in front of her. Both marbles gleam. A combination of lantern and moonlight. But one marble gives off its own light. It is a warm, fiery marble. It emits a comforting glow. This marble would make truth-telling gentle and comfortable. Its neighbour is the opposite. It's trying to suck in the light. The dark and rough black sphere is cold and uneven. Its surface is cracked and fractured. It is the kind of marble that scratches at one's soul, tearing painfully and drawing out the truth in a vomiting retch—a cruel, painful incision.

But Kim-Joy isn't considering which marble to choose. She doubts she really has a choice. Instead, she ponders Samael. The man whose body she knows but whose soul is strange. She lifts her eyes.

"I think I know why you haven't found Her on Earth," says Kim-Joy, a smile sneaking into the edges of her mouth. "You can't get there, can you? Your borrowed body can't withstand traversing into another realm with you."

Kim-Joy interrogates Samael, staring at him. Staring beyond him. And as she does this, she senses his soul wobbling. Wobbling back and forth from the body it resides within.

"How did you manage to hijack another mind's body, though?" she asks him. "What sorcery are you practising? Is it His sorcery?"

Samael says nothing.

"And somehow you despise *Her* because she disrupts the 'natural order'?! Disrupts your one-directional river from death to the heavens? Then, you are hypocrites! Traversing a foreign realm, going against nature, in search of Her… just like He did!"

"Do not blaspheme!" shouts Samael.

"You see the hypocrisy, do you not, Andrew?" Kim-Joy raises her gaze to the Ferryman, who is cowering in the corner of the cabin. "You have succumbed to these souls when they have blatantly lied to you?! They are hunting *Her* because they know She challenges their power, their realm, and their lies."

"Enough!" shouts Samael, blocking the Ferryman from Kim-Joy's sight and stepping up to her. "Then, you have made your choice, Kim-Joy!" He hurls the light, warm marble at the floor, smashing it angrily. "It must be the cruel stone for the dark mind," he rasps, grasping the hair on the top of Kim-Joy's head and throwing her backwards, tearing loose follicles from her scalp, before thrusting two fingers into her mouth.

Kim-Joy tastes the grainy, eroding texture of his skin and braces her body and mind for what is coming.

Samael drops the dark light-sucking marble onto her tongue, making her wince in pain.

Sharp needles scrape through Kim-Joy's veins, as though infesting her body with microscopic vermin which scratch and claw into every corner of her existence, trying to tear out the truth.

"You can feel that, can't you?" says Samael. "Clawing through your mind... It didn't have to be this way... This is our first of many... *conversations*, you know. If you choose to be more compliant, this is the only one that needs to be this painful... your choice."

"Now, let's start this first conversation with an easy question. A simple 'yes' or 'no' will suffice... You are Kim-Joy, landlady of the *Tide and Time Tavern*, yes?"

"Yes."

"Good... and you arrived here five hundred years ago after a fire in the public house in which you and your son left Earth, yes?"

"No."

"No?!" blurts Samael. "Come on, tell the truth! How did you arrive here?!"

"On a cold winter's morning, when I could no longer bear the loneliness of Earth, I hung myself from the lowest branch of a frosty oak tree, stood alone beside a lake in Richmond Park."

"No, you didn't!" shouts Samael. "Tell the truth!"

"That is the truth," says Kim-Joy, calmly.

"Is it the marble, Samael?" one of the silent hooded figures from the door speaks up. "Is it less potent than we thought?"

"It can't be," says Samael. "There is no stronger or more potent stone... I extracted it myself." He looks across at his colleague, concern etched into the sandy furrowing of his brow.

"Perhaps the sedatives are still wearing off?"

"No," says Samael, a whisper of panic cutting in. "Maybe I need to be more direct." He snaps his gaze back to Kim-Joy, whose eyes loll backwards, up to the ceiling.

"Tell me... you have been harbouring Her, haven't you? Where? Where is She? Where have you been hiding her?"

Kim-Joy, her brow glistening, looks back calmly, despite the tension that tears every muscle of her face and body as it fights the pain. Her fingernails claw into the seat. She is resolute and says nothing.

Samael grasps hold of Kim-Joy's head with both hands.

"Tell. Me. Where. She. Is?!" he shouts.

Kim-Joy closes her eyes for a second, then returns to him, sharply in focus.

"She is everywhere. And She is nowhere. She is because, He isn't. And She will be victorious!"

Samael loses his patience. He rocks his head back and smashes his forehead into Kim-Joy's face with a violent crack. But the old lady, despite being bruised and bloodied by this vicious attack, remains steady. The same can't be said for Samael.

The impact with the old lady's skull has cracked off a whole piece of his face, which has crumbled away like sand, leaving a deep, gaping cavern in his head. It is as though he is made entirely of sand.

"Samael?" asks one of the hooded figures by the door, cautiously approaching his colleague.

But before Samael can respond, there is a rumbling. A rumbling in the atmosphere and across the ocean. And a larger, much more powerful presence approaches.

***

Whilst this conversation is happening, east of the *Charybdis*, where the warm night air is also quiet, as quiet as death, and the sea is a perfectly blank, dark canvas, speckled with the reflection of the stars above, the *Guiding Star* sits in the middle of this sphere of light. The horizons are all but gone, and the shape of the hull in the starlight is the only interruption to a full circumspect of stars.

Below deck, Eilish has finally fallen asleep. The trauma of the day has exhausted her mind and her body, which still tumbles through the awful pain of new beginnings. Elijah and Nailah have turned in as well. Leaving just Cyril alone on deck.

On the cabin roof, Cyril has laid out a chart of the seas surrounding them. The starlight is bright enough to read the details on the map and to follow the delicate contours of the sea floor. He takes out a pen lid from his pocket and places it, pointing towards Land's End, a few nautical miles off the toenail of the Meadow. "The *Charybdis* is about here," he mutters to himself.

As he gazes at the chart, Cyril is suddenly aware that he is no longer alone. He senses that another presence has just joined him on the *Guiding Star*.

"Hello?" he says, cautiously, looking around. "I know you're here. Come on, it's only polite… please introduce yourself."

He waits.

"I'm Cyril Spate," he continues, aloud. "Trawlerman of *The Guiding Star*. And you are…?"

He waits in silence.

Then, like a breath on the air, a lady's voice whispers back. "*I'm a friend…*"

"Nice to meet you, 'friend'," says Cyril, smiling. "Have we met before?"

"*No,*" whispers the voice. "*I've not met you, but I am familiar with someone on your crew.*"

"You are?" says Cyril, intrigued. "Shall I go and get them?"

"*No. There's no time…*"

"No time?"

"*He is coming.*"

"He?"

"*Yes… Him.*"

Cyril pauses. "I see," he says, feeling the hairs on the back of his neck prickle.

"I have come to tell you something. Something vital. They are taking your friend to the House of Sand beneath the Source. You must stop them."

"We're trying," frowns Cyril.

"They must not succeed in their mission."

"Their mission?" asks Cyril.

"To find her secret. The future of your rebellion, the future of Well-Wishing, and the future of the Universe depend upon you stopping them."

"No pressure then?" grins Cyril, unable to help himself.

"Help is coming," says the lady.

"It is?"

"Soon," says the lady. *"But…"*

"Go on," says Cyril.

But before the voice can answer, Cyril senses an immense darkness approaching.

He is approaching.

***

Chapter 48

Impotent Rage

The Meadow - The Irish Sea

Knowing, or not knowing, who or what the approaching darkness is, is terrifying to Kim-Joy. It is as though every *thing* around her is overcome with fear. The air, the sea, the old creaking galleon, and the minds, the souls, and the bodies of everyone inside the *Charybdis*.

Kim-Joy is frozen. She has never encountered *Him* like this before. But she knows, it must be Him.

Andrew Callaghan cowers, deeper and lower than when Samael entered the cabin. He basically lies, prostrate on the floor, muttering prayers desperately.

And the soul, called Samael, that clings to the crumbling body of Eric van Koopler, bows low, pulling his fractured head towards the deck.

"My Lord, forgive me!" he shouts, evidently aware of the identity of the presence. Then he drops to the floor and starts to writhe.

Kim-Joy watches, horrified, knowing that the presence is inflicting an excruciating pain on the soul of Samael. His hands, possessed, turn on himself, scratching at his face, tearing away chunks of sandy, crumbling flesh, and scraping into the existing cavernous hole in the side of his head. It is awful. And yet, in the company of this terrifying presence, Kim-Joy finds that she cannot turn away, and she cannot make a sound.

"I'm trying!" shouts Samael, desperately, responding to an unheard question. "We have Kim-Joy, I'm sure of it. She must have done something to break the core of her memory, but it's her, I'm sure!... Yes, yes, we are closing in on Her on Earth as well... yes, I'm sure of it." Then Samael screams out in agony, turning onto his back and convulsing as though having a seizure.

Kim-Joy senses that the soul of Samael is wavering to and from the broken body it inhabits, becoming increasingly vulnerable to losing its grip entirely.

And then, feeling like the atmosphere in the galleon darkens, a voice erupts from the presence. A voice that echoes into every mind in the cabin.

"*Do not return to me without Her!*" it hollers.

In a command of energy, more powerful than the voice, the presence roars. And from the stillness of the air comes a rush of wind. The calm sea outside becomes choppy and angry, and inside the *Charybdis,* the bodies of Samael and his fellow hooded men collapse, creating heaps of sand which are thrown against the wall.

The presence and the souls of all but Samael are gone with the burst of energy. But Samael, his soul fragile, vulnerable, and now without a host body to cling to, is left in the cabin.

"Bring Kim-Joy to the lake house," Samael's disembodied voice calls out desperately. "She has answers, I know it. Do not let her go!"

The Ferryman knows that this command is meant for him.

"Yes," he says, still cowering on the floor. "Yes… I will see you at *The Source* as soon as we can."

"And bring me a new host, damnit!" shouts Samael's voice. "Number Seventeen will do fine."

"Yes," says the Ferryman. "Number Seventeen."

Another breath of wind whistles through the cabin, and this time, the soul of Samael is taken away too.

Kim-Joy drops the black marble from her mouth and stares in silence at the Ferryman. He looks back at her, afraid, and so Kim-Joy offers him a warm, disarming smile.

"You do not have to be afraid," she says, closing her eyes. "There is another way."

The Ferryman looks at the old lady and notices, in the briefest of moments, the beautiful imperfections of her wrinkled face. His head twitches nervously, rejecting his weakness. He carefully gets to his feet and, turning away from Kim-Joy, walks gingerly out of the cabin.

The little old landlady, tied to the chair, her face bruised and bloodied, sighs. '*Thank you*,' she mutters under her breath. And though no presence can be felt, in her soul Kim-Joy is grateful for Her warmth.

***

"So, we *are* going to the Source?" asks Nailah, looking at Cyril, as she and Elijah gather around the trawlerman on the deck of the *Guiding Star*. They had been woken by an unusual squall a moment earlier. It has calmed again now, but a gentle blow has the boat moving steadily forward.

"It seems so," frowns Cyril. "But I think we'd do well to intercept them before they get there. You know, as well as I do, Nailah, the Mountain belongs to the Distillery—the boundary is heavily fortified, and the face itself is treacherously littered with barbed wire, collapsing mineshafts, and unstable cliffs. No one but Drifters get to the Source these days."

"So, how do you propose we intercept them?" asks Nailah.

"I suggest we get as close as we can when they're on land and wait for them to drop their guard."

"You think they will?"

"Everyone drops their guard."

"Even spirits?"

Cyril chuckles. "I'm inclined to think they do," he winks at her.

"You say it was a 'spirit' that told you about the *Charybdis'* destination?" asks Elijah.

"That's right," says Cyril. "Have you ever met one?"

"No," he says. "I didn't actually believe they were real."

"Oh, they're real alright. Shame Eilish isn't up here, she's well accustomed to spirits in the Meadow. In fact, she knows the same one who visited last night."

"Really?" asks Nailah. "How do you know?"

"The spirit told me… well, told me in a way."

"And you're sure they're truthful?"

"I think so," says Cyril. "She wasn't prepared to hang around when the darkness came. And any being that flees darkness is on our side, I presume."

"Where will the *Charybdis* land?" asks Elijah.

"Holyhead," frowns Nailah. Cyril nods. "And there's no way we can land there."

"Why not?"

"Busiest port in the Meadow these days," says Cyril. "Ever since the Distillery struck a deal with *La Prairie,* there have been backlogs of their Drifter barges. You need a permit just to enter the waters around the harbour now."

"So, what's the plan?" asked Nailah.

Cyril grins. "Anyone travelling from Holyhead to the Source will have to get to the mainland via the Menai Suspension Bridge. There's a quick way to that bridge," he smiles. "But it requires some serious seamanship…"

"Not the *Swellies*?!" asks Nailah.

"The Swellies!" beams Cyril. "You know of them?"

"I know enough… I know just how dangerous that stretch of water is… whirlpools, shallow and deep currents, hidden rocks… no end of trouble."

Cyril chuckles mischievously. "But it's a darn sight quicker than the alternatives!"

"If you think we can do it," says Nailah. "You're the skipper."

"We can do it," he says, but a flicker of worry in his eyes betrays him. "So long as Eilish pulls together soon. We're going to need all hands on deck!"

***

Chapter 49

Blind Coincidence

Earth - Mynydd Aaru

Crack!

Marty's mind suddenly floods with consciousness. Consciousness and pain. He's still on the bed. Still incapacitated and lying prone on a prickly and uncomfortable mattress. Still blindfolded with retinas that burn even with his eyes firmly shut.

Crack!

A swirling mountain squall outside is battering the hut, and the door is fighting to hold its latch. Inside, there is an eerie calmness: a quietness that contrasts with the weather and Marty's pain.

"Tea?" says the soft, lilting voice of the woman.

Marty had almost forgotten about her.

He shifts his body towards her voice, testing his threshold for pain. Mercifully, the overwhelming agony seems to have retreated, leaving a throbbing numbness in its wake. He opens his dry mouth cautiously, feeling his saliva sticking to the sharp cracks along his lips, but the skin doesn't break.

"Yes, please," he whispers.

He listens to the comforting and familiar trickle of boiling water splashing onto the dry bag of tea nestled in a porcelain mug. Then a shadow falls over his eyelids, telling him she approaches. He opens his mouth pathetically. He knows he doesn't have the strength or coordination to sit up and drink.

The warmth of the tea that dribbles down his throat is wonderful. His mind, which had felt dull and exhausted, yawns as though waking from a deep sleep, and clicks into gear. It's magical. It's as though the tea has been laced with something.

"Who are you?" he whispers, surprised by how alive he suddenly feels.

The woman doesn't reply. She takes a sip of the tea herself and draws in a long, settling breath.

"I can't say," she replies mildly.

Marty's lip curls with the slightest hint of a knowing smile. A detective's smile. When people say 'they can't', they rarely mean 'they won't'. What they often mean is 'they shouldn't'.

"Why?" he says, his voice finally breaking out of the whisper.

"Because... Because nobody knows who I am," she says softly. "They can't. They mustn't."

Marty is momentarily halted by the lady's cryptic answer, leaving an instant in which the hut is flooded with the distant screams of the storm outside and Marty's senses go into overdrive.

He pushes himself up. Not upright, but less prone, more alert. The pain throbs again, but his voice emerges stronger.

"Why have you been following me?" he asks, catching her by surprise.

"Following you?!" she says, turning away evasively. "I've not been following you... I rescued you!"

"No... before now," Marty clarifies. "I've seen you before... haven't I?"

The lady is quiet, weighing up her options.

"Have I seen you before?" she asks, throwing it back at Marty. "Where?"

"The *Three Knots* at Shoreditch, and the fire..."

"You were there?" she asks, surprised. "Were you caught in the fire?"

"No, I was lucky."

"How do you know I was there?"

"I saw you... And I saw you at the gas explosion in Dagenham..."

"You were there as well?"

"I was there," says Marty.

The lady stops. Marty's interrogation unsettles her, and she stands still, as though trying to work something out. Something unfathomable that she cannot comprehend. She feels in her pocket for something. Something of reassurance.

Behind her, the door rattles noisily again, and a cold wave of frigid air whistles into the hut, ruffling Marty's blanket.

"You saw me in Dagenham?" she asks, carefully, ignoring the storm.

"Just about," says Marty. "I saw you leave the scene."

There is silence in the little hut, contrasting with the impatient, whistling wind outside.

"And I know you were there when that ambulance crashed into the pedestrians at Hammersmith," says Marty.

"That's impossible," blurts the lady. "How could you possibly have been at all three of those tragedies?!"

"I have the same question for you," says Marty. "I'm a detective in the Metropolitan Police… I've been following you for years. I know your 'calling card', your criminal 'signature'… that symbol—the encircled water droplet. You've been leaving it all over the place. And I've seen you, skulking in the shadows of tragedy, fulfilling some kind of macabre fascinations or morbid fantasies… Which is it?"

"Neither!" cries the lady, sounding panicked.

"Did you cause them?" asks Marty.

"No! Of course not!" she shouts. "Never!"

"But you knew they were coming?!"

"I… I…"

"Why didn't you stop them?"

"I couldn't… They… they *needed* to happen."

"What?!"

"I can't explain," says the lady, her voice genuinely apologetic. "You wouldn't understand…"

"Try me."

She pauses. "No… All I can say is, everything you see has happened before. And it *must* happen again."

Marty scoffs, but knows his face betrays his utter confusion.

"It's true, I swear," says the lady. "But it doesn't concern you…."

"It does!" says Marty. "A London bus you marked crashed in Chiswick ten years ago. It collided with my son. It put my son into his coma... And that explosion in Dagenham... it has been pinned on me! I've lost my job in the Met. I've lost my life, my reputation, and I'm on the run. So, yes, it does fucking concern me!"

The strain of Marty's fury sends pain shooting through his mind and into his exhausted body. He cries out.

The lady steps away from Marty and lets out her own long, deep sigh.

"It can't all be coincidence," she says aloud to herself. "There's no way. No way you'd piece it all together. There's no way you'd think to look for me. No. They weren't crime scenes. There are no fingerprints. No. Someone has put you up to this... Who have you been speaking to?" she asks Marty directly, her voice shaky but stern. "Who has put you up to this?"

"No, no," says Marty, "that's not fair. You can't turn this on me. You're the one who has too many coincidences... You're the one who keeps showing up in my life."

"Someone has spoken to you, haven't they?" the lady repeats, worried by how certain she feels. "Someone has pointed you to me?"

"So, what if they have?" says Marty, defiantly.

The lady draws in a sharp breath. "No!" she exclaims. "Not now. Not when I'm so close... Who is it? Please, who is it?!"

"Ha! Why would I tell you that, after you've been *so* open with me?!"

"Please!" pleads the lady. "You have no idea."

"I think I do, actually," says Marty, feeling more certain than he should. "I know all about you."

"You do?"

"You're the one *he's* looking for."

"He?!" repeats the lady. "Who have you spoken to?"

Marty stops. He has been in this place in interrogations many times before. The point of stalemate where both parties know that they each have information that the other needs, but at the same time neither is ready to risk it.

Both Marty and the woman linger in the moment. Both minds whirring, concentrating on what the other has said. Looking for contradiction or clue in the others' comments and questions.

Crack! Smash!

The door's resistance is broken. An explosion of icy air blasts in, and the door clatters into the frame of Marty's bed.

Marty flinches, blindly, feeling the reverberations through his spine and the suffocating cold in his lungs.

"Watch out!" shouts the lady, but too late.

A heavy steel pot that had been resting precariously on a shelf above the bed falls onto the oblivious and incapacitated man, striking him hard, knocking him unconscious.

The lady rushes over to Marty, fearing the worst. But the impact, though forceful, was glancing.

Face down, Marty snorts. His mouth and nose are muffled by the mattress. The lady carefully turns his head, revealing a lump rising behind his ear. He's hurt and unconscious, but he will be fine.

"There's no way you can have come from the Meadow?" she whispers to herself, quietly. "I would know... But someone from the Meadow must have spoken to you."

She looks at Marty. When he sleeps and his mind is disengaged, he looks so peaceful. Just like his son had done.

***

Chapter 50

Time to Talk

The Meadow - The Irish Sea

In the light, before the sun has risen, a silhouette of the land is visible over the starboard bow of *The Guiding Star*.

"That's where we're heading," says Cyril, pointing Elijah to a passageway between the mainland of Wales and the island of Anglesey.

"That's the *Swellies*?" asks Elijah, squinting. "You've been through there before?"

"Never," says Cyril, mischievously. "But I've studied them. And I know trawler folk who have done it."

Elijah looks nervously at Cyril.

"We'll be fine."

"I can't see the *Charybdis* anymore," says Elijah, peering over the bow.

"No, she'll have rounded the headland by now, on her way to Holyhead. But we have plenty of time to get ready to pick up their trail after they cross the suspension bridge."

The hatch of the cabin opens, and Nailah pokes her head out.

"Coffee marbles," she says, passing up rattling ramekins. "Let's have sharp minds for the *Swellies*."

"How's she doing down there?" asks Cyril.

"She's up and talking… but groggy."

"And has *it* worked?"

Nailah smiles. "Come and see for yourself."

Cyril chuckles. "Right, Elijah… keep us heading towards that gap. I'm going to have a little chat with Eilish… make sure she's ready for choppy waters."

*

Eilish is sitting up in her hammock, calmly peering out of the porthole, as Cyril and Nailah enter the cabin. The bucket is empty and dry. It hasn't been used all day, and Nailah has already wiped Eilish clean, bathed her face and arms in warm water, brushed her hair, and given her a fresh set of clean clothes. It has all helped Eilish to feel as normal as possible.

"Governess," starts Cyril.

Eilish doesn't respond.

"Of course," Cyril catches himself. "I mean… Eilish!"

Eilish turns and smiles, seeing the familiar face of Cyril.

"You're looking well."

"I feel it," she says.

"Did Nailah tell you how many days you've been out?"

"Yes!" smiles Eilish.

"And how's that charm coming along?"

Eilish feels into her pocket, touching the sticky lump of resin. "It's getting there."

"And has the resin stopped now?"

"Nearly…. Thank god!"

"Excellent," says Cyril. "Then, I think it must be time for us to have the chat that this whole exercise was for…"

Eilish leans in eagerly. "You're going to tell me about *Her* and the 'secret' Kim-Joy keeps?"

"Yes," says Nailah, grasping Eilish's hand lovingly. "Because we trust you."

Cyril raises a hand. "First, indulge me, Eilish… Tell me your name."

"Elish Callaghan."

"And tell me how you came to be in the Meadow?"

Without hesitating, an image flickers into Eilish's mind, and she recalls it. "I was plagued with self-loathing on Earth," she begins. "My father and brother made my life feel small and insignificant. They bullied me mercilessly. They overlooked me with every opportunity, and they convinced me that every misfortune my family faced it was down to me. Down to my failings.

"One night, I made peace with my sister Ciara, who I know suffered like me. Then I took myself to a cheap hotel on the River Wear in Newcastle, where Ciara was at university. I booked a room on the top floor with one intention. I remember the cold, icy wind that blew through the open window, and the trouble I had unscrewing the restraint that stopped it from opening fully. But I did it. I remember the jump and the dull grey concrete rushing up towards me… and then I arrived here."

Nailah holds Eilish's hand tight, aware of the trauma of recalling such a memory, irrespective of its reality. She bows her head and kisses Eilish's knuckles.

"And what of your brother and father?" asks Cyril.

"What about them?"

"Are they here in the Meadow?"

"Yes," confirms Eilish. "They died in a plane crash."

"But not with you?"

"Of course not!" smiles Eilish.

"Good," says Cyril. "Then you are ready. Let us tell you a story about *Her*. The most important story you will ever hear."

***

Chapter 51

Her Story

Earth - London - The Meadow

This is the story of *Her*. A lady from Earth who died in a fire, set by herself, and who ultimately started a fire of rebellion in the universe. Her death on Earth was just the beginning.

The lady had lived in a cruel world. The city of London in the fifteenth century was only kind to a very few. For the rest, who lived in abject poverty, like Her, survival was the best they could hope for. And even then, for many, survival was just a short-lived dream.

The lady was born in squaller, in a terraced house filled with filth, excrement, and half a dozen siblings. Her father was abusive and always drunk. Her mother, the kindest lady she ever knew, was the family's 'breadwinner'. A breadwinner who made the family's dough by selling her body to the greedy gluttons who polluted the city at night.

And the thing with London, in those days, was that family trades stayed in the family. So, when the lady was old 'enough', she too took up her mother's trade and became, in the hungry eyes of the city's wealthy filth– an undesirable who was desired. A condemned soul that littered the society's underbelly.

In her life, as a young lady who sold access to her body in the slums of Tudor London, she had little sanctuary. And so, like her father before her, she discovered the small comforts of things like alcohol and opium. Comforts that could numb the pain. And there was a pub, just north of the River Thames, which offered women like her a safe place. A place to ply her trade, but a place where her trade did not come with the usual risk to life or risk of jail, and where a steady flow of mead could keep the pain numb enough.

As the lady entered her late twenties, the last of her brothers and sisters, whom she had tried desperately to support, lost their lives to illness and the bottle. And so, by the time she reached her thirtieth birthday, she was alone in the world. Alone, and full of remorse. She was desperate and longed for peace. Peace in her mind and an absence of pain.

In this turmoil, the lady met someone. Or rather, some*thing*. Lodging in the attic room of the tavern, the lady was visited one still summer night by a spirit. A spirit who told her he was an angel from the heavens. He said he had come to comfort her and protect her. And he promised her a release from her pain.

The lady retreated from her outward life in London and became dependent on the promise of freedom from him. And she talked to him plenty. Every night, so long as the air was calm. Even on the nights after she had been out working her trade. And still, the angel comforted her.

And then one day, the angel told her how she could end her Earthly pain. He told her she could join him. Join him, if she chose death. This instruction, despite the lady's desperate situation, caused her great distress. She had seen the pain in her mother's eyes as she faced her final days. She had found the tortured body of her brother after he had taken his own life. And she had been terrified for years that this would be her own fate as well.

Now, the landlady of the tavern in which the lady stayed noticed her distress. She tried to be there if the lady wanted to talk, but she never intervened. It was not her place. And like with all the other women whom she gave sanctuary to in the tavern, the landlady just offered solace and a promise that, no matter what, she always had friends in the tavern.

Then, one night, the lady met with a regular customer. An older man with a temper. He always paid well, but on this night, he became violent. Extremely violent. And the lady decided, enough was enough.

Despairing and without hope, the lady went back to her attic room in the tavern, wishing the world would give her a way out. And, tragically, it did.

Outside, as it was on most nights in medieval London, a bonfire burned in the street. A fire was supposed to ward off the transmission of the plague. But these fires were notoriously dangerous, and every home had buckets of water ready to smother the stray sparks that inevitably danced their way onto nearby roofs.

In the lady's room, there was a full bucket like this. But when the fatal sparks climbed into her attic room that night, she didn't douse them. Instead, she stood back and watched. Watched with joyless and disinterested nihilism as the flames licked up the walls and spread across the ceiling, filling her room and lungs with smoke.

Before the flames consumed the lady, she saw, out of the window, the landlady and her son. She had thought they were out for the night. They were entering the tavern, unaware of the fire above. The lady heard them climbing the stairs, still not knowing of the danger. She wished she could stop the flames, but it was too late. The fire had grabbed hold of the wooden structure and was crackling and hissing. In no time, they were spreading around the tavern, and in the little attic room, the window blew out, allowing in enough air to preserve the lady's life just a little bit longer. Long enough to realise that the landlady and her son had become trapped and doomed with her.

Then, as her life came to its end on Earth, the final thing the lady heard was her spirit. He had been watching it all.

"*Come to me*," he said. "*You will not regret it!*"

And with that, the lady, the landlady, and her son died in the fire.

True to her spirit's word, the lady did find herself free of the pain of her old life. And not dead at all, but alive in a new place—the Meadow. It was like the London she knew, but it was almost empty. Only the occasional soul had entered the Meadow from Earth at that time. Accidents or traumas like hers were, mercifully, infrequent in those days.

But arriving in the Meadow with the lady were the landlady, her son, and the tavern as well. Wracked with guilt, the lady fled the tavern. She fled into the fledgling London. And this is when *he* met her. Her spirit. Though in the Meadow, he was not just a spirit with a voice. He was a man.

At first, the lady could not believe her luck. The spirit, who had given her solace on Earth, now, in the Meadow, took the form of the most beautiful man she had ever seen. A young man with kind eyes and an open soul. But her joy was short-lived.

The man took her to his home, a grand palace, where he introduced himself as a 'prince'—a prince who lived in a palace where she was not the only lady. There were hundreds of other women, all 'saved' by him from their traumas on Earth. All convinced by him to end their earthly lives and take a leap of faith into death. And now that he had collected them, they were in his grasp, literally, and he became cold and controlling.

The prince owned the women in the palace like property. He threatened them, filled them with fear, and made them fulfil his cruellest fantasies. The only peace they got was when he went to the chapel. A quiet place, out-of-bounds to the women, where his mind travelled to Earth to prey on the next vulnerable soul.

For years, the lady lived in the awful reality of the palace. She became haunted by the cruelty of an afterlife consumed by the same fear and despair she felt on Earth. And these feelings almost broke apart her soul. Indeed, it broke the souls of many of the women she lived with, making them become *Flickers*.

But as the lady spiralled into despair, she heard a rumour of sanctuary. A pub, run by a landlady and her son, where they were taking *Flickers* in, and giving them safety and life.

Her mind was made up. One night, when the prince was in his chapel, the lady escaped. She knew where the pub was and how to get there. She just needed time and a pinch of fortune. She scaled the palace walls, no one saw her go, and she fled into the night.

Stained by the memory of her arrival in the Meadow, the lady apologetically approached the pub, desperate to be let in. She needn't have feared. The landlady welcomed her with open arms.

For the second time, the landlady had saved her life. And this, she promised the lady, would be the last time she would need to be saved, for it was time to offer more than sanctuary. It was time to take on the monster.

Together, the two women plotted a rebellion—a rebellion against the prince and his palace. And the tavern became a base for their operations. From dilapidation and despair, the lady found strength.

The prince, angry and undermined by the lady's escape, didn't take long to find out about the pub. And one day, he paid a visit. A visit, in his terms, to 'claim back his property'. But he was not ready for how strong the lady had become.

When his words of persuasion did not convince her to leave, he approached. He lifted his arms threateningly, assuming she would succumb in fear. His body was strong and imposing after all. But she did not succumb. Instead, the lady grabbed a pot from the bar and smashed it into the man's face. And this is where something happened that the lady did not expect.

Instead of knocking the man back, the pot smashed the man. His face crumbled like sand, and his body fell to the floor. The impact of the pot had fractured his very being. For this man's 'body' was not his own. And a body that is not weaved intimately with the soul and the mind, is like sand on a beach, vulnerable to the wind.

The man's soul, his spirit, lingered in the pub over the remains of the body. He roared with fury, but there was nothing he could do. And now the lady knew about him. She knew he was not like her. He did not have a body like she did. And here in the Meadow, like on Earth, he was inescapably vulnerable.

But even though his body was gone, the cruel spirit of the man remained in the Meadow. And every day when the air was still, he visited the lady. He haunted her. And he told her it was only a matter of time before he found another body to inhabit. A better and stronger body. And on that day, he would come for her.

Only, he didn't. And one quiet, windless day, the kind of day the lady was accustomed to expect his awful intrusion, he didn't come at all. In fact, he didn't appear for weeks. And she started to allow herself to believe that he might have died. He might be gone, and her life would finally be free.

It wasn't.

It started as an autumn storm. And, while no one in the cities saw an Opening from Earth, all assumed there had been one, for why else would the weather shift so quickly? But the weather wasn't coming from Earth.

The storm grew and grew, until all of the Meadow was cloaked under dark, billowing clouds, and the rains came down. Heavy, angry rains, causing floods all over the Meadow. Flash floods that wiped out entire settlements. And the River Lethe in London burst its banks.

The Tavern, where the lady and the landlady lived, was under threat from the rising waters. The two women, and all others who claimed sanctuary at the pub, worked tirelessly to pile sandbags to try and protect the building from the floods.

But the rain didn't stop, and soon thunder and lightning filled the sky. It went on for weeks. The flood waters crept higher and higher, and bolts of lightning sparked fires all over the city. It wasn't a stretch for many to interpret it as the end times—the *apocalypse*. People made their peace with their gods and waited to be taken into whatever came next.

But then, just as the landlady prepared to leave the tavern, the storm cleared, and warm still air replaced the angry clouds.

The people rejoiced. In the bright sunshine that settled on the Meadow, they had survived. All who lived rejoiced with a new appreciation for life in the Meadow.

But something had changed. All over the realm, strange things had happened. In one of the Mountains of Wales, the storm never cleared, and a new flow of water burst out from the tallest peak, carving a stream into the Meadow. There were similar interruptions elsewhere in the realm, creating gaping holes into the unknown—fissures in the land, whirlpools in the sea, and bottomless pits in the ground. For new connections had been forged in the storm. Connections to the Beyond. Connections forged by a powerful and vengeful spirit from another realm. A realm called *Elysian* occupied by a group of people who called themselves Angels. An inquisitive people who had found ways to venture into the other realms as bodiless spirits. Angels like Gabriel, who had found his way into the folklore of Earth people.

Soon after the appearance of the links, the awful reality of the connections became clear. Before this day, people had lived comfortably in the Meadow. And only when a person's mind was too tired and ready to leave, did their second life in the Meadow end. It ended at a time when the person chose to fall away. A time when a person went into a gentle sleep and their body, tired and spent, crumbled into sand, while the spark of their soul climbed up into the heavens.

After the storm, this didn't happen anymore. People's minds now tired earlier. And instead of falling into a peaceful slumber, people who had only inhabited the Meadow for a few years or decades went unconscious. And, without thinking, without choice, they now wandered to the Mountains. For the connection between the Meadow and Elysian had been made by him, the prince, to draw souls out of the Meadow and into his realm—a realm where he was strong and could wait to claim his prize.

In the year that followed the storm, losing your mind in the Meadow became a fear that obsessed the people. A fear of losing your marbles and being taken away without will or control, into a realm dominated by vengeful and powerful angels.

And then *He* came back. He came back to the Palace, and this time he wasn't alone. He had a new body and an army of angels from Elysian with him. And he had one objective. He was coming for *her*.

He went to the tavern on the river, the site of his former demise, flanked by his angels. He assumed she would be there. He was ready to settle a score. But when the landlady greeted him, she told him the lady was gone.

The angels searched the tavern from top to bottom and found no one.

"Where is she?" he asked the landlady.

"At the Source," she told him. "She is coming to meet you."

But it wasn't true. The landlady had risked her life and had lied to the Prince. The lady was still in her tavern. Hidden beneath the cellar, in a pit that had formed during the floods. For the tavern, it turned out, was situated above a well. A natural well, unknown to anyone until that storm. A well that only the landlady and the women of the tavern knew about. And crouched in this well, the lady had been saved.

The landlady and the lady knew this was not a permanent solution. The prince would quickly discover that she was not at the Source and would surely return. The lady knew that there was only one way that she could truly escape him. She had to leave the Meadow. But leave like the souls before the storm. She had to disintegrate and let her spark climb into the stars. Like her life on Earth, all those years ago, she would have to instigate her own demise...

***

The Meadow - The Irish Sea

"Quite a story, isn't it?" says Cyril, leaning back on his stool in the cabin of the *Guiding Star*.

Eilish blinks. She had been captivated by the tale and had forgotten where she was. She looks at Cyril and at Nailah, who had both been telling the story. They looked drawn and serious.

"This story," Eilish starts. "This lady... this is the secret?"

"Almost," says Cyril.

"She is the lady from the legend that Kim-Joy told me about, right? ... The lady from the beginning of Well-Wishing?"

"Ah, not quite," says Nailah. "The legend you've heard... that should be taken less literally. Although I understand that believers only started referring to a 'lady' in that legend after *Her.*"

Nailah steps over to Eilish and holds out her hand "Can I see your *Stained Charm*?" she asks.

Eilish nods and passes the resin charm from her pocket.

"They're unique things, *Stained Charms*," says Nailah. "Their sensations never end... imbued with something more permanent than the feelings of a simple marble."

"I know," says Eilish. "Chloe left me hers before she was taken away."

"Yes," smiles Nailah. "And I'm glad you remember her still."

Nailah looks up at Cyril. "So, are we using my piece, or yours?" she asks him.

"She's using her own," says Cyril, looking down at Eilish.

"Her own?"

"Yes... Kim-Joy has given her a piece..."

"What are you talking about?" asks Eilish.

"Yes, Cyril... what *are* you talking about?" asks Nailah.

"Kim-Joy made a charm once—just like a Stain Charm," starts Cyril, looking intently at Eilish. "She has entrusted parts of this charm to the people most important to her... Nailah and I both have a piece... but so do you."

"I do?" says Eilish.

"Yes."

Cyril reaches deep into the pocket of his trousers and pulls out a delicate three-axis sand timer—the *Triaxial Vitaloscope*.

"Kim-Joy asked me to give this to you," he says, holding it up for her to see.

He turns the instrument over carefully, inspecting his own craftsmanship from centuries ago. Then, on the Sand Timer that represents the Earth, where a tiny bronze globe sits on top of the chamber, Cyril twists. He twists and unscrews the little bronze sphere, and as it comes away, into his hand drops a pea-sized piece of sticky resin.

"Kim-Joy knew there was a risk that the *Tide and Time* would fall to the Distillery. Years ago, she broke apart some of her charm into tiny pieces. She has placed these pieces into artefacts that have been sent all around the Meadow... some have even made it back to Earth. All scattered to protect what she knows. And, ironically, there is nothing left for the Distillery to find at the *Tide and Time Tavern*."

"But this," he says, holding up the tiny ball of resin. "This, Kim-Joy left for you, Eilish... for you to hear the rest of the story... and to help you to understand why we... me, Kim-Joy, Nailah, Ciara and others... are risking our lives today."

Cyril carefully offers the pea of resin to Eilish. "You only need to lick it," he says. "As you enter the memory, I'll place it back in the *Vitaloscope* for safekeeping… Are you ready?"

Eilish looks at Cyril and at Nailah, who look back at her earnestly.

"I'm ready," says Eilish, and she leans forward with her tongue poking out, towards the small pea of resin in Cyril's worn leathery palm.

On contact with her saliva, Eilish is transported to another time and another place, long ago.

***

Chapter 52

The charm of a landlady

The Meadow - London - Mynydd Aaru - Earth

A cold blanket of snow lies over London. Its billowing drifts lean against the tightly closed doors of houses and taverns. The people of the Meadow won't be venturing outside today. In the *Tide and Time Tavern,* a roaring log fire burns. Sat around the bar, two dozen women are silent. And by the fireplace beside a young woman is a familiar face, not looking a day younger or older than when Eilish first met her—Kim-Joy.

The women stare at Kim-Joy and the young lady opposite her. Unlike the others, this lady by the fire is radiant. Her hair is clean and plaited. Her clothes are expensive and delicate. Epitomised by a long sapphire ball gown.

The lady in the blue dress smiles at Kim-Joy.

"Ok," she says, in a soft but determined voice. "I'm ready."

"I will give you time to prepare yourself," says Kim-Joy, before embracing the lady and kissing her on the forehead.

The young lady makes her way round the women at the bar, hugging each of them in turn, thanking them, and promising that it'll all be ok. A few are brought to tears. And when she has embraced everyone, the lady in the blue dress wanders to the little door that Eilish knows leads down to the cellar.

While all around her weep, Kim-Joy turns a sand timer on the mantelpiece and waits. She waits until the last grain of sand has fallen. Then she turns to the fire and plunges a prepared torch—a stick with a flammable rag on its end—into the flames. The torch ignites, and Kim-Joy walks with it through the bar to the cellar door where she too descends, alone. Eilish follows.

The cellar is different in the memory. Suffering from recent flooding, the room is cold and damp, the floorboards are rotten, and pools of stagnant water splash under Kim-Joy's feet. And in the corner, sits a well—a deep, cavernous hole falling into the earth below. Above the well is a makeshift frame which creaks under the weight of someone hanging deep below.

The lady in the blue dress is nowhere to be seen. Kim-Joy steps up to the well and peers down into the void. Eilish watches her. She looks deeply sad and tired.

"Goodbye, my dear," Kim-Joy whispers. "Your spirit will live on in me."

Closing her eyes and stepping back, Kim-Joy drops the flaming torch into the well. And in a moment, flames engulf the gaping hole, roaring up the shaft and throwing a harsh, bright light across the cellar. A tear falls down Kim-Joy's cheek.

The flames burn brightly for a few minutes before dying down slowly. As they do, a spark climbs up out of the well, hovering in the room for a moment, before climbing the stairs and making its way out of the *Tide and Time Tavern* and into the sky.

"Good luck," Kim-Joy says to the distant star.

The memory fizzles away, and Eilish braces her mind to return to the *Guiding Star*, but it doesn't happen. A series of shorter memories—flashbacks—now appear before her. Snippets of moments from different people at different times, woven together into a single thread of truth that resides in the resin that touched her tongue.

It starts with Kim-Joy, alone, on a misty mountain. She wears the lady's blue dress. And on the mountain, she wanders to a cliff edge where a roaring waterfall cascades past her. She sits with her back to the rock, looking out into the wall of water. Mist surrounds her, swirling chaotically.

From her pocket, Kim-Joy retrieves a marble. A deep sapphire blue marble, which she rolls in her palm before she drops it into her mouth. Then, cupping her hands, she collects water from the waterfall and sips from them.

Eilish watches as the old lady then droops into a deep sleep—a deeper sleep than she has ever seen anyone enter with a marble. And, to Eilish's surprise, Kim-Joy stands up in her slumber and starts gesturing before speaking with her eyes still firmly shut.

Eilish moves in to hear what she is saying.

"Don't be afraid, Glen... You can trust me. I have been waiting for you... It is awful that you are tormented by this body on Earth... But do not be afraid. You are destined for greatness in another realm... When the winds blow and your voyage is doomed, embrace your new beginning..."

The flashback ends, and another takes its place.

Eilish finds herself on the mountain again. This time, there is an exceedingly tall lady with long, lanky arms that stretch out from her blue gown, who takes muscular strides around a dangerous rocky ledge. Like Kim-Joy before, she reaches out into the waterfall with a cupped hand and drinks the pure water along with a sapphire marble and enters a lucid dream.

Eilish leans in again.

"Nailah," says the lady. *"You have been chosen. Take up the mantle and be ready to thrive in another realm."*

The next flashback is also on the mountain. Not high on the cliffs but somewhere in the foothills beside a cool, clear pool. Nailah stands there in this memory, wearing the long blue dress.

She crouches beside the pool and checks around her. Eilish can hear, in the distance, the clanging of machinery and can just about see the base of the mountain where the Distillery mine stands, collecting resin from the Source.

Like the women in the previous flashbacks, Nailah places a sapphire marble into her mouth before drinking a palm-full of clear water from the pool. She lies down on a slab of rock and enters her lucid dream.

Eilish crouches down beside Nailah to listen and immediately realises that she has heard *this* conversation before.

"Chloe!" Nailah whispers. *"How lovely to meet you. Finally. Your mother has told me so much about you."*

That flashback closes, and finally, Eilish is again on the mountainside, where an angry snowstorm swirls around. She expects to see Chloe this time in the blue dress, but instead, she spots something sliding, out of control, down the slope—a young man.

The man's fall is halted on a cliff edge, as a sack slung around his shoulder gets wedged into a groove of rock, leaving him dangling precariously in the darkness.

"Ashley?" the young man half pleads, half whimpers. "Ashley, can you hear me…?"

There is no response to the man. However, unseen from his position, Eilish observes a sharp flash of white light climbing into the sky—an Opening. And through it, tumbles a young lady with gothic black hair and drawn features, who wears a long silk ball gown and matching blue scarf. Chloe.

Getting as close to Chloe as she possibly can, Eilish watches, mesmerised as her friend walks calmly down to the young man hanging from the cliff. She doesn't say a word to him, but instead reaches towards his waist, where a marble pouch is dangling. She pulls out a tiny marble containing a speck of purple resin inside.

"*Don't suck it,*" she whispers into the man's ear. "*Crack it with your teeth.*"

The man does as he is told, and Chloe watches as a warm, translucent mist fizzes out around his face. The man drops into the marble's memory, closing his eyes and letting his body go limp.

Chloe knows the man is safe. His sack is securely wedged, and his strength will return through the memory. She steps away from the man and strides back up the slope, into the snow and mist.

With the final flashback complete, the resin haze dissolves, and the cabin of the *Guiding Star* comes back into focus. Eilish breathes out, aware of Nailah's and Cyril's eyes bearing down on her, waiting for her reaction.

"That was *Her*, at the *Tide and Time* with Kim-Joy, wasn't it? The Lady who died in the well?"

"That's right," says Cyril.

"But if she's *dead...*, why is He still hunting Her?"

Cyril goes to respond, but Nailah puts her hand out, halting him.

"Let her figure it out," she says, giving Eilish a gentle, trusting smile.

Eilish ponders what she has seen. Kim-Joy, Glenda, Nailah and Chloe, all on the mountain. All in the blue dress.

"He doesn't know she's dead, does he?"

Nailah smiles. Eilish continues.

"She has been kept alive through other people. The lady in the blue dress... she is just a symbol!"

"Well done," says Nailah, beaming. "And because He believes She is still out there, he won't give up hunting. And while He hunts, He leaves the door open to Elysian... a door that we will have to pass through if we want to break Him. Break the stranglehold that He and the warped souls of his angels have had over the Meadow and Earth for centuries."

"It's big, isn't it?" smiles Cyril. "Big enough to do anything to keep it a secret."

"And Well-Wishing..."

"Yeah, it got its name from the well under the *Tide and Time Tavern*."

"Have there been more women who have worn the blue dress?" asks Eilish.

"Many more," says Nailah. "You will only have seen those whose minds you have connected with."

"So, is someone 'Her' right now?"

"I believe so," smiles Nailah.

"Who?"

"I can't know for sure, but I have my suspicions... someone you know well..."

"Ciara!"

Nailah smiles.

"*She* has a funny way of working to bring us all together."

There is a jolt in the cabin, and *The Guiding Star* rocks to port and back again.

"I think the helm might be dozing off," smiles Cyril.

He steps up to Eilish and squeezes her shoulder. "I'm glad to have you on board, Eilish."

Cyril steps out of the cabin, leaving Nailah and Eilish alone.

Nailah looks at Eilish, with the infectious smile of a soul-mate, scanning her face.

"I can't believe you have been *Her*, the lady in the blue dress," smiles Eilish. "Such a secret! I had no idea. No one has any idea!... And Kim-Joy... wow! She is *so* much more than my brother has reckoned with!"

"It's quite a place we find ourselves in, isn't it?" says Nailah.

Eilish laughs nervously, feeling her face flush with Nailah's keen attention. "It's thrilling and terrifying, all at the same time."

"Welcome to *real* Well-Wishing!" says Nailah.

"How do you get chosen to be *Her*... to wear the blue dress?" asks Eilish.

"A good question," says Nailah. "There isn't one way. It generally passes from one person to the next. Glenda found me. I found Chloe. But it doesn't have to be like that."

"And this connection to Earth?" asks Eilish. "Is there some kind of dream state that lets you talk to Earth?"

Nailah smiles. "You must remember stories of hauntings... of ghosts, of spirits from Earth, don't you? There have always been ways of *interacting* across the realms. Communication though. That is much harder. Communication requires intention and awareness... But yes. There is a way. *She* learnt it from *Him*. Lucid dreaming is what the spirits call it. A clear mind and an unconscious body can navigate as a spirit onto Earth. But a blind spirit. A blind spirit that can talk but will blow away with the wind."

Eilish ponders this for a moment, thinking of her angel and thinking of Chloe's memories that she has seen. They are always spirits without bodies, blowing in the breeze.

"But, if you can't see... how can you find someone on Earth?"

Nailah grins. "You're getting straight to the difficult questions!... Show me the vitaloscope again."

Eilish picks it up off the bedside table and rolls the axes of the sand timer.

"The vitaloscope is a great depiction of time in the realms," says Nailah. "Sand only falls through one chamber at a time. The timeline in one realm is independent of the other. And this is true... but it is also *relative*. You see, the vitaloscope depicts the three axes of time from the perspective of the individual. We've learnt this from the Returners. They go back to Earth to the exact moment that they left. The sand has not moved through that chamber while they have been gone."

"But how do you explain when two souls have shared time in one realm, but are separated in another? Well, that's just it. It's *relative*. Between the realms, time warps. It warps around the movement of the souls, creating a consistency alongside relative coherence..."

"I don't think I understand," frowns Eilish, honestly.

"I'll try to simplify... emphasis on *try!*" smiles Nailah, holding her hands out to aid her explanation with gestures. "If you were to leave the Meadow today and go back to Earth, you would go back to Earth to the moment you left. If I were to go through with you, I would go back to when *I* left—a time many years before you. But I would still remember you—someone who is yet to be born. And because of these connections, it is possible to communicate with those we have encountered in another realm *before* they leave their original realm..."

Nailah looks at Eilish, who looks past her, perplexed.

"Glenda knew me," Nailah tries again. "That's how she found me. And I knew Chloe... that's how I found her. And I'm sure, if Chloe were here with us, she'd be able to tell us who wears the blue dress now."

***

Chapter 53

Source of the problem

The Meadow - Holyhead, North Wales

The Ferrymen crewing the *Charybdis* are sworn to secrecy. Nobody on the land knows this is what they do for a living. They are forbidden to tell. And still, the crew don't know the cargo of their ship. They obediently steer the *Charybdis* from the port at Dover to the port in Holyhead, off north Wales, and back. They don't ask questions because they are lucratively rewarded for not doing so. Rewarded in whatever ways their minds desire.

The crew members know something happened last night. When the darkness came, and the calm sea turned to a thunderous ocean. But they aren't about to lose their bounty by asking unnecessary questions. They are here to get their vessel to Holyhead. And right now, the small port town is about half a mile off the bow, the wind is steady, and they should make landfall in an hour. An hour and they'll get their marbles. And so, the crew members in their long black gowns start making ready for the port authorities and the secretive operation of unloading the cargo.

Below deck, Andrew Callaghan inspects the hold, preparing a special delivery. He is one of only a few men who know the *Charybdis'* secrets.

Andrew stands in the long, dark cabin. The cargo bay is deep in the hull. Two dozen beds are occupied by the sleeping bodies of young, athletic men. Asleep through sedation and the consumption of Distillery-produced marbles that hold their minds in stasis. These are the 'missing' men who have been taken from streets all across the Meadow. They will not wake up under any circumstance. Their beds are numbered one through to twenty-four.

Andrew paces through the hold to bed seventeen. The host that Samael requested. Lying in the bed, asleep is a young man with dark blue-black skin. His physique is strong. His muscles bulge under his clothes. His face and head are clean shaven.

Andrew wouldn't usually be in charge of sealing the host. The angels do it themselves. Such is the fragility of their trust in humans. But, without the angels aboard, the task is left to Andrew. He fishes in his pocket for a fresh Distillery marble. A bright purple sphere. Disgusted, he sticks his fingers into the mouth of the sleeping man, drops in the new marble and scoops out the old. This will keep him in stasis until the time comes for his body to be 'hijacked'.

Andrew takes the brake off the bed and wheels it to the front of the hold, to a preparation table. He rocks the sleeping man onto the wipe-clean surface and rolls up his sleeves. He opens a drawer to uncover an array of shaving items, cloths, scissors—everything to remove every hair and clean the body of the man.

Andrew gets to work, cutting and trimming his scalp, then shaving clean to the skin, including eyebrows, beard, and chest. Then, to Andrew's great dislike, he has to get even closer—the legs, the back, and all those other parts with hair. The angels require a clean, hairless body for a host—a body without blemish or identity. Bare life is what they need.

Eventually, number seventeen is prepared, clean, and still asleep. Sweating and repulsed, Andrew rolls the man into a coffin and places a label on top: *'URGENT: House of Sand'*. Now, all he has to do is go back to the cabins and ready the prisoner.

"Right, you," says Andrew, stepping into the cabin where Kim-Joy is still seated and bound in her chair. "You stay with me."

"Are we nearly there?"

"Yes," he says. "And I'm going to need your compliance."

"Am I not already compliant?"

Andrew ignores her and pulls out a needle from his pocket. Another sedative. The same that Kim-Joy was under when she was loaded onto the boat.

"I hardly think that's necessary, Andrew," says Kim-Joy, her eyes following the needle warily.

"Stop using my name," he says.

"Why?"

"Because you don't know me."

"Ah—!" Kim-Joy recoils.

"I haven't touched you," says the Ferryman.

"I know," says Kim-Joy, writhing uncomfortably.

From just below the neckline of her jumper, a wisp of ocean blue mist drifts upwards towards her face. Andrew reaches towards the old lady's neck, and she winces, expecting him to inflict more pain. Instead, he pulls out the leather string of lockets hanging there, intrigued.

The source of the mist is revealed. A marble contained within a locket is cracked. Cracked through to its core and hissing, spewing out a fine mist.

Kim-Joy gasps. "No!" she whispers, desperately. "No. Please, no."

"Whose marble is this?" asks the Ferryman, holding the fizzing locket aloft.

"Please," insists Kim-Joy, her voice cracking. "It is about to expire. Please. Let me enter the mist before it's gone…"

The Ferryman looks at her. His unshakable enemy for so long now, for the first time, looked as frail as her age.

His instinct is to smash the marble right there in front of her. But for some reason, he doesn't do it. Instead, he lowers his palm and gently offers the cloud from the fractured marble to the lips of the old lady.

Before she breathes in, she looks up at him. Her eyes red and afraid. "Thank you, Andrew," she says bravely, and takes the mist deep into her lungs.

Andrew Callaghan watches as the old lady drops desperately into the last utterance of the precious memory. Her eyes, welling with tears, close, and her body goes restfully limp.

Andrew lifts his syringe of sedative. She can't be anything but compliant now. But in the dark, quiet cabin, he feels something unfamiliar that makes him pause—the desperate ache of yearning.

The old lady has something that all the authority in the Meadow hasn't provided him. And he had forgotten just how much he craved it. She is so intimately connected to another soul that it causes her pain. And he hasn't felt that hurt—truly felt its bite—in ten years. He knows why. Because it torments him too much. It torments him too much to think of Ciara.

It isn't long before Kim-Joy wakes from the memory, and Andrew hasn't moved. The wrinkles around her puffy red eyes are writ with melancholy as she looks at her looming captor. But he just stands over her, entranced in yearning, his palm open under her chin.

A moment of unspoken calm passes between them before the Ferryman and the old lady watch the marble in his hand shatter into a constellation of broken pieces. The life and the memory contained within it are gone, and a spark of bright Energy climbs from it, like a dormant fly waking from the depths of winter.

The spark rises up and away, beyond the hull of the Charybdis. Up into the distant sky. Into the heavens to join the Energy of the other souls in the dance of the stars.

"Ok," sniffs Kim-Joy, her gaze dropping to the syringe of sedative hanging from the Ferryman's hand. "Do what you have to do."

Andrew looks at her and hesitates.

"It's ok," she reassures him.

Andrew jabs the needle into her upper arm, and, in a moment, her mind enters a familiar hazy sedation.

Andrew ties a gag around Kim-Joy's mouth and places a hessian sack over her head, before untying her feet and hands, and leading her up onto the deck.

Holyhead Harbour is busy. As busy as it has ever been. Dozens of barges are queued in the entrance to the harbour, their crews jostling for a position against the harbour wall so they can unload their cargo and set back off to sea.

The crew of the *Charybdis* are familiar with navigating the port and find their way through the barges, right into the shallows where a small jetty is reserved just for them.

Waiting for the *Charybdis* is a battalion of Ferrymen. They know the drill. Senior crew aided first, urgent cargo unloaded next, then the rest of the hold is to be emptied. By the harbour-master's quarters, where the jetty meets the land, half a dozen carriages are waiting. Cargo from the *Charybdis* must go straight to the Source without delay.

Stepping off the *Charybdis* first, the Ferryman salutes his battalion, who salute back.

"The prisoner stays with me!" he shouts, pointing at the hooded figure of Kim-Joy, whose hands are fastened to the gunwale. "And there's a single piece of cargo in the hold. Number Seventeen. It's in the coffin. That must come with me, too."

"You're going to the Source, your excellency?" asks an officer on the jetty.

"Yes," says the Ferryman. "I will take the cargo and the prisoner with me. And I'll have you two," he says, wagging a finger at two officers on the jetty. "You two can steer my carriage… and I won't accept any delay."

"Yes, your excellency!" shout the men, stepping forward to assist their boss off the boat.

"Chop chop!" shouts the Ferryman at the remaining officers. "Down into the hull. Number seventeen. Quick!"

The Ferryman strides down the jetty.

"And I could do with a good marble or two. It has been quite a voyage," he says, not even looking over his shoulder to see the officer who scuttles behind in his shadow.

"Er, there's a problem, sir," says the officer, his voice shaking. "Haven't you heard?"

"What?!"

"The marbles, sir. We've… well… we've run out!"

"Run out?! Don't be ridiculous!"

"There are none in the whole of North Wales, your excellency. We've been asking the teams at the Source for the last few days, but they're telling us there's no resin. There hasn't been resin for weeks. It has got desperate, sir."

"You don't have *any* marbles?!"

"None at all, sir."

"Bloody ridiculous!" shouts the Ferryman. He feels into his pocket and pulls out a dark brown marble of his own. "This will have to do," he mutters, chucking it into his mouth.

"What's happening at the Source, sir? Why has the resin stopped?"

"Don't you worry about that," says the Ferryman. "Just do your job."

"Yes, sir. Sorry, sir."

"Now, which carriage are we taking?"

The young officer points to the front horse-drawn carriage.

"Is she ready to go?"

"Yes, sir."

"Good. And I don't want to be disturbed. The prisoner comes in with me. The cargo can go on the roof. And chop chop! There's no time to lose!"

***

Chapter 54

The Swellies

The Meadow - The Swellies

As *The Guiding Star* enters the Swellies, Eilish's mind tumbles over itself like the water beneath the hull. The Distillery's right to govern in the Meadow—her father's right to rule—is a lie. And the Lady who exposed this lie is dead. Dead for centuries. But only dead in body. She is alive in a sisterhood of impersonators stretching back through five hundred years of history in the Meadow. And her latest impersonator—Eilish's long lost sister, Ciara—had been chosen by her best friend in the Meadow, Chloe, to take up the legacy of Her. Ciara had become the Lady in the Blue Dress.

Since discovering Ciara is alive, Eilish has been looking for her. Now she realises *everyone* is looking for her. But where is she? The last place she was seen was on her way to the Source. To the Mountain. And that's where Eilish and the crew of the *Guiding Star* are heading now. It's also where Kim-Joy, the Ferryman, and the spirits from the *Charybdis*—the *Horsemen of the Apocalypse*—are heading. The Source on the Mountain—the fracturing between the realms that He, the prince, had made to lure Her. And now, like fish caught in a trawlerman's net, they are all being drawn to the Source together.

"Cluster of rocks to port!" shouts Cyril from the bow.

Nailah throws the helm starboard, rocking the *Guiding Star* violently.

Eilish is keeping watch on the port side and observes the dark jagged rocks, scoot past them without touching the hull. On the starboard side, keeping watch there, is Elijah. They are all soaked. The choppy waters splash over the deck every few seconds, and everyone's face mask is fastened tight.

"Back to port, Nailah!" shouts Cyril. "The whirly wants to take us down!" He throws an arm to starboard, where the crew can see the rapidly swirling water, sucking debris into the depths, trying to entice the *Guiding Star* into its influence.

Nailah throws them to the port, and Eilish hears plates, bowls, and ramekins clattering to the floor in the cabin.

They pass successfully clear of the whirlpool, and Eilish watches over the starboard bow as the phenomenon falls away behind them. Like a galactic soup of dark ocean water, the mass foams around a deep, dark void.

"Rocks!" shouts Elijah, spotting a dark black mass cresting.

Nailah swings the helm back to starboard.

"Good spot!" shouts Cyril.

They all watch, holding their breath, as the mass of rock misses them by barely a foot.

"Eilish!" shouts Nailah. "Any chance we can swap?"

Eilish looks at Nailah. She is soaked and bedraggled, looking absolutely exhausted from fighting the helm.

"Of course!" she shouts back, gingerly sliding down the deck towards her.

"Thanks, Eilish," Nailah smiles, sweeping her fringe away from her face. "Keep us heading East and do whatever Cyril says!"

Eilish nods and grasps hold of the wheel. It is much heavier in these conditions than on the flat, calm Irish Sea. And it vibrates angrily in her hands. She stares at the little navigation globe in front of her. It chaotically spins left and right, but generally centres around the letter 'E'. She just needs to keep it there. But it's more complicated than it sounds. The swirling waters yaw the *Guiding Star* to port and starboard chaotically, and it's easy to overcompensate, steering one way or the other. Despite giving it all her attention, the best Eilish can do is steer a meandering course that generally takes them East.

From the bow, Cyril shouts an instruction. Eilish mishears, thinking it is a call to port. She throws the wheel around, narrowly skirting between two dangerous rocks. Cyril holds his head in his hands. They are fortunate, this time. Eilish holds her hand up apologetically.

Looking beyond Cyril on the bow, Eilish notices the faint silhouette of a bridge spanning the width of the Swellies—the Menai Suspension Bridge. It towers high over the water, and even from a distance, it is an impressive structure. Eilish had crossed the same bridge on Earth once, on a trip from Ireland. It had been brought to the Meadow in this form as a result of an awful, but sadly, frequent tragedy for the bridge—suicide by jumping. Quite a memorial to the arrival of the *Stained* into the Meadow.

"That's where they'll be bringing Kim-Joy!" shouts Nailah. "We'll land somewhere near the arches."

Eilish smiles and looks to Cyril for verification, but he isn't looking back. Instead, he has a worried look on his face and stares straight ahead intently. He doesn't shout anything to the crew but leaves his post on the bow and bundles himself back towards them.

"We're heading straight for the *Tysilio* whirlpool," he announces, gathering the crew around him. "She's bigger than normal. The waters are higher than I hoped. She'll swallow us whole if we get too close."

"Can't we go round it?" asks Eilish.

"'fraid not," he says. "She's flanked by rocks. We'll have to do all we can to skirt between them and her edges."

"Can we make it?" asks Nailah.

"I bloody hope so!" says Cyril.

A jolt makes them all freeze. It is followed by the awful moan of rock scraping against the hull.

Cyril rushes below deck to inspect the damage.

"She's hurt, but not compromised," he calls up. "Not yet… we certainly won't escape *Tysilio's* hunger if we lie too low in the water though… It's time to lose some weight… anything we can! Let me take the helm, Eilish. The rest of you, get below deck and clear out anything we don't need. Let's get our bow up. We must hit *Tysilio* with our heads held high!"

The *Guiding Star* rocks drunkenly back and forth as Eilish, Nailah, and Elijah clatter around the cabin, scooping up whatever they can into bundles of sail material—ramekins, rubber boots, marbles, spare rigging. Then, straining back up the steps onto the deck, they hoist the bundles overboard, feeding the hungry ocean.

As the *Guiding Star* lightens, the bow does rise, but at the same time, they veer more aggressively in the chaotic waters.

"Have we lost enough weight?" asks Elijah.

"It'll have to be enough," says Nailah. "There's nothing left."

"In that case," says Cyril, "Eilish and Elijah, resume your positions on our flanks. Eilish, you're on the starboard edge, where I'll be skirting us as wide as I can... hold your nerve but keep an eye for any rocks that get *too* close. Nailah, stay on the stern with me. We'll keep our weight back and the bow raised. I'll hold the helm."

Taking up her position, Eilish ducks as great washes of spray are thrown over the gunwale. They are entering the great swirling vortex of *Tysilio,* where even the spray that fills the air revolves hypnotically. They aim to stay on the outer edges, but nonetheless, they are indeed entering the whirlpool's reach.

Eilish, eyes streaming, stares into the centre of the whirlpool where the water dips into a dark emptiness. Like any swirling mass, the edges spin faster and, despite the horrifying emptiness at the core, it looks much calmer than the waters around the *Guiding Star.*

"Hold on tight!" shouts Cyril.

The boat yaws in towards the whirlpool, dipping the nearside gunwale into the black seawater.

Eilish grips tightly to the stanchions of the boat and holds her breath. She pulls her gaze away from the whirlpool and peers down at the clusters of dark black rocks which are semi-submerged off their starboard flank. The rocks seem too close. Eilish can see their sharp serrated edges. Barnacle-ridden blades, ready to puncture the hull without invitation. But Cyril is a master at the helm, and he holds them just clear of danger.

"She's hungry today!" shouts Cyril, grinning maniacally, straining against the aggressive pull of the water.

Another swell of sea water cascades over the deck, rolling the hull of the *Guiding Star*. As it washes away, Eilish spots a blade of black rock jutting out of the sea, right in their path.

"We're going to hit!" she shouts as loud as she can.

In desperation, Cyril throws the wheel to port, and the *Guiding Star* lurches in towards the eye of the whirlpool.

They miss the rock by inches, but now the whirlpool has hold of them. Cyril fights with the helm, trying to regain their position, desperate to steer them out to the edge again. The hull yaws steeply, making Eilish grip tight to the stanchions to stop herself slipping down across the deck. Below her, on the port gunwale, Elijah has the opposite problem. The side of the boat is so low now that he is up to his knees in seawater. He scrabbles with his feet to get out of the fast-flowing water, which tries to pull him overboard.

"She's dragging us in!" shouts Cyril.

Eilish freezes in fear. The *Guiding Star* feels like a coin dropped into a charity donation vortex, tumbling into an inevitable voyage to the bottom of the sea. She looks desperately beyond the bow. The Menai Suspension Bridge is so close. If only they could hang on just a bit longer.

"All hands on deck!" shouts Cyril, waving the crew towards him. His face tells them everything they don't want to know. He looks worried. Extremely worried.

"Listen to me carefully," he says, pulling them in close. "There is nothing we can do anymore. The whirlpool is too strong. She is not going to let go."

"What do you mean?" asks Eilish.

"I mean, the *Guiding Star* is going down."

***

Chapter 55

A Rough Deal

Earth - Mynydd Aaru

It is calm and quiet on the mountain. The door is open, letting a fresh morning breeze breathe in and out of the cramped little Shepherd's hut. Marty sits upright, propped between blankets and cushions so he doesn't have to support himself. He blindly clutches a warm mug of tea, letting the comforting aroma drift up into his nostrils under the blindfold that is still fastened tight to his head. He tries to ignore the dull ache behind his right ear.

"You were sent up here, weren't you?" the lady asks him from somewhere by the door. "You were sent to look for me?"

Marty knows she is fishing for information. She has been doing so ever since he woke up. And that means she is vulnerable. The less he says, the more she'll have to give up.

"In that case, someone knows I'm here, don't they? Someone knows who I am... What were you supposed to do when you found me?" she asks him. "I assume you want more than my name? Your friend must know who I am, so what do you want?"

It's not working. Marty stays silent but listens intently.

She tries again.

"You must see," she says. "I rescued you. I could have left you to die up here. How could I possibly be a threat? Whatever your friend has told you, they are wrong. Honestly, I had nothing to do with *any* of those disasters... I had no idea your son was caught up in it."

"You could have stopped them," says Marty, breaking his silence miserably. "If you knew it was coming, you could have saved my boy."

"True," the lady concedes, "I could have delayed your son's bike and changed his fate. But then what? Disasters would still happen, but their connections to what comes after—connections you don't understand—would be altered forever. I wish I could tell you why that matters. But… well, to do that, I'd need to trust you, and… frankly… I don't. Not yet."

Marty sits there, motionless, no longer straining his eyes to see through the fabric, simply processing in his mind the scattered pieces she is feeding him.

And while he sits there, she watches him intently, wondering. Wondering what his appearance means. Wondering what comes next.

And then, in the still silence between Marty and the lady, the strangest sensation fills the hut. The presence of someone— someone unseen and uninvited—joining them.

'Take her, Marty!' screams the presence. *'Take her now! You have a chance!'*

Both Marty and the lady are taken by surprise and do nothing.

'Why aren't you taking her, Marty? Your son. I can bring Elijah back!'

"Who are you?!" shouts the lady, looking around in blind panic.

'You know who I am!'

"I don't!"

'Don't play dumb, woman!' says the presence with aggressive misogynism.

"I don't know who you are," the lady repeats. "Are you from the Beyond?"

"The Almighty beckons you… He demands you. And you won't escape this time! You can run, but no longer can you hide! We are… He is… everywhere. Your little sanctuary in the Meadow is crumbling. The Distillery are in our palm, and we are smashing every pocket of resistance that protects you. Unless you plan to live out a grim mortal existence on Earth, you must know you are trapped. The moment you emerge in the Meadow. The moment you leave this realm, we will destroy you. And if you don't come, we can reach you here, on Earth. Not a day will go by that you will live in peace. So, give in… Go with Mr Fredrickson… He can take you to the café at the bottom of this mountain. And you can wait for Him… He has sorely missed you."

The lady looks around the hut, terrified.

"You really have no idea who I am, do you?" she says.

"Oh, I do… of course I do… For centuries, I have been seeking you on His behalf… The Almighty will ensnare His prey… His prize. Mark my words."

The lady stands very still. A realisation is dawning on her. A realisation that makes her reach deep into her pocket, feeling for something. But it is gone.

"So, I am *Her*," she whispers to herself.

"Marty!" shouts the presence, the reverberation of his voice shaking dust from the shelves. *"Take her… Take her or kill her!"*

"What!?"

"Kill her, or our deal is off!"

"I can't… I'm snow-blind… You're here, why can't you do it?!"

"Marty, you weak, pathetic human. If you can't grab her, then kill her! Even a blind man can kill. Kill her with anything you have. Kill her in any way you can!"

"No way!" shouts Marty. "You're insane… This wasn't our deal."

From outside the door of the cabin, a breeze starts to blow.

"Our deal, Marty!" shouts the presence. *"Kill her now! Kill her or lose everything!"*

The breeze quickly becomes a whistling wind.

"Martyyyyy!!!!"

The door of the Shepherd's Hut slams hard, but the latch doesn't catch. It slams again. Outside, a squall screams over the mountain, throwing up loose particles of snow and ice, dust and debris. It clatters into the walls of the hut—a frustrated cacophony of noise.

A spray of cold, icy snow bursts through the door, covering Marty from head to toe. He moans desperately. This is the final straw. Bright, hot sun has burnt his eyes shut, his hope of clearing his name and getting his life back has blown away in the wind, and now an icy frost is going to give him hypothermia.

The lady slams the door firmly shut and fastens the latch.

"That's some friend you have," she says to Marty.

"Is he gone?" asks Marty, confused.

"He's gone."

"Why?"

"His type can't withstand the wind."

"What?!"

"You poor, helpless being, Marty. How desperate things must seem to you to put your trust in someone like that. You've risked your life on this mountain for a lie told to you by a stranger." She pauses. "Why did you trust him? Why did you do it?"

"I didn't have a choice," says Marty. "Literally everything I had is gone… And *he* reached out to me… no one else did. There was no other option."

"But you were prepared to risk your life for him?"

"No," says Marty, firmly. "I was risking my life for the chance of getting my son back… for the chance of finding you."

"And you were prepared to *kill* for him?"

"No," says Marty, quickly. "That was never part of the bargain. I would never agree to that."

"But you heard him, that was his instruction… to kill me."

"I know," Marty sighs. "And with it fades my hope… You should have let me die on the mountain."

"No, I shouldn't."

"Why not?"

"Because, like you, Marty, I value life," says the lady.

Marty sighs. What good is life when all hope is gone?

"So, can I assume you're done with your 'friend' now? You're not going to try and kill me?"

Marty relaxes a touch. "I'm a police detective. I don't befriend killers. I catch them."

"Then, detective, will you give me a chance to tell you my story? You can *detect* where the truth lies."

Marty rolls onto his side and lets a slither of light stream into his eyes painfully. Through the bandage, he can make out the silhouette of the lady. She is standing, very still, looking down at him.

"I'm not blessed with choice," says Marty. "I'm blind and incapacitated. Willing, or not, you have my attention."

"I would rather it were willing," says the lady. "In a few hours, your eyesight should return. By then, I hope to have found a friend in you."

"We'll see," says Marty. "I'm willing to listen."

***

Chapter 56

A fallen star

The Meadow - The Swellies

Y ou good?" shouts Cyril as the hull creaks and the *Guiding Star* dips violently towards the eye of the whirlpool.

Eilish and Elijah are on the helm, trying desperately to hold some kind of steady course and slow their inevitable drift to the bottom of the sea. Cyril, near the bow, won't give up hope. With a pair of pliers, he frantically cuts away the stanchions surrounding the hull, pulling away the long coil of strong, flexible wire that makes up the safe perimeter.

The plan is ludicrous, but he is the only one with a plan. As *The Guiding Star* hurtles around the southern edge of the whirlpool, the starboard side will be at its closest to the rocks that reach out from the mainland. Using the stanchion wire as a lasso, Cyril thinks it might be possible to catch an anchor hold on the rocks and ultimately pull them out of the grip of the whirlpool.

As the final piece of the stanchion comes free, Cyril, up to his thighs in fast-flowing sea water that breaches the deck, scrabbles back to the others.

In his hands, he twists the strong, pliable wire into a series of loops. "Hand holds!" he explains. "In case the *Guiding Star* can't hold on herself." At the other end of the coil, he has broken off a handful of stanchion poles and, using all his strength, has bent this cluster of metal pieces into a makeshift grappling hook.

With the main coil of wire and metal held tight in his hand, Cyril feeds the individual loops to the others. "Hold tight," he says. "And do not let go! If you find yourself in the drink, get to the rocks. They are our way to safety now."

Slipping and sliding, he climbs onto the starboard gunwale, which hangs high above the water line now. Following the wire up from the others, he wraps a loop around one of the rigging cleats—

the strongest point on the deck. This will take the strain if he can hook a rock successfully and pull them out of the whirlpool.

With the wire secured, Cyril wipes the spray off his face and wraps his legs over the gunwale before starting to windmill his arm, ready to throw. Right now, they are as close as they are ever going to be to the mainland and the rocks to the south. The longer he delays, the farther they will be from the rocks. It is now or never.

With a heroic launch of his arm, Cyril flings the coil of wire up into the spray-filled air. The others hold their breath, hoping desperately. And, in an astonishing moment, the hull jolts violently. Cyril's makeshift grappling hook has hit its mark, grabbing hold of a semi-submerged fissure in the rocks.

The metal wire tenses, pulling out from the rock to the *Guiding Star* and snapping up into the air. The hull creaks and screams as it starts to tug against the flow of the whirlpool. Stormy waters begin cascading up from the stern, drowning the deck and lifting the crew off their feet.

"Hold on!" shouts Cyril, his own body rocking dangerously over the starboard side of the boat.

Eilish grips both hands onto her loop of wire, tensing from head to toe. Above her, she hears the cleat groan fatally. Then it snaps.

There's no time to make sense of what happens next. Eilish feels a sharp yank against her arms, the solid deck beneath her feet shoots away, and she is plunged deep into the seawater. As she resurfaces, gasping for breath, she can feel the flailing feet and bodies of Elijah and Nailah beside her, also in the water.

Instinctively, Eilish starts pulling herself hand over hand, desperate to get to the rocks. The whirlpool pulls at her, but not nearly as much as she expects, and Cyril has usefully twisted knots into the wire, helping her to anchor her hands as she works blindly upwards.

In the chaos of the cold, thrashing water, Eilish, Nailah, and Elijah slowly make their way up the hundred feet or so of wire. But, as she takes her first grip of the sharp barnacled rock that will save her, a terrible realisation hits Eilish. Cyril isn't with them.

She looks back into the water where the length of wire is flailing helplessly, hoping to spot the trawlerman clinging on. But she knows she won't.

She clambers onto the rock and looks back into the sea, towards the whirlpool where the *Guiding Star* drifts. On its submerged deck, she can see Cyril. He is standing there, looking back, all alone.

He is going down with his ship.

Cyril waves casually to the three crew members on the rocks, smiling gratefully that they have made it. His casual, fearless wave triggers Eilish to burst into tears. He looks so calm, and she knows this is the last time she will ever see him.

Sure enough, in a moment, the bow of the *Guiding Star* descends into the centre of the whirlpool and Cyril offers them his last salute—covering his face with his right hand, the salute of the Well Wishers. Then, without ceremony, the *Guiding Star* and its skipper are gone.

The three surviving crew members stand, shocked. In the awful silence that follows, they witness, from within the void of *Tysilio*, a spark rising from the water—the remaining Energy of Cyril Spate.

The spark climbs high into the sky above them where, even in the dawn light, they can see another star is waiting—the 'guiding star'. Cyril has been reunited with Kim-Joy's son at last. And together the two stars start their dance northwards, onto their next adventure together.

***

Chapter 57

Ciara's Collection

The Meadow - Near The Mountain

The solemn walk from the Swellies to the foothills of the mountains is heart-achingly quiet. Nailah knows the way. She had been here ten years before, taking Ciara into the shadow of the Mountain, but on that day, she had been filled with hope. Eilish would probably have quizzed her in different circumstances, but now the three of them can't bear to break the silence created by the void of Cyril's absence.

Traipsing inland, the hills around them grow into adolescent mountains, and a stubble of foliage becomes a thick beard of forest. Though this is a forest that has been traumatised. The *Mighty Fire* that erupted from the Source ten years ago has scarred the land permanently. The trees standing today are bright and healthy. But in their shadows are the burnt stumps and scorched earth that never forgets the catastrophe and the destruction of the fire.

Whispering amongst the trees, the first slithering of mist starts to weave and dance amongst the branches. Since the Source was opened into the Meadow five hundred years ago, a permanent blanket of this mist has shrouded the area. This mist is a residue that, like the consumption of water, can cloud the mind and too much exposure can be fatal, sending you 'on'. 'On' to make the unconscious jump from the Perihelion precipice on the Mountain, not so far away. A leap into Elysian. Into *His* realm. The same jump which Ciara came to make ten years ago.

Nailah brings them to a crest of the foothills where, through a break in the treeline, they can see out across the mountain range and westwards to the sea, the Swellies, and the Menai Suspension Bridge. This is the perfect vantage point to pick up Kim-Joy's trail again.

They stand and stare for a moment at Cyril's final resting place, before Nailah perches herself on a smooth slab of slate and sighs, beckoning Eilish and Elijah beside her.

"We lost a great man," she says, breaking into the silence between them. "One of the few great *men* of this realm." She lingers on 'men'. Not to hurt Elijah's feelings, but to speak to a deeper wound that Cyril's loss means to her. The trawlerman was the only male soul that Nailah had been willing to trust for these last ten years. She puts her arm around Elijah apologetically before reaching into her pocket and removing a pouch of marbles.

"We should break a marble in his memory," she says. "But first, I need to fulfil his parting wish…"

Into her palm, Nailah empties the contents of the pouch. What falls out are not her own marbles. Instead, it is the bracelet from Cyril's wrist, containing the original identity stone of Kim-Joy's son.

"Why do you have that?" asks Eilish.

"Cyril knew his end was coming days ago," says Nailah. "Your angel told him. Told him that he would be going down with the *Guiding Star* before we made landfall. He did not want either of you to know, fearing you might try and intervene. But he knew it was part of *Her* plan. It had to happen."

Eilish stares at the bracelet. She doesn't know what to say.

"It's ok. He is back with his son now," smiles Nailah, looking up at the sky. "And that's just where he wanted to be."

"*His* son?"

"Kim-Joy and Cyril were together before this realm. Before they changed their Identity Stones. Sachi was their son," says Nailah. She turns to Elijah. "Cyril wanted you to have this," she says, passing him the bracelet.

"Me? Why?" asks Elijah.

"Cyril saw something of himself in you, Elijah. He wanted you to have Sachi's stone, and he told me to remind you that a father always finds a way to his son."

Elijah smiles and carefully pulls the bracelet onto his wrist.

"And with that," Nailah says, raising a marble over her head. "Let's mark our memory of him... To Cyril," she declares, smashing the marble on the ground.

"To Cyril," they respond, following suit with marbles of their own.

The three of them stand for a quiet moment together, letting the mist from their marbles fizzle around the slate at their feet.

"So," starts Nailah, standing up. "They'll likely pass through this valley... The first fortified checkpoint is a mile or so inland from here."

"Is this where we are planning to rescue Kim-Joy?" asks Elijah.

"It better be," says Nailah. "If we can't get to her before the checkpoint, we've got trouble."

"Is there no way past the checkpoint?" asks Elijah.

Nailah glances at Eilish. "Unlikely. It's guarded around the clock—guarded by trigger-happy thermocline-carrying Distillery officers. Their sole job is to keep people off the Mountain—they aren't going to bend for *us*," she says this, but seems to be insinuating maybe Eilish could make it possible. "Anyway, even if we did get past the checkpoint, all the way to the lake beyond, there are traps."

"Traps?"

"Hidden in the snow, coils of barbed wire tangled over the ground. There are even armed guards watching the snowfields... It's like trench warfare. The Distillery aren't letting anyone near the face except Drifters. The Distillery are at war on the Mountain."

"Why?"

"Because of the *Returners*?" offers Eilish.

"Correct. The Distillery know the pure water from the Source was key to the rebellion last time. They aren't going to let anyone near the Source now. And anyway, even if by some miracle we managed to sneak unnoticed and unscathed to the base of the Mountain, then there's the problem of the house on the lake."

"The house?"

"The *House of Sand*."

Eilish frowns. "I've heard my father talk of that place," she says. "Even amongst the Distillery, it is a dark secret."

"Why?" asks Elijah. "What is it?"

"It's the seat of the *Council of the Almighty*," says Eilish.

"It's the seat of the fallen angels," corrects Nailah. "The place where spirits from the Beyond are interfering in the Meadow."

"Interfering?" asks Elijah.

"Nobody knows exactly," says Nailah. "Well, other than maybe Eilish's father. That's one of the reasons Eilish's sister came up here. Anyway, it's also where the angel told Cyril the Horsemen would be taking Kim-Joy—to the prison chambers off the House. Chambers that are hidden deep in the Mountain."

"And I assume it's also guarded?" says Elijah.

"More than guarded," frowns Nailah. "Angels control all access to the House."

"So, how do you plan to get to the chambers?" asks Eilish.

"Haven't you been listening?" scoffs Nailah.

"Intently," smiles Eilish. "And you've never once said it will be impossible… If there's even the slimmest chance, I know you'll have a plan." She winks at Nailah.

Nailah laughs out loud and, for the first time in Eilish's memory, blushes. She reaches into her pack and pulls out a map.

"I've been on the Mountain's slopes once before," she starts, unfolding it to reveal a plan of the mineshafts within the Mountain. "Up on the *Asphodel Face* is a cave. A cave that leads to an old, abandoned shaft. This shaft," she prods a point on the map, "provides access to a point just off from the prison chambers, out of sight and scrutiny of the Distillery. If… and it's a huge and improbable 'if'… we can get to the cave—assuming it hasn't collapsed since I was last there— then yes, we might get to Kim-Joy from there."

Eilish looks at the location of the cave. It appears to be a level traverse, maybe half a kilometre, from a point labelled '*the eye of the needle*', where two sharp spires of rock protrude from the face.

"Is it easy to find?" Eilish asks.

"It should be," says Nailah. "I told this to your sister when I brought her here—the best option, if there is such an option, is to take the Drifter's track up the Mountain. It is well-trodden and risk-free, so long as you can blend in with the Drifters. The cave would be visible as you approach the needles."

Eilish stares at the map, committing the route to memory.

"Talking of Ciara…" says Nailah. She lifts her hand and points to the hillside opposite. "Can you see the little building over there?"

Eilish squints. Nestled amongst the trees, burnt stumps, and scorched earth is a small stone hut.

"What is it?"

"It's where Ciara showed she could be trusted with our biggest secret, too."

Eilish looks at Nailah. She smiles, knowing that the experience she shared with her on the Guiding Star, as her mind was fractured, is as vulnerable as a mind can be in the Meadow.

"You should go and pay it a visit."

***

Eilish trudges up the steep slope alone. Her feet squelch inside her shoes. Her clothes are still soaked from the sea. Nailah and Elijah have stayed on the hilltop to keep watch on the suspension bridge, waiting for Kim-Joy and her captors to cross over towards the mountains.

Up ahead of Eilish, the little stone hut comes into view. 'Hut', diminutive as a term, is still a little grand for the hollowed-out pile of stones. Nailah had told Eilish that it was an ancient hut, used by some of the earliest settlers in the Meadow—those from the legends. Without that history, it was certainly unremarkable.

It appears no one has entered the hut in ten years. Not since the *Mighty Fire*. The stones are scarred with the charred impression of forgotten trees. Eilish doesn't know what she hopes to find. Just something. A sign. A connection. Anything that helps her feel closer to Ciara. But she's also afraid of what awaits her. Ciara had been left here alone, a matter of weeks before the

Mountain and the forests burned. If she were here when the fire broke out, she would surely have died here too.

There is a door to the hut. A miraculous survivor of the fire. It's rotten and creaks as Eilish pushes it open.

Inside, it is damp and dark. There are floorboards—their very existence a surprise—but they are rotten and bow precariously under Eilish's feet. There was once a window, but ferns have grown over it. It lets in a trickle of forest hue, and once Eilish's eyes have adjusted to the gloom, she can make out the shape of the room where Nailah said goodbye to Ciara ten years ago.

There is a pile of something in the corner—wet and mouldy rags, maybe. Or possibly, the remnants of a deceased animal or person? Eilish is too afraid to go poking around in it to find out.

She stands for a moment, taking in the feeling of the hut. Imagining Ciara here. Imaging what is must have felt like to be left alone, not knowing what the future holds. Imagining the smell of distant burning.

One of the floorboards stands higher than the rest. Something is propping it up, stopping it from sagging under its own rotten weight. Eilish drops to her knees and slips her fingers into the cracks beside the floorboard, rocking it to see if it will budge. It does.

She lifts the board carefully, and her inquisition is rewarded. Under the floorboard lies a backpack. A mountaineering backpack that she has seen before. The backpack that Chloe carried onto the mountain before her leap. The backpack that Eilish had seen Chloe carefully pack and unpack in the snow.

Eilish lifts the pack onto the floor. It is cold, damp, and heavy. But it is *not* empty.

She reaches in. Amazingly, the waterproofing has kept the contents dry all these years. The first thing her hand touches is a book. A small book. She lifts it out carefully.

Eilish's heart throbs as her eyes fall on the cover. It is the blue leather, early edition of *Through the Looking Glass and What Alice Found There* by Lewis Carroll. More than a century old, this is the edition that her mother had read to her, Ciara, and Andrew in their childhood. A book that Eilish loved. A book that connected her to Ciara.

Holding her breath, Eilish flicks through the pages. And there it is. The photograph of Ciara and Eilish that Chloe had stowed away on the mountain. A photo of the sister she hasn't seen in years. Her closest friend in the universe.

In the photo, Ciara's face is kind and composed, smiling next to her own beaming face. Just how Eilish remembers her. She remembers Andrew taking this picture on holiday. A happy memory. When the three siblings had spent happier days together. This was before Ciara's depression. Before they lost their mother. Long before any tragedy brought either of them to the Meadow.

Eilish notices that Ciara has highlighted a section of the book.

> 'That's the effect of living backwards,' the Queen said kindly: 'it always makes one a little giddy at first--'
> 'Living backwards!' Alice repeated in great astonishment. 'I never heard of such a thing!'
> '--but there's one great advantage in it, that one's memory works both ways.'
> 'I'm sure MINE only works one way,' Alice remarked. 'I can't remember things before they happen.'
> 'It's a poor sort of memory that only works backwards,' the Queen remarked.

Eilish rereads the peculiar passage a couple of times. She knows it resonates, somehow. Resonates to the world that she is in—a resonance to marbles and memories, and to the strange interconnectedness of the story of *Her*. But the resonance is not entirely clear. Not yet.

Eilish places the open book on the floor next to her and reaches back into the rucksack. Inside her hand falls on the cold metal of a flask and another book. A larger, heavier text. She removes them both.

The flask is unremarkable. A stainless-steel cylinder with a screw-lid, the type that fills discount aisles in camping shops and outdoor enthusiasts receive for Christmas from arms-length relatives. It is much heavier than it appears, as if it were filled with lead. Inside it a cold, contained liquid sloshes back and forth.

The book, though, is more intriguing. Obviously left there on purpose, it is one of the most common textbooks in the Meadow—*The Dance of the Sands* by Professor Pelling. The thick old thesis is familiar to anyone who has received Distillery orientation classes after arriving in the Meadow (and after their weeks or months in the Distillery workhouses or palaces). It's a text that explores, in fine, granular detail, the peculiar relationship that exists in the Meadow between the people who inhabit the realm and the physical properties of the realm itself. The relationship between people's minds, the water that runs through the rivers and oceans, and the deposits of resin that ooze from the skin of new arrivals and the rocks at the border of the next realm.

A fold takes Eilish to a section she had perused not so long ago, though it feels an eternity since she was sitting in Angus' office with Chloe. The section is entitled 'The Source Conundrum'. One line is highlighted.

> *This has left us with one possibility—that not every soul that jumps from the cliffs loses its spark of life into the stars.*

Beside the sentence is a scribbled note. Eilish recognises Ciara's slanting scrawl.

> *A soul that drinks pure water can go back or forth, and still hold its spark.*

Eilish looks at the heavy flask. Of course, it is heavy because it contains Source water. The purer the water, the heavier it is. Ciara must have drunk from this very bottle before heading to the cliffs to fulfil her mission—the jump into the unknown. She sits for a moment, imagining Ciara on the mountain. The same mountain where she had seen Chloe take her life. And as she sits there in the quietness of the damp cabin, she notices something else lying between the floorboards—a shoebox.

Eilish carefully reaches in and lifts out the soggy cardboard vessel, whose structural integrity falls away in her hands. Beneath the cardboard, undisturbed for years and surviving the *Mighty Fire,* is a soft, silky material which flows delicately and folds into her palms.

It is the dress—the blue ballgown belonging to *Her.*

Eilish runs the water-like silk through her fingers, and a trickle of memories witnessed through others' eyes flows through her mind. Memories of women on the mountain. Memories of pain, beauty, and sacrifice. Memories of the origins of the *Tide and Time Tavern.* She is holding history. History of this realm—history of the Meadow. But also, history for all the realms. One of the most important artefacts in the universe. The blue dress of *Her.*

Pulling the fabric through her palms, Eilish feels something hard. An envelope, carefully placed deep in the folds of the dress. And in the envelope, a marble—clear by the distortion of the package.

The envelope is small. Much smaller than Eilish's palm, and on it is a line of text written in ink. Written in Ciara's hand.

I knew you'd come. I've always known. The dress is for you now.
I made the marble before I erased the memory.
It is vital.

From the envelope, a green marble drops into Eilish's hand. A marble that Ciara evidently wanted her to have. She rolls it between her thumb and forefinger. She knows it must contain one of Ciara's memories. A moment of life through her sister's eyes. Potentially a memory of the two of them together. It holds a chance to tumble back into a world with Ciara.

But Eilish knows she should wait. It would be irresponsibly dangerous to enter into a marble memory here, alone in the cabin on the hillside. In the memory, her unconscious body would be vulnerable to anything, or anyone who comes across her. She should wait until she is back with Nailah and Elijah.

But she can't.

The memory, so perfectly captured, is just here, waiting in her palm. A visceral recollection of Ciara's life is right here, looking up at her.

No. She doesn't have access to a safe way to crack the marble. Without a cracking tool, memory extraction is very risky. It is undoubtedly a better idea to go back to Nailah and Elijah.

But maybe she could crack the marble in her teeth? It's risky, but it could work. So long as she doesn't bite too hard and swallow the resin—that would be disastrous. A sure way to send yourself 'on'.

No, she must go back to Nailah and Elijah.

She can't.

Eilish pops the marble into her mouth and crunches down on the brittle glass sphere with her teeth. She feels the pressure of the glass and then '*crack*' and '*hiss*'.

She drops the marble back into her hand in panic. But she has done it just right. A delicate jet of emerald mist whispers out from the marble, creating a tiny cloud in her palm.

Eilish leans in and inhales, entering Ciara's memory.

***

Earth - Dublin

Eilish is in Dublin. In her childhood home on a cold, wet night. She immediately recognises her parents' bedroom. An awful chintzy room full of cheap and cliched ornaments exulting a 'loving marriage'—the shrine her father preserved after his wife, Eilish's mother, died.

But this isn't a childhood memory. Nor is it one Eilish recognises. Ciara is sitting on the bed, alone, her shoulders hunched. She wears a tailored black suit with a green silk cravat draped over her shoulders—an earthy contrast to her long copper hair. This is a memory from a day that haunted Eilish for twelve years. Haunted her, that is, until she altered her own *Identity Stone* and erased this memory altogether.

Although Eilish doesn't recognise it, this is the night she arrived in the Meadow. The night that Eilish and her family took a doomed flight out of Dublin, heading to London.

On the bed beside Ciara is her flight ticket to London, an embossed ticket for Puccini's *Madama Butterfly* at the Royal Opera House, and their mother's old silver vanity mirror. Eilish still holds vivid memories of her mother checking her makeup obsessively in this mirror.

The house is quiet, and Eilish can sense tension. Even without remembering the occasion, she can still recognise the ingredients for pain. Her mother had loved the opera. They had gone as a family every Christmas through Eilish's childhood. But after her mother's suicide, the joy of going went with her. Despite this, her father had kept up the tradition, as if somehow it would keep her alive. Keep him from having to confront the truth. The truth that in his self-obsession, he had contributed to her demise. And each time they went to the opera after their mother's death, Eilish and her siblings could feel their father becoming more deluded about what really happened.

Sitting alone, Ciara looks frightened. Haunted by grief and memory. Tears streak down her face, and her hands shake nervously. And that's when Eilish notices what Ciara is holding. Her stomach drops.

Gripped in Ciara's shaking hand is a small, but far from innocuous, strip of metal—a razor blade.

Eilish rushes forward, crouching in front of her sister, but there's nothing she can do in the memory.

Ciara lifts their mother's mirror and stares at herself in it, blinking quickly. Her eyes are red, her breathing shallow. Then her lips twist into an awfully tragic smile.

"He knows he's killing me, right?" she says to herself. Though it feels to Eilish like she's talking directly to her, which is impossible. "Taking us to the opera like nothing happened. Like I'm still a kid. Like, I don't know how he hurt you. Like you're not gone."

Eilish's chest tightens, and she leans closer, wishing she could wipe away a tear from Ciara's cheek.

Ciara sniffs, but her fingers stay firmly gripped onto the blade.

"You used to sit me up here, remember? When I was just a girl. When we were getting ready for the opera. You would prop me up on this bed while you put on your makeup. And you'd always tell me how beautiful *I* looked. That *I* was so beautiful that no one in the opera would see the show because they would be so distracted by me. You always looked so happy when we were going out." Ciara laughs desperately and darkly. "And even then, you still couldn't see your own beauty. *He* never let you."

Eilish notices her own hands are shaking now.

"You're not like Mum, Ciara," she whispers into the memory.

Ciara stops, almost as if she hears Eilish, but dismisses it.

Then the bedroom door bursts open.

Andrew stands in the doorway. He is agitated and storms into the room, straight for Ciara.

"You're doing this tonight?" he shouts, his voice sharp. "Before we leave? For fuck's sake, Ciara."

Ciara flinches as Andrew bears down on her, but doesn't respond. Not immediately. She just stares at him.

"You don't get to preach at me, Andrew."

His jaw clenches.

"No? If I don't, then who the hell will?"

Ciara shakes her head, exhaling with a sarcastic chuckle.

"You act like you want to stop me, Andrew. But you don't. You just don't want me to leave you behind."

Something dangerous and unsettling flashes across Andrew's face—pain, regret, something old but not forgotten.

Eilish watches her brother and sister curiously. She sees how Andrew won't meet Ciara's eyes directly. That there's something vital hiding just beneath the surface.

The tension in the room reaches breaking point.

Andrew moves towards Ciara, wanting to remove the razor from her hand and neutralise it. Then they could talk. But he's not careful enough.

Ciara, not ready for his approach, jumps backwards in surprise. The blade slips from her grip, tossed dangerously and carelessly into the air. Andrew moves instinctively to deflect it, but his instincts are rash and uncontrolled. The tiny, insignificant slither of metal slices across his cheek.

For a stunned moment, the room freezes.

Then Andrew gasps in shock, his hand flying up to his face. Warm blood trickles between his fingers.

Ciara screams.

"Oh my God, Andrew—no, I'm sorry—"

Andrew lunges forcefully towards his sister, grabbing her wrists, staring at her.

"This is what happens." His voice is shaking. "This is why we said, '*never again*'."

Ciara sobs.

"We said 'never *together*'."

Eilish looks at Andrew. She can see underneath his anger now. She can see fear coursing through his veins.

"Semantics," he shouts.

"You know that's not true," she reacts.

He looks at her. "Together or alone, Eilish still gets hurt," he whispers accusatorily.

And that's when Eilish understands. She always knew her sister was battling an insurmountable pain. A pain more acute than she had ever felt. It came from suffering the cruel loss of their mother. A cruelty compounded by knowing her tormentor—their father—could not see his guilt. It was a pain that craved release— craved an end. And this is why, not for the first or last time, Ciara tried to end her life.

But now Eilish realises something new. Andrew was tormented, too. He might have hidden it better. But the pain he felt was just as acute. Just as destructive. Some time he had tried to take his own life with Ciara. Somewhere, out of sight and hidden from Eilish, their younger, innocent sister. And the guilt of this had driven Andrew and Ciara to make a pact. A pact that they will never leave, never end their lives, together. Why? To protect her. To protect Eilish.

Andrew stands, still clutching his face, and as he does, the tension and fire in his eyes blow out. Like something fighting inside him has finally given up.

"Do what you want," he says to Ciara. "I don't. I *can't* care anymore."

In an instant, Andrew changes. And now he looks like the cruel and distant brother Eilish recognises from the Meadow.

He reaches into his jacket pocket and throws a small, clear pot full of pills onto the bed beside Ciara—the pills she will ultimately take at the back of the plane before the crash. Then he walks out of the room without looking back, leaving her alone on the bed.

Eilish stands in shock. She expects the memory to fizzle away now. She hopes it will. She can't bear any more. But it doesn't.

Instead, Ciara reaches into the pocket of her jacket and pulls out a photograph. She holds it delicately up to her face, her hands still—such a contrast to the blade she held before.

Eilish peers over Ciara's shoulder and confirms what she already half expects. Ciara is holding the photograph of the two of them on holiday. The same one Chloe held on the mountain. The same one Ciara left for her in the backpack.

"I'm so sorry, Eilish," Ciara whispers to herself, clutching the photo to her chest. "I never meant to hurt you. But it's so hard. So hard to keep on going like this."

She reaches into her pocket again, and this time pulls out the little blue leather-bound book Eilish knows so well—the early edition of *Through the Looking Glass*.

"I always loved reading this with you and mum," Ciara smiles. "We would pass it back and forth all night, pretending to be different characters. I hope you remember the good times when I'm gone. I hope we can pass this back and forth again."

Back and forth.

'Back and forth?' Eilish muses.

And with that, the memory fizzles out and comes to an end.

***

Chapter 58

Spiritual Conspiracy

The Meadow - Near The Mountain

In the stillness of the late morning, the dancing mist has settled like a thick soupy fog over the foothills. Eilish had been warned that, should the mist descend like this, she should cover her face. Only a fool breathes in the mist on the Mountain.

Feeling the cool dampness on her brow, Eilish trudges back up through the burnt stumps, saplings, and fledgling trees towards the clearing where she had left Nailah and Elijah keeping watch over the suspension bridge.

Slung over her back, she carries the old rucksack that was passed from Chloe to Ciara and is now in Eilish's possession. She can feel the weight of the flask of pure water and the blue gown inside. The gown that fills her with questions. What does it mean for Ciara to leave the dress? Is Eilish now *Her*? What does *that* even mean? And what about Ciara? Where is she? Has she gone to the Beyond? Can Eilish go there too? And that memory of Ciara and Andrew. A pain from Earth that Eilish has pushed down for years is there again, settled in the front of her mind: the pain that Ciara and Andrew suffered and the connection they shared.

As these thoughts swirl around Eilish's mind, she feels a prickly coldness in her vicinity. A familiar prickly cold feeling. A feeling she has felt many times before—the sense of an angel approaching.

She stops. Is it her angel? The one who spoke to Cyril? Has she followed her here? Has she come to give her instructions or advice? Some clarity, maybe? But it doesn't take long for the realisation to hit her. It is not her angel at all.

"*I know you're out there!*" whispers a sinister ghostly voice. A male voice. A spirit Eilish has not encountered before. "*I know you're there, Nailah… We knew you'd be here sooner or later. There's no point running; the Distillery are everywhere in these parts... and they will get you. So, give in... show yourself."*

Eilish holds her breath, hoping the spirit doesn't see or hear her. Then she feels a second presence entering the mist.

"They've fled," announces the first spirit.

"Both of them?"

"Yes... But the foot patrols will pick them up, sooner or later."

"And you think they're here to try and rescue the prisoner?"

"No doubt."

"It definitely is Kim-Joy then, even if Samael can't get a confession... Do you think she'll crack?"

"She has to... the floods in Elysian will overflow soon if she doesn't... and, my god, that will spell disaster."

"They are already out of resin here, you know?"

"Yes, I know."

"Without marbles, people will start rioting in the Meadow soon."

"Yes, I know... We have maybe three weeks before Distillery control of this realm collapses altogether."

"How do you figure that?"

"That's when the Distillery's own people—their police, their Ferrymen—will be out of marbles too... Then it'll be every mind for itself."

"And did you hear about the Governess? She's missing."

"Yes, I heard. The President is trying to keep it quiet, mind... If the people knew that the Distillery had lost control of their own house, I think they'd collapse in less than three weeks."

"Are they looking for her?

"Not really... Samael has convinced them to put all their energy into helping him... he has convinced them that breaking the landlady's resolve is the only way to get the resin flowing into the Meadow again."

"And has He said anything?"

"He is convinced that finding Her is the only way to stop the floods in Elysian. He is convinced that She is the one flooding our realm again."

"Do you think He's right?"

A moment of silence falls between the two spirits. Eilish holds her breath.

The first spirit speaks, but quieter. Much quieter than before.

"I've heard a rumour," he whispers. *"But it stays between us…"*

"Go on…"

"Have you met Sandalphon?"

"I've heard of him… very tall, right?"

"That's him… Well, Sandalphon thinks that the only way to stop the flood is to break our bridge with the Meadow… to plug the Source. Sandalphon doesn't think that She matters at all."

"But He would never allow that… not while She is unfound."

"Sandalphon doesn't think He needs to know."

"Ah, I see… And with the bridge broken, what, the floods will just recede?"

"Exactly… But not a word… just make sure you're ready to leave the Meadow."

"Understood."

"So, what now? Is the prisoner being taken to the House?"

"For a quick tour? Yes, I imagine so."

"And then to the prison chambers?"

"Yes."

"Will Samael do the interrogation again?"

"No, not this time."

"Then who?"

"Him… He will interrogate the prisoner."

"Will He really come back to the Meadow? After what happened last time?"

"He is already back… Now, come on. Let's get out of here. There is a breeze approaching."

With too much to process, and little clarity, Eilish lies still on her front in amongst the ferns, feeling the damp of the forest floor chilling her skin. She waits until she is certain the spirits have gone, before she sits up and breathes.

***

With Nailah and Elijah on the run, and no way to communicate with them, Eilish is alone. She could wait in the woods, hoping they will return, but it seems unlikely either of them will come back to the place where they were nearly captured. Given this, Eilish decides to push on alone. Her plan is clear, even if her mind is a chaos of confusion. She will try and get to Kim-Joy herself, and hope that somehow her path will cross with Nailah and Elijah again.

The way to the checkpoint doesn't require much navigation. There is only one clear track through the woods. It follows down through the valley heading all the way to the checkpoint. It is the track that the carriage carrying Kim-Joy would most likely take, if it hasn't already.

Eilish knows she'll have to be cautious. At any time, the carriage could appear, and she could do without a reunion with the Distillery.

It starts to rain. Up in the far reaches of the tallest trees, where the mist dances, it takes a while for the droplets to filter through and hit Eilish and the ground she walks on. But soon, it becomes a downpour. And with the rain, the mist also descends towards her.

Eilish knows that this is a dangerous time to be in the mountains. She ties a scarf around her face and tries to keep her breathing slow. The longer she is here, the more likely her mind will succumb to unconsciousness, and her journey into the Beyond won't be a chosen leap but an inevitable walk off the cliffs.

Half a kilometre ahead, Eilish starts to make out the checkpoint. A detached stone building, the fortified Distillery garrison is connected to a gatehouse and the perimeter walls of the Mountain. The dark slate of the building is purple and unwelcoming, with coils of barbed wire and rusty metal spikes decorating every ledge and roof. Lights are on inside, and someone sits in the gatehouse, keeping watch.

Eilish knows that when she gets to the checkpoint she needs to be on the front-foot. It wouldn't take much for someone to question the peculiar circumstance of her appearance, wondering why the governess of the Distillery should be wandering in the foothills in the rain, alone. She needs to approach confidently with demands and questions of her own, such that any enquiry isn't given room to develop.

Eilish strides up to the gatehouse. The tall slate walls tower over her and the Distillery guard sat in the building watches her approach intently. He stays unmoved until she lifts the large iron knocker on the gate.

A moment passes. The rain splashes angrily, chilling her ankles, before a slot in the gate slides open at eye-level.

"Can I help you?" says a voice.

"Yes, you can," says Eilish, confidently and clearly. "You can start by letting me in and out of this awful rain!"

"And you are…"

Eilish drops the scarf from her face momentarily.

"Governess Callaghan?! Your Excellency!"

"Yes," says Eilish, trying to sound frustrated. "Now come on. I need some warmth and some marbles."

"Oh… er… yes, your excellency. I… I, er… I didn't know you were…"

"No, of course you didn't know I was coming! But I'm here now, aren't I? So, let me in."

The man fumbles a set of keys before wrestling with the heavy bolts fastening the gate, and eventually creaking it open, letting Eilish into the checkpoint.

The officer is young, with stocky shoulders and a crop of brown hair. A rifle is slung over his shoulder, but Eilish isn't concerned. Her insider knowledge means she knows it won't be loaded. The Distillery ran out of ammunition years ago - bullets don't often come through Openings with Arrivals these days. He looks like he is trying, against his nature, to appear strong and commanding. He holds his shoulders back and looks at Eilish but doesn't know what to say.

Saving the officer's awkwardness, a door beside him opens and a senior officer steps out. This second officer recognises Eilish immediately.

"Governess Callaghan!" he says, bowing. "I presumed you were your brother coming back. He's just left, you know? He didn't mention you were coming. I hope Henry here has offered you warmth and a new coat?"

The young officer is caught out, and he stammers, trying to respond.

"A new coat would be delightful," says Eilish and, thinking on her feet says, "Yes, my brother does tend to overlook the fine details. I am due to meet the council."

"There is a Council of the Almighty, happening soon?" asks the senior officer.

"Yes," she lies. "An impromptu Council. One to address certain *issues*," she offers, cryptically.

"Ah, yes," says the officer. "The issue with the marbles, no doubt? A very pressing issue indeed."

Eilish holds her gaze steady. She doesn't want to confirm or deny the officer's assumption.

"I'm sure this is on the council's agenda, your excellency, but do you have any update on the resin supplies? The Mountain's been completely dry for weeks now."

"Completely dry?" asks Eilish, concerned.

"Bone dry. And we're almost out of marbles now. We're on one a week ourselves now, and they're pretty risky ones at that." He shows her a bag of dark, dirty marbles—the kind that addicts usually suck. So full of colour that they are likely to burst at any time.

"Here," she says, reaching into an embarrassingly full marble pouch she had been given by Nailah. "One each, if you'll leave me alone to head to the council."

The guards' eyes light up, they are starving for these clean sensations. "Not a problem your excellency!"

"Are you heading straight to the Council now?" asks the more senior officer, the marble rattling gratefully between his teeth.

"Yes. I cannot wait around."

"Then, please, take this," he says, handing her his own long fur-lined coat. "There's a nip in the air."

"Thank you," smiles Eilish, genuinely grateful to have something warm that isn't damp.

"It'll be a quiet walk, I expect," says the officer. "With no resin coming from the mountain, all the working Drifters have been released. The minefield is empty. But be careful, mind. Stick to the Drifter path. None of our armed guards know you're here, and they're on high alert—apparently some high security prisoner was brought in earlier."

***

Chapter 59

Seeing things differently

Earth - Mynydd Aaru

T he lady hoists Marty into an upright position on the bed. Her grip is firm, pushing his back against the wooden wall of the hut. It creaks as it takes his weight.

"Are you steady?" asks the lady.

"Steady enough," he responds, bracing himself with his outstretched hands. It feels good to be upright. Blood can finally dribble down to his fingers and toes again, and he starts to feel more alive. If anything, the blood draining away from his head calms the soreness of his snow-blind eyes.

Out of sight, Marty hears the lady fiddling with crockery. Then there's a sharp crack, like broken glass, and a gentle hiss.

"Here you go," she says, her voice lilting as she re-joins Marty and pulls his hand up towards her, placing a warm mug into his palm. "A cup of tea, as always… It helps the mind and the heart to be more receptive… more willing to listen."

"Cheers," says Marty, raising the mug. Steam washes under his nose and the bandages around his eyes. The smell of tea is comforting. The steam almost intoxicating, filling his mind with calmness.

Something at the bottom of the mug rattles as Marty tilts it towards his mouth. Then he feels the warmth of the tea wash into his dry throat and down into the exhausted chasm of his gut. The sensation is an excellent and distracting relief from everything else.

"Let me tell you my story," says the lady. "If I may?"

Marty gestures for her to continue, and shuffles to get as comfortable as he can.

"Many years ago," she begins. "Years before you first saw me in Hammersmith, I was born and raised in Dublin. I grew up in the city and called it home. But then, one day, just like you, my whole life was turned upside down by tragedy. But my tragedy was different in one significant way… *my* tragedy involved my own death."

"Come again?" says Marty.

"More than ten years ago, I was caught up in a fatal disaster with my sister, brother, and father—a plane crash. You might remember it. It happened over the River Thames one stormy night. It was the night that I died. Or so it would seem to everyone here. Because, you see, that night was also the night I discovered something unexpected. Something incredible which your son will have discovered too… premature death on Earth is not the end… No. For many, it is a new beginning."

"I'm listening," says Marty.

"I discovered that someone who dies on Earth through misadventure, tragedy, self-destruction, or cruelty, can find themselves in a whole new world… a world called *The Meadow*.

"Another world? Like a parallel universe? Is that what you're saying?!"

The lady laughs. "Yes, that's about right. Though it's not what *they* told us when we arrived. They told us we had entered Purgatory."

"They?"

"The government in the Meadow."

"And it's not Purgatory?"

"No. Definitely not. You were close with the 'parallel universe'. It's actually more of a *perpendicular* world to this one. It looks much like here. But the people are different. For a start, they don't age. At least, their bodies don't. It is a realm dominated not by bodies but by the mind. The health of the mind is what matters there, most of all."

"You're nuts," says Marty, conclusively—feeling foolish for allowing himself to be drawn in to start with. "Seriously."

"Think what you like," says the woman defensively. "But let me finish while you're enjoying your tea… and consider this; *I'm* not telling you to kill anyone!"

"Fair enough…" Marty concedes. "I'll amuse you, if you need me to."

"Thank you," she says gratefully.

Marty sighs.

"Right, so if you died and ended up in this perpendicular world you talk about, how are you back here now?" he asks. "Why are you stalking disasters? Why are you here on this mountain?"

The lady pauses.

"I'm here because I discovered something vital in the Meadow, and I came back here to find it."

"What?"

"Love."

Marty yawns. "Go on," he says cynically.

"I had a sister when I was first here on Earth," she continues, ignoring Marty's tone. "The only person I really loved. But it was only when tragedy struck, and I was separated from her in the Meadow that I realised how it was our love that had given my life energy… and it is this same energy that has driven me to be reunited with her again, that is keeping me living."

"Of course," starts Marty dismissively. "Love conquers everything, and all the other cliches… What a load of trite nonsense—no offence. I loved my boy, and it didn't stop me losing him, did it?"

"But it might have saved *you*," says the lady without hesitation.

"What do you mean?"

"I've watched you, Marty. There is something inside you that cannot give up. Something in you that needs to stay alive. And I daresay it's love. A love that cannot give up. Cannot give up hope. It's why you have fought against all the odds to find me. And it's why, if you trust me, well… I can help that thing inside you to do what it needs to do."

"And what's that?"

"I can help you find a way back to your son."

Marty stops. The lady has either just stepped well over the line, or she has just completely changed the odds.

"What do you mean?"

"Your love is still alive and full of energy. I can see it. And love is never singular," she says. "I know that as a fact. To hold such love, your son *must* still love you too. If this is the case… then the tragedy that physically tore you apart on Earth, is drawing you together in the Meadow… And I can take you to him."

"How?" asks Marty.

"Ah," says the lady, with an air of mischief. "Now is not the time to tell you that."

"What?!"

She approaches Marty.

"Are you done with your tea?" she asks him.

"You're seriously not going to tell me?!"

"Not yet. And you're in no position to make me."

Marty sighs. She's right. He lifts the mug to his lips, but nothing pours out. Nothing except for an unexpectedly hard object, which rolls into his mouth. He spits it back into the mug immediately.

"What's this?" he exclaims.

The lady takes the mug from Marty. "Looks like a marble," she tells him. "Nothing harmful."

"What's it doing in my tea?" he asks, accusingly.

"Who knows?" she dismisses. "Would you like me to make you another one?"

"No, I'm good."

"How are your eyes feeling now?" the lady asks. "Still painful?"

"Less so," says Marty.

"Oh, good. And can you see anything?"

Marty pauses. The truth is, he can see things now, even through the bandages. He can see her silhouette clearly, and the outlines of the bed, stove, and furniture around the hut. But he doesn't fully trust her yet. And having sight that she doesn't know about is an advantage he wants to keep.

"Nothing yet," he lies.

"Hopefully it'll return soon. In the meantime, I need to pop out. I have something I need to do on the mountain. Will you be ok if I leave you here while I'm gone?"

"I'll be fine," says Marty. "I'm not going anywhere."

She chuckles. "I won't be long."

"What are you doing?"

"Oh, just preparations," she says. "Preparations for a journey back to the Meadow... I'll explain later if you decide to join me."

"Fair enough."

Marty rocks his head back on the wall, pretending that he is closing his eyes in rest, but he isn't. He watches keenly through the bandages, interested in the preparations the lady might be making.

She gathers some items from the table in the middle of the room. Little items and a bundle of something. Maybe a length of rope? Next, she strides to the far wall where she bends down and lifts the lid off a heavy, creaking trapdoor in the floor.

A cool breath of air blows up through the hole and swirls around the hut, making Marty shiver. He can't really see what she is doing before realising that she has climbed into the hole and has started lowering herself into whatever space sits below.

Marty listens carefully, hearing the lady's straining breath as she descends away. It must be quite a descent as the sounds of her breathing, and the squeaking tension of the rope, take a good few minutes to fade.

Marty waits a moment longer before removing his bandages.

The light of the hut, without his eyes shielded, is a little too harsh, and it stings his retinas. He feels a nauseating ache in his forehead, but at least he can see. He squints to ease the pain and peers around at the hut.

The bed he sits on is an old army camp bed. The mattress is dirty and brown, and the blankets could use a good shake to remove the dust and hair.

The hut is generally depressing. It's the kind of place that you'd assume a recluse might inhabit. Someone opting out of society. Maybe someone with delusions that they have been living in another world for a decade!

'*She's crazy,*' thinks Marty. '*Obviously!*'

He glances at the trapdoor. Cool air still swirls up from the hole. Anchored to an iron ring beside it, the end of a climbing rope is fastened securely. Opposite that is a table and chairs, and beyond them a grimy coal-fired stove. A tin pot with the remnants of tea steams on top, beside a box of tea bags and a bag of marbles.

'*The marble was no accident,*' thinks Marty. '*She is definitely a crackpot.*'

On the wall beside the stove, there's an array of documents pinned to the wood with lines of thread joining them together to form a map. The kind of map Marty had spent his working life constructing. The threads of intelligence that make up a police investigation. A mental map that helps a detective to solve a crime.

The documents are newspaper cuttings. But they don't seem to be arranged as a mind map. Instead, it is simply a timeline. A timeline that stretches back more than a decade.

The newspaper cuttings all report disasters that have occurred around the United Kingdom. A red ribbon is pinned towards the right edge of the documents. It indicates the present day. Surprisingly, the timeline extends *beyond* this point to two further labelled points. The first simply says '*His turn*' and the second, '*My turn*'.

Marty lets the images of disasters on the cuttings filter through his mind. Most are familiar in some way. Terrible tragedies that have affected the nation's mood. There are also some more minor, less well-documented disasters. But these all have happened in London, and Marty remembers each of them.

At the start of the timeline is the story of a plane crash on the Thames. The picture of a plane, its wing reaching into a stormy sky as its fuselage sinks, is iconic. It was a picture that everyone remembers from the night of the infamous Callaghan family disaster. Baron Brendan Callaghan, the financier, had died in the crash with his family. The media circus was phenomenal at the time.

Marty follows his finger along the timeline, looking for one particular disaster. It doesn't take long to pinpoint it. From the *Chelsea Gazette*—'Double Decker Horror: Cops Kid in Coma'. There's a picture of the awful day, too. The red bus stopped in the middle of the street while countless emergency service personnel rushed around, trying to save the young man trapped under the vehicle.

There are some markings on the text surrounding the photo. Marty's name is circled. This is unexpected. Especially when the lady had said she didn't know about him. Maybe she had marked his name after she found him on the mountain. The name of the hospital where Elijah had been kept is also underlined.

Marty scans the other markings and events. There is the fire in Shoreditch, the explosion in Dagenham. The markings don't tell him much. Mostly people or things from the disasters. People like the van Koopler's who died in an ambulance in Hammersmith, and the bandmembers of the *Spirit of Shoreditch* who perished in the pub fire.

Marty pulls up a chair from the table to sit down and ponder the menagerie of disasters before him. He considers the story the lady had told him. The story of another world where victims of all of these tragedies have congregated. Is it even remotely possible it could be true? Could Elijah really be alive in another world?

A coat that rests on the back of Marty's chair slips to the floor. He goes to pick it up before stopping suddenly.

Spilling from the pocket is a handful of visitor permits. Permits that he is all too familiar with. Permits for staying after 'visiting hours' at St. Thomas' Hospital in London. The hospital where Elijah had spent the recent years of his life. It appeared that the lady had been visiting the hospital almost as frequently as he had.

Marty inspects the passes more carefully. The dates are unerringly aligned. The lady had been visiting since the day of Elijah's accident and had stopped going since the Dagenham blast. Coincidence? Detectives don't believe in coincidences. The only possible conclusion is that she knows his son. Which poses the necessary follow-up: why is she hiding it?

***

Chapter 60

The House of Sand

The Meadow - House of Sand

Beside the great lake in the shadow of the Mountain, the Mineralist leans his gaunt body against the veranda rail of the *House of Sand*, protected from the torrential rain. Stretching out in front of him, the cold, icy waters of the lake are calm, and the water is, in his eyes, disturbingly clear, despite the rain that pockmarks its surface. The lake is usually dark and black; the water filled with sediment from the resin-rich waters that flow from the Source and fall off the *Perihelion Cliffs*. But not now. Now the waters are pure and sediment-free. There is no resin coming from the Source at all. This spells disaster for him and disaster for the Distillery. No resin means no marble production. And no marble production means increasingly desperate and frustrated citizens, and the rapid dissolving of the Distillery's power.

The Mineralist yawns. A wide, stretching yawn that pulls at the sinews in the corner of his mouth, reopening a sore that begins to weep. He is exhausted. He travelled through the night to be here, sharing an awful carriage with Founderers from London—the recently unconscious on their drifting journey to the Source. It was the President's urgent instruction that he take the first train out of the city to be here at the House of Sand. Apparently, his *skills* were *needed*.

Peering beyond the lake, the Mineralist glimpses a convoy of horse-drawn carriages approaching at speed. Carriages, he knows, have come from the port at Holyhead. He presumes, and hopes, the occupants of the carriages will explain why he's here with such short and urgent notice.

The carriages skid to a stop on the gravel in front of the house. From the front carriage, the Ferryman climbs out. He looks pensive. Without hanging around in the downpour, he strides earnestly up the stone steps towards the house. The Mineralist runs his hands through his greasy, thinning hair and wanders over to greet the Ferryman.

"Was it a successful voyage, your excellency?" asks the Mineralist, without the niceties of a 'hello'.

"Not really," frowns the Ferryman. "The prisoner is still with us."

"Did the angels not get what they wanted?"

"No," says the Ferryman. "That's why we still have her."

"That is a bit of an embarrassment, I presume?"

"Indeed… There was an incident at sea."

"Incident?"

"When the interrogation failed… Samael cracked…"

"Cracked?"

"Literally, in front of her… His host failed him."

"I see," smiles the Mineralist. "So that is why I've been called here?"

"Yes. Samael is bodiless again. He needs you to work your magic in the sand."

"I'd be delighted," smirks the Mineralist. "Have you got me any fresh samples?"

"Of course," says the Ferryman. "Samael has selected the one he wants."

"Then I can get to work right away…" He looks back out across the lake, in thought. "Are you bringing the prisoner in?"

"I was minded to keep her in the carriage. She's somewhat distraught."

"I'm not surprised," says the Mineralist. "The angels do like to get *close* in their interrogations."

"Mmm," says the Ferryman in contemplation. "She's certainly suffering… She's looking her age now."

"Sounds like she's getting more susceptible to another interrogation."

"Maybe," says the Ferryman.

"An interrogation always works better on a weak and vulnerable mind."

"Of course."

"Then, might I suggest I take her on a tour of the House? Really break her down."

"Wouldn't a tour strengthen her resolve?"

"I don't think so," the Mineralist smiles. "Even the most belligerent minds falter when they witness what happens here."

"Well, you are the expert," says the Ferryman.

"Yes, I am," smirks the Mineralist. "And there is a truth about interrogation that you can only learn from breaking countless minds."

"And that is?"

"Any interrogation can fail… You've seen one of the most notorious interrogators in Archangel Samael. And yet, even he can fail. When a mind is strong, it can resist. This is where the House of Sand can be rather helpful. And it is why, I imagine, Samael has asked you to bring the prisoner here today."

"Why is that?"

"Because there has never been an interrogation that has failed after a soul witnesses what happens in the House."

A vile twisting grin stretches across the Mineralist's face. "If you would like to stay here, Your Excellency, I will happily take the prisoner on my own."

"No," says the Ferryman. "She doesn't leave my sight."

"Then I apologise in advance," says the Mineralist. "What you will witness will not be befitting of a man of your stature."

***

Kim-Joy first heard of the *House of Sand* many years ago. It ranks at the top of the most notorious places to have been developed under the Distillery. What actually happens there, she doesn't know. No one does, except a few people in the inner circles of the Distillery.

Speculations about the House are wild and wide-ranging. Well-wishers like Kim-Joy believe it houses a secret connection between the Distillery and the Beyond. A connection supporting their power, somehow. A connection facilitating the rich channel of resin which comes from the Source and guarantees marble production. And a connection which explains the undocumented individuals who roam in the shadows of the palaces—the *Princes*.

As Kim-Joy is pulled out into the cold, wet rain, in the shadow of the Mountain, gagged and bound, she lays eyes on the *House of Sand* for the first time. The building stares down at her. A sizeable place, like a rural farmhouse, it is not palatial in any way but would nonetheless be accurately described as 'grand'. There are three stories, and though the whitewashed walls are weathered from the winds that batter the mountain, it is clean and imposing.

Hugging the first floor of the House is a balcony which encircles the outer wall, under which a pitched roof shelters a veranda on the ground floor. It looks like the kind of place one might expect to find a retreat. For relaxation or rehabilitation. It is not 'welcoming' in the warmest sense of the word, but there is a calmness to it.

Standing on the steps of the veranda, beside the Ferryman, eyeing her intently, is the Mineralist. He watches as she is dragged up to the house.

"You're keeping her gagged then?" asks the Mineralist.

"I think it's best," says the Ferryman, nervously.

"Oh, shame! No fun!" says the Mineralist. "I'd love to hear what *she* thinks of the House!"

"She stays quiet until Samael comes," says the Ferryman, bluntly.

"Fine… Then welcome Kim-Joy of the *Tide and Time Tavern*… welcome to the *House of Sand*."

He leaves a pause, allowing the imposing building to provide the crescendo to his announcement.

"I will be your 'tour guide' this morning, before your little *chat* with our friend, Samael."

Kim-Joy looks at him with her red-raw eyes. In five hundred years, she hadn't aged a day, until today. Now she exudes the lethargy of someone whose energy is rapidly falling away.

The Mineralist leads them into an expansive drawing room. The floor is tiled with dark purple slate, and the walls are clad in oak. Hanging from the walls are tapestries dominated by religious icons. Images of angels, demons, servitude, and pain, all staring down on them.

A deep chimney breast imposes itself in the centre of the room. In the hearth, a hungry fire burns through a pile of logs, crackling and spitting sparks onto an animal skin rug.

It is swelteringly hot in the drawing room. Warm enough to bring a glisten to Kim-Joy's brow. But not warm enough to justify the attire of the men in there. Two dozen young men, all with immaculate physiques, all completely naked.

The men are silent, passive even, and none acknowledge the entrance of the three clothed figures into the room.

Feeling unable to look elsewhere, Kim-Joy's eyes are drawn to the bodies of the men. Their torsos and wrists are burnt and scarred. These are men who have been through the worst of the Distillery workhouses. But, despite their slavish passivity, these aren't unconscious Drifters or semi-conscious Founderers. They are conscious but placated by deep camomile marbles that rattle inside their perfectly square jaws.

"Do you like what you see?" the Mineralist insinuates, nudging Kim-Joy and pointing at a young man lying on a chaise longue in front of them.

The old lady glares back, unimpressed. Why the *House of Sand* is filled with young naked men makes no sense. The curious incarceration of these men doesn't give Kim-Joy anything other than a sense of despair.

The Mineralist approaches a young man, grabs him by the wrist, and pulls him towards Kim-Joy.

"A perfect specimen, isn't he?" grins the Mineralist. "This one used to have a mop of long blonde hair," he says, sliding his greasy hand over the man's shaved scalp. "He used to work for one of the Water Boards, before he went 'missing'... Amazing, isn't it? So many missing men and I've found them all!" he throws open his arms. "Quite a menagerie, wouldn't you say?!"

"Enough showing off," says the Ferryman. "She's not here to see the Waiting Room, you brought her here to see Surgery."

The Mineralist grins at Kim-Joy. "You wait till you see an operation. You'll never be able to un-see it!"

Behind the Mineralist, another clothed individual enters the drawing room. He is dressed head to toe in flowing dark black robes. Kim-Joy recognises the attire—the same kinds of robes that the *horsemen* wore.

"She has been followed," says the robed man, urgently. "Patrols caught sight of two intruders in the foothills… we suspect they were planning an ambush."

"Have we captured them?" asks the Ferryman.

"Not yet… but we will."

"Who are they?"

"One is Nailah Hussain—her rebel deputy." He spits in Kim-Joy's direction.

"Are we good to continue here?" asks the Mineralist.

"Yes… Just tell Samael, when you see him, that we're on the tail of Nailah Hussain. When we bring her in, I'm sure he'd like to break them together."

"Of course," says the Ferryman.

Kim-Joy is marched from the drawing room through to a clinical ward at the end of a dark corridor. It is dermatologically clean, with white tiles covering the floor and ceiling, and has a scent reminiscent of turpentine-like bleach. A skylight provides surgically precise and unflattering illumination. In the middle of the room, strapped to an angled frame, is a man. Another prisoner from the *Charybdis*. Prisoner number seventeen. The man prepared for Samael.

Until a few minutes ago, the man had been kept sedated with marble after marble. Not anymore. Now on the frame, he is naked, and his mind is clear of the influence of resin. Leather straps hold his wrists and ankles, and his genitalia is exposed to his new audience.

The man looks terrified. His forehead is held to the frame, and his chin is strapped to his chest, forcing his mouth open. He can't speak or move, but his eyes dart around, looking desperately at the people who have entered the room. His throat gargles as though he is trying desperately to speak.

Kim-Joy, her hands bound and mouth gagged, looks desperately, sadly, at the young man. She wishes that somehow her eyes could tell him that everything would be ok. But they both would know that's just not true.

The Mineralist pushes Kim-Joy right in front of the man, a few steps back.

"You don't have to be here for this," he says to the Ferryman.

"She stays in my sight," he reminds the Mineralist.

"Very well," he frowns, closing the door to the ward.

The Mineralist inspects the naked body of the man on the frame. Like a butcher about to prepare a carcass, he is shameless in his inspection. He feels every contour of the man's skin, prodding inside his mouth, lifting the sad eyelids, before cupping the man's genitals and inspecting them also.

In the chill of the room, Kim-Joy shivers.

"He is ready," says the Mineralist, stepping back. He licks his finger and holds it aloft in the room. "Not a breath," he smiles. "Perfect conditions. Samael will be here in a moment."

And almost immediately, the presence of an approaching angel is felt by everyone in the room. A breath in the still air. A prickling over their shoulders.

"*Excellent service, Mr Callaghan,*" rasps the bodiless voice of archangel Samael. "*Well done. I knew I could trust you.*"

In front of them, the naked man starts to moan and, though she can't see it, Kim-Joy senses that the spirit of Samael is rubbing up against him.

Then, without warning or introduction, the most awful thing Kim-Joy has, or ever could, witness starts to unfold.

The man starts to sweat. On his brow to begin with, then his chest, before every pore in his body starts to leak. Next, and much to the man's embarrassment, he starts to urinate out of control. Then he defecates. And soon he starts vomiting as well. He can't retch properly, the straps hold him down, but nonetheless, great waves of vomit pour out of his open mouth and tumble down his body.

It is cruel and disgusting. Kim-Joy turns away, but the Mineralist steps forward and wrenches her head back. Forcing her to watch the brutal ordeal of the man.

Though he is strapped to a frame, the whole body of the naked man starts to shake. Kim-Joy can see the man's heart thumping aggressively in his chest. His breathing is rapid and shallow and, as a final insult to the poor man, his genitalia—against his will—engorge, as though aroused.

Kim-Joy can tell that the man is ashamed and scared. If he could scream, he would scream, and scream, and scream. It is the cruellest, vilest ordeal that Kim-Joy has witnessed in her long life. And this is not the worst. For, as every particle of the man's body disowns him, Kim-Joy senses that the mind of Samael—the bodiless mind of the archangel—starts to strangle the mind of the man.

Strangling his mind, Samael wrenches the man's soul away from his mind and body, making it homeless, ripping the mind from its soul, throwing it into an abyss of nothingness, leaving it floating without an anchor. This is the precious connection that every person has. The connection between the mind, body, and soul that anyone can see when they look into another's eyes on Earth. The connection that anyone can see when they look at another's interrogation stone or identity resin in the Meadow. And here is this man's connection being ripped apart in front of them. And in its place, the soul of Samael slithers into the glove that is the man's body, wriggling its vile nature to the end of the fingers and the tips of the toes. And just like that, the man's body has been hijacked, and Samael is no longer bodiless.

"Clean me off," says the man, Samael. "This is a good body... Perfect for a little interrogation later, wouldn't you say so, Kim-Joy?"

Kim-Joy has no idea how she is still conscious. She feels like her own mind and soul are wobbling precariously with her weak body. She collapses to the floor and starts sobbing.

"Pick her up!" says Samael. "Take her to the chamber. I'll see her when I'm ready!"

***

Chapter 61

The Mountain

The Meadow - The Mountain

Most people in the Meadow will only visit the Mountain once, and they won't remember it, because it is their final journey before the leap into the Beyond. Eilish is like most people, except that, as a Council member of the Distillery, she has been in numerous marble memories from the Mountain. And, of course, she has seen Chloe's memory of her walk on the face ten years ago. So, in one sense, the Mountain and its great allure are familiar. But in another sense, the harshness of its reality is all new.

The spirits had confirmed that Kim-Joy is being taken to the prison chambers within the Mountain itself, beyond the chamber where the Council of the Almighty happens. Eilish had been in marble memories of this council. She knows just how deep into the Mountain she will have to go. Beyond the mineshafts used for marble production and into the core. But thanks to Nailah, she also knows a secret way to get to the chambers, without, in theory, having to come across anyone from the Distillery.

High up on the mountain face is the old and abandoned mineshaft, whose entrance is hidden by rocks. It is a passageway that the group of rebels who ventured this way ten years ago took. The passageway used by Nailah and the notorious individuals known as the Returners. The rebels that Chloe helped on the Mountain.

Eilish looks up at the Mountain in front of her. It is a magnificent sight, climbing high into the sky where its peak is shrouded in mist. Near the base, she can see the lake and just make out the outline of the notorious *House of Sand*. All around that is debris and machinery. The debris of rockfall, unstable cliffs, and barbed wire, coiled like frozen snakes, all over the ground. And the machinery is the abandoned workings of the Distillery marble-mine. The carts, the rails, and the lines used to tether the Drifters who worked the mine—dragging carts and collecting resin from the rock. But, because there is no resin, the minefield is empty. And so, the great vista that surrounds the steep incline of the mountain is a post-industrial wasteland. The only souls that Eilish can see are those in the long line of Drifters who snake their way up the mountain track towards the Source.

There are thousands of Drifters ascending the mountain. Men and women from all eras of history. All obediently marching in one long, silent line, their minds and bodies being pulled upwards and onwards.

Eilish lifts her scarf and fastens it tightly over her nose and mouth. It is still raining, and the mist swirls down low in patches over the minefields. It would do Eilish no good to breathe in the mist now and lose her mind here. She knows that she has been in the Mountain's misty vicinity for long enough already. She can almost tangibly feel the pull of the mountain on her mind, as though already the sands of her sand timer are tilting towards another realm.

Then she remembers Ciara's water. Pure water. *'Nothing clears the mind more.'*

Eilish drops her backpack down and pulls out the metal cylinder, taking a gulp.

The effects are immediate and incredible. She suddenly feels sharp and alert. She feels vibrant in her mind and body. Like she could start running up the mountain. And in this moment of sharpness, a moment of clarity follows—another *jamais vu*.

A vision flashes before her. A vision of the queue of Drifters heading up the Mountain all around her, and a vision of an imposing horse, galloping through the snow towards her. Attacking her.

The vision is gone, as quickly as it came, and Eilish looks up at the queue of Drifters. She knows she should be heading with them on their upwards march. That is how she will ascend the mountain, how she will find the hidden shaft, and start her journey to rescue Kim-Joy.

She crouches down and re-stuffs her backpack, pushing the dress down to the bottom of the bag. The soft blue silk that caresses her skin. Then, without warning, Eilish feels *Her* approach.

Her presence does not feel the same as an angel or spirit. Nor does it feel like a person coming. It is almost as though Eilish's *mind* is seeing *Her.* As though *She* approached within Eilish's mind. And when *She* speaks, *Her* voice is the voice of Eilish's own internal monologue. Incredibly, *Her* voice is also all the voices of the women who have been *Her* before. In one voice, Kim-Joy, Glenda, Nailah, Chloe, and Ciara. They are all speaking within her.

"Now it is your turn, Eilish."

Eilish feels the fabric running between her fingers and, amazingly, it doesn't feel strange when she starts pulling it out of the bag and putting it on. Despite the drizzle. Despite the cold. Despite the long, steep, snowy climb ahead. She will wear the dress.

Eilish has become *Her.*

***

Chapter 62

Strange Preparations

Earth - Mynydd Aaru

Marty's feet touch down on hard ground. It had seemed a good idea at first to follow the lady's rope down through the trapdoor, but his body really wasn't ready for it. Hanging on to the rope with bare hands, and scrabbling frantically with his feet, he had had to lower himself one inch at a time through the seemingly endless darkness. Every sinew in his arms is now tight, almost to snapping, and his breathing is rasping and rapid.

In front of him, Marty can see a route into the mountain, down a path where the lady must have gone. A narrow passageway towards a gentle wash of light. Daylight or torchlight? He's not sure.

He ducks low and shuffles forward. It is cool inside the passage, and a gentle air whistles past. Up ahead, something is knocking. It isn't metronomic. It's purposeful. It sounds like someone is loading or unloading something.

The passageway opens into a wide track. Wide enough to drive a vehicle through—and it looks like somebody has. Tyre tracks are carved into the soft mud, and they look recent.

To Marty's left, the track runs downhill towards an opening bathed in daylight. A wash of gentle grey and white reaches as far as it can towards him. The track is clearly part of the old disused mine. He peers up at the industrial timbers that brace the ceiling. They are cracked and rotten, and recent rockfall piles up against the walls.

Marty had been warned about this mine. The café owner at the base of *Mynydd Aaru* told him all about it. About its partial collapse and imminent danger. He had advised against ever going inside. Recent collapses had shown just how unstable the mine had become. A farmer had lost his life, sheltering with his sheep from a storm. His body, and that of a dozen of his flock, had been found, crushed by falling rocks.

To Marty's right, quite a way up the track, there's the flickering light of a torch where the knocking sounds are coming from. He starts towards it, ignoring the fallen rock debris and the creaks and groans from the timber above him.

Soon, the passage opens into a vast cavern, and the lady comes into view.

She is inspecting something. A motorbike. A Kawasaki ZXR 750. Marty immediately recognises his son's bike. The bike he had left in the bushes far beyond the foot of the mountain.

"What are you doing?" Marty calls out, catching her by surprise.

The lady turns her torch in Marty's direction, forcing him to shield his eyes.

"Marty?!" she exclaims. "How did you get here?"

"Same as you," he says. "What are you doing?"

"I told you… I'm making preparations to go back to the Meadow."

"You're going to *drive* there?"

"Not exactly!"

"Well, before you go, I need some answers," his tone is assertive. He's only a few strides away from her, and he can see, quite clearly, the familiar details of his son's bike.

Hanging from the handlebars is a backpack. It is packed full. Shoved into the pockets are medical supplies, painkillers, dressings, and bandages, as if the lady plans to set up a field hospital.

Marty glances at the cave wall in front of the bike.

'Jesus! She's made a bomb!'

Fifty metres in front of the bike and piled high are dozens of petrol cans and fireworks.

"What the fuck is this?!" he shouts, gesturing to the bike and the vast pile of accelerants.

"I can explain, honestly," she says.

"No," he says, stopping her. "No, first of all, you tell me the truth." He pulls from his pocket the wad of hospital passes from her coat and shoves them into her hand. "You knew my son, didn't you? You visited every single day since he was admitted to the hospital."

"You weren't ready to know," she says, carefully.

"Know *what?*"

She pauses, and even in the low light, he can feel her eyes boring into his mind, wondering if the time is right.

"I know I can take you back to your son," she says. "Because I know him…"

"Come again?"

"I know Elijah in the Meadow. I know that he loves you, and I know that he wants, more than anything, for you to join him… And more than that, *I* need you to join him."

"What do you mean?"

"Everything… and I mean *everything,* depends on you joining him… joining him at the right time."

She turns the beam of her torch onto the cave wall. Up against the rock, away from the explosive material, an old mining cart has been upturned. On it is an array of time-measuring objects. There are sand timers, clocks, and stopwatches. The lady is obsessively timing something.

"At the *exact* right time," she says. "You must go to the Meadow. And then, not only will you see your son, but you will also *save* him."

"Save him?"

"He is being held by a man who is intent on killing him."

"Killing him?"

"Killing him in the Meadow."

"Who is the man?"

"A guard, working for your 'friend'… a guard acting on the instructions of fallen angels to try and stop Elijah from helping us… from helping me."

"Elijah is helping you?"

"Yes. He's helping because he loves you, and because he wants to see you again."

"Why didn't you tell me this before?"

"Because I know what your next question is going to be… and I need you to be ready for the answer."

There is a moment of silence.

"How do I get to the Meadow?" asks Marty.

The lady steps forward and places the torch down beside them, such that they can both see each other clearly.

"Everyone who enters the Meadow," she starts. "Does so, because their mind is still active. And yet their body has failed on Earth… it has been subject to such trauma here that they are taken away… The only people in the Meadow who are there through their own intentional actions are called *Stained*. Stained minds. Stained on Earth to the point of taking their own lives."

"What do you mean?" Marty asks.

"I mean, the only way to Elijah is to take your own life here on Earth."

"Oh… shit."

***

Chapter 63

The Time to Jump

Earth - Mynydd Aaru

The lady throws Marty a warm cloak before pulling one over herself. Then she places a stopwatch over her neck and slings a length of rope over her shoulder.

"Just to be sure," she says, striding to the doorway of the hut.

Leading Marty out into the snow, the lady, her limp exacerbated by the cold, takes Marty past the point on the mountain face where she found him days before. The place where he had said goodbye to life once before.

The weather outside is, once again, calm. The sky is overcast and, so, despite the lingering ache in his temple, Marty's eyes can cope with the whiteness of the world before him.

Now, for the first time, Marty can truly see the lady. He can actually appreciate what she looks like. She is about his age, somewhere between thirty and forty, and her hair is a dark copper red. She has steel in her eyes. A determination. A clarity of purpose. Yet she exhibits no bravado at all. Her strength is a true strength. Marty can see that. And there is something about her strength that gives Marty the confidence to trust her.

The lady leads Marty carefully through the snowfields and around the face, up to a rocky cliff edge where the expansive vista of the Mynydd mountain range opens out before them. It is the most fantastic sight of nature's beauty Marty has ever experienced firsthand.

'*City folk,* ' he mocks himself. But it's true. He never gets to see such splendour from London.

They keep walking until they are scrambling across rocks, heading towards a protruding ledge which reaches out into thin air. On this side of the mountain, they are completely sheltered from the wind, and in the calm, majestic beauty of the mountain, Marty's mind feels the most at ease it has felt in years.

Looking down from the ledge, Marty sees the sparkling lake in the distance, and he recognises the boulder field directly below. This must be the place where *they* jump. He looks out and actually thinks of just how appealing that jump has become now he is there in the peace of the mountain, when all the worries of the world seem so far away.

The lady looks at her stopwatch.

"It's nearly time," she says.

"Time for what?"

She looks at him. She looks deep into his eyes.

"You don't remember me, do you?" she says earnestly.

Marty is confused. "What do you mean?"

"Do you remember what you told me?"

"When?"

"Before the horses came."

Marty looks, and the strangest sensation engulfs him. Like a memory that has not yet happened. A *jamais vu*. And he can see her. But not as she is now. She is wearing a blue dress, and she appears to be scared.

Marty blinks and looks at the lady again.

"You are starting to remember, aren't you?"

"I… I don't know," he stutters.

She lifts the stopwatch from her neck and passes it to him.

"What's this for?" he asks, looking down at the device. It hasn't been started.

"Timing is everything," she says.

"I don't understand."

The lady reaches across and starts the stopwatch.

"Do not stop this," she instructs him. "And when you next see me, tell me I have until two hours forty-three minutes to come back."

"Two hours and forty-three minutes?" he repeats.

"That's right."

Ignoring Marty's evident confusion, the lady unslings the rope from her shoulder and passes this to Marty as well. He takes it, still perplexed. Then she hands him a strange canister from a holster on her hip. Like a deodorant canister.

"Spray the man who holds Elijah," she says.

"What?"

She doesn't answer but instead rocks back on her heels.

"I'm sorry, but you told me to do this."

"Do what?"

Out of nowhere, with an almighty shove, the lady pushes Marty with both hands off the edge of the cliff.

Marty screams at the top of his lungs as he falls through the air.

The last thing that he sees are the rocks of the cliff rushing past him, and up there, the lady's copper hair, blowing in the wind before...

Crack!

And Marty's world falls silent.

***

The Meadow - The Mountain

Far below Eilish, on the track leading from the checkpoint, a horse-drawn carriage hurtles over potholes and through puddles, heading towards the *House of Sand*. Eilish watches intently. The Distillery carriage is certainly not accustomed to such speeds. The rider himself looks to be clinging on for dear life.

When the carriage is half a kilometre from the house, it comes to a clattering halt. And, as the wheels stop rotating, a side door bursts open, and a young man is thrown out.

He lands, face-first, in a crumpled heap on the icy ground. His hands are tied behind his back, and a cloth hood shrouds his face. He's a prisoner.

Following quickly behind the prisoner are Distillery guards. Two of them, dressed in dark purple boiler suits with gas masks strapped tight to their faces. They jump to the ground beside their captive. Without a mask, the prisoner is fully exposed to the tumbling thick mist that swoops around the mountain, but his guards are not. That's the way of the Distillery on the Mountain.

One of the guards throws a decisive, rage-filled kick into the young man's ribs. Eilish can hear his cry of pain from where she stands far above them on the mountain. The kick is a brutal farewell, for the guard jumps back into the carriage, shouting for the rider to move him on towards the house hastily. The prisoner is left with the remaining guard, alone and vulnerable in the rain.

The guard drags the young prisoner to his feet via the knot of rope binding his hands. The prisoner squirms painfully. His arms have been wrenched awkwardly from their sockets, and his weak legs are struggling to hold his own weight.

The guard yanks the hood from the prisoner's head and, up on the mountain, Eilish gasps.

'*Elijah!*' she whispers. '*No!*'

The Distillery guard starts dragging Elijah back along the track, towards the snaking tail of Drifters heading up the mountain. Elijah, beaten and bruised, offers little resistance. And it is wise that he doesn't; in the guard's hand, ready to deploy, is a cannister—a fatal dose of Thermocline Mist, primed to send the young man 'on'.

Eilish feels for the canister she still holds from fleeing her home. If only she could help Elijah with it now.

Then, right in front of the two men, a bright flash of light erupts, stretching from the ground to the sky. An Opening. From it, a man tumbles out. A middle-aged man, dressed in full mountaineering gear with a length of rope slung over his shoulder. He looks like a climber from Earth who has just this moment met his demise. But, in his hand, he holds his own canister of Thermocline Mist.

The man from the Opening looks around, dazed and bewildered, but only for the briefest moment. Almost as though he was prepared for what he would see in front of him, he charges towards Elijah and the guard. He thrusts his canister forwards and, without hesitation, discharges the spray into the face of the Distillery man. The guard doesn't even have the chance or inclination to react.

The mist from the cannister slithers around the guard's face, engulfing him in his own personal cloud, before it draws in through his mouth and nose, making his body arch backwards before falling back and dropping into a lifeless, drifting slump. The guard has gone 'on'.

Eilish cannot believe it.

As the guard starts to wander away to join the line of Drifters, the man from the Opening turns and throws his arms around Elijah in a frantic and loving embrace. This embrace tells Eilish everything she needs to know about the man.

And, as the embrace dissolves into relief and disbelief, the two men turn to look up at the Mountain. The man is telling Elijah something and gesturing wildly and excitedly. Then he throws his arm up, pointing to a location on the Mountain. Pointing directly to where Eilish stands, watching them in wonder. The two men wave excitedly, then start their own walk up the face. They are coming to join her.

***

Chapter 64

Falling Apart

The Meadow - The Mountain

Eilish rubs her hands together, then cups them around her face, breathing on them to keep warm. Her whole body shivers in the swirling wind that now engulfs the cold mountain.

Elijah and the man from the Opening are a few dozen strides down the face. Eilish has watched them the whole way up the Drifter's path, joining the unconscious souls on their way towards her.

Elijah has a deep gouge in his forehead and congealed blood all over his face. His capture by the Distillery was clearly aggressive and brutal. Eilish wonders about Nailah. Has she suffered a similar fate? Or worse? Is she amongst the Drifters? Maybe. But it changes nothing.

Eilish inspects the man from the Opening. He is a tall man. Around his neck dangles a stopwatch which slaps against the zip of his coat. His head is shaved, but it appears to be a recent change. His eyes are red raw, and though Eilish knows she has never met him before, there is something uncanny about him. Something familiar. Something *essential.*

"Eilish!" shouts Elijah, jogging to greet her.

He throws his arms around her.

"You made it!" he exclaims. "I knew you'd keep going… Nailah said you would… I'm sorry we left you. We had no choice. The Distillery came from nowhere. They came with spirits, and we had to run."

"It's ok," says Eilish. "I got through the checkpoint fine. But you… Are you ok?" She looks at the wound above his right eye.

"I'll live," he smiles.

"And Nailah?"

Elijah's eyes drop, and a frown falls upon his face.

"They took her away," he says.

"Where?"

"To Kim-Joy… to interrogate her as well… and… to *burn* them!" he cries.

Eilish embraces Elijah.

"It's ok," she says, over his sobs. "They've not done it yet."

She turns to acknowledge the man who stands patiently, waiting for an introduction.

"Eilish," says Elijah, wiping away a tear. "This is my father!"

"We already know each other," says the man, before Eilish can react.

"You do?" asks Elijah.

"We do?" asks Eilish, mirroring Elijah's surprise.

Elijah's father lifts the stopwatch from around his neck. "You told me the truth," he says, handing it to Eilish. "Thank you. Thank you so much. Now, I've done as you asked… I haven't touched the clock since you pushed me… It's still running."

"I'm sorry, I don't understand," says Eilish. "What push? Why? When?"

"On Earth… Don't you remember? We were here… you told me that I would find my son, and then you pushed me… I'm so grateful you did. Please, don't hesitate when the time comes again."

Eilish looks at Elijah's dad. He speaks with an unerring certainty, but what he says doesn't add up.

"You were with *me* on Earth?"

"Yes. And I must remind you. Now that you have the stopwatch again, you have until two hours and forty-three minutes have passed before you need to leave."

"What do you mean?"

The man chuckles. "I was hoping you'd be able to tell me!"

Eilish looks at the stopwatch, utterly confused. There is just over half an hour to go before the seemingly arbitrary deadline.

"I'm really sorry," she says. "You seem very earnest, but honestly, I don't understand what you're talking about... Shall we keep heading up the mountain? I know a way to Kim-Joy," she says to Elijah. "We can try and tease out some sense as we walk?"

***

Chapter 65

Old Friends

Earth - Mynydd Aaru

The lady doesn't wait to see Marty's impact on the rocks below. She can't bear it. Even if this is how it is meant to be, it is still an awful thing. And, after twelve years waiting for that moment, more than a little seed of doubt has germinated in her mind. Was it even the right thing to do? What if something, *anything*, has changed? If it has, then she may well have just murdered an innocent man.

The lady steps back from the ledge, closes her eyes, and inhales a deep lungful of the cold mountain air. The stop-clock around her neck beeps. Two minutes have passed already. She needs to stick to the plan.

She wanders across the snowy slope, back towards her hut. The sky is now a mottled grey, and the air is still. She smiles. In the distance, she spots two people trudging through the snow up the same mountain path where she first found Marty.

'*Perfect timing.*'

The lady is in the hut before the two walkers approach and has the kettle reaching the boil when there is a knock at the door.

"Come in," she says.

A man enters first. A quiet, timid sort of man. His eyes tell of a life that has seen a lot, but his body betrays the reality. A frail old lady in the twilight of her days shuffles in behind him. It is almost unbelievable that someone like her could have ascended the mountain. And it looks as though it has nearly killed her.

Between the gaps in the lady's thick scarf and woolly hat, the wrinkles of her skin do not detract from the effervescent brightness of her green eyes and her youthful soul.

"You made it," smiles the lady, embracing both visitors.

"Just about," says the man. "Ashley has had a lot of morphine to get up here."

Ashley, the old lady, chuckles. "It makes me feel half a century younger."

The lady smiles back, feeling the infectiousness of her energy.

"Did Mr Fredrickson jump as planned?" asks the man.

The lady pauses.

"He... *fell*... at the right time," she says.

Ashley smiles kindly, knowingly. "Well done, my dear," she says. "That must have been really difficult for you."

"Are you still sure you're up for your part of the bargain?" the lady asks, not comfortable taking credit for Marty's fall quite yet.

Ashley steps up to the bed where Marty had lain and starts removing the warm outer layers of her clothing. Underneath the wool and Gore-Tex, the extent of her frailty is fully revealed. She has cannulas in each hand, with morphine drips strapped to her chest. She has a catheter tied to her waist. And scars. Lots of scars all along her arms, and no doubt all over her body too. Scars from countless surgeries. For Ashley is terminally ill, and she knows it. That is why she is willing to do what she has to do, to help the lady.

"The doctors have given me two weeks, at most," says Ashley. "If anything, the timing couldn't be better."

"What will happen to you?"

"I don't know," says Ashley. "I think there may be plenty of grains left in the sand timer of my mind, even if I'm on to the last few in my body. I would dearly love to see Nailah and Kim-Joy again... But if I can't, well, I'll see what's in the Beyond."

The man steps forward and embraces Ashley.

"Can't I come with you?" he pleads.

"No, Gareth," she says. "You have so much left in your body. And we need people here. People who know the truth. People who can offer sanctuary to *Her*. Please stay here and help *Her* to succeed."

Gareth nods sadly and wraps his arms lovingly around his elderly wife.

"Can we see the dress?" asks Ashley.

"Of course," the lady responds. She reaches beneath the bed where Ashley sits and pulls out a delicate silk ball gown. Both Gareth and Ashley gasp.

"Wow, I didn't think it was real," says Gareth. "I thought I had just imagined it that night on the Mountain."

"My Chloe," says Ashley, running her hands through the silk, "Oh, she did me so proud... Miss Callaghan, it's such a privilege to be part of *Her* plans again."

"Is there anything I can be doing to help *Her* plan succeed?" asks Gareth.

"Just make sure that Ashley falls at the right moment in the right place," says the lady. She lifts the stop-clock from around her neck. "Two hours and forty-three minutes," she says, before pulling open a map and laying it in front of them. "This is where you need to fall," she prods a point on the map at the base of the cliffs.

"Ok," says Ashley. "Good luck, Miss Callaghan."

"Thank you. And you."

"*May the seas warm, and the clouds form...*'"

To which the lady responds, "*...and may the rain fall, filling the rivers of Love.*"

***

Chapter 66

The March of the Drifters

The Meadow - The Mountain

The meandering walk of the Drifters up the Mountain is slow and steady. While Elijah and his father talk enthusiastically, trying to make up on lost time, Eilish strides ahead of them, trying to piece together the fragments of information and the half-formed plan she has to try and rescue Kim-Joy and, if possible, Nailah too.

Eilish knows she only has one canister of thermocline mist. That's one canister to protect them all from attack. Assuming they can get to the prison chambers via the abandoned mineshaft, and don't deploy the cannister on the way, then they will have the bare minimum protection for the escape. Assuming, of course, that they can find the cave, and that the abandoned mineshaft is navigable. Both, very reasonably likely to fail.

'Glass half full,' Eilish tells herself. 'That's the only way to think of this plan.'

And if the plan does succeed and they do escape the chambers with Kim-Joy and Nailah, what then? Well, then Eilish knows where *she* is going next. She is going to follow Ciara into the Beyond. She has the water she needs, and from the cave, it won't be far to the Perihelion precipice. She just hopes she'll have the bravery to jump when the time comes.

Up ahead, the march of the Drifters slows. The unconscious souls are bunching up, forced into single file. And Eilish can see why.

Climbing high above them, two crooked shafts of slate cut into the sky. They are like blades of an open pair of scissors. This is the *Eye of the Needle*—the place where they'll leave the Drifters' path.

As she observes the great feature in the rock, Eilish notices a commotion amongst the Drifters. She strides forward, trying to work out what it is. Then, out of nowhere, four men on horseback emerge, scattering the Drifters, knocking some of them violently to the ground.

Eilish freezes.

The horses canter down the line towards Eilish and the two men. Their hooves sliding in the snow, sending great white plumes up behind them.

'They can't be looking for us, can they?"

Too late. A rider spots Eilish and immediately signals to the other three. Maybe it isn't such a good idea to be wearing the blue dress.

"They're after me!" Eilish shouts down to Elijah. "Go on without me. Get to the cave," she points in the direction they should go. "And use the shaft to reach Kim-Joy and Nailah."

"What about you?" shouts Elijah.

"I don't know," she concedes. "I'll figure something out."

"Remember, two hours and forty-three minutes, then you have to leave!" shouts Elijah's father.

Eilish looks back at him, utterly confused, and then at the stopwatch. If she does have to 'leave' somewhere at that time, she has less than five minutes.

The horsemen are coming for Eilish. She could stay here and let them take her, without a fight. But what good would that do? Might as well give Elijah a chance to disappear.

Eilish starts running down the mountainside, amongst the Drifters, dodging in and out of the unconscious souls. But the Horsemen are gaining ground on her quickly.

'Fuck it!'

Eilish steps away from the line of Drifters and stares up at the approaching horsemen. She looks down at the stopwatch. Two hours and forty-two minutes have elapsed—less than one minute to go.

The horsemen are a few seconds away. Their outstretched arms brandishing cannisters of Thermocline Mist. They have no intention of capturing her alive.

'*This is it!*' thinks Eilish. '*This is the end.*' She feels for the canister of Thermocline on her hip. '*Might as well go on my own terms.*' Only, it isn't the canister. It's Ciara's water bottle.

A clap of thunder makes Eilish jump, almost dropping the bottle. A sharp slice of white light has erupted somewhere near the base of the Mountain—another Opening.

Suddenly, it all makes sense.

Ten seconds to go.

Elijah's dad *does* know her. In one path of the future, she has told him to pass back a message to her, here in the past—a truth.

'*It's a poor sort of memory that only works backwards,*'

Without hesitation, Eilish swigs the pure water from Ciara's bottle, feeling her mind tingle with clarity. Then she tucks the hem of her dress between her legs, drops to the ground, and lies back on the steep face of snow.

In moments, she is sliding, uncontrollably, down the slippery slope.

She hears the horsemen shouting. She can just about make out the chaos of snow, horse, and riders desperately galloping and tumbling after her.

Five seconds to go.

Eilish sees the cliff edge moments before she tumbles off it. Falling down the *Asphodel Face*, she hurtles through the air, unable to think. And before she impacts the ground, the white light engulfs her, and at the exact same moment, another Arrival enters the Meadow.

***

Chapter 67

Twelve years in the making

The Meadow - The Mountain

Five hundred years in the Meadow barely affected Kim-Joy. Her mind had been strong and active. And as she had told Eilish, back in the *Tide and Time Tavern,* the Meadow was where her soul was at home. But since Cyril's marble cracked, and his spark left her, and after witnessing the horrors of the *House of Sand,* Kim-Joy does finally feel old. She feels as though the Meadow is becoming less like home and more like a prison. And, on the surface, that's hardly surprising—she is alone in a cell deep inside the Mountain.

After the trauma of the House, Kim-Joy had been gagged and bound before being dragged to the cells, but she hadn't been blindfolded—that was a slight relief. As a result, she knows exactly where she is. They had followed through one of the resin miners' tracks into the Mountain, and before passing into the prison quarters, they had gone through a vast chamber—the seat of the Council of the Almighty.

The council room was fascinating to Kim-Joy. She had only ever heard of the place, never visited. It was, as expected, a shrine to the beliefs that Kim-Joy despised. It was like a pious orthodox cathedral. Full of aggressive religious icons—strong men slaying beasts, demure women fawning under angels—and passages printed from a variety of scriptures, from the Earthly religions, demanding fear of the wrath of some Almighty power. Nothing like how Kim-Joy sees the universe.

Beyond the chamber, a lantern-lit tunnel led to the cells. The cells were located in the stillest of air, right at the centre of the

Mountain. Even now, when no resin could be extracted in the Distillery mine, the sticky residue of centuries-old resin still clings to the cold, purple slate walls of the cells.

Alone and silent, Kim-Joy sits on the floor of her cell, leaning against the iron bars, containing her. She looks out at the site for her final interrogation. Two chairs opposite each other on a raised platform, arranged to sit in the middle of the crescent of half a dozen cells, so that all the prisoners can see.

A golden throne for the interrogator, adorned with purple felt with its own font of marbles and a twisted golden ladle. Opposite, a rigid chair. A chair of execution. An upright wooden seat, the chair has leather straps on its legs and arms. This is where Kim-Joy will be strapped when the angel Samael is ready.

Kim-Joy calls out to see if any of the other cells are occupied, but her voice just echoes, and no one responds. She will be alone until she gets summoned.

In the flickering lantern light, Kim-Joy looks at her old, tired hands. Her wrists are bleeding from wounds sliced by the ropes that bound them, but the pain is nothing to the trauma.

She feels Cyril's cracked stone on her neck. She has carried this stone for centuries, knowing that it bears a truth that few else know. The truth that she had known the trawlerman before the Meadow. *Loved* the trawlerman before the Meadow. A man with whom she had had a son—a man who took his life on Earth because he couldn't bear to be without her. And now, after five hundred years together, she can't bear to be without him anymore.

From down the tunnel where the council chamber was, Kim-Joy hears voices.

'*It is time,*' she thinks to herself, closing her eyes and breathing calmly. '*Stay with me,*' she pleads.

"Stop struggling!" Kim-Joy hears a guard shout.

She peers out from her cell.

"I said, STOP STRUGGLING!"

Someone is struck hard by the guard.

"Right, that's better. Come on, you, filth!"

Half a dozen Distillery guards appear in the cells. And with them is a second prisoner.

"Nailah!" Kim-Joy's heart jumps for joy, seeing her friend. But the joy is short-lived. Nailah is bruised and wounded. And trapped like her. At least they'll be leaving the Meadow together.

"This is your cell!" shouts a guard, throwing Nailah into an enclosure directly opposite Kim-Joy, obscured from her view by the interrogation stage between them.

Nailah tumbles to the floor and lies motionless.

"Did you knock her out?" asks a guard.

"I didn't mean to."

"They said they didn't want her *bruised!*"

"Oh, come on. She'll be alright. And it's not like *he* won't be bruisin' her!"

"Oi, what you lookin' at?!" a guard shouts at Kim-Joy.

Kim-Joy shrinks away from the bars of her cell—no need to pick a fight.

"Now, not a word between you two!" shouts the guard to his prisoners. "Or there will be trouble!"

"Are we not staying to keep an eye on em'?"

"What, in this shitty, dingy, cold chamber. No, thank you! Unless you want to stay?!"

"No, boss."

"The angel will be here soon anyway."

"So," the guard announces to the prisoners. "We'll see you two girls in a bit, then, shall we? Suspect you might be a bit *sleepy* then… but the flames will wake you up!"

The guard cackles at his own morbid joke, then kicks the cells with his boot as he leaves, spitting in the direction of the prisoners.

Kim-Joy waits until the guards are gone before crawling to the bars of her cell and calling out, as loud as she dares, "Nailah?!"

She waits, listening intently. Hoping just to be able to hear Nailah's breathing at the very least.

"Kim-Joy?" Nailah whispers.

"Oh Nailah, it is so lovely to hear your voice!"

"How are you doing?"

"I'm tired," says Kim-Joy, "But hearing your voice is the best thing."

"Oh, Kim-Joy, I'm so sorry. We tried. We *really* tried to rescue you."

"How did he die?" asks Kim-Joy.

Nailah lets out an uncontrolled sob. "We took the *Guiding Star*. Followed you up through the Irish Sea. Cyril took us into the Swellies to try and get to you before they got you here. But we foundered. And the waters took him."

"Did you see his spark?" asks Kim-Joy, calmly.

"Yes," says Nailah. "He joined Sachi in the sky."

Kim-Joy exhales in quiet relief.

"I'm so glad," she says.

"How are you holding up?" asks Nailah.

"I'm… well, I'm… determined…"

"Me too."

"Then we must hold strong. No matter what they do to us."

"I know."

"And is there *any* hope of escape?"

"Eilish."

"Eilish? The governess?"

"Yes… she fights for us. And she knows the truth."

"About *Her?*"

"Exactly. She recast her resin for us, just like her sister did."

"Wow. And where is she?"

"I don't know. I lost her in the foothills. But if she's still alive, she'll be fighting… I know that much."

Kim-Joy smiles. "Then, I think *She* has a plan."

Without warning, the tunnel leading to the cells flashes with a bright white light. So bright that the two women have to shield their eyes from the glare. And with the brightness, a roar of noise and chaos fills the chamber before a bright green motorbike smashes through an Opening into the tunnel.

The engine of the bike screams as it hurtles towards the cells before its brakes screech and the vehicle comes to a dusty stop.

The hooded rider kicks down the bike stand and, as the bright light from the opening fizzles away, Kim-Joy and Nailah watch in awe as a lady, carrying a heavy backpack, in a long blue hooded ball gown steps off.

"Eilish!" screams Nailah.

Eilish, unsteady on her feet, sweeps the dust from her long copper hair and glances around at her surroundings. A broad grin stretches across her face. She made it.

Eilish rushes to the pannier on the back of the bike, limping painfully, and pulls out a first aid kit. "I have morphine," she says, handing painkillers to each of the women in the cells. She stops in front of Nailah. "I'm so glad you're alive," she beams. "I knew Kim-Joy would be here; I didn't know about you."

"Eilish," says Nailah, stunned, her eyes wide with admiration. "How?!"

"No time to explain now," says Eilish, smiling. "It has been a long twelve years…"

Eilish, in a fury of energy, ties a length of webbed strapping around the bars of each woman's cells. Kim-Joy and Nailah stand, watching her, incredulous and stunned.

Eilish fastens the ends of the straps to a passenger handle on the back of the bike.

"You might want to stand clear," she says, clambering back onto the seat.

Barely giving the two women a chance to step back, Eilish revs the engine and pulls away. With a jolt, the bars of the cells are ripped away, clattering to the ground and skidding across the floor of the tunnel.

Eilish slams on the brakes and, like a person possessed, she runs round back to them, limping awkwardly, pulling out of her backpack her twelve-year-old bottle of pure water.

"What's the plan, Eilish?" says Kim-Joy, stepping through the rubble, approaching her. Her tone tells Eilish that she is ready for anything. Her poise tells her she is impressed.

Eilish grins.

"We're going up to the cave," she says with certainty. "Elijah and Marty are there, ready to hoist us."

"Marty?"

"Elijah's dad… long story," Eilish smiles.

"One for later?" winks Kim-Joy.

"How are you doing, Nailah?" Eilish asks, leaning past some of the rubble.

Nailah is clambering carefully over splinters of chair and dislodged boulders that cling to the iron bars of her cell. She looks up.

"I'm fine," she smiles, throwing a thumbs-up.

"Can you both walk, ok?"

"Better than you," grins Nailah, aware of Eilish's pronounced limp.

"I can run, if needed!" exclaims Kim-Joy, beaming.

Eilish passes her flask between the two women, and they each take a mind-clarifying swig of the pure water.

"Right, let's go!" Eilish shouts.

The three women run down into the candle-lit tunnel, leaving the devastation in the cells behind. The morphine and water have done wonders for both prisoners, and they keep up with Eilish despite their injuries.

Entering the council chamber, Eilish slows momentarily to look around at the vast open space. Standing in the centre of the chamber is the statue of *Him*. A depiction of a muscular man. God-like. Zeus-like.

From her backpack, Eilish pulls out a lump hammer. She had planned to use this to break Kim-Joy free if the bike hadn't survived the crash. But now she has a better plan. She takes a wide swing and smashes the head of the statue into a thousand pieces.

"Woo!" screams Nailah.

"Come on!" shouts Eilish, knowing they don't have time for her wonton urge to destroy.

She has memorised the route through the tunnels. They exit the chamber and take a sharp left back into the Mountain. Nailah had been down this path once before, many years ago, with the Returners.

Somewhere down the track, away from them, their commotion hasn't gone unnoticed. There are shouts of men—Distillery guards. Guards who are now on their way to try and intercept them. But none of the three women is remotely afraid.

They run to the end of the passageway where a mineshaft shoots straight up into the darkness.

"Marty?! Elijah?!" shouts Eilish, hopefully. "Are you up there?"

"Eilish!" Elijah's voice hollers down to them. "You made it!"

"Watch out below!" comes Marty's voice, and a moment later, the end of a rope drops through the shaft, resting on the ground beside them.

Marty has exceeded himself. There are knots and loops in the rope to assist their ascent, making it like a ladder for the women to climb.

"Can you manage it?" asks Eilish, looking at Kim-Joy.

The old lady grins. "I was born for this!"

Kim-Joy places her foot into the first loop and puts her weight through it. Wobbling at first, she steadies herself, then starts to climb into the darkness.

Once Kim-Joy is high enough, Nailah follows, leaving Eilish to take up the rear. She grabs the end of the rope and ties it around her waist, before climbing up behind the others—there'd be no good leaving the rope for the Distillery to follow.

Hand over hand, and foot over foot, the three women clamber carefully and eagerly through the darkness before emerging from the mineshaft into a roughly cut passageway that leads to the cave.

"How did you do it, Eilish?!" asks Elijah, beaming at her as she emerges from the shaft. "We saw you fall! We saw it, didn't we, Dad?"

"That's right," says Marty, encouraging them all to start walking through to the cave, nervously eyeing the precariously unstable beams supporting the old tunnel. "You and the three horsemen must have fallen over one hundred feet! It was awful."

"I'm sorry, that must have been quite a shock," says Eilish. "But thanks to you, Marty, I timed it just right. I fell off the cliff and straight through an Opening, back to Earth."

"What?! That's nuts!" says Elijah. "What are the chances!"

"I'd say zero," smiles Nailah.

Eilish grins.

"Then who made the Opening?" asks Kim-Joy.

"A long-lost friend of yours, actually," says Eilish. "She's very old now. Ashley Arnold."

"Ashley's back?!" says Nailah. "That's amazing!"

"I don't think she's going to be here long," says Eilish. "She was very frail when she jumped."

"Oh, bless her," says Kim-Joy, clutching the lockets around her neck.

"I see your limp is back," says Marty, helping Eilish.

"Back?" she says. "I've had it twelve years!"

"So, what's the plan now?" He asks, beckoning them all into the cave. He seems impatient, almost rattled, rocking clumsily on the balls of his feet. "I've spent too long on this mountain now, in two different realms. And it's freezing!"

Eilish looks at Marty. He doesn't look himself. Aside from the cold, he seems unsteady and queasy. His mind, unfocused and confused. Not at all how she remembers him from before the push. Then it dawns on her.

The mist.

In their haste to get up the mountain, Elijah and Marty have neglected necessary precautions, such as face coverings, although Marty has no reason to know this. Unlike the centre of the mountain where Eilish and the women have been, where the air is still and there is no mist, the two men have been exposed in the swirling mist of the Mountain for hours. It's a miracle they're both still conscious.

Eilish drops her backpack onto the floor and pulls out Ciara's flask again.

"Here," she says, stepping up to Marty. "You need to drink this... And you, too, Elijah. As soon as we leave this cave, you should get your faces covered too."

"Core! That's better!" exclaims Marty, after a big gulp. "Magic stuff, water, isn't it!"

"More so than you can imagine," chuckles Kim-Joy. "So, Eilish... what *is* the plan now?"

"Well, we're all fugitives of the Distillery," she begins. "Except maybe Marty. If we go down the Mountain all together, we will have to fight our way out... And I don't fancy our chances."

So, I assume *She* has a different plan for us, right?"

"Yes... Twelve years on Earth gave me plenty of time to think and understand..."

"And..."

"It is clear to me, now, the awful truth of our times. Strong men claiming a right to rule have corrupted the universe. Men claiming the right to govern. To dominate. Men who have carved themselves into delusions of gods and angels. Men who once had a full grip of the Earth. But *She* loosened that grip. They still have a firm grip on the Meadow. But not for long. The Distillery's power is crumbling, and the rebellion is ready to undermine them. But these men will cling to power and will fight tooth and nail. Because they know, if the Meadow falls, they only have one realm left."

"Elysian?"

"Yes," says Eilish. "I've been speaking with an angel from Elysian... She cannot speak freely. But I am almost certain it is Ciara. Elysian is the realm of the angels. It is the realm controlled by *Him*. The Prince. The powerful one whose lies once gripped the Earth, and still cling to the minds in the Meadow."

"There are no guarantees for any of us if we try and escape down the Mountain tonight. But I believe that is not where I am destined to go..." She lifts Ciara's flask into the air. "A sip of pure water and you can step through an opening back to Earth. The same is true the other way. By sipping and leaping off the Perihelion Cliffs with the Drifters, I believe I can step into Elysian. I can step into *His* realm and take the fight to *Him*... I can find Ciara and carry on what she has started!"

"If any of you are willing to join me, you are very welcome. I plan to jump into Elysian and fight for *Her* tonight! Who's with me?!"

"I am," says Kim-Joy.

"And me!" shouts Nailah, emphatically.

Elijah and Marty look at each other, hesitantly.

"Don't worry," says Eilish. "You two deserve more time together here before you go chasing angels! If you follow the Drifter track down the Mountain until it flattens out, before taking a sharp left, you will find a path that goes straight to a lightly guarded checkpoint. If you go in the dead of night, I rate your chances of getting out unscathed."

"Are you sure, Eilish?" says Elijah. "Should we not come with you?"

"No," she says. "You are not meant to take my path. But promise me this, if you manage to escape the Mountain tonight, get back to London. Spread the word about what has happened here. Spread the word about the missing men. About the torture cells in the Mountain. And about the sacrifice and bravery of Cyril Spate."

"I will," says Elijah.

"And tell them," says Kim-Joy. "That the *Tide and Time Tavern* will be open again soon!"

Elijah smiles. As does Marty, who puts his arm around his sons' shoulders.

"It has been an honour getting to know you both," says Eilish. "Thank you for trusting me."

"Good luck," says Marty, holding out his hand.

Eilish grasps hold firmly and shakes, feeling the warmth of Marty's trust.

"And you," she says.

"So, we're doing this, are we?" asks Nailah, tightening her belt and bending down to re-tie her laces. "We're going up the Mountain and jumping off the Perihelion Cliffs?"

"I think so," says Eilish.

Nailah grins. "This is going to be wild!"

***

Chapter 68

In the footsteps of angels

The Meadow - The Mountain

Wandering around the peak of the Mountain, Eilish, Nailah, and Kim-Joy are overcome with awe. Ever since each of them had called the Meadow their home, they had known of this place—an almost mythical location, laden with a morbid gloom.

The Source.

The spring of water that emanates from the Mountain and tumbles off the Perihelion precipice. A place where every soul for five hundred years has wandered to make their final, fatal jump from the Meadow into Elysian. But walking beside the legendary trickle of water, the warm sunset that fills a kind evening sky, makes the fearful legend of the Mountain fall away. Fall away into the distant mist that surrounds the Mountain but can't reach its peak.

In the distance, the women can see the peaks of the other mountains in the range. And further still, they can see the plateaus and plains of the Meadow.

In front of them, where the water tumbles off the cliffs, they see sparks of light from souls who have just jumped. Sparks that climb up out of the mist and shoot into the sky, joining the hidden dance of the stars beyond.

Without ever being here, on the precipice of the Mountain, awful and terrifying images had filled their imagination of this place. Images of pain, suffering, mist, rain, and gloom. But these projections are wiped clean by reality.

Even the sight of the Drifters isn't awful. They are spread out. They no longer shuffle in a tragic and desperate march.

Instead, each soul walks calmly and serenely to the cliff edge. They walk alone and peaceful. Ready for their next adventure. And Eilish notices, every one of the Drifters is smiling. They are happy and relieved to have met the end of this chapter of their lives.

As the cliff edge approaches, the three women huddle together, walking side-by-side, taking it all in. Then, tentatively, they walk out onto the slab of rock, reaching out over the cliffs. This is the point of no return.

"How are you feeling?" asks Kim-Joy.

"Strange," says Eilish. "It feels like I am about to die for the third time in one day!"

Kim-Joy chuckles. "How about you, Nailah?"

"Oddly," she says. "I'm excited."

"Nothing odd about that," says Kim-Joy. "That's who you are!"

"How do you feel then, Kim-Joy?" asks Nailah.

"I'm feeling ready."

"So, how are we doing this?" asks Eilish. "Who's going first?"

"First?" says Nailah. "I say we jump together."

"I agree," says Kim-Joy.

Eilish smiles and nods.

She looks out at the blanket of mist below them and feels the cool breeze of the air breathing through her hair. She feels so peaceful. The last time she had seen her sister Ciara, it had been tragic, leaving her alone in the universe. Now she is on her way to reunite with Ciara, and she has two amazing women by her side. Two friends who have believed in her, trusted her, and given her a second chance in life.

As each woman shuffles her toes to the edge of the rock, they hold hands, their fingers interlocking. Eilish—the lady in the blue dress—stands between Kim-Joy—landlady from Tudor England, whose soul has lived for five hundred years in the Meadow—and Nailah—a lady who has spent her lifetime fighting cruelty in the name of truth and love. Eilish knows she is in good hands. The best hands. And what's better, *He* doesn't realise it. *He* doesn't realise that the biggest threat to *His* power in the universe is about to step across a bridge *he* made and into *his* realm.

"On three," says Kim-Joy. "One, two, three…"

***

THE HOUSE OF SAND
By *Julian Shaw*

THANK YOU FOR READING

If you enjoyed *The House of Sand*, I'd be incredibly grateful if you could take a moment to leave a quick review.

Even a few words can help other readers discover the book—and your feedback means a lot to me.

Leave a review on Amazon:
      UK: https://amzn.eu/d/9Ly2qcT
      US: https://a.co/d/gHMTKRk

GET A FREE COMPANION EBOOK

Want to go deeper into *The Meadow Series*?

I've put together a free bonus eBook just for readers like you:
Whispers from the Meadow: An Insider's Companion to The Meadow Series

It's packed with background lore, inspirations, and behind-the-scenes reflections—perfect if you're curious about what's behind *The House of Sand*.

Download you free copy here:
https://subscribepage.io/CMivTJ

Thanks again for being part of this journey.

Don't lose your marbles,
Julian